C000156966

THE MEMORY WATCHER
5TH ANNIVERSARY EDITION

MINKA KENT

ALSO BY MINKA KENT

The Perfect Roommate
The Thinnest Air
The Stillwater Girls
When I Was You
The Watcher Girl
Unmissing

All books available here.

ALSO BY MINKA KENT

The Perfect Roommate
The Thinnest Air
The Stillwater Girls
When I Was You
The Watcher Girl
Unmissing

All books available here.

DESCRIPTION

Haunted by memories of the daughter she gave up at fifteen, Autumn Carpenter never fully moved on.

She doesn't have to.

Instead, she lives a life of relative seclusion, content to watch from a distance as the picture-perfect McMullen family raises her daughter as their own. Every birthday, every milestone, every memory, Autumn is watching.

Only no one knows.

But when the opportunity presents itself, Autumn allows herself to become intertwined in the lavish life of the picturesque McMullens. And only then does she realize that pictures . . . they lie. The perfect family . . . it doesn't exist. And beautiful people . . . they keep the ugliest secrets.

FOREWORD

Dearest Reader—

For as long as I can remember, I've gravitated toward stories that center around mysteries, secrets, and good people doing bad things. Humans, quite simply, are the most fascinating creatures on earth. With all of our facets, hopes, desires, buried emotions, and unique experiences, no two of us are exactly alike, and each of us are capable of anything under the right circumstances.

While **THE MEMORY WATCHER** was born into the book world five years ago, the seedling of the idea was planted over a decade ago when I was a newly married, infertile twenty-something and mommy blogs were all the rage.

As each fruitless month passed, I'd find another "perfect" family to watch from behind my computer monitor. With every dreamily posed photograph or charmingly written update, I'd fall quietly in love with these idealistic lives, hoping and praying that one day I'd have my perfect little family too. Enter Instagram shortly thereafter and my eyes were opened to the shiny new world of mommy influencers. With each addictive swipe, I'd grow more invested into the lives of complete strangers—innocently, of course. (I'm certainly no Autumn). They gave me hope. And until I was pregnant with a child of my own, they gave me something to look forward to.

One family, however, was my favorite. I *lived* for their updates. And for years, I watched their beautiful, dreamy little life from behind my phone screen with unapologetic loyalty ... until one day, they closed their account without warning. For a moment, it felt like a huge and personal loss. An emotional sucker punch of sorts. But ultimately it was a wake-up call to step back and focus on the life we were trying to create and not the life other people were already living.

But I digress.

It wasn't long after that when I became pregnant with my first child, life moved on, and all that time spent keeping up with mommy bloggers became a distant memory.

But I never forgot about that family that disappeared from the face of the internet. And to this day, I still don't know why they quit social media cold turkey (though my overactive imagination forks into several plausible scenarios).

Over the years, I'd think about that family every so often and wonder what they were up to now. And somewhere along the line, the inspiration for **THE MEMORY WATCHER** was born.

I'm writing this as we approach the 5th anniversary of this book, after hundreds of thousands of copies have been sold, a spin-off has been published (**THE WATCHER GIRL**), after options, translations, and publishing deals have made their way to my desk. There aren't enough words in the English language to convey my gratefulness to everyone who has read and shared this story, so I wanted to do something special instead. At the end of this book, I've included an extended ending with three brand-new chapters. In addition to that, I've added a list of book club questions and a sample of THE WATCHER GIRL.

Love, books, and gratitude—

Minka

DEDICATION

To K, M, C, and A. This book was a labor of love shaped by your brutal honesty. Thank you.

PROLOGUE

I found her.

It took three years, but I found her.

They call her Grace, and while she may not look like them, she is theirs.

And she is also mine.

Her hair is light brown with a little natural wave, the way mine was at that age, and her dark eyes, round and inquisitive, light up her cherubic face when she smiles.

Her mother, Daphne, dresses her in pink lace and oversized hair bows and poses her for pictures every chance she gets, plastering them all over social media.

The first night I stumbled across Daphne McMullen's Instaface, I stayed up until four in the morning going through all the photographs and status updates, soaking in and screenshotting every last moment and immortalized memory from the day they brought her home from the hospital to the day she blew out the third candle on her double chocolate birthday cake.

1

One thousand and ninety-five days I missed morphed into one thousand and ninety-five days I recovered over the course of one sleepless night.

I hook a leg over the edge of my bathtub, mindlessly scrolling through Daphne's newsfeed for the millionth time in the past week. A million times I've seen these photos, and yet it's like the first time, every time.

Steam rises from the water and sweat collects across my brow. I'm in a trance, and I don't come out until I'm prompted by the sound of my roommate pounding on the door.

"You almost done in there?" she asks. "I put that show on that you wanted to watch. I ordered us a pizza too. Should be here soon."

She's so needy, always clinging to me, always telling me her secrets and whining to me about how hard it is to be her. I read her diary at her bizarre insistence, and believe me when I say she has nothing to cry about.

Her car? Paid for.

Her college tuition? Paid for.

This apartment? Paid for.

Her parents? Overachievers with rigorous expectations. Boo-freaking-hoo.

"Yeah," I call out. "I'll be out in a few."

I don't move. Instead, I keep scrolling, dragging my thumb across the fogged screen of my phone, smiling to myself. I examine another photo, then another and another. I'm not sure how much time passes, but my roommate bangs on the door once more.

"You still in there? Pizza just got here." Her voice is timid and meek on the other side of the door. Over the past few years, I've become her life force. She can't go anywhere or do anything or make any decisions without me. But lately she's been withering away, drawing into her shell. She whispers more than she talks these days, and at night I hear her cry through the shared wall that separates our bedrooms, but she won't get help because the last time she needed it, her parents had her committed.

"Getting out now." I try not to groan as I place my phone aside and reach for a towel.

"You said that twenty minutes ago."

Good God, this girl.

I love everything about her life. I love her overinvolved helicopter parents. I love her dorky little brother. I love her adoring nana. I love her little white BMW and the collection of unused designer purses that fill her closet. I love her drawer full of department store makeup and the way her luxe shampoo smells every morning after she showers.

But I do not love *her.*

She has everything a girl could possibly want, and all she does is fixate on the past, on things she can't change. One unfortunate situation happened three years ago, and she refuses to let it go. This girl dwells something fierce. If only she lived a day in my life, then she'd actually have something to dwell on.

Sometimes I'm convinced I was born in the wrong body, to the wrong family.

I should have been born as her.

"Drying off now," I yell, wrapping a plush towel around my wet body. "Be out in ten."

I finish up, scrolling through photos as I slather her overpriced, fragrance-free lotion on my damp skin, and I do a tiny jump for joy when I see Daphne has posted a fresh picture of Grace.

God, this is addictive.

It's like someone dropped an all-access backstage pass to Grace's life right into my lap.

It's bedtime and my Grace is wearing a princess nightgown that stops just above her chubby little ankles. Wisps of hair hang

3

in her eyes and she's dragging a white teddy bear along side of her.

How I long to kiss her forehead, tuck her in to bed, and tell her how loved she is.

Someday, perhaps.

Until then, this will have to do.

CHAPTER ONE

AUTUMN

7 YEARS LATER...

PRESS, TAP, REFRESH.

Over the years, Instaface's algorithms have learned that Daphne McMullen's posts are my favorite. Her posts are almost always at the top of my newsfeed. But today they're MIA.

Something's not right.

Scrolling down, I pass *@TheLittleGreenCottage* and *@Fitness-Junkie887*. I pass *@JustJustine* and *@CaliMakeupGuru*.

Scrolling...

Scrolling...

Scrolling...

There's no sign of Daphne anywhere.

This is odd.

There's a tingle in the back of my throat, and every nerve

ending is standing on edge. Something's amiss. I feel it all over. Inside. Outside. The core of my bones.

Tapping on the search bar, I type in *@TheMcMullenFamily* and take a deep breath.

No results found.

This can't be right.

Did she block me?

She doesn't even know me. Of course she didn't block me, and I "ghost" follow her. I'm not an "official" follower. Official followers require proof of identification due to Instaface's strict no-dummy-accounts policy.

Just to be sure, I log out of my account and perform the search again.

No results found.

Maybe she changed her account name?

I type in *@McMullenFamily*, *@DaphneMcMullen*, and *@GrahamandDaphneMcMullen*. I type in fifty thousand other variations, all of which lead me to the same dead end.

No results found.

Heat creeps up my neck, billowing to my ears. My throat constricts, and I can't breathe.

Rushing to the bedroom window, I throw back the curtains and slide it open, gasping for air, met with a blast of tepid morning rain on my face that does nothing to calm me down.

This isn't happening. This isn't happening. This isn't happening.

I refuse to believe it.

It makes no sense.

Daphne McMullen has thousands of followers.

She lives for this stuff.

She has so many followers, companies send her free stuff.

She does paid ads for crying out loud.

Why would she just shut it down?

She posted a picture of the kids getting ready for school this morning . . . how could it all just . . . go away like that? With no warning?

My eyes burn, brimming until everything around me is a hazy blur. There's a cry in the back of my throat, readying itself, threatening to burst to the surface if I don't do something immediately.

My knees give out, and I grip the edge of my dresser to steady myself because I can hardly summon the strength to stand. If my boyfriend weren't hogging the bathroom we share, I'd be on my knees in front of the toilet, expelling the shocked contents of my stomach in an attempt to quell the maelstrom inside me.

My gateway to Grace's life has come to a screeching halt. Just like that.

Everything I live for just . . . gone.

"Autumn, you all right out there?" Ben asks from the other side of the door. "I heard a loud noise. Everything okay?"

No. Everything is *not* okay.

I don't answer. I can't. And the bathroom door swings open just as I push myself to standing and clench the lapels of my robe so he can't see what I'm wearing underneath it.

"I'm fine," I say. "Had a dizzy spell. Think I'm coming down with something."

Ben's blue eyes narrow and then relax. He buys it. He buys everything, all the time.

I check my reflection in the dresser mirror, dragging my fingertips through my sandy hair and piling it all into a messy bun on the top of my crown, precisely the way this pretty girl from a gas station yesterday morning wore hers. Gathered. Twisted. Elastic'd. Pulled and yanked into messy submission. I've also managed to scrounge up a sheer white blouse from the back of my closet, and I've slid two chicken cutlet-shaped inserts into my push-up bra. I'm one hundred percent sure Pretty Girl had a boob job.

Everything's hidden under my fluffy gray bathrobe, and the second Ben leaves, I'll stain my lips in bold, electric red. There's a

MINKA KENT

bluish undertone to this particular shade, which I've learned from several fashion and beauty magazines tends to make teeth appear to be the whitest of white. And if there's one thing I've learned in my twenty-five years on this God-forsaken planet, it's that rich people almost always have teeth the color of driven snow.

A cloud of steam floats from the bathroom doorway, wrapping its damp warmth around me and carrying with it a hint of Ben's cologne, which isn't actually Ben's at all. Another man, Dylan Abernathy, wore it first.

I follow his wife, *@DeliaAbernathy*, on Instaface, reveling in their every documented, picturesque moment like it's my own. And it *is* mine. All I have to do is close my eyes and I'm transported to their serene cottage on the Portland coast of Maine. I breathe in, and I can feel the salty air in my lungs, pulling in the scent of the ocean again and again.

I spotted the cologne in the background of one of her photos once, and I had to order a bottle for Ben. It smells like wet moss and rubbing alcohol, but he insists he loves it anyway.

Sometimes I imagine Delia inhaling Dylan's cologne, her nose buried in the curve of his neck, and when I kiss Ben, sometimes I pretend we're them, my hands slinking up his shoulders the way Delia might do. Our lips grazing. His scent enveloping us in a sweet moment of simplistic bliss. And in those fleeting seconds, I'm Delia Abernathy.

Inside and out. All over. Everywhere.

"You sure you're okay?" Ben's hands slink around my waist and his body presses against my back. The warmth of his lips grazing against the side of my neck follows, and I can almost feel the slight arc of his grin. "You need me to run to the store and get you some meds?"

"No, no. I'll be fine." I glance at my phone, which may as well be useless at this point, and I just want him to leave so I can wrap my head around all of this.

"Just take some time for yourself today, okay?" He lifts his dark

8

brows, searching my eyes for confirmation.

All I do is take time for myself anymore. Losing my job as a medical assistant at Children's Medical Group two months ago has given me more than enough time to take care of myself.

"I will," I say.

"Good." He kisses my neck again. "Because I'm getting off early tonight."

My mind spins, trying to recall what we had planned for tonight.

"My sister's birthday?" His dark brows lift as he attempts to jog my memory. "We're taking Marnie out for dinner? You said you wrapped her gift last night."

"Oh. Right." I force a smile, lying through my teeth. I haven't wrapped his sister's gift yet. I haven't even purchased it. Mentally adding that to my to-do list for the day, I rise on my toes, press my lips against his, and send him off to work with a, "Have a nice day, Benny."

He both loves and hates when I call him that, but it always elicits a smile, and I need him to believe nothing's wrong. At this point, I need Ben now more than ever and for reasons he'll never understand.

Sometimes it feels wrong staring into his unassuming blue gaze and basking in his adoring smile while knowing I chose him the way a woman might choose the perfect pair of shoes from a mail-order catalog.

I saw. I researched. I chose.

But he made it so easy; his social media was a click-of-the-mouse smorgasbord.

Before I'd officially met Ben Gotlieb, I knew everything there was to know about him. Where he grew up (Rochester, New York). Where he attended college (University of Vermont). His favorite band (Coldplay). His favorite food (Mexican). What he did for a living (accountant). I knew he was single. I knew he was the oldest child, which meant he was responsible and dependable. I knew he was kindhearted as evidenced by the abundance of inspirational and motivational articles he'd post on his newsfeed. I knew he was a runner who traveled the country for marathons, collecting medals and stickers to showcase on the rear window of his hunter green Subaru. It took me all of an hour in front of a computer screen to ascertain that Ben Gotlieb was a good man.

As Ben would check in to various pubs and restaurants, I would follow.

Keeping back.

Always watching.

Observing who he was with and which kind of women drew his eye.

And Ben definitely had a type.

The blondes never did it for him. Neither did the brunettes or the redheads. But the ones with the Jennifer Aniston sandy-blonde hair caught his attention every time. He seemed to be drawn to the girl-next-door types. Low-slung boyfriend jeans and a V-neck t-shirt. Minimal makeup. Cute ponytail. Bookish glasses.

And so I had to become her.

With a phone full of Instaface screenshots of some beauty blogger named *@EmmaLeeFacesTheDay*, I marched into the salon on Vine and Copeland and had my stylist transform my muddy brown strands into *sandy ash blonde 532*. On my way home, I stopped at the optometrist, grabbing a pair of cute glasses with thick, tortoiseshell frames and a non-prescription lens. I ended my day with an extensive shopping excursion at the Valley Park Mall, balancing my overpriced iced mocha latte, which I was determined to start liking, with an armful of shopping bags and a maxed-out credit card.

It took several days and a lot of practicing in front of the mirror, but by the time the following weekend rolled around, I was ready to officially meet Ben.

Stepping into someone else's skin made meeting him that much easier. The way I walked . . . the way I casually traced my collarbone as I laughed . . . the way I let my stare linger on his just a second too long as my mouth curled into a teasing smirk . . . none of that was me.

And yet it *was* me.

"See you tonight," Ben calls out before he leaves our bedroom, and I watch him grab his leather billfold off the dresser and slip it into his back right pocket. Pulling his navy suit jacket over his broad shoulders, he lingers in the doorway, taking me in the way he has since the moment we first–officially–met. I can almost hear him asking himself how he got so lucky. Ben exhales, his gaze fixed on mine. "I love you, Autumn."

"Love you too," I say. And I mean it. Mostly.

I *think* I love Ben. A girl spends two years with someone and she ought to by now. It's just that he said it so fast. We'd only been dating eight weeks when he blurted it out over Chinese takeout–his choice–and a rented DVD–also his choice. And then he proceeded to ramble on about how he'd never met anyone like me, how he couldn't believe how perfect we were together, how it was as if his dream girl had just . . . manifested from nothing and waltzed right into his life.

Two months after that, he asked me to move in with him, and of course I said yes.

That was the whole reason I scoped Ben out in the first place.

He lived in the charming blue bungalow behind the McMullen family.

And I wanted to watch my daughter grow up.

CHAPTER TWO

Daphne

My blouse is soaked clear through, sticking to my skin and sending a quick shiver down my spine. Graham keeps the house at a frigid sixty-eight degrees year round. It's the way he likes it. Never mind the fact that he's rarely home. When he's not putting in fifty-hour weeks, he's sauntering around the country club greens pretending he's in the company of a quiet crowd who silently applaud his perfected chip shot.

Sebastian splashes in the tub, giggling when it hits my face. I drag the back of my arm across my chin before wiping a streak of running mascara from under my eye. Bathing my four-year-old is worse than bathing the enormous, hypoallergenic labradoodle Graham insisted on getting for the kids last Christmas.

"Come on, buddy. Let's get you out." I turn to grab a towel and ignore my son's whiny pleas.

"Daddy lets me stay in longer." He crosses his arms and brings his knees to his chest.

"Now you know that isn't true," I say, leaving out the fact that the number of times Graham has bathed the kids I could count on one hand. I attempt to tuck my hands under Sebastian's arms, but he's got them locked against his sides. "If you get out of the tub now, I'll read you an extra bedtime story later tonight."

I am that parent. The one who bribes. The one who, somewhere along the line, lost all control and hasn't the slightest idea how to get it back.

"I hate when you read me bedtime stories." Sebastian scowls, his square jaw clenched as he finally stands. He is a mirror image of his father: milky, caramel complexion with chocolate hair and clear blue eyes. On his best days, Sebastian is a delicious little boy, all sweet with a smile that could melt the coldest of hearts. On his worst days, Sebastian is a spoiled monster. "I only like when Daddy reads to me."

Refusing to take a four-year-old's insult to heart, I ignore him, draping a towel around his shoulders and hoisting him out of the tub. The sound of giggling girls coming from Grace's room makes me question whether or not they're changing into their school uniforms like I asked ten minutes ago.

Lifting Sebastian to my hip, I carry him to his room at the end of the hall and place him at the foot of his bed where I had the foresight to lay out his clothes for the day earlier. The sooner I can get him dressed, the sooner I can capture an ounce of my sanity before we hit the grocery store together.

"I don't want to wear dinosaurs. I want trucks." He kicks his legs in protest when I try to slide his jeans on and throws his T-rex shirt across the room.

"Dinosaurs look so good on you though," I say, knowing full well only crazy people try to reason with tantrum-prone preschoolers. I slide his leg into one side and ready the other, but he wiggles out and renders the pants halfway inside out. An exasperated sigh leaves my lips as I try once more. "Your daddy picked this outfit."

It's a lie.

But then again, so is every other facet of my life.

Sebastian's face lights when I mention his daddy. I was hoping Graham was going to get to see the kids before they went to school, but he kissed me goodbye before the sun came up this morning and whispered that he'd see me tonight after work.

"All right." Sebastian crawls off his bed and gathers his thrown shirt before handing it to me. "Sorry, Mama."

It's in these still, small moments I find myself falling back in love with being his mother. I think about the sweet hugs, the occasional unprompted *I love yous*, the lit smiles, and picked dandelions that make me think perhaps my son might actually love and appreciate me after all. I remind myself that maybe it isn't so bad – that it can only get better from here.

"Okay, let's check on your sisters." I take his hand and lead him down the hall, following the trail of laughter to Grace's room. The door is half closed, light from her lamp casting a warm glow that spills into the hall.

I smile when I hear my sweet Rose's giggle. And then a metallic snip follows. I storm through the doorway, the door banging against the wall and bouncing back.

"No, no, no, no . . ." My heart stops in my chest as I reach down and retrieve handfuls of Rose's silky blonde hair. Glancing up, Grace is frozen, shears in hand, wicked little smile fading.

I yank the scissors from her hand with a violent pull that startles both of us and sends her falling back on her bed. My seven-year-old Rose begins to cry.

"Rose . . ." I go to her, cupping her sweet face in my hands, my eyes filling with tears as I examine the monstrous haircut Grace saw fit to give her beautiful little sister. Finger-combing the baby blonde tendrils away from her forehead, her bottom lip quivers.

"Grace was trying to make me pretty, Mama," she says, her blue eyes two perfect glassy pools.

"You're already pretty, Rosie. You're beautiful just the way you

14

are." I kiss the top of her head, taking in a deep breath and inhaling the scent of her vanilla-orange shampoo. Her soft locks lie in a pile at our feet, the same hair she'd been growing out since her toddler years with the exception of the occasional back-to-school haircut. It was past the middle of her back . . . until tonight.

"Mommy, I'm sorry." Grace's voice pulls me from Rose, and I turn to face her. Seated on the edge of her bed, her expression shows no remorse. No regret. Her sandy hair hangs limp around her round face, in a constant state of disheveled tangles no matter how much I comb and tug and pull and braid. "I didn't mean to."

"I don't understand, Grace. You're old enough to know better." I glance down at Rose's hair, my anger coming to life by the second. My stomach is knotted, my fists clenched so hard they ache. This week it's Rose's hair. Last week she let the dog run out the front door and I spent an hour chasing it around the neighborhood like a crazy person. Two weeks ago, she dropped eight of my perfume bottles from the top of the stairs to the wood floor of the foyer to see if they'd break. Six of them did. My house still smells like a French brothel.

My hand grips the scissors so hard they leave indentations in my palm, and when I loosen my hold, I realize I've never seen this pair in my life.

"Where did you get these scissors?" I ask, shaking like a woman who's lost all control of her life.

I've taken every precaution to Grace-proof this house since I first suspected there was something special about her. Graham refuses to believe she's anything but perfect, but he doesn't see what I see because he's never around.

There's something off about her.

"Tell me, Grace." My voice is deeper, my stare harder. "Where did you find these?"

Grace sighs, rolling her eyes. "I took them from Mrs. Applegate yesterday. They were sitting in a cup on her desk."

"You *stole* from your *teacher?* From the *school?*" My jaw hangs for a moment until I can compose myself. "We do *not* steal, Grace McMullen. Do you understand me?"

"Yes." Her ten-year-old voice is chock full of resentment as she stares at the garish Hello Kitty poster on her wall.

"Look me in the eyes when you speak to me," I say.

Her lifeless brown gaze snaps onto mine, her jaw clenched.

"Apologize to your sister. And you're giving the scissors back to Mrs. Applegate today along with a handwritten apology. I'll be back to check on you in a minute," I say. "I want you dressed for school. Teeth brushed. The bus leaves in twenty minutes, and your breakfast is getting cold. Move it. Do you understand?"

"Yes." She stomps to her dresser, yanking the top drawer until it almost falls out, and from the corner of my eye, I spot the eight-hundred-dollar cocktail dress I thought I'd lost last year. I'd even gone so far as to blame the dry cleaner, taking our business else-where and sharing my suspicions with the girls at the coffee shop one frenzied Thursday morning.

"Why do you have my dress?" I march over, yanking her other drawers open to see what other treasures were waiting to be discovered. Just as I suspected, I find my grandmother's antique, diamond-encrusted timepiece resting in a Strawberry Shortcake pencil box. I fired the last housekeeper over this missing watch. Another opened drawer contains a box of chocolate cupcakes and a half-eaten bag of family-sized potato chips, crumbs scattered and sticking to her winter sweaters. Shaking my head, I mutter her name under my breath.

I'd be lying if I said there wasn't a day that passes when I don't regret bringing Grace home. Our bond hasn't been easy, and most days, I'm not sure it exists at all. Everything about her is a chal-lenge, and most days I don't have it in me to conquer those tribu-lations. Adopting a baby was a quick-fix. A marital Band-Aid. Another one of Graham's non-negotiable whims. And I was just a young wife, trying to please the only man I'd ever loved, desperately trying to keep him at any cost.

And if there's anything I've learned in my thirty-six years, it's that desperate people are incapable of making good decisions.

CHAPTER THREE

Autumn

THE WAY I SEE IT, I HAVE TWO OPTIONS: I CAN CRUMBLE TO A dysfunctional heap, refusing to move off the sofa and mourning the loss of Daphne's Instaface account while raising a million red flags with Ben. Or I can carry on like nothing's wrong until I figure out what I'm going to do next.

For now, I need Ben. Ben equals access to Grace, even if we're separated by an acre of yard space and a fence.

I'll figure this out, and I'll land on my feet. Always have, always will.

The supermarket is packed for a Thursday morning. Apparently no one in Monarch Falls has anything better to do this morning. The yoga shop must be closed for renovations? Maybe the coffee shop ran out of soy milk? The bakery out of gluten-free cupcakes?

"Hi." To my right, a man's voice cuts through the cereal aisle, and when I glance up, I see a dopey grin with a laser-sharp stare pointed at me.

For a moment, I'd forgotten that today I'm the pretty girl from the gas station. Red lips. Big breasts. Tight jeans. Sexy, messy bun.

It feels good to be her right now, to step out of my burning, twitching, anxious skin. I almost forget about Instaface for a moment. *Almost.*

I smile the way I imagine she would, eyes half-squinting, lips closed and pulled up in one corner. Lifting my left hand, I give a small wave with just my fingertips and push my cart past him. From my periphery I see him turn, and I allow his stare to linger until I turn the corner.

"Excuse me." An older woman with bushy gray hair and a lavender twin set nearly bumps into me with her cart, wielding the audacity to glare at *me* as if our near-collision was *my* fault.

"I'm sorry," I lie. I saw this woman seconds before she saw me. Her attention was fixed on the wall of oatmeal selections before her as she mindlessly pushed her cart forward one shuffled step at a time.

The woman huffs and keeps moving, giving me side eye as if my look today offends her personally.

Typical Monarch Falls old-moneyed bitch.

I wonder how Pretty Girl deals with people like her? Half of me thinks she's probably too oblivious to notice. Or maybe she's too coked up? I could definitely see Pretty Girl with a two-grand-a-day coke habit. Easy.

Up ahead, a mother with a screaming infant and another mother with a squirrely toddler are blocking the exit of the cereal aisle, gabbing on about something that seems to get the two of them fired up. Maybe preschools or the PTA? Swimming lessons? I couldn't care less. Their faded yoga pants and dark-circled eyes don't interest me. They may as well be invisible. I don't see a mental vacation when I look at them. I see exhaustion.

I would never want to be them.

"Excuse me." I say with a polite smile, staring straight ahead as my cart is pointed in the direction I intend to go.

The women stop yammering and glance up, gawking at me with the kind of stare that suggests they're contemplating how their life would've turned out had they not married their high school sweethearts fresh out of college and popped out a litter's worth of children before their thirtieth birthdays.

Not that there's anything wrong with that.

It's just not my cuppa.

Not my cuppa . . .

I stole that phrase from a woman on Instaface I followed briefly last year. Her posts intrigued me at first. She seemed well-traveled. And her boyfriend was some Italian model who walked runways all over the world. Anytime she didn't like something, she'd politely say it wasn't her cuppa, and it just stuck. Eventually her boyfriend dumped her, her posts dwindled to few and far in between, and after a while she fell off the face of the earth. I unfollowed her shortly after that, and now I can't even recall her name.

The exuberantly exhausted mothers stop gawking long enough to move their carts and let me through. I don't waste my breath thanking them. People who are inconsiderate enough to block a busy grocery aisle with idle chitchat don't deserve common courtesy.

Rounding the corner, I stop at the end of the gift aisle, fighting the smart ass smirk on my mouth.

Marnie. Marnie. Marnie.

If I wanted to be the bigger person, I'd run to the mall and grab something decent. Maybe a giftcard to Bloomies or Victoria's – something she might actually use and enjoy. But I'm feeling very, *very* small today.

The image of Marnie's crestfallen face comes to mind when I envision handing her a cheap stuffed bear and a bouquet of dyed carnations wrapped in pink cellophane.

She would hate it.

She would hate me.

But she already does. And she's made her sentiments crystal clear dozens upon dozens of times behind my back. Never to my face. She's spineless like that. Any time she gets Ben alone, she feels the need to opine that he's too good for me, that I'm using him. Ben shuts her down each time, bless his heart, but it doesn't keep her from bringing it up all over again the next time.

Snickering, I reach for a neon green teddy bear with scratchy matted fur, checking the price tag.

$4.99.

And then I think of Ben.

I can't do that to him. He's a good man. He asked me to get his sister a birthday gift, and that's exactly what I need to do, even if it kills me.

Placing the ugly bear back on its shelf, I trudge ahead, moving toward the card aisle. A pastel yellow birthday card with the most generic inscription draws the short straw, and I toss it in my cart before making a beeline for the gift card section.

I know many things about Marnie Gotlieb.

I know she loves to shop-til-she-drops, and I know her favorite things in the whole wide world are covered in images of dead presidents. I know she likes to be wined and dined by various older men she meets through online dating apps. I know she once slept with her college chemistry professor in exchange for a passing grade.

Pretty sure she has some daddy issues going on as well, though I'm not sure how that came to be since their father is Ward Cleaver reincarnate.

Swiping a couple gift cards from the rack, I grab one for a bookstore, because this woman needs to spend some quality time away from a phone screen, and another for a department store to mask the passive aggressive undertones of the first gift card.

Tossing them in my cart, it occurs to me that I told Ben I had wrapped Marnie's gift last night, which means I need to get her an actual gift. Heading toward the bath and body aisle, I grab a few blocks of organic, hand-milled soap from a low shelf, three for twelve dollars, and then I swipe a bottle of honey almond lotion.

I have no idea what Marnie's favorite scents are, nor do I care.

Rounding the next aisle, I stop in my heels when I spot a familiar image in the distance.

Long legs, red-bottomed shoes, glossy red hair and a screaming toddler paint a portrait of a woman I know like the back of my hand but have yet to meet in real life.

Daphne McMullen pushes her filled cart, slowly perusing organic boxes of macaroni and cheese and loaves upon loaves of gluten-free breads. Her hair glides across her back when she moves, and she turns to the youngest McMullen, four-year-old Sebastian, every few seconds to tickle his chin or give him an Eskimo kiss.

If there is a God, this must be his way of apologizing for this morning. He's sorry her account disappeared. He put her in my path on purpose.

My heart thrums and my mouth runs dry. With a tight grip on the handle of my cart, I watch, jaw loose and eyes glued. She's beautiful in person, which tells me what I've suspected all along: that her Instaface persona is authentic, that Daphne McMullen is exactly who she says she is.

It makes my heart warm, watching her in action with her youngest. Grace is truly lucky to be able to call Daphne her mother.

I chose well.

Sebastian drops something on the floor, and Daphne crouches down to retrieve it, glancing around. My chest tightens, and I turn my head in the opposite direction. I can't stand here and gawk, though if I could, I'd do it all day long.

Behind me, an elderly gentleman clears his throat as if to tell me I'm in his way.

"Excuse me," I say, pushing my cart away.

When I enter the next aisle, I spot Daphne in the distance, making her way to the checkout lanes, so I do the same. Checking the customer congestion ahead, I try and calculate which register she'll choose, and I succeed. Within moments, I've secured a spot behind a round-bellied middle-aged man, who happens to be standing behind Daphne. She doesn't look past him, and she doesn't notice me.

To my back, a woman keeps checking out the other aisles as if jumping to the next one over could possibly save her a lifetime of waiting. She checks her watch, exhales, then glances at my cart. She seems annoyed, whether at this situation or the fact that I'm pushing a full-sized cart for three paper-y items and a few bars of soap. Maybe she's offended that I'm taking up an unnecessary amount of checkout aisle space, and that personally offends her? It's a perfectly reasonable reason to get bent out of shape . . . if you're a miserable asshole.

Two lanes down, a green light flicks on, and a female checker calls, "I can help whoever's next."

The woman behind me scurries off, followed by the hard-bellied man in front of me who nearly topples over the candy display in the process.

People.

This is what's wrong with the world.

And this is why I hate the grocery store: it's a fucking zoo with real, live human animals.

I glance up, readying to take the man's place in line, only my heart drops and my body breaks into a cold sweat when I remember Daphne is standing there, and it takes me a second to realize this is real.

This is happening.

I'm not imagining this.

With my heart pulsing in my ears, I move forward. I move closer and closer still until I'm directly behind her.

If I thought I was star struck before, watching from an aisle endcap twenty feet away . . . that was nothing compared to this.

I observe from my periphery as Daphne chitchats with the checker, some barely-nineteen-year-old kid with acne and auburn hair and a smattering of freckles across his full face. His movements are jittery and uncoordinated, like he's extremely self-aware in her presence, though she's calm as can be. Her skin is the color of bisque porcelain, creamy and flawless, and her golden blonde hair falls around her shoulders in all the right places, shiny and lush.

Four-year-old Sebastian, sits in the front of the cart, kicking his legs and singing some wildly annoying yet equally adorable little nursery rhyme to himself.

"Just a minute, my little love," she says, her voice soft as cashmere and rich as honey as she cups his chubby cheek in her right hand. I think about all the hashtags, and especially her oft used *#mylittlelove*, and my chest expands with warmth. "We're almost done."

Glancing in her cart, I spy things like pomegranates and starfruit, unsweetened almond milk, organic dates, and arugula. These are the foods she'll feed her family.

These are the foods she'll feed my daughter.

It's a far cry from the processed casseroles and frozen, prepackaged dinners and store-brand potato chips I grew up on.

"Two hundred five dollars and eleven cents," the cashier says, clearing his throat after his voice cracks. He pops his knuckles against his green apron and scans the line, avoiding eye contact with the rest of us as Daphne slides her shiny silver debit card through the machine.

Sebastian kicks her again. Harder this time. And she turns to him, leaning down and whispering something in his ear that makes him stop. She makes parenting look like a breeze, and everyone around us is watching in awe.

"Do you have children?" she asks the cashier.

"No, ma'am," he says, clearing his throat again. The color of his face intensifies the longer she focuses her attention on him, and I wonder if she has this sort of effect on everyone she comes across.

Probably.

"I didn't think so," she says with a kind chuckle. "Almost naptime for my little guy."

Checking my watch, I note that it's only ten in the morning. I'm not a parenting expert, and I only worked at the children's clinic for a couple of years, but I'm pretty sure four-year-olds don't take morning naps.

"Thanks so much." Daphne takes the receipt from the red-faced teen, folds it in half, and slips it into her wallet in a hurry. In the process, a twenty-dollar bill falls out, fluttering to the cement floor as her heels click away.

A swift tap on my shoulder from the man behind me pulls my attention from Daphne momentarily.

"You going to give that to her?" A mustachioed Good Samaritan points to the lifeless bill that has come to a stop a few feet before me.

Up ahead, Daphne is almost to the exit, and without thinking, I reach down to grab the twenty before chasing after her.

"Ma'am," I call out, though Daphne McMullen is much too youthful and beautiful for such a common formality. "Excuse me . . ."

Her heels, because of course this beautifully enigmatic creature would grocery shop in heels, come to a quick stop, and she scans the area around her until her gaze stops on me. My hand is outstretched as I move closer, my heart pounding so hard in my chest, I struggle to breathe.

"You dropped this," I say, marveling at how such a simple exchange could knock the wind out of me.

Her lips, shaded in rich mauve, pull into a smile that lights the rest of her face. Smoothing her hand along her flat belly, she saunters toward me, taking her time and meeting me halfway, and I'm amazed at how a person can strut along in heels the same way anyone else would strut along in tennis shoes.

"Thank you so much," she says, her eyes searching mine as if they're vaguely familiar. And they should be. Grace, *our* Grace, has *my* brown eyes. She has *my* wide forehead. *My* round face. *My* muddy brown hair.

I nod, releasing the breath I'd been sheltering and finding myself uncharacteristically incapable of forming a response.

Daphne smiles, releasing me from this moment when she turns back to her impatient Sebastian. Just like that, our exchange is over, and the only mother my daughter has ever known walks away, pushing Grace's little brother in her overflowing shopping cart, loading the organic groceries in the back of the SUV that hauls my daughter from soccer to ballet, heading to the home my daughter runs to after the bus drops her off from school at three fifteen every afternoon.

Returning to the checkout lane in a daze, I retrieve Ben's credit card from my wallet and pay for Marnie's gifts. The cashier doesn't fumble and flit in my presence. He doesn't clear his throat or crack his knuckles. His eyes don't dart around. He only stares at me with dull, vacant eyes, and then he calls out, "Next!" before I have a chance to gather my things.

Within minutes, I'm seated in the front seat of my car, slamming the visor down to take a good look at myself. Or rather, Pretty Girl. My red lips are fading, some of the lipstick smudged beyond my lip line, and my perfectly messy bun has fallen loose in several places, sagging past my crown. I can never get these things to stay in place for more than an hour or two.

I'll never figure out how these women make it look so easy, but I'll never stop trying. After all, they're proof it's possible.

I start my engine and blast the AC. Autumn, the one who does not turn heads or make teenage boys nervous, stares back at me from the rearview mirror, a stark reminder that she was always there, hiding beneath the façade. Being Pretty Girl was fun for all of two hours, but the second I get home, I'm retiring her in favor of Daphne.

Daphne trumps them all.

The years have come and gone. I've followed and unfollowed more people than I can recall. I've tried on a dozen personas purely for fun and neatly placed them back in their box when I was done. I've been inflicted with all-consuming obsessions and morbid fascinations that have dissipated just as quickly as they began, but it's different with the McMullens.

They're practically family.

And they're the only true family I've ever known.

Even if they don't know it.

———

"You're not ready yet?" Ben stands by the front door at four o'clock, dropping his keys in the small ceramic bowl on the console table. His expression is laced with a miniscule hint of frustration, but I know him, and he isn't angry with me. In fact, he's never been angry with me for anything. Ever.

He may be frustrated with the situation . . . but not with me. Not with his dream girl.

Marnie steps out from behind him, sighing audibly and avoiding eye contact. It doesn't matter how many times we've been around one another, the first fifteen minutes, give or take, are always awkward.

"Babe, we've got dinner reservations in the city at six." Ben yanks on the cuff of his jacket, checking his watch, and then he claps his hands. "Come on, let's go."

His sister meets my gaze in passing before settling into Ben's favorite leather chair and whipping out her phone like an addict in desperate need of a fix.

"I just have to fix my hair," I say. "And throw on something different. I'll be quick."

I disappear upstairs for a while, frantically pulling myself together. I feel bad, I do. I feel bad for Ben. I should've been ready, but I made the fatal mistake of checking Instaface at two o'clock this afternoon and getting sucked into profile after profile, each click of a picture leading me to another and another. Before I knew it, I was in too deep and had completely lost track of time.

By the time I return downstairs, Ben and Marnie are standing next to the door, Marnie firing off a scathing text. I bet she's bitching about me to their mother, accusing me of intentionally causing us to be late.

I saw his mother's phone once, at a family dinner. She'd left it unlocked on the bathroom counter, and I read through all of her text messages with her daughter. Marnie would vent about me and his mother would half-heartedly agree, giving general affirmations and never once coming to my defense or saying she disagreed with her propaganda.

"Sorry," I say. *To Ben.*

He gets the door, and we file out to his Subaru. It's an hour and a half drive into Manhattan this time of day. The only reservations we could secure at Marnie's favorite restaurant were for six o'clock, and we had to make them almost seven months ago. God forbid Marnie celebrates her birthday at a *local* restaurant. Monarch Falls, in all its uppity glory, apparently doesn't contain the kind of options that best suit Marnie Gotlieb's sophisticated palate.

"Shotgun!" Marnie calls out, because apparently we're in high school tonight.

I groan silently while forcing a smile across my face. "Of course. It's your birthday."

I would've given it to her anyway, but now it feels like an irritating obligation.

I wanted to stay home. I even insisted to Ben that this night be about the two of them. I lobbied for a brother-sister bonding experience despite the fact that I knew thirty-six percent of the night would be spent with Marnie passive aggressively ragging on me and Ben changing the subject. But alas, Ben slipped his hand into mine, kissed my forehead, and teased me that I wasn't getting out of it.

He doesn't see what I see.

He doesn't hear the snide comments or see the side-eyed glances. He doesn't pick up on the ice queen body language or the fact that the two of us enjoy each other's company about as much as someone with a hatred of sharply pointed objects would enjoy an acupuncture session.

It's not that being around Marnie makes me uncomfortable. I'd just rather avoid it if I could. It isn't pleasant. Knowing I have to see her is akin to knowing I have a gynecological appointment coming up. It just isn't something I look forward to, and it's one of those things I just want to get over with. Plus, she reminds me of those high school bitches, the ones that ran the school and tormented me every single day of my pathetic teenage existence. She's one of *them*. One of those plastic girls. It's like they're cut from the same cloth. There must be some secret central brain somewhere that girls like her feed off of because they're all the same carbon copy snobby legionnaires.

Privileged. Insecure. Entitled. Mean.

Ben can be so oblivious sometimes. It's probably his best–and his worst–quality. But I knew that going into this. It was one of the reasons he was so perfect for me; for my objectives.

Sliding into the backseat, I buckle up and fix my gaze out the passenger window. I'm seated directly behind Marnie, appreciating that the headrest does a sufficient job of blocking my view of the back of her annoying, egg-shaped head.

I stifle my annoyance when I watch her fiddling with Ben's radio. That's what Marnie does when she comes around. She messes with things. She touches everything. Like it's hers. Like she owns it. She's like a goddamned cat rubbing her scent all over everything. She makes herself right at home. It doesn't matter where we are, if Ben's around, Marnie runs the show.

And Ben laughs!

Like it's *endearing*.

Never mind the fact that his sister took it upon herself to rearrange our silverware drawer shortly after I moved in with him. She also rearranged our living room, insisting that he throw away some of my things because they just didn't go with anything. She kept using the word "clash," and it was fitting, that word. Because she and I clashed from the second we met.

"Do you remember this song?" Marnie squeals from the front seat, placing her hand on Ben's arm as she bounces. "Summer before you went to college, we used to drive around listening to this CD over and over again."

She sighs, resting her head back and grinning at her brother the way she usually does . . . looking at him like he hung the moon. I suppose it's easy to understand why she's so infatuated with him. He's the only man, that I'm aware of, who pays her any mind. He's the only man who puts up with her annoying little nuances and desperate cries for attention. If they weren't brother and sister, and if he were about a decade or two older, he would *so* be her type.

I chuckle to myself at the thought.

It both sickens and entertains me.

Maybe this is normal behavior for a brother and sister? I wouldn't know. I have an older brother, and he's a giant dick. Always has been. Probably always will be.

"What's so funny back there?" Ben turns the music down, glancing up at the rearview mirror.

I wave him off, biting my thumbnail because he thinks it's

cute. "Oh, nothing. I was just thinking of something funny I saw online earlier."

Marnie's posture is tense now, her head slumped against the passenger headrest as if I've just sucked all the air out of her birthday balloon.

"Can you turn the music back up, babe?" I ask. The last thing I need is to give Marnie more ammunition against me. "I love this song."

I hate this song.

Marnie sits up, clearing her throat. Her favorite song is blasting, but she isn't dancing or singing along anymore. It makes me think, for a moment, that she'd forgotten I was back here.

Retrieving my phone from my bag, I check my Instaface feed for the tenth time today in hopes the McMullens' profile will instantly be restored, but no dice.

They're probably gearing up for dinner about now, and within the coming hour, Graham will pull in the drive and the kids will pile into his arms. I've seen it through their windows time and time again. They clobber him, scaling up his arms and legs and nearly knocking him over. It makes me smile every time.

I used to get a tiny electric ping in the center of my stomach whenever I'd see there was a new image. It was like a little fix every time. Every little mundane detail of their perfect little life lit my soul in a way I could hardly put into words.

It was all feels. Nothing but feels.

Closing out of Instaface, I pull up my photos, flipping to a screenshot from last week of Grace licking a beater covered in mashed potatoes. Below it, the caption reads, *"Dinner time! Behind the scenes with my little sous chef!"* Sebastian and Rosie, the McMullens' middle child, are in the background waiting patiently for their turns. Grace is grinning ear to ear, staring up at Daphne with the kind of love and adoration that both melts and breaks my heart.

Seeing Grace so happy, so nurtured, so loved, and watching

her live the kind of childhood I only ever dreamed of is all I could ask for in this life.

I'll find a way back to her, to my baby.

A mother always does.

CHAPTER FOUR

I FIND DAPHNE'S CELL PHONE NUMBER ON SOME PAY-PER-RESULT online directory during the drive home from the city. My entire body is humming and buzzing with a vibrant shade of hope, and I have to force myself not to smile in case Ben notices my bizarre mood shift.

First thing tomorrow, I'll buy a burner phone and some prepaid minutes, use the star-six-seven feature to block my number, and call once the kids are out of school. If I could hear her voice, and theirs in the background, that would be better than sheer nothingness.

Darkening my screen, I exit the backseat and climb up front as Marnie waves goodbye–to Ben. She saunters up the sidewalk to her colonial townhome on the north side of town, stumbling slightly thanks to the expensive bottle of red wine she enjoyed with her steak dinner. Ben waits, watching as she fumbles for her keys, and then he shifts into reverse the second she disappears behind the front door. I'm not sure he knows, but his parents

33

bought this place for Marnie straight out of college, hoping, at least I assume, that unloading this kind of responsibility on her might spark a little ambition.

I fail to see their logic, but I digress.

Ben has no idea. Or if he does know, he's never once complained. Over the past two years, I've come to learn that Ben mostly worries about himself. He minds his own. He doesn't notice that he could probably use a new car. He doesn't concern himself with obtaining the latest model iGadget or the most stylish wardrobe despite the fact that his handsome income could afford him anything his simple heart desires.

Ben is securely and contently in his own little world.

"You okay?" Ben slips his hand into mine as he backs out of Marnie's driveway. "You've been quiet all night."

I darken my screen and slip my phone into my bag, turning and offering a reassuring, sleepy smile.

"Of course," I say.

Ben slaps the steering wheel, a move that catches me off guard and sends my heart temporarily into my throat.

"What?" I ask.

"You know what I just realized?" he asks. "We forgot to give Marnie her gift."

Damn it.

"Maybe you can drop it off tomorrow?" he asks, brows lifted.

I'd love nothing more.

"Sure," I say. I'll get right on that as soon as I buy my new phone.

He gives my hand a thankful squeeze.

Somewhere on the other side of town, Grace McMullen is snuggled beneath warm covers, her belly full from dinner, a sleepy smile on her face. Closing my eyes, I send her my love the way I do every night.

"Are you happy?" Ben's question causes my eyes to flick open, and headlights from an oncoming car send a sharp sting to them.

"What are you talking about?"

"You were so quiet tonight. It's like you cut yourself off from the conversation. And really, Autumn, you've been distant these last couple of months." He slows to a stop at a yellow light, turning his attention my way. "Every since you lost your job, it's like you're pulling into this shell, and I don't know how to get you out of it. You don't talk as much as you used to. You walk around in a daze. You're forgetful, and you never used to be forgetful. Are you depressed? Do you want to talk to someone?"

If that's his perception of me, I had no idea. I was quiet tonight, yes, but the last couple months I thought things were better than ever between us.

"Ben." I force a smile, exhaling through my nose and tilting my head to the side. "There's nothing to worry about."

The car behind us honks, and we both gaze up in tandem at the green light. He releases my hand, placing his at two o'clock on the steering wheel, and presses his foot into the accelerator with gentle patience.

"All I know is you're not you anymore." His lips press into a flat line. "It's like I wake up with one person . . . and I come home to someone else. One minute you're up, the next minute you're down."

Clearing my throat, I scoot closer to him, resting my head against his tense shoulder.

"It's weird not having a job to go to every day," I say, searching for the words that will put his mind at ease. "I guess I'm still settling into this routine. Trying to figure out what I want to be when I grow up."

I glance up at him and spot a smirk.

"What *do* you want to be when you grow up?" he asks.

Daphne McMullen, but since that's not an option . . .

"I don't know." I shrug one shoulder, sitting up straight. "Maybe I'll go back to school for nursing? I loved working at the clinic. I love kids."

"What about teaching?"

I shake my head. Standing in front of thirty pairs of eyes all expecting me to be some kind of shining example for them sounds like a recipe for disaster. And I'd have to be myself, every single day. Day in. Day out. I'd die of mental fatigue by the end of the first school year.

It's exhausting being me.

Living with my thoughts.

Hiding my vulnerabilities behind someone else's clothing.

"Well, take your time," Ben says, resting his hand on my left thigh and squeezing my knee. "I kind of like having you home more, especially on the weekends."

Me too. I hated working Saturdays.

"Your hours were terrible too." His face wrinkles, and I think about all those times I'd come home to Ben eating canned soup for dinner or a bowl of cereal. Which always struck me as odd, because Ben knows how to cook. I make us dinner most nights now, most of the time imitating something I watched on TV that morning and taking all the credit. He hasn't explicitly admitted this, but I know Ben enjoys coming home to a hot meal like he's some 1950s husband. And I know that he secretly loves that his dream girl no longer comes home in snot-covered scrubs with tired feet, and instead she pounces into his arms at five thirty with a smile on her face.

He gets me all to himself now.

At least as much of me as I'm able to give.

Yawning, I press my cheek against the cool glass to my right, my eyes growing blearier by the minute and the distance hazing over. I want to go to bed. I want to lie in Ben's arms, feeling his warm breath on the top of my head as he pulls me against him. I never used to like it. The smothering. But I've gotten used to it. I can tolerate it now, and on the rare occasion, I even crave it.

I'll probably close my eyes, pretending we're Graham and Daphne like I do most nights. There have been times when I swear in the dark, through squinted eyes, Ben could pass for Graham. They share the same square jaw and dimpled chin, the same chocolate brown hair and vivid baby blues.

Ben turns the corner to our neighborhood, and for a fraction of a second, a sliver of warmth runs through me. It's very possible that this is what contentedness feels like. I have to admit I am comfortable with the way things are. More so than I've ever been.

Sometimes I wonder what this would feel like if what we had were real. If we'd met on the street or at the grocery store. If our friends had set us up on a blind date and neither of us could deny the chemistry.

But it is what it is now, and I am what I am: his fantasy girl.

Letting him beyond my façade would shatter the illusion I've worked so hard to create. And the second that illusion is shattered, Ben isn't going to want me anymore. He's a rational, logical man, and he's generous and forgiving and annoyingly optimistic and understanding.

But he wouldn't understand this.

And I'd lose the only things I have left in this life; the one person who's ever genuinely loved me. And a front seat view into Grace's life.

CHAPTER FIVE

DAPHNE

THE SOFT HUM OF THE GARAGE DOOR WAKES ME FROM A TWILIGHT sleep. The blurry numbers on the alarm clock beside me read 9:52 PM. Sitting up, I throw the covers off my legs and tiptoe to the bathroom before Graham comes upstairs.

The night before our wedding some twelve years ago, my mother-in-law sat me down and gave me an earful of advice: *Never dress down. Wear makeup to bed. Keep your hair long. Always try to impress him in the bedroom, it'll keep him from growing bored with you. Stay the beautiful girl he married, not false advertising . . .*

Standing in front of the sink, I grab a boar-bristle brush and re-shape my blonde waves. Patting on a bit of breathable mineral makeup and brushing my teeth again, I give myself a once over and adjust the white satin nightgown that covers my matching teddy, both of which are new and both of which were purchased on a whim this afternoon.

We haven't made love in three weeks; a concerning record.

The swoosh of the door against plush carpet tells me he's on the other side of the wall.

"In here," I call out. Not that it's an invitation. Another one of my mother-in-law's *Marriage Rules* included never becoming too comfortable in front of one another in the bathroom, so we've adopted a closed door policy during the tenure of our relationship. "Be right out."

My heart pounds in my chest the way it always does before I see him.

I push the bathroom door open a moment later, standing in the doorway and watching the flicker of the TV as it paints colors across his bare chest. The covers are drawn to his waist, and his brawny arms open wide when he sees me.

My striking, handsome husband wears a dimpled smile just for me. The same one he's always worn. The one that still makes my stomach do backflips and somersaults. The smile I've never grown tired of.

And the smile I'd foolishly assumed all these years would only ever belong to me . . .

"You're home late this evening." I say it with a lilt in my voice, as if I'm making a simple observation and not a pointed accusation. I don't think there are many women who can do what I do. Who can see their husband with another woman and continue like it never happened at all. Maybe there are more of us, hidden away, silently keeping calm and carrying on because it's what you do when your entire world rests in the palm of one man's hand. Or maybe I'm the only one, and I'm completely crazy. "Kids missed you."

They say it takes a strong woman to leave. I say it takes an even stronger woman to stay and fight for what's rightfully hers.

He lifts the covers, and I crawl in beside him, taking my place in his arms and wondering if these arms held *her* tonight. Graham leans over, kissing my cheek, his eyes glued to the sports highlights on the glowing TV screen.

"Sebastian wanted you to read him a bedtime story," I say with a smile.

"That's adorable." He offers a distracted laugh and doesn't seem the least bit affected by having missed out on tucking his son into bed.

I lean against him, nuzzling my bloodhound nose into the bend of his neck and breathing him in–the way I do every night–comforted by the fact that his cologne still lingers, faded from his morning shower, and there isn't a trace of perfume to be found.

He wasn't with her tonight.

I exhale, shoulders loosening and feeling slightly better, existing in this space with my husband and trying my hardest to focus on the here and now. He isn't perfect, and yet he is. He's all I've ever wanted, and I know I can forgive him, even if he doesn't ask for it, because that's what you do when you love someone so much you can't breathe when you think about losing them.

We built one hell of a beautiful life together.

We can fix this.

I can fix this.

I can remind him that the things he has here, our beautiful home, our twelve-year marriage, our three children . . . those things have permanence and substance and value. This girl he's been seeing . . . she's the equivalent of a leased Porsche. There's no real commitment and the fun will wear off soon enough. She might steal him away on lunch hours, but at the end of the day, he still comes home to me, and that has to count for something.

I even paused my Instaface account recently after much deliberation. Graham always complained that I spent too much time with my nose buried in my phone, so this is my attempt to be more present, more focused. My paid ads were generating me an easy few hundred dollars a month, but it was only ever a fun little project for me, a way to beautifully document my children's childhood.

"Grace cut off Rose's hair," I blurt. "It's awful. Short in the back, long on the sides. Some semblance of bangs."

Graham's attention whips to me, his brows lifted. "How? Where were you when this happened?"

"Bathing Sebastian," I sigh.

"We need to get you some help around here." Graham unfolds my arms, slipping his hand into mine and squeezing it. He's sorry. He's always sorry, even if the word doesn't care to exist in his vocabulary. "I know the kids are a handful sometimes. I don't expect you to do it all. And Rose's hair will grow back. I'm just happy nobody got hurt. I should've been here to help."

I could cry.

It's been months since Graham has recognized that I don't have it easy, that being a housewife and stay-at-home-mom is work. Plus, hiring help would mean I could dedicate more time to my budding social media empire. I'm up to eleven thousand followers, growing by hundreds every day. Companies are starting to send me products to sponsor, and I might have a shot at making an actual career out of my little hobby some day.

"I hate that you work late, especially on Fridays." I pout, missing the days when we could paint the town together or venture off to the city for a long, romantic weekend without worrying about hiring a babysitter equipped to handle Grace if she's in one of her moods.

"Me too." He brings my hand to his lips, depositing a kiss as his gaze affixes to the screen once more.

"I think Rose has strep again," I say, visually tracing the outline of his strong jaw, chiseled cheekbones, and perfectly straight nose. "She came home from school with a sore throat and those little red bumps all over her belly."

When I met Graham in high school, he'd just moved to our little town from Manhattan, and I'd never seen a boy so gorgeous before. He was worldly, wielding charisma and exotic unfamiliarity even at eighteen, and I was a girl who tended to blend into the background most of the time, daydreaming about the day he might notice me but never expecting it to happen in my wildest dreams.

And then it happened.

He saw me. He asked me on a date. And another and another. He became fixated on me in a way that no one ever had before, leaving love letters in my locker and commandeering my evenings and weekends as we became inseparable. Graham made me feel beautiful and worthy, and for some wildly inexplicable reason I don't care to explore, he still does.

Now I cling to that feeling like it's my lifeline.

I exist wholly in this space he has created, this space where I'm the most wonderful thing he's ever loved, and he's the only man I ever want to be with.

"One of us is going to have to take her to the urgent care clinic in the morning. She needs antibiotics," I add.

"Okay."

"But I'm scheduled to play Bunco at Heather's, and I have to pick up a French silk pie on my way. If I can't go, I'll need to find a replacement," I say. "And on top of that, I have a hair appointment I can't reschedule. I had to cancel last time because Grace forgot her field trip permission slip, and I had to run to Brinkman Academy before the bus left. Anyway, the salon will charge me a fee if I cancel again. They might even blacklist me, and that would be a shame because nobody in this town does hair like Mario."

"I'll take her," he says, turning to me, his expression softening.

My shoulders are lighter with those three little words.

"Really? Are you sure?" I try not to get my hopes up because he's done this before, but I think he means it this time. He must sense the exhaustion pouring out of me. He must smell the heartbreak and the undying devotion, its silence urging him to do the right thing and come back to me. "You'll have to take all three of the kids. Dr. Harrington likes to test and treat all three of them when one has it, otherwise they'll keep spreading it back and forth."

"Not a problem." He says it like it's nothing, but I'm so happy I could kiss him.

So I do.

I crawl into his lap, reaching for the remote and clicking off the TV. He attempts to protest until he realizes what's going on, and then his full-lips arch into a delicious smile – one he wears just for me. At least tonight.

"Is this new?" He's tuned to me now, and he slips a finger under the spaghetti strap of my teddy, releasing it and letting it fall off my shoulder. He breathes me in and cups my face, and just like that, he's mine again. His attention belongs to me. His body belongs to me. I possess him and he possesses me.

And I'm never letting go . . .

. . . at any cost.

And maybe, if I kiss him hard enough, I won't think about what I did last week.

CHAPTER SIX

DAPHNE

Tonight I'm cheating.

I stopped at Lucco's on the way home and picked up a pan of Tuscan lasagna, roasted vegetables, and homemade carrot cake. If I can slip in through the back door, I can re-plate everything before Graham sees, and if I'm lucky, he'll be busy with the kids.

Greta will be gracing our presence at seven o'clock sharp tonight. The first Saturday of each month is reserved for my mother-in-law and only my mother-in-law. She prefers to spend a half hour with the kids before their bedtime and the rest of the evening sipping wine on the back patio, her gaze and attention obsessively fixed on her pride and joy son.

Graham's only-child status has been both a blessing and a curse over the years. When his mother passes someday, he'll inherit a kingdom's worth of assets. Until then, we're stuck bending to her every desire, keeping her content to ensure our future, and our children's futures, are financially secure.

Slipping in the back door, I hear the drone of the TV from the family room mixing with girl giggles. In under five minutes, I've transferred the food and placed it in the oven on a warming setting.

"I'm home," I call out.

The thunder of little feet around the corner precedes a barrage of hugs. Six little arms wrap around me, all fighting to get the best grip. They only miss me when I'm gone. They only hug me when they haven't seen me all day. The rest of the time, I'm just a fixture. A milk-fetcher. A peanut butter and jelly sandwich-maker. A toy picker-upper.

"Hi, Mommy." Grace releases her hold on me, standing on her toes and puckering her lips. I lean down, giving her a light peck, when her hands drag through my hair. And she giggles, getting that maniacal look in her eyes. She covers her mouth and points at my hair.

Reaching for my silky soft strands, the ones Mario spent the better part of this morning combing, conditioning, highlighting, cutting, and blow-drying into perfection, my fingertips drag along some sort of sticky substance.

"Grace." My jaw clenches so tight it hurts. She holds her hands up, fingers spread wide and covered in melted chocolate. Nice of Graham to ignore my no-food-outside-the-kitchen rule. "Why did you do that?"

My salon-day hair is ruined.

The kids trample off, their bare feet leaving footprint-shaped smudges in my dark wood floors. I've begged and pleaded with Graham to let me replace them with something lighter, something with a matte finish that won't scratch or show every speck of dust and pet dander, but he refuses, always claiming he doesn't see what I see, and that I'm just being dramatic. Never mind that he comes home after the sun goes down each day.

The darkness naturally hides the things we don't want to see.

A cursory glance at the kitchen clock tells me Greta will be here any minute, and I haven't even had a chance to set the table or arrange the flowers. I tie my hair back, twisting it into a messy low bun, and retrieve a bouquet of red peonies from a brown paper bag on the counter.

"Nana's here!" Rose squeals from down the hall.

I place myself firmly in the last remaining seconds before Greta takes over my house, relishing in them as best I can.

Cocoa, our chocolate labradoodle, blazes through the kitchen and barrels down the hall, tail wagging fiercely. If I don't try and stop her, she'll knock Greta to the floor, and then I'll never hear the end of it. I abandon the flowers and chase after the dog, intervening at precisely the right moment.

Greta doles out grandmotherly hugs to the children, and she's nothing but smiles until Grace tries to tug at the giant pearl necklace that circles her wrinkled neck. She swats Grace's hand, giving her a stern look, and Grace backs up to the wall, arms crossed.

"Daphne." Greta gives me a once over, her mouth a reserved smile but her gaze clearly displeased with my frazzled appearance. For as long as I've known Greta, she's always deemed dressing down as a sign of disrespect. If she had her way, I'd be greeting her in nothing less than Pucci or Dior.

Rosie and Sebastian each take one of Greta's hands, pulling her toward the kitchen, and I move quickly to close the front door before releasing Cocoa's collar.

"Now where's that devilishly handsome son of mine?" Greta releases the children's hands, wandering away toward the family room in search of Graham. I'm quite positive she'd be perfectly fine not seeing the children at all. The grandmother thing is all a ruse. A familial publicity stunt.

The younger two children follow her, disappearing around the corner, and I head toward the kitchen to grab the plates and napkin rings from the butler's pantry before she comes back.

"Flowers," I say under my breath. I was in the middle of arranging the flowers just a second ago . . .

With an exasperated sigh, I leave the pantry with a stack of plates and place them on the island, which is now completely clear and void of any trace of red peonies.

Resisting the urge to yell out Grace's name, I quickly scamper from room to room until I come across a pile of pulled petals that bloom into a trail that leads behind the dining room table. I spot her dirty foot sticking out from beneath a chair.

"What are you doing?" I speak in a yelled whisper, my eyes hot with angry tears. "You destroyed those flowers, Grace. Why?"

Her leg tucks in, but she doesn't mutter a word.

"Grace," I say, jaw tight.

No response.

Falling to my knees, I meet her gaze under the table. A single red peony flower rests in her hands, and she lifts it to her nose.

"I'm going to ask you one more time," I say. "Why did you destroy those flowers?"

Her dark eyes settle on mine, unblinking. "Because they were for Nana Greta, and I don't like Nana Greta because she doesn't like me."

"Of course she likes you, don't be silly." I'm lying. I'm lying through my teeth. I've seen the way Greta looks at Grace, and there's no love in her eyes, only forced smiles and careful distances.

"No. She doesn't." Grace sighs, her shoulders hunched. "You don't have to lie to me, Mama."

For a moment, I don't see my troubled child. And I don't think about all the things she does that drive me up a wall or how she's ruined far too many beautiful family moments to count.

She's hurting.

And right now, she needs her mother . . . the only one she has.

The only one she'll ever have.

"Come." I open my arms, staying put and waiting for her to move toward me. That's how it's always been with Grace. Everything has to be her idea.

Hesitating for a few seconds, she eventually decides to crawl out from under the table, curling up in my lap. She may be ten, but she still fits. Her arms wrap around my waist and she presses her cheek against my shoulder.

It's been a long time since I've held her. In fact, I can't recall the last time. Years ago, perhaps.

Together we breathe, sitting in silence.

"Daphne?" Graham's voice calls from the next room.

I look down at Grace. "We have to get up now. Want to help me set the table?"

She shakes her head, squeezing me tighter. She doesn't want to move, as if she feels safe and protected in this dark space beneath the table; in my arms.

"Come on, don't do this," I say, gently pushing her off my lap.

Grace whines the way Sebastian does when he's not getting his way, but I ignore it, rising up until she slides off my lap and lands in a flaccid, protesting puddle on the floor.

"I'd love your help, Grace. It would mean the world to me." I inject lightness into my tone, clasping my hands together and feigning excitement when really I'm worried she's going to intentionally smash a few pieces of china when I'm not looking.

She groans, rising up, dragging her feet as she follows me to the kitchen, her arms limp and shoulders slumped forward.

"Mommy, can I tell you something?" she asks.

"Of course."

"And promise you won't be mad at me?" Her dark eyes are wide, scared almost, but I'm the one who's afraid here. I'm afraid of what she's about to confess.

I exhale. "Okay."

"You know when you were looking for your keys the other morning, before school?"

I nod. Lips tight. The girls were on their way to the bus stop and I was running late for Sebastian's preschool drop off. Graham had to run home to give me the spare from his key ring, and he underhandedly lectured me on not being so forgetful.

"I hid them in the flower pot." Her chin tucks against her chest, but her eyes hold on mine.

"Why did you do that, Grace?" I inhale deeply, trying to contain my frustration. I want her to feel like she can tell me everything, and this could be a make-or-break moment for us. "Do you want to tell Mommy why you'd do that? You made your brother late for school, and that wasn't very nice."

She bites her lip, glancing at the ground and back. "I wanted to take your car for a drive the night before."

My jaw hangs. *She's ten years old.*

"I thought it would be fun. And I took your keys from your purse, but then Daddy came home from work, and I didn't want to get in trouble, so I hid them in the flower pot."

"Why didn't you tell me where they were? You saw me looking for them."

"I didn't want you to yell at me."

"Grace, I've never yelled at you." I don't yell. It was never my mother's style and it'll never be mine. My fists are clenched at my sides, my jaw tight too, but I try to maintain a calm and loving gaze as best I can.

"I took money from your wallet too," she says quickly.

"How much?" I suppose the amount is irrelevant.

"I don't know. It's upstairs in my nightstand. You can have it back."

Damn right I'll be taking it back.

Lowering myself to her level, I brush her dark hair from her round face and tilt my head. "Is something going on that you need to talk to me about? You've been stealing lately, and getting into trouble, and not listening."

Grace shrugs, and I remember reading in a parenting book once that children, at this age, are incapable of knowing why they do the things they do. They react to things in their own ways, and acting out can be a cry for help or it can be a basic cry for attention.

I need to spend more time with her.

"Let's go eat, okay?" I slip my hand in hers. "We'll talk later. Just the two of us."

"Promise?"

I nod.

Greta is seated at the head of the table in the next room, sipping a glass of pinot noir Graham must have poured for her. We have a small reserve in the wine cellar, bottles hand-picked and kept in stock for Greta's visits.

"Dinner smells wonderful, Daphne," Greta says. "When are we eating?"

I look to Graham, then back to his mother. "The kids don't go to bed for another forty minutes or so. Didn't you want to spend a little more time with them? They only see you once a month."

Greta's lips purse, her pink lipstick bleeding into tiny wrinkles. Graham shoots me a look, silently sharing his frustration at me for putting Greta in her place.

"The kids really look forward to it," I say with a smile. My phone buzzes in my bag, but I ignore it. An unknown number has called me three times since this afternoon, but I refuse to answer a blocked call. "They miss you, is all I was trying to say."

"My, my." Greta twirls her necklace around two manicured fingers. "I suppose I was getting ahead of myself, wasn't I? That's what I get for showing up hungry and expecting to eat."

She rises, ruffling Sebastian's hair and taking his hand. Greta leads him to the family room, and Rose follows, Grace several reluctant steps behind.

"Need any help?" Graham stands at the marble island, a glass of pinot in hand, picking off a stray piece of lint from his charcoal-colored cashmere sweater.

Cocoa scratches at the back door. I stand frozen, waiting for him to take the initiative to let her outside for once. He does. To my surprise.

"Can you set the table while I run upstairs and fix my hair?" I ask.

He scrunches his nose. "Your hair looks fine."

I drag my palm across one side. "Grace ran her sticky fingers through it a little bit ago."

"So now you have to wash it again?" He seems annoyed by his assumption.

"No," I say. "I just want to get the chocolate out."

"Are you going to be up there all night?" He exhales, sipping his wine. "I know how you get. You say you'll be down in five minutes and you're up there for an hour."

My arms fold across my chest. "I don't understand the attitude tonight. Did something happen today?"

He stares over my shoulder, out our back door into our pristinely landscaped backyard oasis. Graham is standing before me, yet he's somewhere else. Maybe he wishes he were with *her* tonight.

My chest tightens when I think about him missing her. Preferring her.

After an endless minute of silence, his gaze flicks to mine. "It's just been a long day with the kids. I could use your help down here."

Welcome to my world.

"But your mother is here," I say, brows lifted.

He cocks his head to the side. He and I both know Greta doesn't lift a finger when it comes to the kids, but he'd never come out and admit that.

"Five minutes. I promise." Before Graham has a chance to protest, I run upstairs.

Peeling off my jeans, I slip into a pair of black leggings and pull a cream-colored tunic over my head. Grabbing my phone from my jeans pocket, I hurry toward the bathroom, determined to fix my hair at warp-speed just to prove a point.

Brandishing a round brush, an ionic hair dryer, and a can of super hold hairspray, I'm hard at work when my screen lights up with a text. It isn't a number I have stored in my phone, but it's one I instantly recognize.

I NEED TO SEE YOU AGAIN.

Swiping my phone off the counter, I clear the message and turn my phone off.

CHAPTER SEVEN

DAPHNE

I PARK THREE BLOCKS AWAY TUESDAY MORNING, BEHIND AN OLD brick building that used to house a tattoo parlor. It's empty now, and no one ever uses the alley except on Sunday nights when the corner deli gets its weekly bread delivery.

I send a text and check my reflection in the visor mirror.

Hiding my phone and purse in the glove compartment, I grab my keys and climb out, double checking that all my doors are locked before tucking my hair under a baseball cap and slipping on a pair of oversized sunglasses.

A minute later, I'm stepping lightly with one destination in mind. My heart beats, my throat constricting with every step that leads me closer to the leaning yellow house at the corner of Johnathan Street and North Fourteenth.

My eyes scan the streets, my body freezing every time a car passes and relaxing every time I realize it's one I've never seen before. Up ahead, the screen door on the side of his house gets caught with the wind and slams against the vinyl siding. I walk faster, almost entering a full trot, and breathe a sigh of relief when I see him peeking through the crack in the door.

Last time I came, I waited outside for three full minutes while he finished up some business inside. They were the longest three minutes of my life.

The door pulls just wide enough for me to slide in the second I approach, and the darkness behind it lures me in.

"Nice disguise." He snickers, drawing on the end of a lit joint and handing it to me. His eyes drink me in as I remove my sunglasses. I secretly like it. "You got here just in time."

I wet my lips and take it, puffing greedily twice before handing it back. I glance down at my casual ensemble fit for a day of errand-running, my throat burning as I hold the smoke and then exhale.

Slicking a palm down my running tank top, I ask, "What's wrong with my outfit?"

His mouth draws into a slow grin. "Nobody dresses like that in this part of town. What are those, ninety-dollar yoga pants? And someone's going to yank those hot pink sneakers right off your feet if you're not careful. They look brand new. And expensive as fuck. You can't dress like that around here."

"I don't have anything else." At least nothing fit for a quick sneak into the bad part of town.

"Make the hubby take you shopping." He laughs, taking two puffs and passing it back, and then he motions for me to follow him into his living room. It's dingy as per usual, Grateful Dead blankets hanging like curtains from the picture window and tin foil covering the three small diamond-shaped windows in his front door.

In here, I'm a world away.

I may not be soaking my feet in the crystal blue waters of Aruba, but a mental vacation is better than no vacation at all.

I take another hit before sinking down into an arm chair. This high should last a good ninety minutes, and as soon as it wears off, I'll have to head home. But I don't want to think about that.

I want to be here.

Escaping my existence.

I'm not Daphne McMullen in this house. There are no carpools, no appointments, no nail salons, bake sales, bath times, or infinite hampers of laundry. No permission slips. No gourmet dinners on the table by six. No screaming kids. No fires to put out. No dressing up just to go to bed. No cheating husband to preoccupy my thoughts.

"You get my text last weekend?" he asks, settling into his saggy leather sofa. He kicks his feet up on his coffee table, shoes and all. There's a black light shining from a lamp behind him, and it makes the laces of his sneakers glow bright.

"I did."

"You ignored me." He says it with a pained smirk. "That's cold."

"I was with family. You're not supposed to text me on the weekends, remember?" I lean forward, handing the joint back and waving to signal that I didn't want anymore. Too much and the high will last too long. I don't want to be stuck here longer than I have to be, and I need to get home in time to throw my clothes in the wash, shower, and get this sweet, skunky smell out of my hair.

"I was missing you was all." He shrugs, and when I look at him, all I see is the cherry red end of the joint in the dark. It nearly extinguishes before glowing brighter as he sucks on the end. "Your song came on."

"Which one is that?"

"You know the one." He chuckles a relaxed, stoner chuckle and begins to hum. Within a few bars, I recognize the tune as Billy Joel's *Uptown Girl*.

"That's not my song." I sink back into the chair, blanketed in something extraordinarily other-worldly. My heart beats hard in my chest, but my body is melted, merging with the shape of the chair beneath me. My eyes close softly, and a smile claims my lips.

"Everyone needs to do this. This is what the world needs. The world needs more of this."

He laughs. "Relax, Mama. I got you."

Within seconds, the mellowness of Pink Floyd pumps from speakers in the corners, filling the tiny confines of his living room, drowning out all my thoughts. I focus on every element of the music right down to the bass notes as they build and reverberate through my chest and rush through the end of my fingers and toes. I experience them. Really experience them. I'm one with them. One with this moment.

Higher than a kite.

Higher than a bird.

Higher than the clouds we used to fly through when Graham used to sweep me off to a weekend in wine country when it was just us two.

In the span of a four-minute song, I'm swept away. When it ends, my eyes part, two weary slits, and he comes into focus.

"Why are you staring at me like that?" I attempt to sit up straight, body hardly cooperating.

"I dunno." He's lying on his stomach across the couch, hands tucked under his chin like a child and eyes glassy. "There's something kind of sad and beautiful about you. Trying to figure it out."

"Don't waste your time." I adjust my position, eyes focusing on him. His smile is boyish, but his body is all man. The way he looks at me, his attention deposited like a lump sum in my direction, reminds me of Graham in our younger days.

"You want to take some of this home with you when you leave?" he asks. "On the house."

"What kind of question is that?" I snap at him, and I instantly feel horrible for it. But what was he thinking? I'm not leaving here with drugs in my possession. All I can picture is red lights in my rearview, my teary-eyed mug shot, my children being ripped from me, Graham leaving . . .

He sits up. "Just feel bad about last time. You gave me . . . I just feel like I owe you something in return."

"Last time was a mistake." My words slice through the thin smoke that lingers between us.

I'm not sure what I was thinking.

I wasn't thinking. That was the problem. I was high out of my mind. I was having a god-awful day. I was lonely. Doubting my marriage. Doubting my ability to raise these children into adulthood. Doubting every choice I'd ever made up to that moment.

It all happened in a blur of desperation and despondency. He kept telling me how beautiful I was, how lucky my husband must be to have me, and I lapped it up like an eager puppy, like a woman starved of love and affection.

And then his hand found my hair and his lips found my mouth, and before I knew what was happening, I was on my knees, my hands unzipping his fly. His satisfied moans were music to my ears. He had nothing but praise of the filthy variety. For the first time in a long time, I felt wanted. Desired. Appreciated. Carnally needed.

When it was all over, I bolted out of his house like a crazy person.

I cried so hard on the drive home, I had to pull over to the side of the road to catch my breath.

"Must not have been that big of a mistake," he says with an air of arrogance that doesn't quite suit him. "You came back."

"Forgive me, but I don't exactly know a lot of . . ."

"Dealers," he huffs, dragging a hand through his messy, dishwater blond waves that stop just above his shoulders. "You can say it. Or is it not in your country club vocabulary?"

"I can't tell if you're trying to be cute or insult me." My brows meet. "Either way, you're ruining this high, so can you please stop?"

"As you wish, Uptown Girl." His eyes flutter closed, the length of his lean body stretching so far his feet hang off the arm of the sofa.

"Why are you always in shoes?" My body drips over the side of the chair, or at least it feels that way. "Every time I see you. You have shoes on."

He puts his joint out in a nearby ashtray, mouth half-smirked. "Never know when you're going to have to run."

I smirk, readying a clever comeback, and then I stop myself once I realize he isn't joking.

"Plus have you seen this floor?" he adds. "There's a reason it's so dark in here all the time. The dark hides shit."

"You live alone, right?"

"Forever and always."

"Doesn't take much to tidy up every once in a while. You know, I think I have a spare vacuum in one of my storage rooms. I could give it to you if you'd like."

He sits up, elbows resting on his knees, his expression fading. "Yeah. That's just what I need. Some lady in ninety-dollar yoga pants pushing a goddamned Dyson down Johnathan Street to my house. Like *that's* not obvious."

I laugh. He doesn't.

"Sorry. I . . . I'm new to all this," I say. "I don't think like . . ."

Our eyes catch, and my mouth stops moving. I'm not sure I can finish my thought without insulting him.

"You can say what you need to say. Not much offends me. Thick-skinned over here." He leans back, slipping his hands behind his head, never taking his eyes off me.

Five weeks.

That's how long I've been coming here.

"I don't think like someone trying to stay out of trouble," I blurt. "I've never been in trouble before."

We have a standing date of ten o'clock each Tuesday morning. He has my phone number if he has to cancel, otherwise he knows I'll be here as promised.

"Mama, I've spent my entire life trying to stay out of trouble." He snorts, eyes fixed on me. When he inhales, his shoulders loosen and he studies me. "I've got it down to an art."

"Can I be honest with you?"

He shrugs. "Of course."

"I don't like when you call me 'Mama.'" The room spins, but I don't mind. "I've got three that call me that all day long. I come here to get away from that."

Dragging the back of his hand under his nose, he sniffs, mouth twitching. "Okay then. What am I supposed to call you? Been over a month now and you still won't tell me your name."

Right.

I rear-ended him last month on the east side of town when I was driving past Graham's office to make sure his car was still there. He'd canceled our lunch plans at the last minute, seeming distracted and uncharacteristically giddy on the phone. Not wanting a police report to be filed or Graham to see the insurance claim, I offered to give this man cash. He was reluctant at first. And then I fished a hundred-dollar bill from my wallet as a down payment as well as the gold Bulgari timepiece on my wrist. The damage to his car was noticeable; streaks of white paint on his chrome and a good-sized dent. My car was more or less unscathed.

After a quick deliberation, he scribbled down his number and address, and I showed up the next day, an envelope of cash in hand, not expecting for this man to invite me in, offer me a peace offering in the form of a freshly rolled joint, and present the solution to my problems in the form of a simple, temporary escape.

"You tell me yours first," I say. I didn't want to know his at first. It seemed pointless to exchange names. Plus, not asking for his name made it easier for me to withhold mine. But it almost seems silly to keep it up at this point.

"So if I tell you my name, you'll tell me yours?" He lifts an eyebrow, his face all angles and edges in the dark. He tucks his hair behind his left ear and clears his throat, lips holding his constant smirk.

"Yes. Your *real* name," I say. Inhaling, I readjust my position in the chair, soaking in the last half hour of this magically euphoric state. "Not your street name."

"I kind of like the mystery between us. It's hot," his mouth pulls at the corner, and I spot a dimple, "despite the fact that you're a married woman. Normally I'd respect the hell out of that by the way, but . . ."

My cheeks blush, even in my high state. "Oh, really? Is that why you let me put your . . . in my mouth."

His face winces. "Just call it a cock, all right? And yeah. I was blazed out of my mind when you did that. And you're sexy as hell. You think I was going to say no to that shit? What'd you expect? My dick wasn't going to roll into itself just because you're rocking a giant diamond on your finger."

"So then you *don't* respect that I'm a married woman." My eye catches the glint of my ring.

"No, you didn't hear me. I said I *normally* do. But the whole problem is that *you* don't. Because if you did, you wouldn't be here."

"I come here to get high and *only* to get high. You caught me in a moment of weakness last time. It won't happen again."

His head tilts to the side. "You know how many times people say shit like that? *It won't happen again. This'll be the last time. It was a one-time thing.* They never mean it. They keep doing the thing they said they weren't going to do because it makes them happy. Gives 'em what they *need*. Doesn't matter if it's right or wrong."

My mind goes back to that day, the cold wood floor against my knees, his hips thrusting as I choked on his length, his hands knotted in my hair. I felt free. Alive. Un-numbed.

I wasn't thinking about Graham. I was thinking about me; something I probably haven't done enough of these last few years.

"You can't compare that little indiscretion with the promises of the drug addicted and criminally corrupt." I brush a loose strand from my face, tucking it back under my cap.

"That's right. You're above that shit. I forgot."

"I'm not above anyone."

"Then why do you park three blocks away every time you come here? Why do you stuff all that fancy blonde hair under a baseball cap? Everyone else, they just come as they are. They park out front. Get their shit. Get on with their lives."

"I can't be seen here. You know my reasons."

"And yet you keep coming back."

"It's complicated."

"Life," he exhales, "is complicated. But please, by all means, keep believing that yours is some special snowflake."

"I don't expect you to understand." My high is fading fast, and I'm clinging on with everything I have. The moment I return to my car, it's all over. I'll be re-immersed in the very reality I came here to escape.

"What do you see when you look at me?" His question catches me off guard.

"I beg your pardon?"

He laughs. "Jesus. Not even a high can keep you from sounding like some resort wear broad. Let me rephrase my question. When you look at me, do you see some dope dealer or do you see a person? A human being?"

"Why do you want to know?"

"I've always been curious about your type. I figured you rich people walk around judging everybody else all day. Just curious how you judge me."

"That's a really strange question." I try to concentrate, swallowing against my smoky dry throat. "When I look at you," I begin, eyes focused in his direction, "I see someone who's taken an alternate route in life. You're intelligent. You don't let people push you around. I see someone I can be real with. You're not fake. I like that. You call things the way you see them, and you don't sugarcoat. You're probably the only person I can be myself around."

He's quiet, his eyes focused on the half-smoked joint in his ashtray. Digging in his pocket, he produces a lighter and then reaches for the joint.

"Well, then," he says, lighting up and speaking through pursed lips. "I'd say that's a crying shame. A real tragedy."

"I'm confused."

His gaze flicks to mine.

"It's sad you can't be real with anyone but me."

"Are you being sarcastic?" The hands of the clock on his TV stand glow under the dark light. It's time for me to go. I feel around for my keys, digging in my front pocket and wrapping my fingers around the metal. I'm not sure what I'd do if I got so high I lost them.

He takes a puff before placing the joint between his thumb and pointer finger, offering it to me. I shake my head and wave my hand.

"Not being sarcastic but for the record," he says, exhaling. "I don't feel sorry for you."

"I don't want you to feel sorry for me." My words snap back at him.

"Good," he says. "If you can't be real with people, that's *your* problem. Not theirs. Don't be one of those assholes who blame their problems on everyone else."

"Now you're making assumptions."

"Lady, you've been coming here every Tuesday for the last five weeks pouring out your heart and soul. All you do is take a few puffs and the filter comes off." He takes another toke. "At first I thought you had it rough, but now I'm convinced you do it to yourself."

My nose wrinkles. "You don't even know my name. How can you judge the way I live my life?"

I stand, hands gripped on my keys, eyes scanning the dark room to ensure I don't trip over something on my way out.

He rises, moving toward me. The sweet, stale scent of pot ash and smoke circles us. "I know enough. I know your husband doesn't appreciate you. I know your kids are spoiled little shits. I know your friends are a bunch of fake bitches. Your life, Uptown Girl, is a joke. Coming here is the realest part of your week, and you know it. It's why you keep coming back. I give you something you *need*, one way or another. Something you can't get anywhere else."

"I have to go." I shuffle in the dark toward the back door by the kitchen, with the sound of his sneakers scuffing the carpet behind me.

He walks me to the door, following so close I feel his hot breath on the back of my neck.

"Mitch," he says, his hand on the door knob a moment later. "My name's Mitch."

CHAPTER EIGHT

AUTUMN

GRAHAM MCMULLEN JOGS BY AT SEVEN FIFTEEN MONDAY
morning. Shirtless, tan, and taut, his muscles gleam and glisten
beneath the late May sun. Wrapping my hands around a steaming
mug of coffee, I peek through the blinds, watching until I hear the
soft tromp of Ben's footsteps as he makes his way downstairs.

So close, yet so far away.

Our lives barely seem to intersect anymore, and it's as if the
McMullens are slipping out of reach.

My attempts at calling Daphne from my burner phone have
led me no where. She doesn't answer. Ever. It doesn't matter what
time I call. Twice now she's sent my calls straight to voicemail,
and of course I listen to her greeting in its entirety and then hang
up before it beeps.

"Morning," he calls out, leaning against the oak bannister. It's
Memorial Day and the office is closed, as evidenced by the Coldplay
t-shirt and ripped jeans Ben has chosen to wear today. It's a far cry

from his usual suit and tie uniform, and I decide I like him better dressed up. I also decide never to tell him that just like I'll never tell him that the collection of ties in his closet were heavily inspired by ones worn by Graham in several of Daphne's Instaface photos.

Graham wears a lot of gingham, a lot of complementary colors. Gray suits with pink and green plaid ties. Navy suits with burnt-orange buffalo check shirts. Graham is a walking department store billboard in the best of ways. Classic, cool, and effortless, he reminds me of those smiling dads in the Sunday flyers, the ones smiling and throwing footballs in their polo sweaters and pressed suit pants.

"Morning," I say, lifting my mug to my lips. "You want some coffee?"

Ben's not a coffee drinker, but I always offer. He likes to know I'm always thinking of him, that he's always on my mind.

Some days I wish that were the case.

My life would be much simpler if it were.

"What do you want to do today?" He hops off the bottom step and heads into the kitchen, rifling through the refrigerator. He makes a lot of noise, and part of me wonders if he's doing it intentionally . . . perhaps he wanted to wake up to a nice breakfast this morning? But I brush off the notion because Ben isn't like that. He isn't passive aggressive.

"You want to take the dog for a walk?" I ask. I could use a reason to pass the McMullen's house and Ginger's the perfect excuse. "It's really nice out."

The doorbell chimes and the dog yaps, startled from her soft place on the back of the sofa. Seconds later, the mail truck drives away. Before I have a chance to stop him, Ben strides across the kitchen and through the living room to the entryway, stepping outside to grab the package from our doorstep.

"You order something?" he asks, reading the label. "Trina's Trinkets?"

Tucking a strand of hair behind my ear, I paint a casual expression on my face and take the small box from him.

"It's just a charm." I tuck the box under my arm, and Ben doesn't question the fact that he's never seen me wear a charm bracelet in the entire two years we've been together.

Taking my package with me, I climb the stairs and shuffle to the guest room at the end of the hall. It's sort of unspoken, but that room belongs to me. My things fill the closet. My dresser rests against the far wall. My bed anchors the middle. When we moved in together, I didn't want to sell *all* of my things on the off chance it wouldn't work out. Everything I own, which isn't much, is in this room, and Ben, as far as I know, steers clear. He has no business being in here anyway. Nothing in these four walls could possibly interest him.

Softly closing the door, I fall to my knees and feel around beneath the bed until my fingers rake across a small wooden box. Dragging it across the carpet, I lift the top off and push it aside while I open my package.

The gold locket I ordered from a small shop online is displayed neatly in a small, gray velvet box. It's an oval, maybe an inch and a half long, and the letter "G" is inscribed in the center in cursive. Carefully sliding my thumbnail between the clasp, I pop it open, smiling when I see the laser-printed portrait of a grinning Grace staring back at me.

I give myself another moment to admire my small treasure, and then I tuck it neatly into the wooden box along with some other "mementos." A sample-sized bottle of Daphne's signature Jo Malone orange blossom perfume. A tube of Chanel lipstick she once recommended. A Tom Ford pocket square embroidered with Graham's initials. Various photos of Grace I'd copied and saved and had printed. A letter for the McMullens from a distant relative, mistakenly mixed up in our mail. Various items Daphne had recommended via Instaface . . . hand creams, shampoos, detox teas, stationery, and facial creams.

Everything in this box is a materialistic, three-dimensional embodiment of that family.

Ben's heavy footsteps return me to the present, and I quickly place the locket into the gray box and slide the gray box into the wooden one. Securing the lid, I push it back beneath the bed and pull the bed skirt down to keep it from plain view.

Holding my breath for the sake of making the least amount of noise possible, I listen closer, my ear pressed against the guestroom door, until I hear him go back downstairs.

I have to stop being so sloppy.

CHAPTER NINE

Daphne

"What'd I miss?" Graham strides into the kitchen Monday morning, grabbing an apple from a fruit basket on the island. He bites into it, wiping a drip of juice from his lower lip, and grins. His dark hair is still damp from his shower and his skin glowing from his AM jog.

I don't tell him about Grace stealing Rose's last pancake, and I don't tell him about Sebastian stabbing Grace with his fork. He should have been there, refereeing breakfast this morning as I cooked and served, but I decide to pick my battles.

"You're in a good mood this morning," I say, rinsing breakfast plates in the sink before making my way to the table. With a damp wash cloth, I wipe Sebastian's sticky face and fingers. He climbs down, running toward his father and wrapping himself around his left leg.

Graham reaches down, ruffling Sebastian's hair, and I catch the hint of a black glove sticking from his chino shorts. His tan arm plays nicely off his teal blue golf polo. He's dressed for eighteen holes.

"Golfing?" I ask. "On Rose's birthday?"

He nods.

"Didn't you golf Thursday morning?" My back is to him now, my hand clenched on the sprayer nozzle.

"It's just a quick nine holes with Trey DuMont."

I've never known Trey DuMont to do "a quick nine holes." It's always eighteen and two rounds of beer at the Pueblo Cantina. On the days he spends with Trey, I'm lucky to get him back before dinnertime, and even then, he's usually so loaded up with beer and bar food he isn't hungry for the elaborate family dinner I've prepared.

The jingle of Graham's keys tells me there's no changing his mind, and I won't bother. It was a waste of time the last time I tried, and the time before that. I'm rarely able to convince this man to spend a quiet day off with his family, and I'm not sure why.

"What time will you be back?" I ask, as if it'll make a difference. When Graham gives me a time, I usually know to tack three or four hours onto it.

"Not sure."

I turn to him, eyes hot and stinging, but I refuse to cry. I refuse to look pathetic and lonely in front of my own husband who somehow always has it together.

"The party starts at three, so . . ." my voice trails. I don't know why I bother.

"I'll be back before then. What are you guys doing today?" he asks.

You guys.

He sees us four as one unit. It's not just me and the kids. It's always *you guys*, like he's separate from us.

I don't answer. He should know I'll be baking a cake from

69

scratch, assembling gift bags for the guests, setting up games, and minding the children all at the same time.

"Okay, well . . ." He's looking down at his phone, gliding his thumb up and down like he's scrolling through a fascinating article that's worth his full attention. "You know, kids these days don't get enough exercise."

"That's random," I exhale my words and roll them into a small groan. He doesn't notice.

Our kids get plenty of exercise, but of course Graham wouldn't know. He's not around when I'm carting them from dance practice to soccer to karate.

"So when are you going to be back again?" I try my question again, hoping for a better answer this time.

Graham looks up from his phone, eyes squinting. "Just depends, honey. Holidays at the club are busy. We've got our tee time, but it depends on the people ahead of us, and whether or not Trey's bringing his A-game today."

He chuckles, padding across the kitchen to the garage entrance.

"Maybe after the party, we can open a bottle of red and watch a movie when the kids go to bed? Just us?" He flashes me a dimpled half-smile, his gaze intense and direct, and I temporarily forget my irritation and the fact that he's snubbing his family on his daughter's birthday. "How's that sound, yeah?"

I nod, wiping my hands on a dry dish cloth.

"When was the last time we had a real date?" I ask.

He glances to his left, mouth pursed. "Good question, honey. I don't know. It's been a while."

"Why don't we get a sitter next Friday? There's a Broadway show I've been dying to see, and it's a limited run. We could get tickets. Have a nice dinner. Maybe even stay at a nice hotel? Make a weekend out of it? Like a mini vacation?"

Graham pauses by the door, his fingers loose on the knob. "Next weekend, next weekend . . ."

"I could ask my mom to watch the kids."

"Your mom's in Boca Raton."

"I'll fly her up for a couple of days. She'd love to see the kids." My brows lift as I wait for his approval. My lips curl into a smile, almost willing him to show an ounce of excitement about my proposed weekend away. "Especially if it's on our dime."

He exhales, pulling the door open. "Yeah. Give her a call. If you set it up, we'll go."

Graham's monotone response slices through my enthusiasm, and in an instant, he's gone. The gentle clamor of the garage door precedes the near silent departure of his Tesla. Within seconds, he's zooming down our shady, tree-lined street.

I'm losing him.

Or maybe I've already lost him.

Maybe I'm clinging to the ghost of what once was and what will never be.

My skin is on fire, eyes burning. When my lower lip trembles, I know I'm fighting a battle I won't win. The sound of my children laughing from the next room is the last thing I hear when I yank the back sliding door and find myself on the patio, struggling to breathe.

I need a minute to myself. I need to let it out, and I don't want them to see me upset. They're just children. They're my babies, and I don't want them to worry.

Collapsing in a wicker chair under the covered patio, I bury my face in my hands and have a quiet cry, my palms muffling escaped sobs as best they can.

I miss the Graham I fell in love with.

This Graham, this increasingly self-centered version, is a stranger to me.

I don't know him.

I don't recognize the man he has become.

What does it say about our marriage when I can't recall the last time he held my hand? The last time he planned a special date night? The last time he whisked me off to some business dinner and slipped his hands under my dress at the table?

We used to be inseparable.

We used to be insatiable.

When did I stop being enough?

When did I stop being the apple of his eye?

Over the course of a few minutes, I let it all out. Our lot is oversized, a little more than half an acre, and surrounded by large shade trees and wrought iron fencing that separates our section of the neighborhood from the older, quainter homes behind it. We've always meant to replace it, to put up a privacy fence that matches the rest, but over the years it slipped off our to-do list once we realized we'd yet to actually see a neighbor from the homes behind us.

When I've had my cry and my fill of shameless self-pity, I dab my tear-streaked cheeks on the back of my hand and draw in a breath of foggy morning air. Rising from my seat to head back inside, I stop when I notice something in the distance.

A woman.

Staring out the window of the house directly behind us.

At least I think it's a woman. I can hardly be sure from this far away.

Good god, I'm an idiot. I should've run up to my room and had a cry like a normal person, but there are days when my sanctuary feels more like a prison cell, and today was one of them.

My cheeks burn, and I offer an apologetic smile before heading back inside. I'm truly sorry she had to see my meltdown.

At the last moment, I stop to offer her a wave.

She stands there. Sullen. Unmoving. Watching.

And without warning the blinds close, and she's gone.

CHAPTER TEN

A<small>UTUMN</small>

I<small>T'S JUST BEFORE DUSK WHEN WE PULL INTO OUR DRIVEWAY, THE</small> entire day gone just like that. Poof. One minute I'm sipping coffee and admiring the *view*. The next minute I'm being forced to shop for vintage teacups for Ben's mother in Forrest Hills because he insisted on a day trip to get us out of Monarch Falls for a bit.

At least lunch was good: tomato bisque and a house salad for me. Ben inhaled his plate-sized quiche Lorraine like a starving man-child.

I pretended it didn't embarrass me.

I'm sure to anyone else we looked like your average, run-of-the-mill, Caucasian, twenty-something couple. Boring and ordinary in every way. We look like the newlyweds who just moved in next door, ready to lend a cup of sugar or the use of our shiny new lawnmower.

Sometimes I wonder if Ben has secrets. If he does, he does a grade-A job of hiding them. I don't think he has any though, and I kind of wish he did, if only to spice things up a bit. He doesn't disappear at odd hours. He never has a cat-who-ate-the-canary look on his face. He doesn't have any quirks or idiosyncrasies that make me question who he is or who he claims to be.

The man doesn't even have a hidden porn folder on his laptop, and believe me, I've looked. He doesn't have any kinky requests between the sheets. Ben, in all his simplicity, just likes plain vanilla sex. His favorite position is missionary.

Guess that makes things easier for me.

"What do you want to do now, babe?" he asks as the car creeps into our garage. He kills the engine, unfastens his seatbelt, and turns to me. "You want to get ice cream or something?"

No.

No, I do not want to get ice cream, *Ben.*

We just got home. I want to *stay* home.

Besides, not all of us were blessed with the metabolism of a twenty-year-old Olympic swimmer. Ben can eat anything. And he does. I've seen him put down an entire large supreme pizza, half a pan of cheesy breadsticks, two-thirds of a package of chocolate chip break-and-bake cookies, and still complain that his stomach is growling.

If I ate the way he did, I'd be the size of a house by now, and yet Ben is strapping yet lean, miraculously wielding a runner's physique despite the fact that he doesn't run nearly as much as he used to.

Not all of us have the luxury of good genes.

Some of us were born with less desirable junk that clutters our DNA.

Some of us were born with DNA that makes us want things we shouldn't have and do things we shouldn't do, and at the end of the day, it boils down to the fact that we are all made a certain way, there's nothing we can do to change it, and that's just how it is.

Ben and I climb out of the car and make our way inside. I can already hear the dog scratching at the door, so I hurry in to let her outside. Grabbing her leather leash, I hook her up and step into the backyard, grateful for some alone time and a bit of familiar fresh air.

She wastes no time doing her thing and returning to my side, jumping on her hind legs and whimpering for me to pick her up. I scoop her up in my arms, letting her lick my face as I linger outside a little longer. Her breath smells like shit. Literal shit. But I don't mind because she's my baby, and she can get away with murder and I'd still love her just as fiercely.

Love is cracked like that, I suppose.

Gazing across our lot, I peer through the iron fence that separates our land from the McMullens. Party lights are neatly strung, hanging from their covered patio, and a woman whom I don't recognize, hired help probably, is cleaning up abandoned pool floaties and wrinkled towels.

Sighing, I take a seat on one of the patio chairs and let the dog cuddle in my lap.

"I missed it all," I say to her, nuzzling my nose into her ear.

A light chill runs through me as the wind picks up, and the leaves of the oaks that canopy the McMullens' backyard paradise rustle as if to signal a storm is coming. A flash of lightning zips across the sky, followed by droplets of water that land on my nose and cheeks. I love a good summer rainstorm, its nature unapologetic and intense.

Ginger jumps from my lap, trotting to the back door and scratching. She hates thunder, and she knows it's coming. I follow, stealing once last glance at the remains of Rose McMullen's seventh birthday party.

Ben is seated on the sofa when we step inside, already dressed in sweats and his favorite Red Sox t-shirt. He's hunched over, elbows on his knees and eyes glued to the sports highlights flickering across the TV screen. Ginger takes a running jump to his side.

Traitor.

"It's starting to storm," I say, heading upstairs to change.

"You didn't know that?" he asks, keeping his attention on the screen.

I don't watch the news. Ever. I couldn't care less about weather and current events. It's too depressing. I suppose that's why I gravitate toward social media. Everything posted is picturesque because most people only share their highlight reels and never the ugly, unusable footage that lands on the cutting room floor. It's the exact opposite of the evening news.

It's always sunny on Instaface, even if that sun is artificial.

Save for Daphne. She's as authentic as they come. She doesn't need to hide behind faux news stories and staged pictures of her family. They are, in not so many words, genuine perfection.

You can't fake their kind of love.

CHAPTER ELEVEN

DAPHNE

"You again." Mitch pretends like he's unhappy to see me, but that slow smile spreading across his face gives him away. He pulls his side door open, and I inhale a lungful of sweet marijuana smoke. "How goes it, Uptown Girl? You have a nice, uh, Memorial Day weekend? What'd you do? Go boating? You guys boat at all? Shit. What do rich people do in their spare time?"

"You live in this house," I say, following him to the dingy room with the Grateful Dead blankets, "but I refuse to believe you're as poor as you claim to be."

He chuckles, plopping down in the middle of his sunken sofa. "Never said I was poor."

"When you use the term *rich people*, it has an insinuation of exclusivity," I say. "You can't tell me you're dealing because it's a lifelong passion of yours. The reward has to outweigh the risks or you wouldn't be doing it."

"You're not wrong." He grabs a small baggie of weed and pinches some leaves between his thumb and forefinger, dropping them along a single rolling paper. "You can't live like you've got money over here. Not in this part of town. I'd need security and some vicious dogs, and truth be told, I just want a simple kind of life. I don't want to worry about some knuckleheads breaking into my house at night looking under floorboards and mattresses. Trying to keep a low profile."

"That's smart."

"And *rich folks* like you don't need guys like me setting up camp in your fancy neighborhoods."

He rolls the paper then licks the seam before retrieving a lighter from his pocket. His thumb flicks it twice, a flame appearing the second time. His eyes find mine as the joint rests between his lips.

My body craves this release, this high, and my fingers drag edgily along the arms of the chair I've taken. Mitch takes two slow drags and hands it off. I'm all over it, greedy and desperate. I'm well aware that this isn't a good look for me, but in here, with Mitch, none of that matters.

He accepts me exactly as I am. My carefully crafted exterior doesn't fool him. He sees through it all: my flaws and imperfections, my ugliness and inadequacies. And still he doesn't push me away.

"You ever going to tell me your name?" he asks, peering down his nose. "Thought we had a deal last time. I tell you mine, you tell me yours, remember? I told you mine and then you bolted."

"I wasn't *bolting*. I told you, I had to go."

I take another drag from the joint and lean back in the chair, my body starting to feel lighter with each slow second that drips past.

"Anyway, I kind of like when you call me Uptown Girl," I say.

"Not cool. You tricked me. That shit wouldn't fly on the streets, just so you know. Nobody deserves to be baited and switched. That's just disrespectful."

"It's not that I don't want you to know my name," I say. "I just don't want to be me when I'm here. Does that make sense?"

"Nothing about you makes sense." He sits forward, elbows resting on the ripped knees of his jeans, studying me. "And that's kind of the best thing about you."

"I can't tell if you're insulting me or not." I take another drag. He hasn't asked for it back, but he seems preoccupied. *With me.* "I can never tell with you. You're impossible to figure out."

"Good," he says. "I don't want to be the kind of guy people can figure out. Nothing good can come of that. People figure you out, they take advantage. That's how it works. They find your weaknesses and they exploit them."

I wonder if Graham has figured out my weaknesses. Maybe he's known them all along. Maybe he's been exploiting them, and I've never even noticed.

"Am I easy to figure out?" My relaxed body braces for his answer. If there's anything I know about Mitch, it's that he's incapable of sugarcoating.

He leans back in the couch, arms loosely folded and head cocked as he pulls in a hard breath.

"Yes and no," he says. "Certain things about you are mysterious. Other things . . . incredibly cliché and predictable."

"Ouch."

He finally reaches for the joint. "You asked. Don't ask if you don't want to know."

"Fair enough."

A warm peacefulness sinks into my bones. My body feels like it's been sliced open at the cellular level with an obsidian knife, but in the most enlightening way.

"I feel different with this," I say, my voice just as mellow as my body. "I feel like I could . . . I don't know, paint something."

I realize I sound utterly ridiculous, but I don't care. I'm not sure I'm capable of having a care in the world right now.

Mitch laughs, his hand resting on his flat stomach. "We're

smoking Lamb's Bread today. It's new to the area. Just got it in last night from my West Coast supplier."

"Lamb's Bread?" For a moment, I consider how something like this would have traveled across the country, where it would've been stuffed and hidden to make such a trek.

I decide I don't need to know.

"It gives you more of a euphoric high," he says. "Makes you introspective and creative and shit. Bob Marley used to smoke this."

"Oh." I settle into the worn cushions of his chair, arms relaxed at my sides. Closing my eyes, I wrap myself up in this amazing, exultant state. "What do you normally give me?"

"Blue Haze," he says without pause. "For your anxiety."

"My anxiety?" I smirk. "You think I'm anxious?"

"Are you joking right now? Good god, woman, I've never met anyone more tightly wound than you. You make me all tense just looking at you."

"Just stop talking," I say, eyes slowly rolling to the back of my head as I inhale. "I want to actually enjoy this this time."

Mitch switches on some music that makes me feel like I'm in some secret, underground club in Manhattan. The beat is relaxed, ambient. Crazy how Mitch knows exactly what I need, and he hardly knows me.

Last night, Graham brought home flowers for me after work. It's been months since he's done that, so I kept my mouth closed, opting not to correct him when he proudly declared he'd searched high and low for a bouquet of yellow tulips because he remembered they were my favorite.

He used to bring me daffodils.

Daffodils are my favorite.

I guess they're both yellow.

He knew me well once upon a time. I'm not sure how a man just forgets the favorite flower of the woman to whom he's been married the last twelve years.

I'm weightless and anchored at the same time, my body and mind joyously separated. The sound of feet shuffling on the floor force my eyes to open. Mitch is standing in front of me, his heavy gaze examining me.

"What?" My shoulders jerk, and I sit up. "Why are you looking at me like that?"

My mind goes to last week, when I caught him staring at me like this for the first time.

"Is it weird?" he asks. His shoulder-length sandy hair is tucked behind his ears, and there's scruff on his chin. He's the opposite of Graham's signature, clean-cut style, and yet I can't help but to secretly find him alluring.

My palm rests on my chest, my heart speeding up for a moment. When I try to speak, my mouth is dry.

"I'll stop if it creeps you out," Mitch says with a benign chuff. "You're just really fucking pretty is all. Like a Hollywood actress. One of those vintage pin-up ones from the forties. When I get high and I look at you, it's almost trippy. Makes me lose track of time. Or maybe it's the weed."

I clear my throat, body tensing slightly. "Yes, it's weird."

And it's weird that I kind of like it.

"That's cool. No worries. I won't do it anymore." He makes his way to the kitchen. The sound of clinking glass is followed by the slamming of a fridge door. When he returns, he has two beer bottles in his hand. "I know it's the middle of the day, but there's nothing like a little Lamb's Bread and pale ale."

It's been seventeen years since I've had a beer. The last time was my freshman year of college, when Graham dragged me to a frat party where everyone was doing keg stands, including me.

I'd never been so sick after that night.

And Graham took me home, stayed by my side all night, holding my hair back as I hugged a toilet bowl. He brought me cool towels and clean pajamas and never left me for more than a minute at a time. The next morning, he made me buttered toast and ran to the store for ginger ale, still cursing himself for taking me to that party.

That man used to move heaven and earth to make sure I was okay. He was protective of me. Gentle with my heart. Sensitive to my feelings.

"No, thank you." I wave him away, the memory of that beer and vomit taste coming back to me in small waves. My stomach churns.

"Suit yourself." Mitch shrugs, placing the extra beer on the coffee table and twisting the cap off his own. He plops down, kicking his sneaker-covered feet up one by one. His lips wrap around the bottle, then a hint of his tongue, and he releases a satisfied sigh with his first gulp. The liquid sloshes as it returns to the bottom of the bottle.

"I don't think I'll be here after the next couple of Tuesdays," I say before I forget.

He huffs. "Sure."

"No, I'm being serious. Once school's out, I'm on my own with the kids. I don't know when I'll be able to get away again." God, I'm going to miss this. *This*, my standing Tuesday morning date, is what keeps me going each week. This is what I live for lately, and I take full responsibility for how screwed up it makes me sound.

"Why don't you take some home with you?"

"I can't." Sitting up, I pull my legs under me, curling up in his chair. I want to take a nap right here, curled into a little ball. I want to sleep for a million years in this foggy, exuberant haze. "I wouldn't know how to transport it, where to hide it . . ."

"Uptown, geez, I'll teach you all that." He stands, running his hands down his ripped jeans and eyeing the hall. After a second, he leaves, returning with a small plastic bag filled with a fair amount of rolled joints. "Going to have to start charging you now, just so you know. This bag's a hundred bucks, and that's the discounted rate."

"I don't have any cash on me," I say, wondering if it'll fit in my front pocket without bulging too much. Shaking my head, I silently scold myself for even considering this. This is insane. I can't. This is why I come *here*. "It's okay. I shouldn't."

He sighs, letting the baggie fall to his side, his hand tight around it. "All right, fine. That's on you."

"I can't smoke in the house," I say. "It just feels wrong. I can't do it around the kids. And if my husband ever found out . . ."

"Yeah, yeah, yeah. I know you have your reasons. Mother of the Year and all that."

I huff. "I'm hardly Mother of the Year."

"I doubt that." His eyes drag the length of me. "I bet you make homemade cookies and read bedtime stories. I bet you're the kind of mother every kid dreams of, the kind that only exist in Hallmark movies."

I roll my eyes. "I wish I was a Hallmark mom. Maybe if I were, my oldest wouldn't be acting out all the time."

"Acting out? Or acting like a kid."

I tell him about Grace. About the pancakes and the stealing and the disobedience. I tell him about her penchant for doing horrible things and making *me* feel guilty in the end, as if her behavior is a direct result of my inferior parenting skills.

He laughs. "Shit, Uptown. Pretty sure my mom would tell you you've got it easy. She sounds like a kid. A handful. But a kid. And you're doing the best you can. Everyone's always doing the best they can."

"Do you have any kids?"

He shakes his head. "Nope."

I think about asking if he wants kids, if he even likes them, but I stop myself when I remember his lifestyle is a glaring example of the kinds of priorities that do not involve becoming a father.

"Sounds like you need a break is all," he says. "And that's why you come here, am I right?"

I nod.

"Anyway," he says. "I'm not going to pressure you. I'm not one of *those* assholes. Plus weed's not addictive. If you were hooked on the hard stuff, I might try to turn a buck or two."

He winks, and I assume he's joking.

"I appreciate it." My mellow is fading faster than I'd hoped. "How come you've never charged me before?"

"You've been paying with your company."

"My company?"

"Yeah. I like hanging out with you for some insane reason. You're like the last person on earth I'd be friends with in real life, and I'd totally lose my street cred if I were seen around you, but you're interesting to me, Uptown. I like you. And that says a lot, because I really don't like anybody."

My jaw loosens as I try and decide if I want to be flattered or insulted. I settle on a little of both.

"Thanks, Mitch. I like hanging out with you, too."

"Yeah, well. If you miss me, you've got my number."

"You know I can't text you."

"Then you know where to find me."

Mitch flops down on the couch, and we sit in enlightened silence for the better part of the next hour, soaking in the last fleeting moments of our time together. When it's time for me to leave, he walks me to the back door, and I begin to regret not asking more about him when I had the chance.

All I ever did was come here and blab about myself, ranting and raving about trivial things like some self-loathing, self-pitying lunatic, and he sat beside me and listened. From time to time, he'd offer his sage advice, which always resonated no matter how screwed up it was, but most of the time, he'd listen in silent support.

Never once did I have to pretend to be who someone wanted me to be. Never once have I had to apologize for speaking my truth no matter how crazy it made me seem.

It's been five weeks since I met Mitch.

And in five weeks, he's become one of the best friends I've ever had.

"The kids go to their grandmother's for a week in the middle of July," I say when we're standing at the side door. "You'll see me then."

"I'll see you before then." He moves closer, his hand braced on the wall behind me. Mitch's scent is a combination of marijuana and drugstore shower gel. He's everything Graham is and nothing he isn't, and it feels dangerously wrong to be this physically close to a man who isn't my husband. Mitch's mouth curls up at the sides when our eyes meet, and then he digs into his front pocket. "Almost forgot."

Lifting a single rolled joint, he places it in my hand and curls my fingers around it. He doesn't let go, and there's a tightness in my chest as I remember just how much I've missed holding hands with someone who looks at me like I'm the most splendid thing they've ever seen.

"Consider it your emergency stash," he says. "It's small enough you can hide it anywhere. You have an attic?"

My brows furrow. "Yes, I have an attic. Why?"

"When you need a little Mommy break, take this guy up to the attic. Smoke rises. Wrap yourself in a towel and cover your hair. Nobody'll know."

The thought of hiding drugs in my house makes my body quaver, but the thought of going the next several weeks without this miraculous and divine intervention is even more terrifying.

Last summer I went to the doctor after breaking out in hives. She said I had a stress rash, and then proceeded to accuse me of being depressed because I admitted I wasn't sleeping lately. It made no sense, but she was adamant that I take a pill that combatted both depression and anxiety. I went home and researched the side effects: weight gain, decreased libido, headaches, and brain zaps. Life was already a challenge without those extra little extras, so I never called her back.

Besides, I'm not depressed or anxious, I'm desperate. I'm at the end of my rope.

And there's a huge difference.

"Fine." I tuck the joint down the front of my sports bra. "All right, I'm going."

"Take care, Uptown," he says, holding the door open. "When life gets too crazy, you come see me. I'll make it all go away."

CHAPTER TWELVE

AUTUMN

TODAY'S SUNRISE PAINTS THE SKY IN SHADES OF PINK AND ORANGE, but it may as well be gray. Seated in the kitchen, I pull my knees up against my chest, resting my chin on top of them as I stare into the backyard. The McMullens are probably getting up now, Daphne about to fix breakfast in the kitchen before the kids traipse down the stairs one by one. If I had to guess, I'd bet Graham ran out to fetch the paper and a latte from Daphne's favorite coffee shop, and I'd bet the kids are just starting to wake, rubbing their sleepy eyes and washing up for the breakfast their mother so lovingly prepared.

If it were a week ago, all of this would be documented for the world to share.

I've always been of the opinion that if you have a beautiful life, you should share it with the rest of us. Not everyone has the privilege of living the kind of life most people only ever see on TV.

The McMullens were real.

They *are* real.

And now they're holed up in that oversized McMansion of theirs, hiding away like they're too fucking good for social media now.

My hand trembles, probably from my lack of sleep catching up with me, as I reach for my coffee which has turned lukewarm. I'm not sure how long it's been sitting there. Could be hours for all I know.

It hit me last night, after seeing the remnants of Rose's party, that this is my new reality, and there's nothing I can do to change it.

I stayed up all night. Pacing. Crying into the sofa pillows. Forcing myself to fall asleep and failing miserably. At three in the morning, I crept upstairs to the spare room and pulled out the wooden box, scattering all my photos and mementos across the floor, mourning the days when a *press, tap, and click* was all it took for me to step inside Grace's life.

I needed to think.

I needed to be alone.

I needed to figure out what I'm going to do.

At four in the morning, it dawned on me that I could pretend to be a prospective parent at Brinkman Academy where Grace and Rose attend school. I could make a phone call as soon as they open today and schedule a tour, and maybe I could see them, see where they eat lunch and swing on swings at recess. I could see their classrooms and their lockers and their teachers and maybe even see Grace.

The creaking of the stairs tells me Ben's up now, but I can't bring myself to turn and face him. I'm sure my face is puffy and my eyes are swollen and red. There's nothing I can do to hide them. I should've been icing them hours ago, but I wasn't thinking straight.

"Babe." His warm palm cups my shoulder, and from the side of my vision I watch him crouch down. "You didn't come to bed last night."

I nod, biting my bottom lip and feeling like opening my mouth to speak would be a very bad idea right now. If I so much as try to make a noise, it won't be words that come out.

"What's wrong?" He presses his lips against the side of my head, wrapping his arm around me. His question smells like morning breath poorly concealed with mint toothpaste, and it makes me want to vomit. "Okay. You don't have to talk."

He moves away from me, but he doesn't go too far. Sliding into the seat next to me, he rests his elbow on the table and reaches his other hand for mine. His arms are long, like his legs, and they stretch across the table.

"Will you do me a favor and talk to someone this week?" he asks.

My gaze flicks onto his.

Ben's mouth flashes into a quick smile. "I know you don't like to talk about your feelings, and you don't open up too much, but I think it would be good for you."

Talking to someone is the last thing I want to do right now.

Nobody would understand.

Nobody has ever truly understood me.

"Do it for me?" he asks, his lips curling into a coaxing smile. "Please?"

Staring hard into his pale blue eyes, a hard ball of resentment fills my tense stomach. I hate that I need him, that I'm stuck here without a choice.

Ben, and this house, are my only gateway into the McMullens' lives now.

Clearing my throat, I summon all the strength I have and let him take my hand.

"Just feeling depressed about not having a job," I lie. "It finally hit me last night."

His head tilts, and I truly believe the sympathy in his gaze is genuine, but none of it matters because none of this is true.

"I'd been wondering," he says with a delicate timbre in his

voice. "You just haven't seemed like yourself ever since they let you go. You're more withdrawn. I really think you should talk to someone."

I wave him off, rising and lifting my coffee mug to my lips. I take a sip, ice cold, and swallow the bitter liquid before returning to dump the rest in the sink. Peering across the backyard, I see that the kitchen light is on at the McMullens' house, and it sends a tight squeeze to my chest when I think of all the memories I've already missed.

My shoulders sink, my hope deflated.

"I'm going to start looking for a job again, and I mean really look. And I'll start on Monday," I say. I'll say anything if it means not seeing a shrink. I've never liked them anyway. Don't trust them. They're snakes in the grass. Professional manipulators. "I'll take the first job I can get."

I don't want Ben to worry about me. I don't need him prying. My plate is piled to the roof with things I have to concern myself with right now, and I don't need anything else added to the mix.

He rises from the table, moving behind me, cupping his hands around my waist as we both face the kitchen window above the sink. Ben buries his chin into the bend between my neck and shoulder before hugging me tight.

"I like having you home," he says. "But I like it even better when you're happy. I just want you happy again."

Yeah. Me too.

CHAPTER THIRTEEN

DAPHNE

"Be good for Gram." I wrap my arms around my children as they cling to my leg Friday afternoon, and then I glance up at my mother, her suitcase resting at her side as we stand in the foyer. A flash of yellow passes the front window as her cab drives away. "Thank you so much, Mom. I know it was short notice, but we really appreciate it. We just need to get away for a bit. You know how it is."

Never in all my life have I been able to slip much of anything past my mother. She stands, arms still thick from years of weekend waitressing and forty hour weeks at the tire plant.

Her sparse brows rise, and her mouth lifts in the corner. "Everything okay in paradise?"

"Of course." I smile and swat her away. I don't want her to worry. Leaning down to kiss the top of Sebastian's messy brown mop, I realize he's in desperate need of a haircut, but now that school's out and I'm dealing with everything else, it isn't a priority and it'll have to wait. "Are you going to be a good boy this weekend?"

He nods, wearing a sheepish grin.

"Grace, will you be a good helper to Gram?" I run my hand along Grace's arm, stopping to unfasten her hand from my hip. She squirms, trying to cling tighter. "Grammy loves when you help her. Please be the good girl I know you are this weekend."

"I don't want you and Daddy to go," she whines into my shirt, her voice muffled. "If you leave, I'm not going to be good."

I glance at my mother, exhaling with relief when I see she didn't hear my daughter just threaten me. Had I ever so much as threatened my mother growing up, I'd have been shipped off and sent away to some military boarding school on the other side of the country. She'd have taken on a third job just to pay for it, too.

"I'll bring you back something, Grace," I say. "Daddy and I will bring something back for each of you, but you have to be good. If Grandma tells me you got in any kind of trouble, I won't bring you anything."

My threat is empty, and she knows it. Her hollow brown eyes stare up into mine, blinking once, not showing any sign of excitement or willingness to agree to my rules. I'm not worried about Rose and Sebastian. They'll behave. But in my heart of hearts, I know Grace won't. And I can't come home with only two presents.

Even at her young age, Grace already feels like an outsider. I can tell. And while we've yet to tell her she's adopted, she's getting to the age where she's going to start asking why she doesn't look like anyone else.

The hum of the garage door signals Graham's return home from work. Our packed bags are already resting by the back door. I spent the better part of today preparing a road trip playlist; mostly songs we used to listen to back in the day. Before we had kids. When the spark was still alive and well with no end in sight.

The clink of Graham's keys on the kitchen counter are followed by the soft tromp of his shoes on the wood floor.

"Hey, hey." He wraps his arm around my mother's shoulders, giving her a kiss on the cheek. She lights up like a Christmas tree, the way she always does around him, and runs her fingers mindlessly through Rosie's hair. "Looking good, Graham."

"Not as good as you, Mom." He smiles wide, giving her shoulder a squeeze before bending down to scoop Sebastian up. "Hey, little buddy."

Enter *Super Dad.*

"Daddy!" Grace leaves my side, drawn like a magnet to Graham. Rosie clings to my mom, probably enjoying the fact that for once she doesn't have to share her with anyone. "Can I come with you guys?"

Graham bends to kiss the top of Grace's head and then cups her chubby cheeks with one hand. "Sorry, Gracie. It's a Mommy and Daddy kind of weekend. We'll be home in two days. It'll go by so fast. Be over before you know it."

My jaw slacks. The way he speaks to Grace, it's as if he's trying to remind *himself* it'll be over before he knows it. There's nothing excitable about Graham right now. Nothing that tells me he's dying to get away, just the two of us. He's acting as if he's about to go on a business trip and this is business as usual. An obligation.

I brush it off, chalking it up to hormones or something else that could cloud my judgement and sensitize my feelings.

"You ready, honey?" I ask. Mom smiles at me. She's happy for us. She always has been. The day we married, she pulled me aside and told me I was the luckiest girl in the world to have found a man who loved me as much as Graham did, and she told me to never let him go, not for anything, or else I'd spend the rest of my life regretting it.

Graham looks up at me, like he's seeing me for the first time – like he didn't notice me until now.

"Yeah," he says. "We all packed?"

I nod. "Bags are by the back door."

Graham checks the bold-faced watch on his left wrist before clapping his hands and slicking them together.

"Let's hit the road." He smiles, and I question his authenticity. But only for a moment. And then my excitement takes over.

This weekend, I get Graham all to myself.

I couldn't ask for anything more.

———

"OH, LOOK AT THAT ACURA." I SWAT HIS HAND AND POINT TO THE red car passing on our left. We've been on the road forty-five minutes now, and I can almost see the lower Manhattan skyline in the distance. "It looks just like the one you drove in high school."

Graham's mouth pulls wide and his gaze follows the speedy little car. "Look at that. Same model year and everything."

"Same color too. Matador red." Crazy how I remembered the name of his car's paint color, but back then I knew everything about him. His shoe size. His favorite gum. The name of his hair products. The brand of chinos he liked best. I was obsessed. Suppose I still am in many ways.

"Huh." He watches the car until it fades into the distance, disappearing over a hill. "Those were the days, weren't they?"

"I'd give anything to know what simple and carefree feels like again." I close my eyes, resting my head against the seatback.

My world tilted on its axis the day Graham showed up at Northville High. At the time, I was a reserved seventeen-year-old who mostly kept to herself, nose buried in a book or behind a camera lens. I got good grades and had a small group of reliable, plain Jane friends who never caused any trouble. The first time I saw Graham, I was eating breakfast in the cafeteria because my mother had to drop me off early that morning, and she needed my car because hers was in the shop. A dark-haired boy in gray slacks and a fitted navy polo strutted past me with a leather messenger bag hanging from his shoulder. I stared, unabashedly, figuring I wouldn't be detected since I never was.

But without warning, he turned, *noticed me*, and then smiled his dimpled, easy-going smile.

I remember glancing to my right and then my left to make sure he wasn't looking at someone else, but I was all alone in my corner of the cafeteria, and that moment marked the first time in my entire high school career that a boy didn't look right through me.

My cheeks burned, and I couldn't meet his gaze. He was head to toe confidence, dressed for prep school and walking with purpose, and before I could muster the courage to look his way again, he was gone.

For the remainder of that day, I watched for him everywhere I went. I even broke free from my silent demeanor to ask around about him and get his name. I knew he was new. Our town didn't produce anything that looked like him or dressed like him or walked like him. For the better part of the hours that followed, I half-wondered if I'd dreamed him up.

He found me again after sixth period, stopping me in the hall and telling me he liked my sweater. It was a thrift-store find, though he didn't need to know. He said everyone at his old school wore that brand, and he instantly recognized the little embroidered lizard on my left breast.

He said I reminded him of home.

By seventh period, I could think of nothing but the new kid. And by eighth period, he walked into my photography class, my sacred space, and took the chair beside me. By the time the three o'clock bell rang, he'd finally introduced himself and asked if he could take me on a date that Friday.

Months passed, and I maintained my place as the apple of Graham McMullen's eye.

Most days it felt unreal.

Unquestionably too good to be true.

I wasn't just lucky; I was the *luckiest*.

By Christmas, I was drowning in crazy, teenage, hormonal love and Graham was my lifesaver. My love for him was the kind that made me write cheesy love letters and obsessively daydream about the future and walk around in a dumbfounded stupor. The kind that made me float everywhere I went; made me feel like I was some kind of special for the first time in my life.

In many ways, we were all wrong for each other. His family was wealth and luxury and I was the latch-key only daughter of a working single mom. He said I reminded him of a famous actress, and that he had this thing for long-legged girls. Graham liked to have the kinds of things no one else had, and he joked that I was exclusively made just for him. He'd traveled the world with his parents. He'd seen a lot of things and met a lot of people. He even spoke four different languages.

He was only eighteen, but he knew exactly what he wanted.

And for some insane reason, he wanted me.

Rich, charismatic boy. Quiet, underprivileged girl. He offered me the world. Who was I to say no?

At seventeen, my love for him knew no logic, and I don't suppose that part of it has changed much over the years.

At thirty-six, I'm still as obsessively, unreasonably, and irra-tionally head over heels with a man who can't even remember what kind of flowers to get me anymore. A man who traitorously fulfils his physical needs in the bed of another woman.

"Don't say that." Graham's voice carries a scolding tone.

"Pardon me?" I snap out of my nostalgic haze.

"Don't say you miss simple and carefree," he says. "It sounds like you wish our children were never born."

His accusation stuns and silences me, and I swallow the shame that rises like bile in my throat. It wouldn't be the first time I've longed for the days before Gracie. Before Rosie. Before little Sebastian. It wouldn't be the first time I've wondered what path our life together would've taken if it was only ever us against the world.

Our trajectory took a one-way detour the day we adopted Grace.

"How could you suggest such a thing?" I throw his accusation back in his face. "Do you honestly think that I regret my children?"

"No." He laces his fingers through mine. "I'm sorry. That was uncalled for."

I've never felt such an intense amount of emerald-green jealousy as I did the first time I saw Graham with Grace. He looked at her the way he used to look at me: nothing but the deepest love humanly possible.

Oh, how I wanted to be her, wrapped tight and safe in his arms, placed on a pedestal so high only he could reach me.

Graham adored her, *worshipped* her. She was all he talked about from the moment he woke up until the moment he fell asleep each night, and I was no longer the only one for whom his heart swelled.

"I love those kids with all my heart," I say. I do. I love them in my own way, as much as a mother who never wanted to be a mother could love her children.

"I know you do." He releases my hand, fixing both of his to the steering wheel as we approach heavy traffic.

Shortly after we married, Graham's father passed. He was forty-seven when he and Greta welcomed Graham, their only child, into the world. When Arthur died, Graham became obsessed with the notion that he should have children at a young age. He didn't want to wait. He didn't want to have them later in life and miss out on all the momentous occasions in their lives. A man's legacy, he was suddenly convinced, was the whole point of life, and it killed him that his father would never have a chance to hold a grandchild in his arms.

My heart was breaking for Graham. We'd always planned to

start our family once we hit our early thirties, after we'd had an entire decade to explore the world together tether-free, but Arthur's death changed things.

Graham was determined to start a family as quickly as possible, and I was young and terrified and less than ready, so I lied. I never stopped taking the pill, hoping I could draw things out a few more years.

Never one to back away from a challenge, Graham insisted I seek a fertility evaluation and proceeded to go full speed ahead with the adoption route in the interim.

The agency said we could be waiting for years.

I thought we had time.

We got the phone call about Grace within three months.

I'd never seen Graham so excited about anything in his life. Wrapped up in nervous energy and blinded by his contagious excitement, I quickly climbed on board, and we rushed to the hospital, waiting anxiously to hold our new daughter as some teenage girl from Connecticut signed away her rights.

The adoption was closed, and we never met Gracie's biological mother. But I think about her often, to this day, wondering what circumstances brought Gracie into the world. Wondering if Gracie's mother, too, was *special* in the same kind of way Gracie is.

I suppose we'll never know.

And maybe it's for the best anyway.

CHAPTER FOURTEEN

D APHNE

"H OW ' S   YOUR   STEAK ?" I   ASK ,   WATCHING   G RAHAM   SLICE   INTO   HIS
filet with quiet determination that night. He hasn't uttered more
than a handful of words to me since we arrived at Jocasta. It's as if
his mind is somewhere else entirely, and it's taking all the strength
I have not to show my frustration. I'm not exactly looking
forward to spending a weekend with his shell. "My fish is incredi-
ble. I *live* for their sea bass."

He glances up, eyes squinting and trained on me. I bet he's
thinking about work. You can take Graham McMullen out of the
office, but you can't take the office out of Graham McMullen.

"Honey?" I release a nervous titter, my thumb worrying the
handle of my knife.

Graham blinks, shaking his head and chewing his steak.
"Sorry. Was thinking about something."

"You can give yourself a day off, you know." I fork a piece of
fish and give him a wink. "You work too much."

"Wasn't thinking about work for once." He gives me a half-smirk before returning his attention to his entrée. His narrative ends there, and I find myself questioning the timeline of our marriage, wondering at which point he stopped opening up to me, stopped caring about himself a little more and me a little less.

"Everything okay?" I ask.

"Yes, Daphne." His brows meet in the middle. His shoulders tighten, a sign, I've learned over the years, that he doesn't want to talk about it.

I finish my meal in silence, ordering a second glass of wine the next chance I get. When the server shows us the dessert cart, I look across the candlelit table at my husband. His elbows rest on the table, hands folded and covering his nose and mouth.

He doesn't want to be here.

"No dessert, thank you." I wave the server off with a polite smile and reach for my purse. Graham retrieves his wallet, grabbing some large bills. "I'm going to run to the ladies' room. I'll meet you in the car."

I don't give him time to protest, though I'm not sure he would anyway. Gathering my things, I dash toward the restroom, hoping I can keep the tears at bay until then.

Flinging the door open, I inhale sharply when I see the restroom attendant. She locks eyes with me, a middle-aged woman with short gray hair and wide-set eyes.

"Good evening," she says.

"Hello," I say, lips wavering and eyes welling. I find a stall and lock the door, whipping out my compact and grabbing a wad of tissues to keep any mascara streaks from getting the best of me.

It was a mistake, coming here. Planning this little getaway weekend. I see now that he'd rather be anywhere but with me.

Pulling in breath after breath, I count to ten. And I count to ten again. I repeat it until my shoulders no longer shake with each inhalation, and I'm confident I can pull myself together enough to get out of here without causing a scene.

When I exit the stall, the attendant is still looking at me. I give her a quick smile, eyes honed on my reflection in the mirror, and she clears her throat.

"Everything okay, miss?" she asks.

I mentally thank her for not calling me "ma'am."

"Yes," I lie, washing my hands.

The woman hands me a warm towel.

"Forgive me for saying this," she says. My heart sinks to my shoes. When someone prefaces their statement with an apology, it never goes well. "But you're the other woman, aren't you?"

I scoff at her audacity, meeting her deep stare with one of my own. "Excuse me?"

I splay my left hand against my chest, but she doesn't look at my diamond ring. She looks me in the eye.

"You're here with Mr. McMullen, aren't you?" she asks.

My jaw hangs. How this random woman knows my husband by name is beyond me. We come here once, maybe twice a year. It's a two-hour drive from Monarch Falls. I would hardly call us regulars.

"How do you know my husband?" I ask.

"Your husband?" Her brows lift. "Oh, my goodness. I shouldn't have said anything. Please, forgive me."

I step closer to her, my ears growing hot. "Please answer my question."

Her eyes avert to the floor and she reaches for a white towel, cleaning up the sink area.

"I won't say anything. I'm not going to get you in trouble," I say. "How do you know my husband?"

She's quiet, and our eyes catch briefly in the mirror. I reach into my purse and flip open my wallet, retrieving a small stack of good-sized bills and handing them over because everyone has a price and judging by the looks of her scuffed shoes and wash-worn blouse, I'm guessing she could use a little assistance.

Her shoulders hunch over the counter and she sighs before

turning back to me. "He comes in here every Thursday night with some blonde woman."

I can't breathe. My chest is tight and my skin is overheating.

"I . . . I thought it was his wife. I see them together all the time," she says. "The way they act . . . everyone loves them here. We all know them by name. I . . . I thought *you* were the other woman, and I was about to give you a piece of my mind."

My lips are numb, like the rest of me, and I bite them so I can feel something, anything, in this moment. I need to know this is real because right now, it feels like a lucid nightmare.

And it is. This is my nightmare. This is my living hell.

"What does she look like, this woman?" I rub my wedding band between two fingers, twisting it over and over. I saw her once, from a good distance, the day that Graham cancelled lunch plans. I saw a flash of yellow hair, a face covered in giant sunglasses, and a sexy little coupe speeding off into the distance.

"I've already said too much." She waves me off, turning her back to me. "Please. I don't want to be involved. It's none of my business. I was prepared to defend Mrs. McMullen. I didn't realize you were her."

This affair ... it's more than physical. If he brought here, to our special place, she must mean something to him. That or he's simply replacing me. Trading me in for a younger, newer model.

With dried, burning eyes, I storm past the attendant, purse flung over my shoulder, and make my way to the valet stand where my husband sits in our idling car.

Pulling the door open so hard, it nearly comes back at me, I drop myself into the front seat. I'm seething. Nostrils flaring. Heart racing. My vision is tinted red, fading to black with each second that passes.

"You okay?" Graham places his hand on my knee, and I flinch. That hand . . . the one that held mine as we said our vows, the one that held my hand as I gave birth to Rosie and Sebastian, the one that touched me in ways no one else ever has.

I fling his hand off me. "Don't."

I wanted to save this; I wanted to save *us*. I wanted to believe all was not lost.

"Daphne." He laughs. He thinks this is a joke. "Is this about dinner? I'm sorry I didn't have much to say. We're working on this acquisition at work, and it's stressful. It's like a game of chess. I shouldn't have been preoccupied when you planned this little date night for us. I'm sorry."

Graham pulls into the honking, chaotic Manhattan traffic, veering around the corner and leading us back to our hotel.

The thought of sleeping next to him, his duplicitous hands caressing my body, his greedy fingers slipping down my panties as his lips claim my flesh, makes me nauseous.

"Night is still young. Let me make it up to you," he says.

I don't know if he can.

CHAPTER FIFTEEN

Daphne

When Grace was born she had thick, dark hair and wide, round eyes like two endless black holes. They turned a shade of ordinary brown after a while, but looking at her was slightly unnerving at first. She wasn't one of those babies who garnered comments from complete strangers. No one stopped us to tell us how beautiful she was. No one offered to babysit, and no one fawned over her for very long. It was as if she gave off this force-field that kept anyone from getting too close.

For the first three months, she was fussy and cranky. The doctors said she had colic, but she was never like that when Graham was holding her. Just me.

In a desperate attempt to bond, I took her to Mommy-and-Me classes that first year. Music. Yoga. Baby signing. Anything I could get my hands on, I signed us up for. All the other moms seemed so effortless with their babies. All the other babies cooed and laughed, reaching for their moms.

Clinging to their moms with their sticky hands and grinning their drooling smiles.

Not Grace.

She'd crawl off every chance she got, and when she wasn't curiously exploring, she was having the mother of all meltdowns. Somewhere along the line, I lost track of how many classes Grace had disrupted, how many times I had to sneak out with her and get her home where she could continue on with her hissy fit.

Every day was a struggle.

And then Graham would come home.

Grace would light up and giggle, and Graham would smother me in kisses, unable to keep his hands off me, telling me motherhood looked gorgeous on me, and how he couldn't wait to get home to his little family every night. He'd scoop Grace up in his arms, kiss her tiny forehead, and carry her off to the family room while I fixed us dinner.

I could hear him counting her fingers and toes from the next room, all the while I was counting down the minutes until her bedtime so I could breath again . . .

So I could have Graham to myself again.

So I could feel normal again.

Everything about motherhood felt unnatural. It was a poly-ester suit I could never remove. Scratchy. Uncomfortable. It pulled in all the wrong places and looked horrible on me, I was sure.

It didn't help that Graham moved us to Monarch Falls, where I knew not a single soul. My days were Grace. My nights were Graham. I existed solely as a wife and a mother. My hope was always that I'd meet some other mommy friends, but it never happened. Those women stayed away from me the way everyone else stayed away from Gracie.

There were days, that first year, that I wasn't sure I could do it. I'd page through various mommy blogs all day, convinced these women knew what they were doing because they looked ridiculously happy all the time with their exuberant grins and Eskimo kiss photos. I studied their recipes, their discipline methods, bought the clothes they bought, and followed the trends they raved about. For a period in my life, it was an obsession.

I became one of them, and I imagined a whole nation of moms, all faking it until they made it, all trying to get through each and every parenting tribulation with smiles plastered on their faces and gentle, silent reminders that nothing lasts forever.

And then I came across a defunct blog. A woman and her husband had a beautiful baby girl, chronicling the first two years of her life, and I could see that they weren't trying to be some kind of picture perfect family. They genuinely loved and adored each other. They genuinely loved life. Their daughter had a contagious smile, white-blonde curls, and big blue eyes. They called her Emmy, and like Grace, she was adopted.

As the blog posts progressed, I almost clicked away until something in the side bar caught my eye. It was a link to a post simply titled, "Funeral."

My heart sank, and I found myself poring over a dozen or so posts detailing the accidental choking death of their sweet Emmy. Her mother had taken her to a park one afternoon, feeding her sliced strawberries when one piece got lodged in her throat. When she couldn't get it out, other park patrons tried, and 911 was called. Emmy was unconscious, and after a few days at the hospital, she was pronounced brain dead.

The blog posts stopped after "Funeral."

I cried for hours after reading about Emmy and her parents.

And I looked at Grace differently from there on, reminding myself every single day that we were lucky to have her. That she was given to us for a reason. Those parents will never get to tuck sweet Emmy to bed again, and I get to spend every waking minute of my day with my daughter.

Things were a little better when Grace turned eighteen months and began to talk more. Word by word, we could communicate. We could see eye to eye. She became fascinated by everything I did, shadowing me, suddenly inseparable.

With each day that passed, I felt more at ease in my role, and Graham noticed. He called me a natural, said he'd never loved me as much as he did when he watched me with her.

It felt good to see him happy, to feel his appreciation and admiration. So when Grace turned two and Graham insisted we try for one of our own again, I didn't say "no."

Over the year that followed, Grace was a sweet little angel. She picked flowers, skipped down sidewalks, accompanied me to baby yoga, and twirled in the frilly dresses I picked out for her. We shopped and lunched and made friends with the neighbors. Grace smiled more than she cried, and complete strangers would stop me to rave about how well-behaved my child was.

Life was grand.

And then Rose came along. Conceived after a single try, Graham never once questioned my earlier "infertility diagnosis," but he did push for me to see a doctor as soon as possible, just to make sure everything was normal.

The day I gave birth to Rose, I saw that darkness in Grace's eyes again. The smiles stopped. The tantrums started. The doctor said it was a phase, that she was jealous of the baby. But as a mother who knew my daughter, I could sense it went far beyond any of that.

And I was right because seven years later, nothing has changed. If anything, she's only become worse.

My house is quiet on this Monday morning, and it gets like this toward the end of the school year. The kids know summer break is just around the corner, and they lose all desire to get moving in the morning, even little Rose.

Graham left before the sun came up this morning, saying he had an early conference call with London.

He still doesn't know I know about the mystery blonde, and I'm not sure when I'm going to spring it on him. Besides, I want to have my facts straight. I can only imagine him laughing at me when I tell him his liaisons were casually confirmed by a bathroom attendant. By the end of the night, he'd have me convinced the woman didn't know what she was talking about, and then he'd probably call and have her fired.

I was thankful for the dark of the hotel room that night, but hurt and simultaneously relieved when Graham didn't initiate love-making. We spent the better part of Saturday doing our own thing; me at the spa and him catching a televised Royals game at his favorite Manhattan sports bar.

Saturday night, we attended a Broadway show, each of us ignoring our awkward, stilted conversation during the intermission, and I let him hold my hand when he reached for it during the second act. Graham yawned and checked his phone throughout the night, but he never complained.

Then later in the hotel room, out of absolutely nowhere, he held me in his arms and told me he loved me. We were lying in bed, the glow of the TV flickering on our faces. He apologized for working so much, promising me the deal he was working on would allay that. Graham gave me his word that he'd be home more, saying his kids were growing up and he felt like he had a birds-eye view when he really wanted a front row seat.

I'd closed my eyes and listened to the gentle softness of his voice in the dark, breathing him in and trying not to lose it against his chest. Never had my husband felt so physically close, yet so emotionally far away, and it was a kind of pain that seared straight through me.

This life – this *beautiful* life – we've built together means nothing if he isn't a part of it. I can't be a single mother. I can hardly be a married mother. I can't do this without him. I can't do it on my own.

But I also can't stick around like some doormat while he's taking his little whore to *our* restaurant, sneaking around, coming home late, and filling my head with a million different plausible excuses like I'm too dimwitted to question him.

To be honest, I'm shocked that I'm not completely falling apart at the seams. If anything, I'm numb.

I'm in survival mode.

If the kids were in school today, I'd have time to think on this. I need to make a decision. I'm well aware of the fact that I need to figure things out. I can't flounder around in this murky gray area forever, straddling the lines of two very different existences.

My head pounds despite the two cups of coffee I've already inhaled this morning. Two thumps are heard from above followed by the creak and whoosh of a bedroom door opening.

Grace is finally up.

I wait for her footsteps to trail down the stairs, pouring myself another cup of coffee in the interim. After a couple minutes go by, I head to the bottom of the stairs to check on her, repeating her name in a yelled whisper.

Nothing.

Taking the steps as carefully and quietly as I can, I see her open door at the end of the hall, and then my gaze travels to the double doors to the master suite, which are wide open.

I know I closed them this morning.

Tiptoeing to my room, I don't see Grace, so I duck my head into the master bath, freezing and drawing in a long breath when I see her sitting on the counter, a tube of toothpaste in one hand and her other smearing it all over the mirror and faucets.

"Grace McMullen." I say her name through clenched teeth. "Why?"

"I'm making a design!" she says, brows furrowed as if I have no right to be upset with her right now.

I storm to her side, hooking my hands under her arms and pulling her off the counter. She laughs, eyes dead and lifeless, and reaches like she's going to smear her sticky hands all over my hair and face. Yanking her to the tub, I draw a bath and begin peeling her clothes off.

"Stop it! Don't touch me!" She struggles against me, jerking her arms away.

And then she strikes me, her hand sticking to my face.

I pull her close again, and this time her little chubby face is red hot, twisted, looking at me like she hates me. Like I'm the worst mother in the world.

Reaching for me, she grabs a clump of my hair and tugs me toward her. I lose my balance and fall into the tub of running water, wondering how I ever doubted her strength and watching her take off running.

"Get off me," she screams, frantic and crying. She's in another one of her moods, and I haven't the slightest clue how to fix this because I can't understand it. Sebastian and Rose don't behave this way, and I've raised them all the same. "I hate you, I hate you, I hate you."

"Grace! Get back here." I climb out of the water, my pajamas drenched, and chase her down the hall, my feet slipping every which way when I hit the hardwood floor. She's already thundering down the stairs, skipping steps and jumping off the bottom.

Grace disappears around the corner, and I'm standing at the top of the stairs, sopping wet, cold, hair sticky and white. Defeated.

I can't keep doing this.

Something's got to give.

CHAPTER SIXTEEN

Autumn

THE BIG YELLOW BUS ROUNDS MAGNOLIA DRIVE AT A QUARTER TO eight Monday morning. My hand grips Ginger's leash, and we pick up our pace. A group of schoolchildren are gathered on the corner, jumping and giggling as they wait for their ride.

Keeping to the other side of the street, I watch the kids, searching for Grace's dark hair and cherubic smile. My heart flutters when I see her, but I pull my baseball cap tight over my forehead and adjust my sunglasses. My hair is gathered beneath my hat, and I'm in one of Ben's baggy sweatshirts and a pair of frumpy jogging pants. Each time I walk Ginger, I try to dress a little differently. I wear mostly grays and blues. I like to blend in. I want to be that nondescript neighbor taking her dog for a morning walk.

Practically invisible.

The bus comes to a squeaky halt and the doors creak open. From my perspective it looks as if the thing is swallowing them

MINKA KENT

whole, one by one. Within seconds, they're off to school, and a little boy with white-blond hair points at Ginger and waves to me.

In a flicker of a second, I try to imagine his parents. What they're like. I bet they're good people who teach him manners and self-sufficiency. I'll bet he's an only child. Friendly and intelligent.

But clearly his parents screwed up somewhere because he should know better than to interact with strangers.

Stranger danger.

"Sebastian, come back here." A ball rolls into the street, followed by a running child, and it takes a moment before it fully registers that Sebastian McMullen is headed in my direction - and his mother is frantically, obliviously following after him.

Daphne is on her phone, one hand pressed against her ear and the other outstretched, hysterically screaming as she yells for her son to stop.

The ball rolls across the street, bumping against the curb and coming to a halt maybe ten feet ahead. Daphne is gravely unaware of everything else as she runs after her son, including the blue sedan that nearly clipped her when she ran out between two parked cars.

That's a real mother for you, willing to put her life on the line and ignoring everything around her just to focus on the safety of her baby.

My heart pounds in my ears as I watch her calmly take Sebastian by the wrist and pull him back to their driveway where her SUV is parked neatly on her side, the right side, with the rear passenger door ajar just the way she left it.

"I don't know," she says, exhaling into the phone as she lifts Sebastian to her hip. She's winded, I can see that from here, but whoever she's talking to probably has no idea that seconds ago, she and little Sebastian McMullen was almost roadkill, and something tells me Daphne doesn't intend to tell her. I don't blame her though. I wouldn't want to relive a terrifying moment for anything. "Graham mentioned hiring someone, but I feel like at this point all the good summer nannies are taken. We really some-one. I'm going to make him handle it. I just don't have the time."

I walk straight ahead but keep my gaze fixed on the two of them as she fastens Sebastian into his car seat, shuts the door, then walks around the back. Within seconds, the brake lights flash to red for a moment and the car rolls down the driveway.

"Come on, Ginger, let's go home," I say as we round the corner past the McMullen's house.

I have to admit I'm confused . . . Daphne has never once mentioned a nanny in the past. Is it a new thing? Has she always hired a nanny for the summer but kept it under wraps? I did always wonder how it was that she could keep a house spic and span, cook gourmet dinners each night, raise three healthy, happy children, and not have so much as a single dark circle under her sparkling blue eyes.

Of course.

Rich people always have hired help!

I can't believe I could be so naïve to think that the McMullens did it all themselves.

Ginger makes a pit stop by a mulberry bush, but the second we get home, I'm opening my laptop and pulling up every nanny agency in the area until I find their ad. All I need to do is become everything they're looking for and the job is as good as mine. Then screw Instaface and living my life between snapshotted moments.

I'll have access to the real thing.

Visions of helping Daphne in the kitchen and braiding Grace's hair and chatting with Graham about the stock market and running errands in one of their luxury SUVs flood my mind all at once.

This is going to be laughably easy. I'll be the best thing that's ever happened to them.

And they're going to *love* me.

CHAPTER SEVENTEEN

Daphne

I'm shaking.

I did something I've never done before, and I don't know if it makes me human or a monster or something in between.

Graham texted me earlier, saying he wouldn't be home until after nine tonight. I slipped the kids each a dose of chewable melatonin and put them to bed at six o'clock so I could have a little bit of a breather.

After the toothpaste incident this morning, Rose and Sebastian woke up. I poured them all cold cereal for breakfast and spent the better part of the morning scrubbing down my bathroom and trying to get the paste out of my hair before I got them out the door.

When the kids got home from school today, I grounded Grace from everything she loves . . . her books, her CD player, her dolls, her tablet filled with educational games. Anything I could think of. I stripped her bedroom bare and made her stay up there all afternoon, alone, like a prisoner in solitary confinement. I even made her eat dinner in her room all by herself, which she probably enjoyed.

But I felt like a merciless monster all afternoon for it, until she emerged, without permission, at six o'clock, screaming at the top of the stairs and crying. She threatened me left and right, promising to turn me in for child abuse. When I marched up the stairs to deal with her, I found her arm covered in self-inflicted bruises and bite marks.

I can't do this. I can't do this all summer. This can't be my life for the next ninety days.

I always thought the older the children got, the easier this would get, but it's only proven to be worse with each passing birthday. They're all on varying pages, pulling me in different directions every time I turn around.

I'm seated in the front room of our home, cloaked in late-evening darkness, sipping a double Belvedere on ice. Soaking up the sound of silence, I slowly feel my sanity grabbing hold of me again. My mind's been fixated on that emergency joint since earlier today, though I refuse to touch it just yet because something tells me the worst is yet to come.

After my drink is finished, I make one more and then trek quietly upstairs to draw myself the hottest bubble bath I can stand.

Earlier today, just before I picked Sebastian up from preschool at noon, I passed Graham's office. His car was gone, and I was certain because I circled the parking lot three times. When I called his assistant and asked to be patched through, she fumbled over her words and told me my husband was in a meeting.

I gripped the phone so tightly I thought it might shatter.

And then I thanked her. And told her to have him call me when he could. An hour passed, and he called and said he wouldn't be home until later.

The more I think about it, the more I'm absolutely positive he's in the city, with *her*.

I would give anything to know what he sees in her. I want to know what she has that I don't; what she gives him that I can't. Does she make him smile a little bigger? Does she make him laugh a little louder? Does she make his cock a little harder?

And then there are the phone calls.

Every day, around four o'clock, a blocked number calls me.

I have half a mind to think it's her. Maybe she wants to hear my voice. Maybe she's just as curious about me as I am about her. Or maybe she wants to torment me, make me go insane so I'm that much less appealing to Graham.

Either way, I still refuse to answer.

Upstairs, tucked away in the back of my closet, rests a miniature cedar chest, maybe five inches tall by eight inches wide. Folded and stacked inside that box are dozens upon dozens of "love notes" Graham has penned for me over the years, each one filled with promises and professions of his undying devotion spanning from our younger years until just a few months ago.

I'm so lucky to have you in my life, Daphne . . .

You're the best thing to ever happen to me . . .

How did I get so lucky?

You're perfect for me . . .

I'll never love another, Daphne. I promise . . .

I'm going to spend the rest of my life with you . . .

I wonder if my husband has always been a world-class liar and cheat, or if his wants and needs and desires pivoted the day he met *her*.

Earlier I dug the letters out of the box and ripped them to shreds. It didn't feel as satisfying as I thought it would, my anger replaced with mourning.

I toss the remains of my Belvedere back, and I wait for it to hit my bloodstream, and then I fix myself another because I can't stop thinking about what they're doing right now, and I want to be thinking of anything but the two of them.

I wonder if she knows she's stealing someone else's happiness?

Ruining other people's lives? I wonder if it's all worth it to her, if she even cares?

Dread settles in the pit of my stomach as the room spins. In all my ruminating and contemplating and fixating about saving our marriage, I never once considered the fact that Graham may very well be planning to leave me or that I may very well be fighting a lost cause.

I need to make a decision.

CHAPTER EIGHTEEN

AUTUMN

"YOU'RE IN BETTER SPIRITS TODAY." BEN DROPS HIS WORK BAG BY the front door and steps out of his shoes. He's home later than usual today and he smells like beer and O'Tool's pub. If I weren't so exhausted, I might have the energy to be offended by the missing invite, not that I would've wanted to go. He's looking at me like he expected to come home to a ragamuffin, shocked to see me dressed in jeans and a cute t-shirt, my hair pulled into a half-taut ponytail and just enough makeup on my face to give me a healthy glow. "You're smiling. You have a good day today?"

He should know by now that the answer is yes. Today was a good day. Today restored my hope and quelled my anxieties. As soon as I located the McMullen's nanny ad, I spent the better part of the morning crafting the perfect resume. By noon, I received confirmation that it had been received and acknowledged.

They're going to be calling any day now, dying to pull me in for an interview, and I'm going to knock their socks off.

I spent the rest of the afternoon studying and practicing what

I'd say, trying to come up with the kinds of questions they might ask. Their want ad explicitly stated: *Monarch Falls family seeking full-time summer nanny for our three children, ages 10, 7, and 4. You must love children, be mature and responsible with a clean driving history, and CPR/First-Aid certified. Hours are Monday through Friday from 9-4. You must be punctual and well-presented. We're a non-smoking household with one non-shedding pet. Must be comfortable around dogs. Previous experience with children and a background check required. Please email your resume to admin@mcmullenandhenrycorp.com.*

Piece. Of. Cake.

It's almost like they were looking for me specifically.

"How was your day?" Ben asks, plopping down beside me on the sofa. I'm surprised he hasn't mentioned the smell of pot roast in the slow cooker. It's all but polluting our house with its onion gravy stench. I hate pot roast. Always have. But I made it for him because it's his favorite, and I want to forget about yesterday. I want to forget about my meltdown. I want things to go back to normal.

Ben and his dream girl.

Two boring little peas in a perfect fucking pod.

"Great," I say, leaning into him. Even after a day at the office, he still smells like Dylan Abernathy's cologne, which I don't love as much as I'd hoped to. I'm counting down the days until that bottle's empty. I just might have to accidentally knock it off the bathroom counter one of these days. "Spent all day applying for jobs. Feeling really good about things."

Ben slips his arm around me, pulling me into him. "All you needed was a little push in the right direction."

"Yeah," I lie, leaning against him. "I'm so lucky to have you. Thanks for always knowing exactly what I need."

He smiles like a teenager whose coach just high-fived him after shooting a three-pointer with four seconds on the clock. I want to puke.

Ben pops up, our moment over before it barely began, and shuffles toward the kitchen. He disappears around the corner, and then I hear him say, "Oh, sweet. Pot roast. Thanks, babe!"

Simple Simon.

The clinking and clambering of silver on china precedes his return, and he plops down beside me, mouth full of carrots and potatoes, and pats me on the knee.

"I made you an appointment," he declares.

"An appointment for what?" My stomach unsettles.

"Thought you could talk to someone." He shovels a bite of roast onto his fork.

"About . . . what? Exactly?" I smile and bat my lashes like nothing's wrong because nothing *is* wrong.

"You've been so down lately. Just thought it'd be good for you to talk to someone," he says. "You don't really have any friends, so . . ."

I rise.

I don't want to have this conversation.

I *know* I don't have friends. *Well aware.* And for good reason.

I don't need him to point it out to me.

"Sorry." He slumps his shoulders, glancing away and exhaling as if I have no right to see myself out of this conversation. "Didn't realize it was such a sore subject for you."

Crossing my arms, I stare past the sliding door, eyes squinting until the McMullens' back patio comes into focus. I take a step closer. Lights are strung and lit above their dining set, and in the dim light, I spot Daphne setting the table.

"I'm going to eat outside tonight." I head toward the kitchen and fix myself a bowl of cold cereal. I'd rather eat sugary processed corn flakes than Mrs. Gotlieb's "famous" pot roast recipe anyway.

Ben takes his dinner to the living room, and Ginger follows, hopping beside him on the sofa and begging for scraps. Ben happily obliges despite the fact that I constantly tell him not to feed her. She's a purebred Cavalier and she has a sensitive stomach. He doesn't care. He thinks it's cute when she climbs up on her hind legs and swipes her paw at his shoulder. When they realize I'm headed outside, the two of them stop what they're doing and stare in my direction like they're waiting for an invite.

"It's nice out. You want to eat outside?" I extend an invitation, fingers crossed they leave me be.

Ben hesitates before rising to join me, and I go on ahead because I see the McMullen children filing out their back door and taking their places.

"You ever drop off Marnie's birthday gift?" Ben asks, taking the spot beside me a moment later. Ginger's inside still, scratching at the glass and looking like she's about to murder someone for a tender scrap.

Shit. No.

"I completely spaced it off." I inject an apology into my tone, but my gaze is focused on the other side of the fence, trained on the real-time family portrait in the distance. They do this from time to time. They dine al fresco. I only wish I could go inside and grab my binoculars because Daphne's tablescapes are to die for. It's as if she studied under Martha Stewart herself. "I'm so sorry. I'll get it to her this week."

"Okay, yeah, back to that appointment. The guy's name is Dr. Barringer and it's tomorrow at noon. I emailed you with his address this morning. His receptionist was going to send you the paperwork."

"Ben, come on." I laugh, swatting at him. "Seriously, I don't need to talk to anyone. I'm better now. You said so yourself."

"You're better today, but what if something changes tomorrow? Or the next day. You need to talk to someone, babe. You don't really open up to me, but maybe you could open up to him? Get it all out. It'll feel good."

The thought of sitting in some shrink's office baring my soul and spilling my secrets is about as appealing as paying someone to rip out my entrails sans anesthesia.

"Ah, look at that," Ben's attention follows mine. "That's adorable."

"What?" I play dumb.

He points.

Points!

If they were to look up right now and see him pointing at them, I would *die*.

Gently, I loop my hand into his elbow and pull his pointed finger to the side.

"Don't point, babe," I say softly. "They can see us, you know. If they look up."

He shoves a forkful of meat between his lips and laughs out his nose.

"My bad," he says after he's chewed and swallowed. "It's good to see families eating together, you know? Some of my guys at work, the ones with kids, they say nobody does that anymore."

"It's probably true," I speculate. "People are so busy all the time anymore. Nobody sits down for a good, old-fashioned home cooked meal."

Except the McMullens.

They're as close to perfection as anyone's ever going to get, I'm convinced.

It's like someone cut them out of a 1950s Better Homes and Gardens magazine and breathed life into them. Gazing across the fence line, I see Graham and Daphne at opposite ends of the table, the children quietly slicing away at the food on their plates. Daphne pours herself a glass of red wine and Graham leans toward little Sebastian and ruffles his hair.

"Maybe someday that'll be us?" Ben nudges his shoulder against me before leaning down to kiss my forehead.

"Yeah, maybe someday." I wrinkle my nose, cute like a bunny. I don't tell him I don't want that with him. I don't want to settle down and be his girl-next-door wife for the rest of my life.

I'm already getting bored with this shtick. It's eating away at me like a flesh eating disease while simultaneously killing me from the inside. It's not who I am. It's not who I want to be.

Maybe for now, for necessitated reasons.

But not forever.

CHAPTER NINETEEN

DAPHNE

I'M LYING IN BED, WRAPPED IN PITCH BLACKNESS, WHEN THE DOUBLE doors swing soft against the carpet. I recognize Graham's steady strides and keep my eyes squeezed closed. He's missed most of our dinners this week, and tonight he left after dinner to go "run some errands," though I can't imagine what kind of errands he would need to run at eight o'clock at night.

I have nothing to say to him.

All I've been thinking about – all I've been dreaming about – since I put the kids to bed tonight was taking off for a few days.

I deserve better than Graham. The kids deserve better, too. We're living this life he created for us, a life we created together, and he's off doing his own thing, like none of us matter anymore.

I'm a prisoner in this outwardly beautiful life, and I'm a slave to its inward ugliness.

For hours today, I silently stewed, obsessing about Graham's affair more than ever, asking myself questions to which I'll probably never find the answers.

Half of me wants to finally confront him, to create a scene, to put my hurt on full display and let him see the ugly aftereffects of his illicit affair. The other half of me reminds myself I have no money of my own, at least not in any large amounts. No job. No way to support three children by myself. I have no way of leaving just yet and nowhere to go. The only family I have is my mother, and she lives in a one-bedroom condo in Boca Raton with her new boyfriend, whom I'm convinced is a closet pervert for . . . reasons.

"Daphne, you awake?" Graham slides under the covers, occupying his side of our enormous king bed. The bed shifts with his weight as he moves closer, slipping his hand over my waist and pulling me into him. "I'm back now. I had to get a card for my assistant. It's her birthday tomorrow." He chuckles. "Usually she does all my running around, but I didn't think it'd be fair to make her get her own card."

I keep my eyes shut, hoping he'll leave me alone if he thinks I'm still sleeping.

"How was your night?" he asks. He knows I'm up. I'm sure my ragged breathing gave it away. "Were the kids good? They go to bed on time?"

My mouth forms a straight line, and I burrow my cheek against the pillow, rolling away from him just enough. He pulls me in, nuzzling his nose against my neck. His sudden affection is baffling, unnerving.

"I don't want to do this anymore." My declaration is a whisper that silences Graham but doesn't remove his touch.

"Daphne." He releases a firm breath. His hand grips my side, and he rolls me to my back. My eyes part and find his, and for the first time in years, Graham looks genuinely hurt. "What are you talking about? You don't want to do *what*?"

I don't know where to begin, and I'm exhausted, so I push him off me and move to my side of the bed again.

"What's gotten into you?" His hurt tone has morphed into

annoyance. I'm sure he's not used to his perfect little wife showing a full spectrum of emotions, but I've reached a point where it no longer matters. I even washed every last bit of makeup off my face before coming to bed tonight, a non-verbal act of revolt, though it's so dark in here he'll never be able to notice.

"Bad day?" he asks.

I don't answer, and it isn't because I'm into giving him the silent treatment or I'm in the mood for some juvenile guessing game.

I haven't the energy.

He's not worth *my* energy.

And what energy I have left, I need to conserve for tomorrow morning, because Gracie isn't going to stop being Gracie, and I need to ensure Rose and Sebastian's lives don't suffer because of that.

"Good news," Graham's voice is lighter now, his lips pressed against my ear and the heat of his body warming my back. "My assistant posted the want ad earlier this week for the nanny. I told her it's the last week of school, so this needs to be priority one."

I'm fully awake now. I didn't take him seriously the first time he'd mentioned hiring help for the summer. It wasn't the first time he'd suggested it and let it fall to the wayside in favor of other priorities.

Graham, being the old-fashioned type, has never once seriously or genuinely proposed any kind of nanny arrangement, and if it buys me more time to figure out what I need to do, then so be it. I'll play the part a little while longer.

"Any good applicants?" I ask, exhaling and trying my hardest not to get my hopes up.

Graham chuckles. "You don't sound excited."

"Of course I'm excited. I'm just too exhausted to show it." I yank the covers up to my neck and scoot another couple inches toward my side of the bed. "The kids ran me ragged today."

I close my eyes with a little more hope and a little less despair, daydreaming about what I'll do with my sudden windfall of free time.

Maybe I'll open Instaface again. I'll take up running. I'll get massages and shop – alone. Untethered to a stroller or a restless preschooler.

And when I'm not busy spoiling the hell out of myself on Graham's dime, I'm going to find out exactly who it is my husband's screwing when he thinks no one's looking.

And in between doing all of that, I'll finally figure out what I'm going to do with the shattered remains of our marriage.

"My assistant's calling applicants and scheduling interviews this week," he says, rolling away. "I'll handle everything."

Before I fall asleep, I think about all the times Graham has given me credit for my hard work and long days, praised me when I least expected, and shown sympathy out of nowhere. I'd always basked in his acclaim for me, lapping it up like a kitten to milk.

But it's crystal clear, now, it was only ever a manipulation tactic, and I fell for it. Every. Single. Time.

CHAPTER TWENTY

Autumn

I pass Cotton street on the way to the pharmacy. One left turn and I'd be at Marnie's townhouse. Her birthday present sits in the front seat beside me, the packaging slightly bent and battered from being handled and moved around five too many times.

At Ben's insistence, I attended my evaluation this morning with Dr. Barringer, who asked me a series of questions and diagnosed me with anxiety. I left with a written prescription for Ativan and feeling exactly the same as I did when I went in.

I don't think I'm anxious.

This morning while Ben was in the shower, I read his text messages and discovered that Dr. Barringer is a fantasy baseball friend of his, and that recently Ben complained that he isn't getting laid as much anymore. Dr. Barringer replied that I "may be experiencing some situational stress from her recent job loss and there are medications that could help her relax."

So there. Ben has a dirty little secret after all: he just wants sex.

The stoplight ahead turns red. I'm in the middle lane. My hand reaches for the blinker, though I doubt anyone will let me over this time of day.

I should do the right thing.

I should drop off her gift.

The blue corner of my prescription sticks out from the zippered pouch on my purse, and I'm hit with the sting of betrayal.

Ben . . . Ben who kisses the ground I walk on . . . went behind my back and convinced his shrink buddy to drug me up so I could go back to being his perfect, pliable dream girl.

And fucking Marnie with her fake tan and bleached hair, always looking down her smug little pig nose at everyone.

The car behind me honks, and I gaze up to see the car in front of me halfway down the next block already. Pressing my foot against the pedal, I lurch ahead, leaving the turn to Marnie's road in the dust.

My hands grip the steering wheel, clammy and moist, and my heart thumps hard in my chest. Rolling down the window beside me, I swallow lungful after lungful of humid June air that only serves to make things worse.

Reality tastes particularly bittersweet today.

All this time I was using Ben, he was using me too.

He doesn't care about me. And he probably never did.

And maybe it's not fair for me to have such a double standard, but if he only knew how much I sacrificed for him–how much I sacrificed to be everything he could ever possibly want in a woman . . .

That ungrateful bastard.

Kingman Avenue lies ahead, and in a split-second decision, I maneuver myself between a mini van and a rusty Oldsmobile and hang a right. Up ahead lies Brinkman Academy, where Grace and Rose McMullen attend school.

I almost called the other day to schedule my tour, but I took an additional look at their website and saw that all prospective parents need to complete paperwork before requesting a tour, which includes two written referrals.

Kind of hard to get a referral when your kid is imaginary.

The clock on the dash reads a quarter past one, and a quick glance toward the distance shows an abundance of children running around a fenced-in playground. It must be recess.

I pull ahead, parking beneath a shade tree on the opposite side of the street.

My eyes scan it all, from the slide to the monkey bars to the swings, where little girls stand in line patiently waiting their turn.

It doesn't take long for me to find Grace, swinging higher than everyone else on the fourth swing on the left. She's grinning so big, her dark hair airborne each time she swings forward.

I smile along with her, clasping my hand across my chest.

That's my girl.

My sweet, happy Grace.

And then it happens so fast.

A boy stands in front of her swing, daring her to kick him, only she drags her feet along the scooped out rocks beneath her, coming to a quick stop. I can't make out what they're saying, but she looks angry. He reaches for her hands, yanking them off the chains, and then another little boy appears out of nowhere, arms crossed as if he owns the place.

My heart races in my ears.

Where are the teachers on duty?

Why are they letting this happen?

The second little boy pushes Grace off the swing from behind, and she lands on her hands and knees. Standing, with ruddy, wet cheeks, she brushes the gravel from her knees and hangs her head.

A teacher with a whistle comes running.

About damn time.

My chest rises and falls in quick succession. I had no idea I was breathing so fast. But my ears are still warm to the touch, and I can feel the scowl formed across my face.

My baby wraps her arms around the teacher, crying into her shirt as the teacher pats her back and waves for another one to deal with those snot-nosed menaces.

Those boys hurt Grace.

I've never felt this way before, but every bone in my body wants to kill them for hurting her.

CHAPTER TWENTY-ONE

Daphne

Graham's hand on the small of my back as I butter the children's toast this morning startles me out of my thoughts.

"Who is she?" he leans in, whispering into my ear.

I glance over my shoulder, toward the family room where my friend Elizabeth's daughter sits on the carpet playing with the kids.

"Her name is Addison," I say. "And she's watching the kids."

"I told you I was handling everything."

"Yes, and that was over a week ago. The kids have been out of school for five days now, and I need help."

"My assistant's scheduling interviews today," he says with a scoff.

I look toward Addison to ensure she isn't hearing our exchange. She's merely a Band-Aid until we find someone a bit more qualified, though she's been here all of an hour and the children do seem to like her already.

Graham lifts a hand to his hip and follows me as I move about the kitchen. Wiping my hands on a Grecian dish towel, I turn to him.

"Interview your applicants and if we find someone better, we'll make a decision then. In the meantime," I say, "we have Addison."

I neglect to inform him that in addition to being a quick fix Band-Aid, Addison is also an insurance policy. I wanted someone here on the off-chance that Graham didn't follow through with this whole summer nanny business promise of his.

"Addison," I call over the island. She pops up, her tiny little waist peeking out between her short shorts and tight tank top. Maybe that's how girls this age dress these days, I'm not sure. I'm going to have to tell her to tone it down, but I'll wait until she's been here longer. The last thing I want is for her to feel uncomfortable. Or for her to run back to Elizabeth complaining about me. A woman's reputation in this city is worth her weight in gold. "Can you bring the children over? It's time for breakfast."

She claps her hands and grins and talks to my kids as if they're puppies, but they seem to respond to it and they follow her like ducklings, all in a row. It's amazing how well-behaved my children are with everyone but me.

"Addison, this is Mr. McMullen," I say.

"Nice to meet you." Addison extends a lean, tan arm toward my husband, and my soul dies a little when I watch his eyes light.

I think I'm going to be sick.

"Okay, I'm leaving," I say. "I'll be running errands all morning. Call my cell if you need anything."

"Will do, Mrs. M.," Addison rises on her sneaker-covered toes, shoving her hands into her back pockets and jutting out her perky breasts. She's a walking, talking teenage cliché, but it isn't her fault. She is her mother's daughter, and Elizabeth is as cliché as they come . . . white colonial, two children, doctor for a husband, cooks a mean veal parmesan, and keeps a Volvo in the garage.

———

"I want to know who she is." I take a hit from a freshly rolled joint and squint across the dark of Mitch's living room. Even in the dark, I feel his gaze drinking me in.

He's missed me.

He said so the second he opened his door.

"Does it matter?" he asks.

I exhale, a wispy halo of smoke rising above my head, and then I sink back in my chair.

"I don't know," I say. "I feel like it does."

Mitch lifts his hands behind his head and kicks his legs out. His flat stomach caves. His tie-dyed shirt is probably a size too big, but it's soft and faded and comfortable, and that's exactly how I feel when I'm with him.

"I don't think it does," he says.

"I just want to know what he sees in her."

"You'll never get an answer to that. Only way is if you go straight to the source, and even then, why would he tell you the truth?"

Mitch has a point. I groan, taking another drag. "I hate when you're right about things."

"It's not about being right or wrong, Uptown. It's about not giving a fuck. The second you stop caring is the second you free yourself from all this shit." He reaches for the joint, takes a greedy puff, then passes it back.

"That sounds really great and all," I say, an edge of sarcasm in my tone, "but it doesn't make me any less curious."

"You know what they say about curiosity."

"It killed the cat?"

"Curiosity can be as dangerous as a butterfly over an open flame." He reaches for the joint again, only this time he snuffs it out in a crystal ashtray on the cluttered coffee table.

"Why'd you do that? I wasn't finished."

Wrapping his fingers around my waist, he gently tugs me to the sofa. Bob Marley's raspy croon plays from the speakers behind us, telling us that every little thing is going to be all right.

I want to believe him.

"What are you doing?" I ask as Mitch pulls me into his lap. I laugh, as if this is the funniest thing in the world. And though I know it's the weed, I couldn't stop if I tried.

The warmth of his palms flanking my hips captures my attention, and the giggles begin to subside. Mitch's eyes, honey brown and as deep as his philosophical ramblings, hold my entire existence for what feels like forever, and for the first time in weeks, I am still.

"You're a beautiful woman," he says. "People would fucking kill to look like you, you know that? People spend a lot of money to look the way you do."

I lift a hand to my warming cheek, but he pulls it away.

"But it's your insides that are all fucked up." His words sting, but I feel their truth in the darkest parts of me. "I think that's why you're so hard to figure out. Your insides don't match your outsides. It's all off-kilter or something."

Tucking my chin, I release a nervous chuckle and glance away for a second. "Okay, I see what you're saying, but I don't know why you needed to pull me into your lap. Kind of overkill, don't you-"

Before I can finish my sentence, I'm silenced by the taste of his smoky mouth on mine. His tongue, warm and unfamiliar despite what we have or haven't done in sessions prior, sends tingles that settle in my middle before radiating to my fingers and toes.

I press my chest against him. I want to be close to him. I want to be close to anyone. I want the kind of exclusive intimacy I've only ever known with one other man before.

My hands gather the fabric of his t-shirt, and I begin to lift it over his head until he stops me.

"I'm not going to fuck you," he breathes, his lips against mine.

Now I'm hurt, my ego bruised. He can't pull me into his lap, silence my words with a hungry kiss, put his hands all over my body and then act like *I'm* the one who wants to go too far with this.

Pulling myself off his lap, I tug my shirt into place and scan the room for my things. I'm high as a kite and unprepared to drive home, but if I can just sit in the car for the next hour, hopefully it'll wear off and I can be on my way like none of this happened.

"It was a mistake coming here," I say.

"Shit. Uptown. Wait," he says, though it's unconvincing.

I swipe my bag from the far end of the couch and fling it around my shoulder.

"Don't go," he says.

He's following me now, and I'm standing in his kitchen. A sink full of dirty dishes and an old sack of fast food on the counter make me nauseous. The basement door is open, and the smell of must and cat litterbox wafts up. I wonder if he has a roommate? I wonder how much there is about Mitch I've yet to discover. And most importantly, I wonder what the hell I ever saw in him.

He's dirty and his house is filthy and he smells like pot ash and smoke, and he's the biggest know-it-all I've ever encountered in my life, and that includes my mother-in-law.

I move to the door. He's one step behind me. His hand splays across the deadbolt.

"It's not that I don't want to," he says with a dissatisfied sigh. "God, you're so fucking sexy. I'd nail the fuck out of you."

I turn to face him, arms crossed tight.

"God." He buries his face in his hands, rubbing his eyes with the heels of his palms. "I don't even know how to tell you this."

My heart sinks into the pit of my stomach, its fall cushioned by a pillow of sheer dread.

"When I'm with you," he says, "I don't feel like Mitch, the deadbeat pot dealer."

I roll my eyes.

"When I'm with you, I feel like the man you think you see

when you look at me," he says. "And I know that doesn't make sense. But let me explain."

My brows meet. "Go on."

"When you look at me, it's like you have so much hope or some shit. It's like you want me to have all the answers, to be everything you need me to be, and the truth is, I'm just some guy who barely made it out of high school and happened to make the right connections so he could get by selling dope." Mitch's hands fall against his sides. "I'm not special. I hustle and bullshit people for a living. But you don't look at me that way. And I want to be that guy you see when you're looking at me. I wanna be him. But I'm not."

"So that's why you stopped me from taking off your shirt? Right. Makes perfect sense."

"That's part of it," he says, biting his full lower lip. His head falls and his eyes won't meet mine. He drags his fingers through his greasy hair and then blows a heavy breath. "I have a girlfriend."

"You son of a bitch." I taste the irony of my words the second they leave my lips. But it's too late now.

"I know, I know." His honeyed eyes lift to mine. "Look, I *love* my girl. We've been together a long time, since we were practically kids. She'd do anything for me, and she'll always have my back. But at the end of the day, I'm a man. I have needs. I get bored. I want to escape every now and again, just like anybody else. I want to be someone else every once in a while. And I found that with you."

Silence engulfs us. I don't know what to say. I don't know whether to be flattered or infuriated or a violent mix of the two.

Twisting my fingers around the doorknob, I try to leave, but he flattens his palm across the door.

"Wait," he says.

I face the side, not wanting to look at him.

"Your husband," he says, "I'm sure loves the hell out of you. I'm sure you're his number one. And this other chick? He must get something from her he can't get from you, and it's probably something you'll never be able to give him because what you have is so deep and so rooted. I speak from experience when I say this, so I hope you're listening."

I nod.

"My girl, I know she deserves better than me," he says. "But I know I'm not going to do better than her, so I'll never let her go. She's got me for life . . . if she wants me. Your husband, if he's got any brains at all, probably feels the same way."

"Can I go now?" I pull back my sleeve and glance at my watch. "You're trying to make me feel better and you're trying to smooth all of this over so you can feel better about what you did . . . what you've been doing for the last several weeks . . . and I just want to go, so can I go now?"

"Uptown," he says, smirking and head tilted. He thinks I'm cute when I'm angry, I can tell. His hand moves to my arm, but I smack it away. "I'm sorry. I really am. I . . ."

"You let me suck your cock," I blurt.

He laughs. "God, I know. I'm a fucking scumbag, aren't I?"

I twist the knob and yank the door open, finally, and he squints and shields his eyes as daylight blinds him.

"I was always honest with you," I say, staring outside. My mellow is wearing off quickly. "I told you everything. I confided in you. I trusted you. I thought you were different. I thought you were the most genuine man I'd ever met. So when I looked at you in a certain way, Mitch, it was because I thought I was looking at the one man who could prove to me that not all of you are selfish assholes."

"I'm sorry. I really am." He follows me outside, under the carport. "Let me make it up to you."

I laugh, my shoes scuffing his cracked, weeded driveway. "No thank you."

"I mean it," he says. "You want to know the name of that girl? I've got people who can find out."

Rolling my eyes, I say, "And I should believe you why?"

"Tell me where she goes, what she drives, what she looks like," he says. "I can put one of my guys on it and get you a name in less than a week."

Tossing my head back and moaning, I turn to face him again. "I'm not normally in the habit of doing business with lying sacks of shit. But I feel like this is the least you could do after everything."

"Text me the details," he says. "I'll get it done."

I strut away not knowing it was possible to feel like less than half of the woman I thought I was when I came here an hour ago.

Now I feel flimsy and insubstantial, like a bough about to snap in the midst of a torrent.

CHAPTER TWENTY-TWO

AUTUMN

I COUNT THE REMAINING PILLS IN THE BOTTLE, EATING MY WORDS and swallowing my ego.

It's been a week since I sent my perfect resume to that nanny agency in response to the McMullens' want ad. And it's been weeks since I last had the pleasure of enjoying a decent McMullen Instaface story.

I'm going through withdrawals.

And anxious as fuck.

I toss back one of Dr. Josh's little yellow pills, chasing it with a glass of white wine despite the fact that there's a bright green sticker on the bottle that explicitly states, "DO NOT DRINK ALCOHOL WHILE TAKING THIS MEDICATION."

Alcohol intensifies the effect, therefore, I take my pills with alcohol. Besides, I've already done my research. I know the exact ratio of booze to pills that would kill me, and I'm not that stupid.

I don't have a death wish.

I just don't want to feel anything right now.

It's as if my life has become a void wasteland filled with noth-ingness.

If there are no McMullens, there is no point, and that's the cold, hard truth.

The clock above the TV quietly informs me Ben will be home in approximately fifteen minutes. He's going to want sex tonight. God forbid he goes more than a week without a release, and I'm not sure how much longer he's going to buy the whole, "these new pills are zapping my libido" lie.

God, I love when karma comes full circle.

I top off my wine and toss back my pill before settling onto the sofa with Ginger by my side. If I'm lucky, I can catch the end of Ellen on the DVR before Ben comes home and commandeers the remote control.

Lying on my side, I flatten my cheek against a throw pillow and let the booze and pill do their thing. Relaxation floods my body, sinking deeper and deeper until I no longer care.

My eyes are glued to Ellen. She's laughing, but I'm too zoned out to know what she's laughing about. From my periphery, Ginger pops her head up, looking at me, and then I hear the faint chime of my phone, ringing from the kitchen.

Sliding one heavy leg off the sofa at a time, I make my way to my phone, not recognizing the number flashing on the caller ID.

Clearing my throat and injecting as much soberness as possible into my tone, I answer. "Hello?"

"Autumn Carpenter?" the woman on the other end asks.

"Yes. This is she." I always hate when people speak like that. It isn't natural. Nobody talks like that in real life.

"My name is Harriet, and I'm Graham McMullen's assistant," she says, causing me to almost drop my phone.

Glancing around the spinning room, I search for the nearest seat and take it. Immediately.

"Yes?" I say, silently begging her to continue.

"He wanted me to set up an interview for the nanny position you applied for," she says. "That is, if you're still interested."

My mouth is dry, and I can hardly contain my excitement, but I manage to blurt, "Yes, of course. When was he thinking?"

"He's doing interviews Monday."

My heart sinks. She said interviews. Plural.

How could they even need to consider anyone else? I ticked off every requirement they listed. There's no one more perfect to watch those children than me.

"What time?" I ask, feeling my voice break and quickly reminding myself that I still have a shot. All I have to do is go in there and charm him and show him that he can't afford not to hire me . . .

"Would nine o'clock work?" she asks. "You'll be the first one if that's okay."

"Perfect," I say.

"Great. I'll put you down," Harriet says. There's a sweet, benign quality in her voice. She doesn't sound like a woman who hates her job. I'll bet she loves working for Graham. I'll bet he's good to his people. He appreciates them. "The interview will be at the McMullen-Henry building in downtown Monarch Falls. Are you familiar with our location?"

"I've seen it, yes," I say. It's hard to miss a building covered in blue glass and shaped like something out of a science fiction movie.

"Perfect. Come to the eighth floor and check in at the front desk."

"I'll be there," I say before ending the call.

I wouldn't miss it for the world.

CHAPTER TWENTY-THREE

Daphne

I text Mitch the plate number, XHW 771, and make and model of her car, Alfa Romeo 4C, and I sink back in my seat as I watch her exit Graham's building under a midday sun. They don't even try to cover it up. Their affair is on full display, out there for the world to see.

My body burns when I think about how many times I've stopped into the office and made idle chit chat with some of the employees. All this time, I bet they've known. All this time, I bet they looked at me with pity in their eyes the second I turned to leave.

It's *humiliating*.

I wait until she's gone and her tail lights fade to nothing over the hill, and then I climb out of my car and head inside with a boxed chocolate cupcake from Graham's favorite bakery. I used to do this, back when things were better. I'd show up at his work in the middle of running errands and drop off a sweet treat just to let him know I was thinking of him.

The only difference between then and now is that I used to call. I used to give him a heads up. But today I'm popping by unannounced. I'm bypassing his assistant, and I'm showing myself to the gargantuan double mahogany doors he insisted on having installed two years ago because he thought it would help with impressing potential clients.

I make my way across the parking lot, through the lobby, and up the elevator. When I reach his floor, I give his assistant a quick wave, ignoring her when she tries to stop me, and then pushing through the giant doors at the end of the hall.

He's on the phone, not noticing me. He's laughing, and I hear him talk about his nine iron and a new golf course opening up next spring in the next town over. There's something relaxed and satisfied in his tone, and for the first time in my entire adult life, I resent his happiness.

I want to take it away from him, drown him with it. I want to boil him in it until he's nothing but a shallow reduction of the man he used to be. He doesn't deserve to be so casual and confident and collected.

"Daphne." His eyes flick up onto mine. He doesn't flinch. He doesn't look like the cat that ate the canary, and there isn't so much as a hint of slick sheen across his brow. "What are you doing here? Everything okay?"

I stand, in awe of how this man can fuck his mistress across his desk and then greet his wife ten minutes later like nothing happened.

He tells the person on the phone he'll call them later, and he rises, coming around his desk and moving toward me. Graham adjusts the Windsor knot of his tie and clears his throat.

"Just wanted to drop this off." I place the small cardboard box with the bakery logo on top at the edge of his desk, and then I turn to leave.

He chuckles. "That's it? God, you scared me. I thought for a second . . ."

How he can stand there with his haughty smirk and preten-tious smile and that untouchable aura is beyond me.

"See you tonight," I say, showing myself out.

This isn't normal, and he knows it. I would never stop by unannounced and walk away in a hurry, but I can't stay.

I can't keep doing this.

"Daphne." There's a darker quality to his voice, one that suggests that maybe, just maybe, he sees his kingdom crumbling before his very eyes.

And he should.

Because by the time I'm done, there'll be nothing left of his perfect little life but ash and smoke.

CHAPTER TWENTY-FOUR

Autumn

I WOULDN'T BE HUMAN IF I WEREN'T NERVOUS RIGHT NOW. I CATCH my ankle bouncing as I wait in the lobby of Graham McMullen's office. His secretary phoned him the second I checked in, and I heard her state, "Yes, sir. She's a bit early." I had to bite my lip to keep from smiling because so far, so good.

Must be punctual.

Check.

I grab a magazine from a small side table to my left and page through. My eyes scan the pictures and sentences, but nothing registers. I couldn't possibly read an article about Roth IRAs at a time like this.

For two days I prepped.

Every waking minute of every day. Right beneath Ben's nose, too. I kept my tablet angled so he couldn't see it as I Googled and read dozens upon dozens, if not hundreds, of articles on the art of acing the interview, and I immersed myself in the language of families who use nannies and au pairs, their expectations, their code of conduct.

I purposely avoided the horror stories, as they didn't seem to apply.

With a family like the McMullens, I don't anticipate a single off-putting scenario. It's not their style, and it wouldn't be in good taste. If there's anything I've learned over the years, it's that everything Daphne McMullen touches is gilded in style and good manners.

"Autumn Carpenter?" A man's voice fills the quiet waiting area. I glance up, expecting to see a pimple-faced intern drowning in his father's three-piece suit, only I'm met with the chiseled features and chocolate-brown hair that can only belong to one person.

I rise, swallowing away any hint of fear and self-doubt, and place a warm smile on my face. A black leather portfolio rests in my left hand, and I slowly extend my right to meet his.

My palm slides against his, fitting perfectly in that warm, tight space. These are the hands that caress the cheek of Daphne, the hands that gather Grace and Rose and Sebastian after a long day's work. These are the hands that drive the family to the lake on summer weekends, and these are the hands that teach the children how to fish and throw a baseball.

"I'm Graham." His voice resides comfortably in his broad chest, and his full lips part into a welcoming smirk. Not a smile. Smiles are for casual strangers. Smirks are for people with whom you have an unspoken understanding. I can't help but feel a connection already, and I can't help but wonder if he feels it too. "This music out here is awful, isn't it?"

I don't answer immediately. It wouldn't be polite to say yes, but it wouldn't be in my best interest to disagree with the very first question he throws my way. Plus I don't want to seem insecure or overly agreeable, as those are some of the worst qualities a childcare provider could have. Children sense weakness in adults. It's practically their sixth sense.

"My business partner insists on this channel," he says. "Makes me sleepy. Anyway, let's head back to my office. You need anything? Water? Soda? Coffee?"

"I'm fine, but thank you." I follow him, my heels carefully tapping against the polished Carrara tiles.

He holds the door open once we reach his suite, and he lets me enter first. A guest chair upholstered in crackling, aged leather is already pulled out. Smoothing his emerald green tie, he points to the chair and tells me to make myself at home.

I lean my portfolio against the side of my chair and run my palms along the underside of my thighs, smoothing my skirt as I take a seat.

I watch him: the way his hand gently rubs the underside of his jaw as he studies my resume, which rests atop a small pile on the center of his desk. His brow raises, as if he's discovering something new, and I have to question whether or not he hand-selected these interviewees or had someone else do it for him.

A man like Graham McMullen, who manages millions of dollars in assets on a daily basis, a man who owns his own corporation, surely has enormous fish to fry, so I don't blame him for outsourcing, but I can't ignore that niggling twinge of disappointment that accompanies the fact that for once, he didn't put his children first.

"You live on Willow," he says, his blue eyes gliding over the table and stopping on mine. My heart stops cold. The corner of his mouth pulls. "We're on Linden. We must be neighbors."

I exhale slowly, so as not to make it obvious. "You're on Linden? No kidding?"

My jaw falls slightly, my lips twisted upward.

"Small world," he says.

"Indeed." I resist the urge to point out the obvious, that he should hire me because I'm literally a stone's throw away . . . that I would never be late because I could walk to work. But I don't want to seem presumptive. And we've only just begun.

"Says here you were a medical assistant at Children's Medical Group until this past March?" he asks next.

I zip my posture and give a slight nod. "I was. And I loved that job more than anything. I love working with children, and I was actually the lead medical assistant in my department. My supervisor would constantly call me a 'mother hen.' She thought I was too mature and responsible for my age, so she put me in charge."

I give a small chuckle. He does too.

Must love children.

Check.

Must be mature.

Check.

Must be responsible.

Check.

"Impressive," he says in such a way that I believe him. "So I assume you're CPR and First Aid certified and all of that?"

"I am," I say.

Another check.

"What was your favorite thing about working with children?" he asks. "I'm sure it had to have been stressful at times? Sick, screaming babies and all that?"

I offer a polite giggle. "We had our well children as well, the ones there for check ups. And actually, the children were my favorite part of that job. Everyone always said I had a way with them. They'd tend to give me the most difficult ones sometimes because I was the only one who could put them at ease."

His eyes flick to mine, and for a moment, he appears lost in thought.

"What did you do before that, Autumn?" he asks. "This is the only job listed on your resume. Did you babysit? Dog walk? Any of that?"

"I attended college after graduating from high school. Children's Medical Group was the first job I landed," I say proudly. "I worked there for several years, until they were bought out by a group of doctors who were bringing on their own nurses and assistants."

"I see." He bites his lower lip. "Have you thought about applying at another clinic? I feel like we've got one on every street corner here."

I don't understand why he's asking this question. We're not here to discuss why I haven't applied at another clinic. We're here to discuss this job. This nanny job. The one I applied for.

"I suppose you could say I'm sort of in limbo right now," I answer.

Good save.

"I was thinking of going back to school in the fall, for nursing, and I've been on the fence about it. In the meantime, I still want to work, and when I saw your ad for a summer nanny position, I got excited again at the prospect of working hands on with children. I just felt like the stars aligned."

He leans against his wingback chair. The thing is massive, upholstered in brown tweed with leather buttons, and fit for royalty. He forces a breath past his nostrils and turns his attention toward my resume once more.

My chest tightens.

I don't think he likes me.

I don't think he's impressed.

I glance down at my attire. White, button-down blouse. Grey pencil skirt. Black kitten heels. Conservative makeup.

Must be well-presented.

Check.

Should I have shown up in clothes better suited for running through a sprinkler? For Play-Doh and finger paint?

My mind processes everything all at once, going a million miles an hour. I spent all weekend preparing for this. I expected to stride in here, say all the right things, and be met with a gleam in his eye and a smile on his face that tells me he's thinking, unequivocally, *"She's the one!"*

The phone on his desk rings, startling us both. His eyes flick to mine.

"I'm sorry. I need to get this," he says, yanking the receiver and cradling it on his shoulder. "Yes. I remembered. I've worked it out. I'll be there. All right. Thank you."

Graham hangs up, pushing the resume across the table and sinking into his chair. He rests his arms across his taut stomach and gives me a casual smile. I can tell he doesn't like interviews. He seems like a simple, straight shooter, and in interviews, you have to be someone else entirely, at least to a point.

"That was my lovely wife," he says with a chuckle, "reminding me to pick up the dog from the vet on the way home."

"What kind of dog do you have?"

He blows a breath past his lips, staring off to the side. "I don't know. It's one of those big hypoallergenic dogs that supposedly don't shed, but they really do. Kids named her Cocoa."

"I love dogs," I say with as much enthusiasm as I can muster. It's true. I love dogs. But my heart is breaking right now and my stomach is twisted and my confidence is disappearing like air from a tire with a slow leak. "I have one of my own, actually. A Cavalier King Charles spaniel."

He smiles, flashing his perfect, dazzling smile. "I have no idea what those are."

"Here," I say, reaching into my purse on the floor and pulling out my phone. "Let me show you. She's beautiful. Her name is Ginger, and she's . . . she's my everything."

I pull up my photos and hand my phone over. He cradles it gently, bringing it to his face, which lights up when he sees my baby.

"She's quite the darling little dog, isn't she?" He hands the phone back, and our fingers brush.

Must be comfortable around pets.

Check.

I spot a family portrait on a table behind his desk. "Is that your family?"

He spins in his chair, retrieving the photo. It's one I haven't seen before, one not posted on Instaface for all the world to see, and my heart is going to burst if he doesn't hand it over immediately. I've been jonesing for a fix something fierce lately.

"This is last summer," he says. "We took a road trip to the Black Hills. My wife wasn't the happiest. She tends to get motion sickness in cars, but I wanted to treat the kids to a good, old-fashioned family vacation, you know? No planes. Just the five of us spending quality time crammed into a rented mini van."

Funny, Daphne didn't share anything about this on Instaface last summer. I'd have remembered if she traded in the Mercedes for a week in a Dodge Caravan sans leather and a moon roof.

"The kids look like they're having a good time," I say, resisting the urge to trace my finger over Grace's cherubic face. She's grinning so hard the apples of her cheeks are bright pink, and her arm is hooked around Rose, practically knocking her over.

"Kids had a blast," he says, chuckling to himself as if he's recalling some fond memory that I'd give anything to experience right alongside of him. "Hope to take them back again soon."

I've heard of families traveling with their nannies.

I wonder if the McMullens would take me along with them if they take another family trip this summer?

My heart flutters at the thought.

A beep comes over his desk phone, and the voice of his receptionist plays through the speaker. She tells him his next appointment is here, and I feel my mood evaporating into the thinnest air.

This isn't fair.

It's over before it even began.

He hardly asked me any questions!

How could he possibly be able to make a confident decision

about my ability to care for his children when he barely scratched my surface?!

Graham rises, offering me a tight-lipped, silent apology. "I'm sorry about that. Looks like that's all the time we have."

"Oh?" I pretend it doesn't bother me, tittering as if I find the situation amusing. "Well, if you'd like to talk more, you know where I live."

We both laugh, as if I've just made the funniest joke, and I feel a wave of hope rushing through me. He may be interviewing a half a dozen nannies today, but none of them will make him laugh the way I did, I'm sure of it. And none of them live on Willow street. He passes Willow on his way home from work every single night, and he'll think of me, and subconsciously, he'll know, I'm the one for the job.

I gather my things, letting Graham follow me to the door. When he places his hand on the small of my back, an electric zing pulses through me.

We have a connection.

I feel it.

"Thanks for coming in," he says. "We're hoping to make our decision as soon as possible. We'll definitely be in touch."

He extends his hand, and I meet his shake, giving a confident squeeze and locking eyes.

"It was my pleasure, Mr. McMullen," I say.

And I mean it.

He'd be a damn fool not to give me this job.

There's nobody, and I mean nobody, better suited to take care of these children.

Nobody else is going to love them like they're family.

Nobody.

CHAPTER TWENTY-FIVE

Daphne

The family room TV is blaring when I walk in the door this afternoon. Dropping two filled paper grocery sacks on the island, I peek my head into the next room. Sebastian is jumping on the sofa and Addison is sitting on the floor between the girls. Coloring books and crayons are scattered all over the Baluch rug, and a flash of heat passes through my body.

Clearing my throat, I say. "Hi, guys. Coloring needs to be done at the kitchen table, okay?"

Addison whips around, her jaw slack, and I see her shove her phone under her left thigh. She was texting.

"Sure, yeah. Of course," she says, frantically gathering the books in her arms.

"Thank you." When I turn to leave, I spot an open bag of crackers sitting on the coffee table as well as a bag of M&Ms Addison must have brought from home. I button my mouth, hard as it is, and return to the kitchen to begin dinner prep.

This is a trade off, I remind myself. And having Addison to

watch the kids is better than not having anyone at all. It's been nearly two weeks since Graham claimed he was going to make hiring a summer nanny priority one, and so far I've yet to hear him mention a single applicant's name.

I'm sure it was just another manipulative tactic.

I'm sure he figures we're keeping Addison, and he doesn't care that she isn't quite good enough for the job because he assumes I've handled it the way I've always handled all matters of the home and children.

Typical Graham.

I'm not sure why I expected that leopard to change his spots.

I preheat the oven to three seventy-five and head upstairs to change into something comfortable. Before, I'd always make sure I was dressed to the nines when Graham came home from work. I'd touch up my lipstick, squeeze myself into skinny jeans, and fix my hair, reveling in anticipation because I always looked forward to seeing his face and the way his eyes took me in the second he walked through the door.

But screw that.

Changing into yoga pants and a basic T-shirt, I glance out the picture window in the master bedroom. This has always been my favorite view of our street. The weeping willows and majestic oaks and the gorgeous houses lining both sides have made living here somewhat of a fairytale.

Now I know it's just a bubble with a false sense of security.

Ten years ago, we moved here from the next town over, when Graham decided to start his financial advising firm downtown and Grace was a newborn. This house wasn't yet for sale, but our real estate agent had word that it was coming on the market soon, so she got us an early look.

I knew this house was going to be our home the second we stepped inside. Dark and cozy in all the right spots, light and airy where it counts. The sweeping foyer and grand staircase in the entry were fit for a Southern Belle and the in-ground pool out back was fit for a sunny, New England summer. A year into living here, Graham let me lead the charge on the kitchen remodel, saying "yes" when I insisted on a Viking range and double refrigerator, a chef's island, and honed Calcutta marble as far as the eye could see.

I used to love this house.

I used to be one hundred percent certain I'd live here forever, that I'd take my last breath in this bed, that my children's children would visit here every Christmas, filling the house with laughter and the tangy sweet scent of gingerbread cookies.

I used to be certain we'd grow old together here.

Drawing in a long breath, I reach for the curtain to draw it closed, only I stop when I spot a car slowing down. It's not one that I've ever seen in this neighborhood before, and I'd remember a car like that. Jet black with seductive curves and round tail lights, I instantly recognize this car as *hers*. It's the other woman's Alfa Romeo.

The car slows to a near stop in front of our house, though I can't see though the privacy tint on her windows. It lingers for a few beats, and then it zooms away like it wasn't there at all.

My heart is beating, wrapped in confusion.

Why the hell would *she* be driving past our house?

CHAPTER TWENTY-SIX

Autumn

MARNIE'S CAR IS PARKED IN THE DRIVEWAY WHEN I RETURN FROM the grocery store.

Today, of all days, is not the day.

This morning marked two weeks since I interviewed with Graham.

That's two weeks of inexplicable radio silence.

A group of boys fly down the sidewalk on bikes with "school's out for summer" smiles on their ruddy faces and playing cards in their spokes.

I finally broke down and called the office around noon today, and much to my surprise they patched me through to Graham, who was immediately apologetic.

"I meant to call you," he said. *"Things have been so hectic here lately, Autumn. I'm so sorry. Anyway, we filled the position, but if it doesn't work out, you're on our shortlist. Number one, actually."*

I thanked him, wondering if he could hear the shake in my

voice, and when I hung up, I collapsed on the sofa, refusing to move for three straight hours.

I slam my car into reverse and back into the driveway, blocking Marnie's fancy little sports car, the one afforded to her by one of her many suitors. From the driveway, I see Ben and Marnie sitting in the living room, I see the flicker of the TV, and I see the two of them laughing, lost in conversation.

Ben's home early.

I hate when he does that. I hate when he shows up from work early, without a phone call or text message. He thinks he's surprising me. He thinks I *like* it.

Ugh. Please.

Pulling the keys from the ignition, I pop the trunk and slam the driver's door. If I make enough racket, there's a tiny chance he'll come out and help me, as he usually does, but I'm not going to put my money on it today. He's with her. *Kid sister extraordinaire.*

Nine plastic sacks filled with groceries anchor my arms a moment later, but I manage to make it to the front door, jimmy my key in the lock, and kick the door open. I'm met with doe-eyed expressions and not a single offer of assistance.

"Autumn," Ben says. "I wondered where you were."

If he *really* wondered, he could've texted me.

Marnie won't make eye contact. Her shoulders slouch as she exhales. I've interrupted their brother-sister time, and that makes me the world's biggest bitch.

"Hi, Marn," I say, shortening her name like we're besties and sounding chipper as hell.

She pulls her phone from her purse, still avoiding my gaze, and mumbles back a half-hearted hello.

"What are you two up to?" I pretend to be happy, because a wise woman once posted a bombshell-esque photo on Instaface with the caption that happiness was the best revenge. And because it's all I can do to keep from falling apart in front of the last two people on earth I'd ever want to fall apart in front of.

"Just hanging out," Ben says, sinking into the sofa cushions and stretching his hands behind his neck. "You want to go get some beer and wings at O'Toole's?"

I see Marnie shoot him a look, as if he should've known better than to invite me, and as much as I'd love to be the cog in her wheel, I'd rather sit alone, at home, and wallow in a scalding hot bath of self-pity because that's just the kind of mood I'm in tonight.

Plus, I need to figure out my next move, and I can't do that with Ben buzzing in my ear all night long, rambling off sports statistics and asking what I want for Christmas even though it's six damn months away.

"Ah, thanks for the invite, guys," I emphasis my last word. "But I'm just going to chill at home tonight, if you don't mind."

Ben pouts, finally coming to my aid with the grocery bags. He follows me to the kitchen, putting away the milk and standing back while I do the rest. Was he always this lazy or am I just now noticing it?

"I want you to come, babe," he says.

My eyes flick up, and I crumple a plastic bag in my hands. "I've got a headache. Just going to lie down and watch TV, I think."

"You've had a headache almost every day for the past two weeks," he says. "It's like the meds aren't even working."

He mutters his last sentence under his breath, as if he doesn't want his sister to know I'm taking meds of any kind. And it makes sense if I think about it because I'm sure she's told him time and again that I'm crazy. In fact, I know she has. I've heard her from the next room. The only thing I can't understand is why she would think that. I've been nothing but kind and generous to her since the day we met, getting emotionally stonewalled in return.

I've never uttered a single unsavory word about that bitch, as much as I'd love to. At least not to Ben. Family comes first to people like the Gotliebs, and I know my place. Me trash-talking Marnie is different than Marnie trash-talking me. That's just the way it is.

"Please?" I lift my brows and slink into his arms. "Let me stay home tonight?"

God, I sound like a pathetic, submissive little see-you-next-Tuesday, and I want to crawl out of my skin and slither away from Ben, from his wicked sister, from this house on Willow Street.

But I stay.

I always stay.

Because of *them*.

And now I don't even have them.

I have nothing.

I am nothing.

"You've been so down lately," he reminds me, because I guess I wasn't aware? "A beer would cheer you up, don't you think?"

I laugh. If he genuinely believes a *beer* would cheer me up, then I've truly hit the lottery of idiot boyfriends.

"Ben, she doesn't want to go, don't make her," Marnie chimes in from the next room. Good to know she's got her listening ears on.

"Thanks, Marn," I call back, deadpanned.

"Welcome," she says.

If anything, I guess we can bond over our mutual hatred of one another and our common annoyance when Ben refuses to take "no" for an answer.

Ben lets me go, and I tend to the groceries, putting away the final bag of canned goods when Marnie shows up in the doorway.

"I'm starving," she whines, pressing her hand over her caved-in stomach. I believe her. She looks like she's starving. Girl probably hasn't had a decent meal in weeks. I bet her flavor-of-the-week likes her on the skinny side. "Hey, Autumn, Ben said you interviewed for a nanny position?"

I whip my attention in her direction, peering at her through my periphery. I'm ninety percent sure she's going to make some underhanded remark about how there are hundreds of medical assisting jobs in the tri-county area and how I'm wasting my education (like she has any room to talk).

It bothers her, I'm quite sure, that I'm playing house with her brother while he foots the bills, but if she only knew this is what he wanted . . . then she wouldn't be able to villainize me for it.

But that's Marnie. Always making assumptions. Always thinking she knows everything. That girl thrives on drama and feeds off conflict.

It's probably why she's so skinny: zero carbs in gossip.

"Yeah?" I ask. "What about it?"

"The McMullens, right?" she asks.

"How'd you know?" I hook my hand on my hip, as if she has no right to know this family.

"Ben told me," she says, her gaze grazing my shoulder and landing on her brother. "I know them."

I swallow the hard ball in my throat, simultaneously trying to wrap my head around this.

"You know them . . . *personally?*" I need context, and I need it now.

She rolls her eyes, fighting a smile. "I interned at McMullen and Henry my senior year of college. I worked with Graham."

Huh.

First name basis.

I need to sit down, I think. Or I need a drink and a little yellow pill. But instead I stand, soaking in what are quite possibly the nicest words this faux-lashed wildebeest has ever uttered to me.

"They didn't pick me." I turn away, arranging condiments on the fridge shelf so I don't have to look at her anymore, though I feel the weight of her stare.

"Really?" She sounds shocked. Though she's probably being fake. I should know better than to think, for one moment, that Marnie Gotlieb is capable of being genuine about anything.

"You want to make a phone call? Put in a good word?" I ask, my words drenched in friendly sarcasm, and for the first time ever, I feel like we're speaking the same language. "Tell them they made the biggest mistake of their life?"

Marnie chuckles. "I'm not in a position of influence with them. I'm just some intern from once upon a time. I doubt Graham even remembers me anymore."

Her voice tapers as she tucks a strand of blonde hair behind one ear. And then she takes a step closer, as if she actually wants to engage in a conversation with me for once.

"Daphne's really particular." Marnie speaks like she knows her personally, and my curiosity is surrendering, clinging to every word this woman speaks. "I never officially met her, but that's the vibe I always got. She was always telling him what to do and where to go. She can access his calendar from home. Needs to know where he is at all times. Total control freak."

"Daphne?" I lift a brow, my belief completely suspended. I *refuse* to believe this.

"I mean, all of this is stuff I heard secondhand, so who knows," she covers her tracks. "So you know her? You know Daphne then?"

Shit.

Shit. Shit. Shit.

I wave my hand. "Anyway, none of this matters because they didn't choose me, so . . ."

"Well, that sucks." Marnie folds her arms across her chest and stares out the sliding glass doors, toward the McMullen house. Has she known all along that they lived there?

Maybe had we not been so hellbent on hating each other, we might've become friends years ago, and maybe I'd have been able to siphon information from her or worked my way into that circle? Maybe things would've been different now?

God, there's way too much hate in this world.

And I'll admit, right here, right now, that at times, I can be my own worst enemy.

"Marn, you ready?" Ben asks, clearly bored with our conversation. He glances up from his phone. I'm not entirely sure he caught the gist of our exchange anyway, because he sure as hell hasn't offered his condolences on my not getting the job.

Marnie removes her gaze from the back door and saunters toward the kitchen island, rearranging the salt and pepper shakers.

"Salt on the right, Autumn," she says. "Pepper on the left. You should know that. It's common knowledge."

And just like that, nothing has changed.

CHAPTER TWENTY-SEVEN

Daphne

"Kindly ask your mistress if she could not drive past our house in broad daylight." I crawl beneath the covers tonight, keeping a careful distance between myself and my husband.

The air is thick with silence, and he doesn't move.

"What?" he asks a moment later.

"You heard me." I reach for my lamp and turn out the light, rolling to my side, my back toward him.

It's been a day.

Addison left early today because she had college cheer camp, which I didn't know was a thing in the summer, and I'm pretty sure she was lying about it just to get out of work early. The kids were hopped up on candy and junk food, and they didn't want to sit still for dinner, let alone eat dinner. By bedtime they were all whining that they were hungry, but I told them the kitchen was closed and sent them off to brush their teeth. Grace and Rose fought over who got to use the sparkly princess toothpaste first, and Sebastian jumped on his bed, kicking off the blankets and pillows and refusing to stop.

And Graham . . . Graham was "working late" once again.

"Can we just stop?" I spit my words, pressing my cheek hard against the pillow. The warmth of his hand on my shoulder makes me shudder.

"Daphne," he says. I brace myself for a torrential downpour of excuses, lies, and alibies, ones he's practiced for months, readying himself for this moment. "How long have you known?"

Flinging the covers off me, I scramble out of bed. I can't be next to him right now.

"A while," I answer once I'm standing before the window.

The soft pad of his bare feet on carpet follows, and though I don't see him, I feel him behind me, breathing, existing, wasting this beautiful space we've created.

He doesn't say anything, which tells me he's deep in contemplation, and it hits me that perhaps I'm going about this all wrong. Maybe he's been one step ahead of me this whole time, being careless with his activities because he wants to get caught. In his mind, maybe if he gets caught and I'm the one who ends things, he won't be the bad guy.

God damn it.

"Daphne-"

"Save it." I grab a silk robe from the back of an armchair in the corner and drape it over my shoulders. I'm going to go downstairs, pour myself a drink, and sit in the dark.

There's a thump behind me, and when I stop and turn, I find Graham on a heap on the floor, his elbows resting on his knees and his hands hiding his face.

I've known this man almost twenty years, and I've *never* seen him like this before. *Ever.*

"What are you doing?" I don't go to him. "Get off the floor."

"Daphne, I'm so sorry." He cries, like a man-child, into the palms of his hands. His shoulders rise and fall, quick jerks between near-silent sobs. "Forgive me."

"Seriously?"

He glances up at me, his blue eyes red-rimmed and bloodshot, and then he brings himself to my level, reaching for me. I take a step back.

"The damage is done," I say, arms folded. "I don't know how we'll ever be able to recover from this."

"We can fix this," he says, not bothering to dab the tear sliding down his left cheek. All these years together, and I never knew my husband had a penchant for theatrics.

I say nothing.

"I don't love her," he adds.

Still, I say nothing.

"She's a mistake. A . . . a fling. She means nothing," he says. "You . . . you're my world. You're my everything. You're the only woman I've ever loved. I need you."

His words are just that: words. They mean nothing.

"You were with her tonight," I say. It isn't a question, and he doesn't respond. "So you expect me to believe that you love me and you're so remorseful, when hours ago you were with her."

His face is red, and he brushes disheveled strands of dark hair from his brow. I feel like I'm seeing him for the first time all over again, only this time I'm not attracted to him. Looking at him doesn't make my heart press against the inside of my chest. Being next to him doesn't make me feel weightless and effervescent. It's as if his charm, his magic, his allure, has dissipated and all that's left is this tragically flawed human version of a man who sold the world.

"I was with her," he says, voice low, "because I was ending things tonight."

"Convenient."

"I don't expect you to believe me, but that's the truth." His hands clap against his sides. "I've been trying to end things for a while actually. And each time, she makes threats. She says she's going to harm herself. Or she's going to tell you."

I laugh. "So you're being manipulated by a twenty-two-year-old?"

I don't know how old she is. I can only assume.

"She isn't right," he says. "She has some issues. And I never should've gotten involved with her, Daphne. For as long as I live, it'll be my deepest regret. I hate myself for hurting you. You didn't deserve it. You've never been anything but perfect and wonderful."

I'm not sure when it happened, but Graham closed the gap between us. He's standing so close I can smell this morning's aftershave, and his hands are reaching for my hips.

"I love you," he says, "so much."

I don't return the sentiment.

"How can I fix this? I want to fix this. I *have* to fix this." Desperation is a terrible color on him. "We can't throw this away. Not because of a stupid mistake."

"I've been seeing another man," I blurt. I don't tell him it's a drug dealer, and I don't give him details or context. I want him to assume the worst. I want to shove the knife in and give it a good twist. It's only fair.

Graham's expression fades, and I'm quite certain I've given him the shock of a lifetime. He finally blinks. Then swallows. His entire aura is awash in deep pain, and I so badly want to ask him how he likes the taste of his own medicine.

He slips his hand into mine and leads me to the edge of the bed, where we both take a seat.

"So we're even then." He snorts through his nose, pulling on his lower lip and staring ahead at the carpet.

I jerk my hand from his. "No. No, we're not *even*. Not even close."

"Who was he?"

"You have a lot of nerve." I rise and make my way around to

my side of the bed, yanking my pillow. "I'm sleeping in the guest room. I'm exhausted, and I don't have the energy to listen to how sorry you are and how much you love me. If you actually loved me, Graham, you wouldn't have thrown me away in the first place."

"Are you going to tell the kids?" he asks.

My jaw hangs. Of course I wouldn't. I don't want to traumatize them for the sake of vindication. I'm not evil.

"We'll figure everything out another day," I say, yawning.

"What do you mean, figure everything out?"

"The separation, the divorce, the splitting of the assets," I say. "Everything."

"No, no, no." He strides across the room, his hand splayed. "We're staying together."

"Oh, so you're just going to go ahead and make that decision for the both of us?"

"Of course not," he says. "But can't we try? Can't we do counseling and work on our marriage before we throw it all away? Think about the kids, Daphne."

I close my eyes and pull in a long breath. Such a manipulator.

"I think about the kids," I say. "I think about the kids every second of every damn day unlike someone else I know, so don't you dare try and exploit them to get what you want, you pathetic son of a bitch."

Graham's jaw drops. I've never called him a name in my life, at least not to his face, and never with clenched fists and gritted teeth.

"Okay." He breathes in. Breathes out. "You need some time to cool down. I get that. I'm going to give you some space, and then tomorrow, we'll start fresh, and things will be better. I'll make this up to you. I'll spend the rest of my life making it up to you. And I'll prove to you that I meant every word I said tonight."

CHAPTER TWENTY-EIGHT

AUTUMN

HE NEEDS TO KNOW.

I mean, *I* would want to know . . . if they were *my* kids.

My vision blurs. I squeeze my eyes, and he comes into focus again, his hand resting on his jaw as he scans the flower cooler and eventually settles on a bouquet of daffodils. It's as if the last two hours didn't happen. I have no memory of parking my car outside McMullen and Henry Corporation. I have no memory of watching employees file out the front door, shuffling to their cars until the last remaining vehicle in the parking lot was a familiar black sedan with University of Pennsylvania plates. I have no memory of watching Graham McMullen climb into the driver's seat of his car, and I certainly have no memory of following him here, to Hiland Grocery and Deli on Pepper street.

I feel like those things happened . . .

But I have no memory of them.

And now here I am.

Standing back as Graham selects a bouquet of flowers for his wife after a long day's work. Maybe it's a special occasion? Maybe they have a date tonight? It is a Friday, and that would make sense.

"Excuse me, miss." There's a tap on my left shoulder that startles the bejeesus out of me. "Are you in line for the flowers?"

Before I get a chance to respond, Graham McMullen spins on the heels of his polished dress shoes and spots me immediately.

I stand, frozen, searching his eyes for a sign that he recognizes me from our interview a couple weeks ago.

"Hi," I say, my hand gripping my plastic grocery basket. It's a prop, really. I even went so far as to throw a few items in there: tangerines, a pack of bubble gum, and a rum raisin pie.

Looks legit enough.

"Autumn? Autumn, is it?" His face lights, and my world tilts on its axis. I forget, for a moment, how hurt I was that he didn't choose me. I forget about how botched my interview was. How my time was unfairly cut short by the arrival of the next person on his list.

"Yes!" I smile and laugh, lightly smacking my leg like I'm suddenly remembering who he is. We step aside and let the others have at the floral arrangements. "How's it going, neighbor?"

He chuckles, his gaze captured on mine, and I wonder if he looks at everyone this way . . . like they're the only person in the world.

How lucky is Daphne that she gets to wear his ring and his name. How lucky is she to raise his children and sleep in his arms each night.

I imagine the sweeping, romantic gestures a man like Graham might make for his true love. Flowers when she's least expecting them. Last minute tickets to her favorite sold-out musical. Surprise getaways to wine country.

"How's everything going with the nanny?" I cut to the chase.

"Good," he says, nodding. And staring, still. "Everything's going really well. Her name is Addison. She's the daughter of one of my wife's friends. Kids seem to like her."

Nepotism.

Nice.

Did I even stand a chance, Graham?

I watched this girl, this "Addison," the other day from across the fence. The children were in the backyard swimming, and she, while dressed for the water, sat in a lounge chair, slathering her taut body with suntan oil and texting on her phone.

The words are right there, on the tip of my tongue.

He needs to know.

My jaw hangs, and my heart pounds in my ears. This can either go really well for me. Or he'll see right through it.

"This nanny of yours," I lean in, lowering my voice, and he meets me halfway. "Is she blonde? Rather petite?"

He studies my face.

Oh, god, he's onto me.

Maybe?

"It's just that, I saw her the other day. I was outside with Ginger, and she was outside with the kids." I glance around, buying time. The longer I wait to reveal my information, the more he might take me seriously. And he should. His children are in danger if she's running the show this summer.

"What is it?" His shoulders square, and his jaw flexes. When his brows meet in the middle, I know he's officially concerned. "Did you see something?"

I lift my thumbnail to my lip, pretending to hem and haw, and then I say, "Yes. I . . . I don't want to get anyone in trouble."

"What did you see, Autumn?" He's impatient with me, and fatherly impatience looks beautiful on Graham McMullen.

I fight a pleased smile in favor of a worried frown. "The kids were swimming, and I guess I was surprised to see your nanny sunbathing."

He smirks.

And everything changes.

"I'm sure it wasn't what it looked like. She was probably taking a break. Those kids are enough to wear anyone out." He grips the flowers and eyes the checkout lanes.

"She was on her phone," I blurt.

He stops, returning his attention to me.

"It looked like she was texting, and I saw her make some phone calls," I say. "The kids were swimming and doing their own thing. Even your boy – your youngest. And she was sitting in a lounge chair rubbing oil all over and paying more attention to her screen than your children."

He's silent.

"Anyway," I say. "I wasn't going to say anything . . ."

Liar, liar, pants on fire.

"I guess, if they were *my* kids, *I'd* want to know," I add. "And since I ran into you, I . . . I'm sorry. I felt I had to take the opportunity to say something."

I turn to leave, offering an apologetic smile.

"No, no." He captures my wrist gently in his hand and prevents me from moving. "I'm glad you told me. I wouldn't have known otherwise, so thank you."

"Okay, well." I smile, pulling in a deep breath and exhaling as I switch my plastic basket to my opposite arm. "It was good seeing you. If you ever need a cup of sugar, you know where I live."

He smiles, and I feel him watching as I walk away. If I had to guess, I'd say he's thinking about what I shared, wondering how he's going to break it to his wife. They'll probably discuss it after dinner tonight, once the kids are in bed.

The McMullen children are everything to their parents, that much I know.

They're going to ditch Addison, I can feel it. I see it written all over Graham's face, chiseled in the worry lines that spread across his forehead when I broke it to him.

And then they'll replace her with me.

CHAPTER TWENTY-NINE

DAPHNE

"WHAT'S THIS WOMAN'S NAME AGAIN? THE ONE WHO SUPPOSEDLY saw these things?" I'm rinsing a head of broccoli under the faucet as Graham leans against the island behind me, arms folded, a proud look on his face.

"Autumn," he said.

"And where did you find her?" I transfer the broccoli to a wooden cutting board and retrieve a knife from a tall cupboard where I keep all sharp things out of Grace's reach.

"She was an applicant," he says. "Former medical assistant at a children's clinic. Basically like a nurse."

"Not the same thing, but continue." Each spear of broccoli is met with a satisfying chop.

"Believe it or not, she lives one street over, did I tell you that? Anyway, I ran into her when I was picking out your flowers today," he says, handing me a bouquet of lilies wrapped in brown paper, "and we got to talking and that came up."

I knew Addison was less than ideal for this position, but the fact that neighbors are watching and seeing things and saying things, it tells me it's time to cut her loose. The nanny a family chooses is a reflection of them, and I can't have my reputation tarnished by some nineteen-year-old who can't put her phone away for a few hours.

"She's still looking for a job, and she could start tomorrow," he says. "She interviewed well, and she was one of my top candidates. If you want her, I'll give her a call. She knows it's a short-term position, and she's fine with that. Loves kids. CPR certified. More than qualified."

"How old is she?"

His brows meet. "Not sure? Mid-twenties? Very mature and professional for her age, I'll give her that."

Sighing because I don't have a choice but to trust his judgement, I place a lid on the steaming broccoli and return to the sink to rinse the carving board.

"I'm trying here." His voice is low and he's right up on me, speaking softly so the children can't hear. "Seems everything I do lately isn't good enough for you. You're walking around lately like you hate life, and I'm trying to make things better. I'm trying to fix things. At least meet me halfway?"

"Can we not have this conversation right now?"

Rose skips into the kitchen, her timing impeccable. "When's dinner, Mommy?"

"Soon, sweetheart." I run my fingers through her glossy hair before bending to kiss the top of her head. "Go play. I'll call you when it's ready."

Rose returns to the family room, and I begin pulling dishes and silverware.

"Graham, be a dear and set the table, will you?" I've never asked him to set the table until now, and the look he gives me makes me question whether or not he comprehends my request. "I could really use a hand."

The man walks the dog every night and acts like he should get a gold star on his sticker chart for it. He loaded the dishwasher once, and it was all I heard about for almost an entire week.

"You know, I decided to reactivate my Instaface account," I say.

"I never knew you deactivated it," he says, breathing loudly as he hoists a stack of plates off the counter and doles them out around the table. He doesn't care about my social media platform. He never has.

"Really? It must have slipped my mind," I say. "Didn't you notice? I've been on my phone less? You were always saying my nose is buried in my screen."

He says nothing.

"Anyway, I'm hoping to pick up some sponsorships again," I say, though I may as well be talking to myself.

When he's finished setting the table, he struts to the next room without saying a word, hiding out in the den with a finger of Scotch until I call out that dinner's ready.

We eat mostly in silence, the five of us. I made sure the children swam for hours today in the backyard with Addison. They're hungry and tired, and that equals an early bedtime sans medication so I won't be inflicted with mommy-guilt the rest of the evening.

When dinner's finished, I ask Graham to bathe the kids, and he responds with the same stupefied look he gave me earlier.

"It's either baths or dishes," I say, a dish rag bunched in my hand, ready to toss his way. "Your choice."

If he wants to earn brownie points, he can start by lending a hand.

His jaw sets, and he rises from the table and moves toward me. When our hands touch, he yanks the towel from me and proceeds to the sink.

"What's wrong with Daddy?" Grace asks from the table.

"Nothing, sweetie," I call back, eyes on Graham. "He's just doing what good daddies do."

"But why is he mad?" Grace asks, yawning. It's a good sign

when she's tired, and it's usually a good indication that she won't be fighting bedtime. "He was stomping. You said we're not allowed to stomp in the house."

"He wasn't stomping," I lie. He was definitely stomping. "Run upstairs and strip down. I'll be up in a minute to run your bath."

I clean the younger children up, then stop myself before I begin to clear the table. Graham can do it. His arms aren't broken.

"All right, run upstairs," I say, and then I turn to my husband. "You got this?"

"Of course," he says, voice muffled and back toward me. His displeasure is suddenly my pleasure. If he could turn around now, he'd see the ridiculously oversized grin covering my face for the first time in years.

The kids are going to bed without a fight tonight.

My husband is doing dishes, and tomorrow, I'll let him be the one to break it to Addison that her services are no longer needed.

I grab my phone and snap a picture of Graham, posting it on Instaface with the hashtags *#BestHusbandEver, #DontBeJealous, and #LuckiestWifeAlive.*

They're sarcastic little hashtags, of course, but no one needs to know.

Within seconds, I'm up to eighty-seven "likes." My photos of Graham have always gotten the most attention out of everything I post. It's almost as if these bitches follow me just so they can ogle my husband.

My fingers hover over the keyboard, and I'm half-tempted to write, "Ladies, if you want him, you can have him. #AllYours."

CHAPTER THIRTY

AUTUMN

I KEEP MY PHONE BY MY SIDE ALL DAY.

Waiting.

Watching.

And when the phone rings at twenty-five past two in the afternoon, I nearly knock Ginger over in the process of answering it.

"Hello?" My voice is sweet, innocent, and unsuspecting.

"Autumn?" It's a man's voice. But not just any man.

My soon-to-be-boss.

I bite my lip.

I know what's coming.

"Yes?" I answer.

"It's Graham McMullen," he says. "How are you doing?"

"I'm well, thank you," I say. I sound like Donna flipping Reed. If my phone had a cord, I'd be twirling it around my fingers and twirling in my knee-length skirt. "Everything all right?"

"I just wanted to thank you," he says, "for yesterday. For telling me what you saw."

"Of course," I say, breathless and concerned, my voice low.

"Daphne and I spoke last night," he says, "and we've decided to let Addison go."

My heart trots, and I can't feel my face.

There may as well be confetti flying through the air. I need a glass of champagne and a handsome gentleman to kiss whom does not taste like beer and chicken wings and smell like Dylan Abernathy's mossy cologne.

"If you're still available," he says, "and if you're still interested, we'd love to have you work for us for the summer."

I hold my silent applause. And I hold back my response.

I don't want to seem too eager.

That would be suspicious.

And I don't want him to think I've been sitting around all day, waiting for this moment.

That would be pathetic, and I need my credibility to be perfectly polished.

"Oh, Graham," I act shocked at the prospect.

"You were my first choice, actually," he says.

How could I possibly say no, now?

I'm grinning so wide my face hurts.

"I'm sure it would be fine," I say. "Let me just talk it over tonight with Ben when he comes home. Can I get back to you first thing in the morning?"

"Of course." Graham clears his throat. "We were actually hoping you could start Monday."

"Of course. It shouldn't be a problem, but I'll let you know as soon as possible."

"Thanks, Autumn."

"No, thank *you*. Talk soon." I end the call on a sweet note and toss my phone aside. It bounces on the couch cushions and wakes Ginger from her half-asleep haze.

My body is ringing, practically vibrating. It's on a whole other frequency. I've tuned into something miraculous. I can't recall the last time everything felt so right in my life. Things don't always work out for people like me . . . the underprivileged. The less fortunate. The ones society forgot. The ones who blend into the background.

The ones who matter to no one.

Before I realize what I'm doing, I find myself at the top of the stairs and then the end of the hall. Bursting into the guest room, I belly flop on the bed and reach beneath to grab my secret stash of McMullen mementos.

Only I don't go for the small box.

It takes two hands to drag the big one across the carpet, and I retrieve the box cutter from the nightstand to slice through the tape. Each time I peek into this box, I tape it up to prevent easy access on the off chance Ben would go snooping.

Plopping on the floor and sitting cross legged, I fish a few things from the bottom of my collection.

A pair of J Brand jeans, exactly like the ones Daphne wore in an Instaface photo last year, a pair of Swarovski crystal encrusted Louboutins complete with unscuffed red bottoms, a black silk blouse that serves as a near replica of a vintage Chanel piece Daphne found at a thrift shop. I couldn't find the exact one, given that the original was born in the 70s, but I found the next best thing via some Etsy shop out of Canton, Ohio that specializes in reproducing old clothing designs based on photos.

Within seconds, I've peeled out of today's clothes and stepped into Daphne's.

My old dresser rests against the north wall, and I step over my box, making my way to the unfamiliar reflection in the distance.

From here, minus my sandy blonde mane, I look like her.

I complete the look with a set of pearl earrings and a matching necklace, and I tie my hair back, twisting it into a low chignon. A slick of pink across my lips finishes my look, and in the blink of an eye, I'm officially transported.

In the coming days, I'll get to set foot inside their world.

I'll get to see what they see, smell what they smell, touch what they touch, and hear what they hear.

And my daughter . . .

My Grace . . .

I'll get to meet her all over again.

Maybe we'll bond over our love of mint chocolate chip ice cream and brown-haired Barbies, and maybe when she's not looking, I'll count the freckles on her arms – just because I can. I'll get to breathe in the sweet scent of her soft skin, and I'll get to hear her giggle in person, which will be a million times better than some thirty-second Instaface video, and she'll get to know me – even if she won't actually *know* who I am.

I abandon my moment the second I hear Ginger carrying on downstairs. It's too late for her to be freaking out over the mailman, and it's too early for Ben to be home – unless of course he's "surprising" me again.

Creeping down the hall, I take the steps with caution, dipping down and peeking over the banister toward the living room where Ginger is yipping from the back of Ben's armchair. She's facing the front door, and the sound of a car door slamming makes my heart stop cold.

I run back upstairs, to the room I share with Ben, and peek outside only to see Marnie's black coupe in the driveway.

Lovely.

If I don't answer, if I pretend to be gone, there's nothing she can do. She'll leave soon enough. Taking a seat in the middle of our queen bed, I bide my time by making faces in the dresser mirror, manipulating my brows a little bit higher and pinching my cheeks until they're a little bit rosier, imagining if it's possible to shape and mold my face into a Daphne McMullen replica.

For a split second, I stare and my reflection and see her.

But I blink.

And she's gone.

And it's just me.

I must be incredibly exhausted because I find this entirely too amusing, and before I know it, I'm laughing out loud.

The tinker of Ginger's collar in the hallway brings a stop to my shenanigans, and a second later, she's pouncing on the bed, licking my face.

"Why didn't you answer the door? I rang the bell, like, ten times." The "angelic" voice of Marnie Gotlieb nearly scares the shit out of me.

My hand flies to my chest as I twist in her direction. Ginger wriggles free from my arm, and I regret that I must have been holding her too tightly.

"What the hell are you doing?" My voice is shrill, uncool. "How did you get in here?"

"You didn't answer. I called Ben, and he told me where the hidden key was," she says, hand on her hip. "I came to get my birthday gift. Ben said you were going to drop it off weeks ago, but surprise, surprise, you never did. I was in the area, so I figured I'd stop by and take it off your hands. I know you're super busy doing . . . what do you do again these days? Sit around and play house on my brother's dime?"

It takes everything I have not to roll my eyes or spit in her smug little face or yank those platinum extensions clean out of her hair.

"You can't just show yourself in like that," I say. "This isn't just your brother's place. I live here too."

Marnie, for some ungodly reason, flips on the light, and illuminates my . . . *get-up.*

I really, *really* hate this bitch.

"What the hell is that?" She has the audacity to point at me and wrinkle her nose. "What are you wearing? Are those . . . are those *Louboutins?* Does Ben know you have those? Did you buy those with his credit card?!"

"Get out!" I charge at her, wiping that smart little smirk off her snotty little face and sending her stumbling backward. She nearly loses her balance until her back smacks against the wall in the hallway. She says nothing, her eyes squinted, glaring.

"I'm onto you," she says through gritted teeth.

"Onto me?" I mock her, adding a haughty laugh at the end.

"There's something not right about you." Her finger is pointed in my direction, trembling slightly as her chest rises and falls. She scans my outfit one last time, and we're both suddenly breathless and adrenaline-fueled, two alley cats preparing for a territory showdown.

"Why? Because I dress up once in a while? *Puh*-lease, Marnie, get a life." I cross my arms. "I think there's something off about *you*. You have some sick obsession with me, and clearly you need to find better things to do with that busy little brain of yours."

"I've been asking around about you." Her voice is low, frightened almost. "Nobody has ever heard of you before. Not in this area. Where did you say you went to high school again?"

My jaw tightens.

"You're lying about … something," she says, straightening her posture. "And the second I figure it out, I'm going to tell Ben. I'm going to tell him *everything*."

"Good luck." I hook my hand into her elbow, and I realize this is the first time she and I have ever actually touched. She's bonier than I expected. And as much as I hate to admit this, she smells good. Like expensive flowers. And vitamin E lotion from The Body Shop.

It makes me loathe her even more.

"You don't deserve my brother, and you know it," she spits her words at me as we near the front door.

"That's where you're wrong. I deserve him because I make him happy. I'm everything he could ever want," I remind her. "We're in love, Marnie. And I know that bothers you because you have this disturbing little crush on your big brother that I've yet to fully comprehend or figure out, but he's mine. And there's nothing you can say or do to change that. So stop. Fucking. Meddling."

Her jaw hangs, and I grab the door, swinging it open so hard the knob hits the wall behind it.

"Next time, I'd appreciate a phone call before you come barging in. A nice, proper girl like you should know it's common courtesy," I mock her infamously condescending tone.

"What about my birthday gift?" She hooks a bony hand on her skinny hip and cocks her pencil thin brows.

Groaning, I stomp to the kitchen and swipe her stained card and wrinkled gift bag from the counter before returning and handing it over.

"*Happy birthday, Marnie.*" My lips smile, but my eyes glare.

I'm so bored with . . . *this*, and I'm in too good a mood to let Marnie "Basic Bitch" Gotlieb ruin my high.

Besides, she couldn't begin to dig up my past if she tried.

It's dead and gone, just like the girl I used to be.

CHAPTER THIRTY-ONE

Daphne

Flowers again? I don't mean to seem disappointed, but this flowers after work every other day thing is getting old. Can't he think of something else to do? Jewelry? Chocolate? If he's going the full cliché route, the least he can do is mix it up a little.

I will say, though, he's been pulling his own weight. The first couple days were challenging, but he's been helping out more and grunting and groaning less, and a girl could definitely get used to this.

Today he brings me blue hydrangeas, wrapped in paper and tied with a bow. They're beautiful, and they smell like a million dollars.

"Thank you," I tell him, letting him kiss my cheek.

He's trying. I'll give him that. He's trying harder than he's ever tried before, which isn't saying much because he's never really had to try, but still. The effort hasn't gone unnoticed.

"Why don't you go upstairs and get changed," he says, leaving his hand on the small of my back.

I glance down at my yoga pants and t-shirt, readying myself to bite his head off for criticizing my outfit.

"I have a surprise for you," he says. "Sitter's going to be here in an hour. I'm taking you out tonight."

I swallow my words before they have a chance to come out, and I turn to face him.

"Out where?" I fight a smile. I don't know why I'm smiling. Wait. No. I'm an idiot. *That's* why I'm smiling.

"Wear that little black dress, the one you wore last year on our anniversary," he orders, leaning in and brushing his five o'clock shadow against the side of my neck. He deposits a biting kiss and then gives me a look, that look he always used to give me, and then heads to the family room to sit with the kids.

I climb the stairs still wearing that dumb smile, and there's a hint of butterflies in my belly. Hope, perhaps. And as messed up as it may be, there's a rather large part of me that still loves that moron of a man, who still wants to grow old with him. There's a rather large part of me that's still longing to capture everything we've lost before it's gone forever.

And I can't raise these kids alone.

I can't do this without him.

I round the corner at the top of the stairs and shuffle into our bedroom, closing the double doors and heading straight for the closet to pluck his favorite dress of mine from the far back.

He gets one more chance.

One.

CHAPTER THIRTY-TWO

Autumn

TODAY IS, QUITE POSSIBLY, THE BEST DAY OF MY LIFE.

And I'm not being facetious.

I mean it with every ounce of my heart and soul.

My ears ring and my fingertips vibrate as I tap the knocker against the McMullen's wooden front door for the first time in my life. I've never stood at this door before, under this awning, but in many ways, it feels like coming home.

A canopy of trees lines their lot, and this time of morning, everything is dappled in soft sunlight that trickles through swaying, leafed tree branches.

There's a warm fullness in my chest, and it feels so full it could burst.

Daphne answers the door dressed in skintight jeans and a sheer white blouse. Her long, buttery blonde hair shines in the late-morning sun and her face lights when she sees me.

"Come on in! You must be Autumn." She pulls the front door wide, and I step inside the McMullen home with wobbly legs.

If this is a dream, I never want to wake up.

My gaze catches on the marble console table in the foyer, instantly recognizing it from Instaface photos, and then I glance at the sisal rug beneath my feet. The one she ordered last spring from some fancy catalog and they sent her the wrong size, so she got to keep it for free. Resting in a milky white vase on the console is a small bouquet of pale pink roses. They're not her favorite, but they look exquisite in this natural light, and the vase is an antique Baccarat she purchased at a Manhattan boutique two years back.

I know every square inch of this house.

I don't even need a tour.

"Nice to meet you." I extend my hand, searching her eyes for any hint of recognition on her part. It's been several weeks since I saw her at the grocery store, but I'm the spitting image of Grace. Just being here is risky, but it's a risk I'm willing to take because I'm a woman who has run out of options, and I cannot be without this family. They've become a part of my daily routine. A part of my existence. A part of me.

And I can't live with the idea of missing another cherished moment of my beautiful Grace's sweet little life.

Daphne meets my hand with a firm shake before calling the children's names. They thunder down the stairs, all dressed and ready for the day, all of them staring at me with wide, curious eyes.

A giant, curly-haired dog steps across the foyer, her nails clicking as she comes to my side. I let her sniff my hand, and then she sniffs my shoes.

"She must smell my dog," I say.

"Cocoa, go lie down." Daphne claps her hands and Cocoa retreats into the next room. "Kids, this is your new nanny, and her name is Autumn. She's going to be watching you during the day for the rest of the summer. Now, Autumn is in charge. I want you to listen to her and respect her, and if I hear that any of you have disobeyed, there will be consequences. Do you understand?"

The children nod, though their little gazes are still fixed on me.

Daphne spins on her heel, pulling the coat closet door open and retrieving a pair of beige Chanel ballet flats. She steps into them, brushing her glossy hair from her face.

"I'm going to give you a quick tour, and then I've got to head out." She takes confident, runway-model strides with her impossibly long legs, and then she motions for me to follow her into the next room. She smiles, glad to give me a tour, and her tone is warm and welcoming.

I truly feel as if I belong, as if this was all meant to be; some kind of divine intervention.

An arched doorway leads from the two-story foyer into a vaulted family room. Windows galore provide a view to the backyard pool. To my home, too. To the left of the family room is an eat-in kitchen area complete with booster seats for the smaller children and an over-the-top floral arrangement centering the table.

She doesn't show me the formal living room, Graham's den, or the dining room, though I could easily find them on my own.

I follow her blindly around her gourmet kitchen, and she spouts off something about organic macaroni and cheese. She laughs, but I missed the joke because I was too busy becoming completely immersed in this home.

Seeing something in a photo, and then visiting it in person, are two completely different experiences. I'm still reeling, absorbing everything all at once. Sensory overload.

The scent of freshly baked bread fills my lungs, and I imagine Daphne waking before the sun rose this morning and tiptoeing downstairs to make a fresh loaf of whole grain artisan bread for the children's breakfast.

They are *so* loved, and I hope they'll always know that. They're the luckiest.

Nodding and trying hard to pay attention to everything she's saying, I continue following her as she leads us to the stairs. I get a tour of each of the children's rooms. Sebastian has some sort of nautical theme happening with shiplap walls and anchors and whales. Rose's room is pale pink with stuffed ballerina dolls on her bed and a dollhouse in the corner. Grace's room is blue and dark and not at all what I expected. And it's the only room in the house that isn't picked up and neatly organized.

No wonder Daphne hasn't shared this room in her newsfeed before.

I try not to linger too long, and I tell myself I'll be spending plenty of time in this house over the coming months. I can gawk later. I follow Daphne back toward the hallway. She's still rambling on, telling me about the children's schedule and how there's a manual on the table in the foyer for me. It contains the children's daily routines as well as their likes and dislikes, and a discipline guide expertly catered to each child.

The double doors leading to the master are closed tight. She doesn't take me in there, and while I completely understand, I let myself wallow in disappointment for a few moments.

"I think that's everything," she says when we're standing at the top of the stairs. The kids keep a careful distance behind Daphne, eyes still glued on me. "Oh, do you have a swimsuit? You'll want to bring one. These three love to swim just about every day, weather permitting of course."

"Of course." My mouth is dry, and I'm speechless. So much is happening all at once.

I wish I could blend in with the wallpaper for a bit. Absorb everything I've just seen. Get my bearings. Put my head on straight.

Everything about the McMullen home is impeccable. The hardwood floors show hardly a speck of dust, and the carpet is plush and cloud-like beneath my toes. Every picture hanging from the wall is perfectly straight, and although the house is several decades old and recently remodeled, it still holds that 'new house smell.'

"My number's on the side of the fridge," she says. "Call or text if you need anything. Graham's number is written there as well, but please only bother him if you're unable to get through to me and it's an emergency."

"When are you coming back, Mommy?" Rose pipes up, her voice angelic and shy.

Daphne hesitates, her eyes flicking from me to her kids and back. "I'm not sure. I'll be running all over town today. Might not be back until dinnertime."

"So you're leaving us again?" Grace asks. "Like you did with Addison?"

Daphne chuckles. "Of course not. Autumn is here. Grace, I explained all of this."

Her patience with Grace seems to be somewhat worn, though she smiles through it.

"This is their first summer with a nanny," Daphne says to me, her tone apologetic. "They're not used to not having me at their beck and call twenty-four seven. It's an adjustment for all of us."

She exhales, and I detect a hint of freedom in her eyes, though I can't, for the life of me, understand why she wouldn't want to spend these precious days with her babies. If they were mine, I'd never leave them with anyone. Ever.

"Anyway. Like I said," Daphne descends the switchback staircase, smiling with her eyes, and I decide she's a million times more amazing in person than I ever thought. "Call if you need anything."

Within seconds, the back door clicks and a hum comes from the garage. Nothing about her screams "control-freak" like Marnie said. I don't get that from her at all. She's in control, but she isn't a freak about it.

Then again, Marnie lies. She lies about me all the time.

"So." I rest my hands on my hips and turn to the kids. "What do you guys like to do around here?"

Rose and Grace chatter over one another and Sebastian stands back, hiding behind his biggest sister. He has a finger in his mouth and his chin tucked against his chest. Crouching to his level, I reach for him and pull him close.

"Hi, buddy," I say.

He doesn't answer, only stares back at me with those clear blue eyes of his that match Graham's fleck-for-fleck.

"He's shy," Grace says. "But I'm not."

I laugh. "I see that."

"I like your hair," Grace adds, wrapping her own around her fingers. "It's kind of like mine."

"It is. You're very observant."

"I want to be a hairstylist when I grow up," she says. "I gave Rose a haircut last week, but Mommy didn't like it."

My gaze switches to Rose, her hair cut into a short bob. In the last photo I was able to see of the kids, her hair was down to the middle of her back. Shiny. White blonde. Downy soft.

"We should always leave haircuts to grown ups," I say gently. "Kids shouldn't give other kids haircuts."

"Can I show you my dollhouse?" Rose asks.

"Of course you can, Rose," I say.

She takes my hand, sliding hers between my fingers, and pulls me to the big room at the left of the stairs. Her room is yards nicer than Grace's, with a window seat and a crystal chandelier.

Rose takes a seat on the floor in front of her pink dollhouse and begins retrieving various dolls, showing them to me with an ear-to-ear grin and zero commentary. I tell her what I like about each one, and that seems to please her.

"Can I show you my room, Autumn?" Grace asks.

I turn to my daughter, my sweet Grace, and rise. "Absolutely, sweetheart."

Grace clips her chubby fingers around the crook of my arm

and pulls me through a door that leads to a Jack-and-Jill bathroom. On the opposite side of the bathroom is the entrance to her room. It immediately feels darker in here. The walls are almost a grayish blue now that I study them more closely, and the furniture is some kind of dark-stained wood. Espresso maybe. It feels more like a little boy's room.

Or a dungeon.

With as much sharing as Daphne's done over the years, she never once shared Grace's room, and now I can see why. It doesn't mesh with the rest of her open, airy house. It's dark, while the other rooms are light. This room is almost tacky in comparison.

Grace's bedroom sticks out like a sore thumb in the McMullen house, therefore Daphne treats it like it doesn't exist.

"Did you decorate your room, Grace?" I ask.

She nods, wearing a proud beam and upright shoulders. "Mommy let me pick out the colors. She wanted pink, but I hate pink. Pink is gross. I wanted blue."

My jaw is tight, and I'm not sure what to say. The color is ugly, that's for sure. But for Daphne to hide it? As if it's some kind of shameful secret? While she clearly has no problem sharing the rest of her house?

"Daddy made Mommy paint my room blue," she declares. I detect a bit of smug victory in her tone, and I wonder if she ever pits those two against one another. "Blue is my favorite color. It makes me so happy!"

"Then that's all that matters, baby girl." I ruffle her hair, and she jerks away, giving me a scowl. "Sorry."

"You can't touch my hair," she snips. Her expression softens. "But it's okay if you call me baby girl." Grace flops onto her bed, belly first, and rests her chin in her hands. "I miss being a baby."

Chuckling, I ask, "Do you even remember what it was like? That was a very long time ago."

"Kind of." She stares ahead, frowning. "I just remember my mommy used to love me more when I was her baby."

Grace's big brown eyes water, and my heart rips in two. I want to hold her, comfort her, but then I hear a crash coming from down the hall, and I remember Sebastian, and I have no idea how long he's been unattended in the next room.

Shit, shit, shit.

Speeding down the hallway and careening into his room, I find him sitting amongst a pile of giant plastic blocks. There must be a thousand pieces scattered all over his otherwise picture-perfect and overly-organized room.

"Hey, buddy, I don't think we're going to play with these right now," I say. "Let's pick them up and head downstairs."

His arms cross over his chest. "But I want to play blocks."

"I was thinking the four of us could go downstairs and do some arts and crafts. I'll even draw you a monster. Would you like that, Sebastian?" I ask. I need to learn his language, and I will. I just need more time. In the meantime, I recall from my days at Children's Medical Group that little boys love silly monsters something fierce.

He gives me a single head bob and crawls on his hands and knees, shoving large plastic blocks in his clumsy little hands and tossing them in a large, nautical-striped storage bin. Rose lingers in the doorway behind me, watching in hesitation before stepping in. Without saying a word, she begins to help with clean up.

"Thank you, Rose," I say. "It's very sweet of you to help. Where's Grace?"

Rose peers up at me with her pretty blue stare and points down the hall. "She's in Mommy and Daddy's room. And she's not supposed to be in there."

Shit.

Squeezing past Rose and through Sebastian's door, I spot the double doors of the master suite at the opposite end of the hall. And they're wide open.

"Grace?" I call from the doorway.

Looking around, nothing seems to have been touched. The

193

bed is made with perfect precision; fluffed euro pillows, creamy duvet, and all. The top of the dresser is neatly arranged with stacked decorator books, assorted perfumes, and silver picture frames of smiling children. The lamps on the nightstands are centered, silver mercury with creamy linen shades, and the drapes on the windows are pulled open, letting in a fair amount of natural light.

Beyond that, two doors are open: one leading to a bathroom and one leading to a closet.

"Grace, are you in here?" I call again.

Walking carefully like some kind of trespasser, I move toward the closet first, peeking my head in. It's pitch black inside, so I move to the bathroom.

At first glance, I see nothing. Then I spot the top of her brown head peeking up from inside a freestanding tub.

"Hey, sweet girl, your sister said you're not allowed to be in here," I crouch down beside her. "How 'bout we head downstairs and – oh, god."

She's covered in makeup.

Red lipstick. Black mascara. Huge pink circles of blush on the round apples of her cheeks. Pulling in a calm breath, I react with laughter instead of anger, and her expression lights.

"You look so pretty, Grace," I say. "But let's get that off your face, okay? I don't think your Daddy wants to be chasing off boys just yet. You're still a little young for that stuff."

"Do I look as pretty as my mommy?" She bats her lashes, which are unfortunately sparse and stumpy. It's those Carpenter genes that will forever plague us both.

"You look even prettier. You're the prettiest thing I've ever seen." I reach for her hand and help her out. "Do you know where your Mommy keeps her makeup wipes?"

Grace shrugs, and we both scan a marble vanity covered in various products: expensive creams, fancy-looking makeup brushes, organic hair products, and a spread of department store cosmetics.

"Probably somewhere over there," Grace points to the elaborate display.

"Um, okay." I pull in a hard breath and do some light snooping. Taking a seat at the vanity, I scan the endless arrangement of bottles for some kind of makeup remover product. A cleanser. Micellar water. Anything. The kind of makeup Daphne McMullen wears isn't the kind that washes off with basic soap and water. It's better quality. Higher pigmented. We need real-deal cleansing agents.

I lift a small Lucite tray, sitting it aside and lifting another, hoping to God I remember to put these things back exactly the way I found them.

"Hang on, Grace," I say, unzipping a small, monogrammed makeup pouch. There's a beautiful diamond lotus necklace sitting on top, and I pull it out to examine it before gently searching through the rest of the contents: nail clippers, tweezers, a highlighting pen, mascara . . .

. . . a joint.

Blinking hard, I refuse to believe this is what it looks like.

But what else would it be?

Skinny, rolled, and tapered at the ends, there's no denying that Daphne is hiding a marijuana cigarette amongst her pricey cosmetics collection.

"Did you find it yet?" Grace hooks her hand on her hip, her head tilting impatiently. Rose and Sebastian are probably done cleaning up now, and I need to get us all downstairs. I promptly end my search for makeup remover and carefully put everything back where it was. Except the lotus necklace, which is tangled around my fingertips. "Where are we going?"

"We'll just wash you up downstairs," I say, and without thinking, I shove the necklace in my jeans pocket when she turns around. I'll use dish soap if I have to. That stuff cuts through grease; it can cut through Chanel makeup.

———

THE KIDS AND I ARE QUIETLY COLORING AT THE KITCHEN TABLE when Daphne returns. It's a quarter 'til four, and she's been gone almost seven full hours without so much as a check-in.

"Hello, hello." She waltzes in, shopping bags in hand and red hair curled into giant waves that bounce off her shoulders when she walks. Her nails are slicked in a fresh coat of mauve that wasn't there this morning, and I can't help but picture a lit joint pinched delicately between them.

It's a jarring image, and it doesn't suit her at all. It's tacky. Classless really. The epitome of everything Daphne McMullen does *not* represent.

It reminds me of my mother, of her dirty fingernails and the stench of stale pot smoke wafting from her and clinging to me. I never could quite wash it off completely.

Depositing the bags at her feet, she pulls off her oversized sunglasses and strides to the kitchen table.

"What are we up to?" she asks, resting a hand on Rose's shoulder.

"I colored you a picture, Mommy." Rose hands her a page ripped from a princess coloring book. Each of the sections are colored neatly, as she was determined to stay inside the lines.

"Me too, me too." Grace lifts her paper so quickly it whacks Rose in the face.

"Careful, Grace." Daphne scolds her, walking away before she can acknowledge Grace's picture. She moves to her son, ruffling his dark hair and squeezing his cheeks. He smiles, and I'm pretty sure he has yet to say more than twenty words to me today, but he did seem to be warming up to me this past hour or so. "Autumn, would you mind hanging around another fifteen minutes with the kids while I get dinner started?"

"Not at all," I say.

"You're the best." Daphne pulls a brown paper bag from the ground and hoists it onto the counter, pulling out fresh produce and an assortment of random ingredients. "I'm trying out this new recipe tonight, and it's just so nice to not have to worry about keeping the kids entertained, you know?"

She has yet to ask about their day.

"I've got about twelve thousand Instaface followers eagerly waiting to hear how this turns out." She flits about the kitchen with a hint of exhilaration, and I'm not entirely sure if she's talking to me or to herself.

"Twelve thousand followers? Wow," I say, feigning shock. "Are you a blogger?"

"Something like that." She turns, two cans of organic stewed tomatoes in hand, and winks. "I don't have a blog per se, but my posts have a lifestyle focus to them. Home design. Recipes. Family life. All my followers are one-hundred percent organic. Most of my recipes too."

She laughs as she retrieves a small carton of heavy cream from the bag.

"What is your Instaface handle?" I play dumb.

"At . . . *MeetTheMcMullens*," she says. "All one word. You should look me up. Are you on Instaface?"

For a second, I'm momentarily speechless. Last I looked, I couldn't find it anywhere.

Was I delusional? Did I dream all of that up?

"I'm not," I lie.

"Oh, really?" Her voice raises. "That's too bad. You're missing out. You should join. It's so much better than those other sites, you know? No fake profiles. No spammers. It's completely legitimate."

"That's what I hear."

"Go on, look me up! I love getting new followers."

With her permission, I pull out my phone and look her up.

Her profile isn't private or search-restricted or MIA anymore, and I'm confused, stunned. I offer a timid smile, my face numb with excitement, and I turn my attention to the children. "Grace, are you good on crayons?"

Grace looks up at me, batting her short lashes. "Yes, Autumn."

Ever since this morning, she's been a little angel, and we both promised not to mention the makeup situation to Daphne. It's our little secret. And she promised me she wouldn't go wandering off without me ever again.

I know this girl like the back of my hand, and maybe it's a combination of watching her grow up over social media the last decade or maybe it's because she's a part of me.

But I *get* her.

I speak her language.

She's the most perfect little girl I've ever laid eyes on, and I'll cherish these summer days with my Grace for as long as I live.

"All right." Daphne peruses the spread of ingredients along her marble island. "I think I'm good here if you want to call it a day, Autumn? I'm sure you're exhausted."

I laugh through my nose. "I had a blast today. See you guys tomorrow?"

"Bye, Autumn!" Rose calls from the table.

Sebastian says nothing. Typical.

Grace hops down from her chair and runs at me, wrapping her arms around my waist. My back is to Daphne, and all I want is to run my fingers through her hair and squeeze her tight.

My eyes mist, but I blink it away. "See you in the morning, sweet girl."

It makes it slightly easier to leave tonight knowing I've got weeks' worth of photos to catch up on tonight.

CHAPTER THIRTY-THREE

DAPHNE

"Hey, Uptown Girl." Mitch wears a devious smirk on his face when I show up at his house in the middle of Wednesday afternoon. "Wasn't expecting to see you today."

When I woke up this morning, I didn't plan to come here, but I also didn't plan to decide I'd randomly crack into my husband's email and read all of his messages to hotpinkpout at gmail dot com.

The most recent message was sent yesterday.

A simple, "I miss you. I want to see you again."

This comes after the fact that my husband has been nothing but doting and adoring, showering me with gifts and tokens of his appreciation, sweeping me off to surprise date nights and reminiscing with me about the good old days.

"Are you alone?" I ask, the last of my breath mint disintegrating on my tongue. My chest rises and falls, my entire body electric with anticipation.

Mitch tucks his wavy blond hair behind his ears. "Of course."

He pulls the door open and lets me in. The place is cleaner now, and the curtains are pulled on the living room window. The place looks completely different in natural light. A little less scary, a little less dark, a little more . . . real.

"She left me," he says. "My girl. She met some pathetic fucking car salesman at the dealership where she works. He wears suits to work and hits his monthly quotas like a good boy. Guess I'm chopped liver."

"He's still fucking her," I say.

It happens so quickly, his hands tugging at my waistband, pulling at my skirt. His mouth against mine, I accept the sweet, ashy taste of his tongue between my parted lips as it mingles with the spearmint on mine.

"This means nothing, by the way," I whisper between kisses. His hand finds my ass, giving it a greedy squeeze. "I still think you're an asshole."

"And I still think you're fucked up on the inside." His lips move against mine, and he backs me up against a nearby wall, sliding his hands under my thighs and hoisting me up.

I don't disagree.

Everything about this feels wrong.

And right.

And dirty.

And delicious.

I've never felt so alive.

"You have no idea how long I've wanted to do this," he says, his lips grazing mine.

"Stop talking." I silence his mouth with another kiss, my hands digging for his waistband, feeling a hint of what I've done to his body already. Retrieving a condom from my bra, I tear it with my teeth and hand it over. I may be in a bad place, but I'm not reckless. "Now's not the time for your philosophical bullshit. Just fuck me."

"Right here? Against the wall?" he asks. I can practically taste the eagerness in his voice, and it's a libido-quelling reminder that he's seven or eight years younger than me. But I shake those thoughts from my mind, wrapping my hands around the back of his neck as he grinds his hips against me.

His fingers gather the hem of my skirt, inching it higher and higher, to the point of no return.

Mitch takes me against the floral-wallpaper covered walls of his kitchen, next to a vintage spice rack and a yellow wall-mounted rotary phone that looks like it's been there for decades. I'll bet this was his grandmother's home at some point.

His style is simple. He has no fancy tricks up his tie-dyed sleeves. His sex is no-frills and back to basics. He fucks me like an eighteen-year-old fucks their high school girlfriend, no eye contact and soft grunts between bouts of silence, but it's enough to get me off.

I didn't come here expecting sexual fireworks, anyway.

I came here to protest my marriage.

I came here as an act of rebellion.

A call and answer to the last twelve years of my life.

We're a sweaty, heaving mess when we're done, and Mitch carefully pulls himself out of me, letting me slide down the wall.

"Jesus, Uptown. What was that all about?" he breathes against my ear, nose nuzzled in my hair.

I wear a grin for the girl I used to be.

This . . . this was for her. This was for the woman she was painstakingly groomed to become. The perfect little housewife. This was for the girl she never got to be. The girl thrust into the illusion of domestic bliss when all she wanted was to travel the world with the boy who claimed he loved her when in fact, he never did. Not in a true sense.

For the first time since meeting Graham McMullen, I'm free.

It turns out, all along, I was never actually afraid of losing him.

I was afraid to be alone; afraid no one else would ever want me.

But there's a huge difference. And I was wrong.

"I'm not afraid anymore," I answer Mitch. "That's what this was about. I'm not afraid to be the person I've always wanted to be."

"God, you're fucked up, you know that?" Mitch laughs, his breath warm on my neck. "You want a smoke?"

"What kind of question is that?"

CHAPTER THIRTY-FOUR

Autumn

"I think it's going to be a while before Sebastian warms up to me," I tell Ben over dinner that night. We're celebrating my new job – at his favorite restaurant. The Red Sox happen to be playing on all the TVs here, and it's dollar wing night. Ben also felt the need to invite three of his buddies.

And Marnie.

But of course everyone's late and we went ahead and ordered wings and beer without them.

"Did you hear what I said?" I ask sweetly, scraping the Carolina sauce from a wing.

He peels his gaze from the TV screen over my head and directs his attention at me.

"What'd you say, babe?" he asks.

"I was telling you about the McMullens' little boy," I say. "He's shy. He doesn't know what to think of me."

"He'll warm up to you soon." Ben smiles.

Yeah. That's what I just said.

"I just adore Grace," I say, not wanting to overemphasize how I really feel. "And Rose is a sweetheart. They're good kids."

"No one caused any trouble today?"

"Not at all." I leave out the part about Grace getting into Daphne's makeup. A child could do far worse things in my opinion, and we should all be forgiven for our mistakes, especially mistakes made when we're innocent children and don't know any better.

"You're glowing." Ben smiles, chewing. Staring.

I hate when he stares, and I especially hate when he stares at me.

"I love my new job." I glance down at my plate, trying to distract myself from the weight of his gaze.

"You're so good with kids, Autumn." He reaches his hand across the table and takes mine, giving it a squeeze. "You're going to be a great mom someday."

My eyes flick onto his. No one said anything about motherhood.

"I'm way too young to be thinking about babies," I say with a laugh.

"You're twenty-five," he counters. "My parents had me when they were twenty-two."

"Well, that was almost thirty years ago. Times have changed." I fork another wing from the plate between us and deposit it on mine. "It's going to be a long time before . . ."

I glance up, only to see his crestfallen face.

"You never know," I change my tune, but only for him. I need to be agreeable Autumn, the one who rests happily on the same page as her doting lover at all times. "I don't like to talk about the future, Ben. You know that. I'm a spur of the moment kind of girl."

I toss him a wink and release his hand, reaching for Daphne's diamond lotus necklace hanging from my neck. It's tucked beneath my t-shirt where he can't see, though I doubt he'd ask about it anyway. Two years now and he's yet to comment when I've donned something new or different.

My oblivious Ben.

"There they are." Ben stands from our corner booth as three of his best friends from high school file into O'Toole's. Ben is exactly the kind of guy who would be pushing thirty and still hang out with his old high school friends. As far as I can tell, they all went to the same college together, roommates of course, and they all settled back here in Monarch Falls.

They were the popular guys in school. Athletic. Smart. Attractive. They were the ones I would've avoided and made fun of, because they were the types of boys who tended to make my existence less than enjoyable.

It's funny how things shake out sometimes.

"Hey, Autumn. How are you?" Ben's friend, Matt, takes a seat beside me. I like Matt. He's always asking how I'm doing and what's new with me. If I get skipped over in group conversations or sidestepped or ignored (which happens often), he always steers things back to me.

Ben could take a page from Matt's book.

"Hey, Matt!" I scoot over, making room. He's a bigger guy. Balding on top but still benignly handsome with sparkling green eyes and dark blond hair. I saw his photo in one of Ben's yearbooks a while back. He was Monarch High's homecoming king and starting quarterback. Matt married (and later divorced) his cheerleader girlfriend because most of the inhabitants of Monarch Falls are living, breathing banalities. His current girlfriend is a raging bitch, and I'm truly shocked she's not here because she usually feels the need to accompany him everywhere he goes. Apparently her last boyfriend cheated on her and now she's insecure and Matt doesn't mind because his ex-wife cheated on him and he "gets it."

Ugh.

I wish Matt would grow a pair.

He'd be the perfect catch for someone who'd actually appreciate him if he'd stop being so damn nice all the time.

"Hey, guys!" Marnie makes her grand entrance in an itty bitty tank top the color of bubble gum and hot pink lip gloss. I swear she dresses younger whenever she's around these guys, like she feels the need to really play up the whole kid sister bit, and it's clear as day she had a thing for Matt once upon a time and she still does.

His girlfriend hates Marnie, and his girlfriend is a bitch, but she's a smart bitch.

She's onto her. Just like I am.

"I'm thinking of booking one of those singles cruises," Marnie announces a few minutes later, completely out of the blue. It's as if she expects any one of them to talk her out of it, which of course doesn't happen. "I think it'd be a lot of fun."

It'd also be *a lot of fun* if someone were to accidentally push her overboard.

She reaches for a single wing drenched in Carolina BBQ sauce, places it on her plate, licks her fingers, and then doesn't touch it.

"I found this one," she continues. The guys are glued to the TV sets that surround us, none of them paying attention to the conversation. "You fly to Sanford, Florida and you leave from Cocoa Beach, then you cruise to St. Thomas and Jamaica and a bunch of other little islands. It's ten days."

Ben clenches his fist in the air and grunts, and there's a collective moan from the guys. Something must've happened in the game. I have no idea. I wasn't watching.

Marnie has her phone out now. Surprise, surprise. And she's firing off a text message. Her screen lights a moment later, her eyes scanning the screen and her mouth fighting a sly smile.

And then I see it.

Dangling from her neck.

A diamond lotus necklace, exactly like the one around my neck.

"I like your necklace," I say to her.

She glances up at me, as if I'm being sardonic, and she says nothing.

"Where'd you get it?" I ask.

Marnie shoots me another look, like I'm inconveniencing her, and her long nails click against her phone screen.

I continue waiting for my answer, watching.

After a moment, she sighs. "It was a gift. I don't know where it's from."

"Your parents get it for you?" I ask, genuinely curious.

Her big blue eyes land on mine, and her nose wrinkles. "Why are you asking so many questions? It's just a necklace. Seriously. Get over it. Stop being weird."

"I like it, that's all." I stab my chicken wing with my fork and scan the table. The guys are still focused on the game. A quick glance at the TV over Ben's head tells me the Sox are in the outfield and the Yankees have three runners on base. "Who gave it to you?"

Marnie sits her phone down and groans. "I don't know, some guy. It was a while ago."

Marnie waves her hand, prompting us to move aside so she can scoot out of the booth, and our waitress approaches the table, smiling wide when she sees all the men because she knows she can flirt her way toward better tips.

She's smart. A hustler. I see it in her eyes.

I don't hold it against her. Men plus flirting equals money.

She has common sense.

I have respect for common sense.

There's not enough of it in this world.

Everyone's too self-centered and ego-driven. And lazy. God, are we lazy as a society. It's disgusting really. We're fed information, we don't question it, and we allow it to shape our thoughts, our wants, our desires . . . our life decisions.

And then we wonder why we're so fucking miserable all the time.

Our waitress smiles.

I don't think she's miserable.

Marnie disappears into the bathroom a moment later, as if that were the only place she could go to get away from my questions.

She isn't the smartest. All she had to do was lie about the damn necklace. Had she told me she bought it at a boutique, I'd have thought nothing of it. But now I'm curious. And now I *need* to know. And I'm going to find out. And she better hope to God it's a coincidence.

CHAPTER THIRTY-FIVE

Autumn

Monday is chlorine and sunscreen scented with a high in the upper 80s. The McMullen children have been poolside for the better part of the afternoon. We had an early lunch (organic turkey and homemade apple butter on ancient grain bread with a side of baby carrots, unsweetened applesauce, and almond milk), a quick rest, and then we suited up and grabbed our towels.

Sebastian clings to my back, his floaties snug on his skinny arms, and he rides me as I swim across the shallow end chasing the girls. They want to pretend I'm an alligator and they're duckies. Each time my fingers graze their little feet, they giggle and laugh and we have to start over again.

I haven't had this much fun in ages.

I check the clock constantly, ensuring the children's sunscreen reapplications are timely. I won't have the McMullen kids burning on my watch. Besides, Grace has my fair complexion, and we're especially prone to sunburn.

"Should we rest for a sec?" I ask them after a bit.

Grace pouts, and I hate to see her sad.

"Okay, give me five minutes," I say.

She smiles and swims to the opposite end of the pool to grab her snorkel and flippers. Rose follows. Sebastian clings onto me tighter. He likes to be in the water, but he's also deathly afraid to be in by himself, I've noticed.

I start to swim toward the ladder when I see the sliding glass door to the patio begin to move. A second later, Graham steps out. The outdoor clock reads a quarter past three.

"Oh, hello," I say with a friendly smile.

"Daddy!" Sebastian waves. "We're playing alligator with Autumn. Want to get in with us?"

"Sorry, buddy," he says, crouching down poolside. Even with all the Coppertone and chlorine in the air, I catch a whiff of his cologne. It's fresh. Clean. Sexy. Graham's eyes find mine. "Everything going okay? Kids being good for you?"

"Of course. They're little angels," I say. I don't tell him I'm tired and I'm going to sleep like a rock tonight, because I don't mind. Honestly. I love this. I'm deliriously, pleasantly exhausted. But my legs and lungs and arms and back need a breather. I lift Sebastian up the ladder and he runs to a nearby lounger, wrapping himself up in a Grecian-striped towel. Climbing the ladder next, water rushes off me in rivulets and the weight of gravity takes a hold of me. For a split second, I almost lose my balance, but Graham is there, hooking his arm into my elbow and pulling me into him so I don't fall.

I'm embarrassed.

And also, transfixed in his calming oceanic gaze.

"You all right?" he asks, peering down his nose with a concerned stare.

"I'm fine," I assure him. "We've been in the water all day. I'm probably just a little dehydrated."

I leave his side and go to my water bottle, which is resting on a teak table between two cabana-style loungers. I swig and gulp until my stomach is full, and my eyes never leave Rose and Grace for one second.

I'm a good nanny.

When I turn to face Graham again, I catch his stare resting in a place it doesn't belong. It's only for a fraction of a second, and for a moment, I wonder if I'm imagining things, but then he smiles and mutters something about it looking like it's about to rain, and then he turns to his children.

My hand slicks down the side of my modest, black one-piece. I went with something conservative, because a nanny should never steal the show, and showing up with some glitzy gold bikini is more like something Marnie Gotlieb would do.

This thing leaves plenty to the imagination, and there was Graham. Imagining . . . something.

I don't want to believe it.

I don't want to believe he has eyes for anyone but Daphne.

She's a good wife. A great mother. She's his everything. And he is her whole world. They have a marriage for the ages, and a beautiful family to show for it.

He must have been lost in thought, and his eyes just happened to be on my ass.

"All right, I'm headed back to the office," Graham announces. "Autumn, when you see my wife, can you please remind her I won't be home for dinner tonight? I've got a conference call with China at seven o'clock."

"Of course."

CHAPTER THIRTY-SIX

DAPHNE

THE HOUSE IS DARK AND STILL, AND I SWIRL A FINGER OF MY husband's prized bourbon in my left hand while checking my Instaface feed for the day.

Graham is back to "working late."

That didn't last long.

Closing my eyes and sinking into my chair, I picture him with her, and I imagine they're both conspiring to drive me to the point of insanity. And some days it feels as though it's working.

My phone vibrates and a text message displays across the screen.

Mitch.

My heart rate quickens. That thing we did . . . it was a one-time thing. But he's been texting me almost daily, telling me how tight I was, how wet I was, telling me all the dirty things he wants to do to me again.

I think he's a lot better in his head than he is in real life, but I don't want to be the one to tell him that.

My thumb drags across the screen, and I close out of Instaface and pull up my messages.

FINALLY GOT HER NAME, he writes. YOU STILL WANT IT? GOT HER ADDRESS TOO.

CHAPTER THIRTY-SEVEN

AUTUMN

BEN GRUNTS AND GROANS, PUSHING HIMSELF INSIDE ME, HIS BODY shaking and quivering before his grand finale. He doesn't ask if I'm close. Never has. Probably never will. I used to think he was oblivious. Now I know he just doesn't care. And why would he? Our relationship has been about him from day one. From the moment we met.

He finishes, his face buried into my neck because he's never been one for eye contact during sex.

I sink into the bed we share, pretending to be spent because it was *sooooo good*, and he smiles his proud, puppy dog smile before hitting the shower.

Once a quarter Ben travels to Tulsa, Oklahoma for work, and once a quarter we have goodbye sex, which is when we have sex and I whisper in his ear how much I'm going to miss him and it makes him feel loved and special.

As soon as I summon the strength, I join him in the shower,

purely for efficiency reasons, and he uses that as an excuse to cop a few more feels.

"I love that you're back to your old self again," he says, his hand on my left breast like it's no big deal. He has yet to say anything about how toned and tan my body's been looking lately, and I wonder if he's even noticed. I've been nannying for the McMullens for two full weeks now, and lately every afternoon's been spent poolside.

"I love my new job," I say. And it's true. I *love* this job.

"What's going to happen when summer's over?" he asks.

I feel my smile melt from my lips.

I haven't thought that far ahead.

My hope is that I become a sort of babysitter-on-standby. Maybe they'll need me after school? Maybe Graham and Daphne will take more trips and they'll need someone to watch the children overnight? Maybe since we're neighbors, we'll become sort of . . . friends?

The possibilities are endless.

"We'll deal with that when the time comes," I say.

"I just don't want you to go back to the way you were before." He plops a handful of shampoo into his palm and lathers his hair with brute force. I wonder if anyone's ever shown him the proper way to bathe himself or if he'll forever shower like an uncoordinated orangutan.

"Back to the way I was before?"

"Moody. Sad. Closed off. Annoyed with me all the time." He laughs, as if my blue phase was comedic. "It was like it was that time of the month twenty-four seven."

Ha, ha, ha. Women and their hormones! Hilarious.

"I'm so sorry I put you through that." I've learned over the last two years that sometimes the best way to deal with Ben is to say the opposite of what I really want to say.

"It's okay, babe." He turns to face me, depositing a damp kiss on my mouth. "I still love you. Always will."

"Love you too."

He washes his body and steps out, leaving the water running for me. When he starts humming *Sweet Caroline*, I have to tune him out. Not because of the song. The song is fine. But the man can't hold a note to save his life.

And to think, I used to find that endearing.

There was a point, earlier in our relationship, when I really did like Ben. And I genuinely felt lucky to be with him. I loved his lack of complexities. It was refreshing. Different. Safe. But now I feel nothing. I feel nothing, and I feel trapped.

We finish getting ready together, making small talk, and bumping shoulders in our tight bathroom. By the time I slip into my jeans, he's wheeling his suitcase down the hall. His flight leaves in two hours and the airport is thirty minutes away. I hate how close he always cuts it. One traffic jam could cause him to miss his entire flight, and I'm really looking forward to some alone time this week. These quarterly trips are my breathers from Ben.

I meet him by the front door when I'm ready, and he kisses me on the mouth then slips me the tongue because there's nothing like a Monday-morning make out *sesh* to kick off the week.

"I'm going to miss you," he says, his lips grazing mine. He's trying to be sweet. And it *is* sweet. I'll give him that. He presses his forehead against my forehead and smiles his goofy Ben smile. "Love you, babe."

He gets like this anytime he travels. He acts like we're never going to see each other again, and he needs to make damn sure I know he loves me and I love him. It's as if he thinks he's going to return to some kind of toxic wasteland where our happy home once was.

For as carefree as this man claims to be, he worries too much about losing me.

"Love you too," I say, slapping my hand on his broad shoulder. "You should get going. You're going to miss your flight."

He twists the door knob, shooting me a lingering look, and then he's gone. I'm smiling. And I feel evil for it. He may annoy the hell out of me, but I'm not soulless. I'm not a monster.

I'm only human.

———

WHEN DAPHNE OPENS THE FRONT DOOR, HER HAND IS MOTIONING for me to hurry up, and she almost slams the door behind me. Someone is crying in the next room.

Grace.

Daphne checks her watch, her brows arching. "I'm going to be late."

A coldness runs through me.

"Did I miss something?" I ask. "Was I supposed to be here earlier than nine today?"

"No, no." She places her hand on my shoulder, her eyes suddenly merciful. "My acupuncturist messed up my appointment. It was supposed to be for nine thirty and they set it for nine, and it takes ten minutes to get to that side of town, so I'm just . . . ugh. It's been one of those mornings."

I feel you, Daphne.

I wonder if she and Graham ever make love in the morning, and if they're really into it. I wonder if he asks if she's close and if he looks into her eyes and if she smiles when he kisses her and if her heart aches when she sees him leave.

"I'll be out most of the morning," she says, sliding her purse over her shoulder. "I've got errands to run, and then I'm meeting a friend for lunch in the city."

Grace is still crying.

As soon as Daphne leaves, I'll go to her. I'll wrap my arms around her, and I'll tell her she can talk to me about anything. I'll listen. Daphne seems too busy to listen this morning.

"Are the kids okay?" I ask.

Daphne's expression falls, as if I've shoved my nose too far up the wrong side of her business.

"Oh." She laughs. Then rolls her eyes. "The crying. Yes. Grace clearly woke up on the wrong side of the bed today. Monday mornings are always rough, aren't they?"

I bite my tongue and everything flashes red for a second. She isn't going to ask what's wrong? She thinks her daughter's just having a Monday morning fit?

There's a small corner of my heart that's shattering as we stand here, bathed in sunlight in the McMullens' foyer.

I know what it's like to be the emotionally neglected daughter. To have a mother too preoccupied with everything else to take the time from her busy schedule with you as you cry.

"All right," Daphne says. "Anything you need before I go?"

I press my lips together, stare up at the two-story ceiling, and then shake my head. "I think we're good, Mrs. McMullen."

She still hasn't told me to call her Daphne, and I haven't asked. I've yet to call either of them by their first names, opting to not use a name at all when I speak to them most of the time. How are they ever supposed to see me as an extension of their family with all of these constant formalities?

The second Daphne leaves, I follow the sound of Grace's cries into the family room. Rose is sitting quietly on the end of the sofa, reading an Amelia Bedelia book, and Sebastian is sitting quietly on the opposite end, playing an educational game on his tablet. Grace's cries die down when she sees me, and tear tracks line her chubby cheeks. Before I have a chance to ask what's wrong, she lunges toward me, landing in my arms. Her little hands lock behind my back and she buries her face into my t-shirt.

Running my fingers through her hair, I ask in my best motherly tone, "What is it, sweet girl? Why are you crying?"

"Mommy and Daddy were fighting this morning," she sobs.

I watch the other two children, who are as oblivious as Ben is on the best of days. Maybe they're too young to notice. Or maybe

Grace heard something because her room is so close to the master suite.

"Sometimes grown-ups fight," I say, my voice a gentle whisper. "It's nothing to cry about."

"But my Mommy and Daddy never fight," she says, sniffing. "My friend Alexis said when her mommy and daddy fought, they got a divorce. I don't want my parents to get a divorce."

I lead her to the sofa and sit her down beside me, keeping her hand in mine. "Your parents won't . . ." I don't want to use the D-word in case the other two hear it and repeat it later on.

"How do you know?"

"Did they say it?"

"No." She scratches her nose, and I tuck a strand of loose brown hair behind her ear.

"If they didn't say it, then you have nothing to worry about," I make a promise to my daughter I have no business making. But I can't have her worrying. I can't stand to see her sad, heartbroken.

I gave her up so she could have a better life.

This beautiful, innocent little soul deserves to be happy.

She did nothing wrong.

Our eyes hold, and I never want to let hers go. She reminds me so much of myself at that age. Young, carefree, blissfully unaware of reality looming on the horizon. Cupping her face in my hand, I smile.

This is what Daphne should have done earlier.

How hard is it to take two seconds from your morning routine and sit down with your crying daughter and ease her tiny little worries?

Is Daphne really that selfish?

I hope to God, for her sake, that she was just having an off day because nobody treats my daughter that way, especially not her own "mother."

CHAPTER THIRTY-EIGHT

DAPHNE

MARNIE GOTLIEB.

The homewrecker finally has a name.

I expected something, I don't know, prettier. Something younger? Britney or Caitlyn or the kind of name you'd see one of those god-awful reality shows about pregnant high schoolers.

Her face doesn't match her name. With a name like Marnie, I expected someone bookish, maybe Harvard educated. A schoolteacher with a married man fetish, I don't know.

But that isn't her at all.

I spent all day watching, seeing where she went and what she did and who she was with. It's amazing what all you can learn just by observing someone. Marnie started her day at the gym, and she's one of those girls who works out in a full face of makeup and an itty-bitty hot purple sports bra with matching booty shorts. After the gym she went home, and she emerged two hours later, still with a full face of makeup, and headed to the Starbucks drive-thru. After she finished her coffee, she headed to the mall on the west side of town, disappearing into a department store entrance and coming out two hours later with an armful of bags and her phone plastered to her cheek. I'm not sure who she was talking to, but her face was pinched and as soon as she got to her car, she threw the bags into the passenger side with little care.

From there, I followed her home to her little white townhouse. She disappeared inside all afternoon, which was the least interesting part of her day, but I took that time to do a little online research.

According to the assessor's page, her parents own her place. Her name isn't anywhere on it. And according to LinkedIn, she graduated from college three years ago, but not without completing a semester-long internship at McMullen and Henry Corp.

Graham does like convenience.

Her resume is scant, and she doesn't appear to have ever held a real job. Mostly internships and volunteer work. I don't see a single award or scholarship listed, and her connections are extremely limited.

Marnie's Instaface profile is wide open and under her full name, *@marniegotlieb*, so it was ridiculously easy to find. I scroll through over five hundred photos, ninety-three percent of them selfies or flat lays of random things she bought at the store mixed in with designer sunglasses and tubes of expensive lipstick.

Unoriginal.

I breathe a sigh of relief when I get to the last photo and can confirm that there are none of the two of them together. At least there's that.

I sit my phone aside after a couple hours. Marnie still hasn't left her townhome, and I check my watch. I need to get home soon and relieve Autumn.

That Autumn is a saint, truly. I couldn't have picked a better nanny for my children. Graham, shockingly, knocked that one out of the park. They adore her. Sometimes I think they might even

like her more than they like me. And she's so good. She's so observant and respectful. She makes the kids mind their manners, and
she never feeds them junk food or lets the TV blare in the family
room all hours of the day.

They listen to her, and she listens to them. There's a kind of
mutual respect thing happening that I didn't know my kids were
capable of.

Reaching for the ignition, I start my engine. So many questions were answered today, yet so many still remain. Mitch is
right: I'm never going to know what he sees in her. I could watch
her day in and day out and still never know. It's a waste of time,
and my time is precious. At least I know her name, and I know
there's nothing special about her. She's just a young girl who
makes Graham feel like the middle of his life isn't sagging.

Oh, well, though.

She can have him.

I pull out of my parking space and look both ways, stopping
short when a red Corvette veers into a nearby spot, almost
swiping my front.

That'd be a disaster.

The man, dressed in gray pants and a white button down,
climbs out and hurries toward the sidewalk, checking his
periphery to see who's around. A moment later, he's knocking at
Marnie's door. And she opens, her painted mouth pulled into a
Cheshire grin. He reaches for her, placing his hand on her hip,
and she hooks her arm into his, drawing him inside. The door
closes, and I sit in my parked car for a second, asking myself if
that actually just happened.

CHAPTER THIRTY-NINE

Autumn

"You're home early." Daphne's face lights when she sees Graham the next afternoon. It's as if yesterday had never happened. She's been flitting around, rambling happily about this new soufflé recipe she wants to try, and how she's in the middle of planning a nice family vacation.

I'm confused, but maybe this is how the well-to-do handle things? They wallow in their problems with self-pity and expensive wine, and the next day it's back to business as usual?

"I'm golfing, remember?" he says, moving toward her. He places his hand lightly on her hip, leaning in to kiss her forehead, but keeping a careful distance between their bodies. It's cold, his kiss. And her eyes fall toward the floor. She's disappointed.

My heart breaks. For her. For Grace. For Rose and Sebastian.

They're too young to know what's happening. They're too little to see the writing on the wall.

This is how two adults fall out of love, and watching it in real time is almost too hard for me to manage. My eyes burn and I look away, grabbing a crayon from the box between Sebastian and me and turning my attention toward the coloring book Rose abandoned in favor of a Barbie sticker book.

All the anger and resentment I felt toward Daphne the other day has dissipated.

She's broken, not selfish.

She's a woman who tries so hard and fights so hard and works so hard . . . for a man who doesn't even appreciate it.

I wasn't imagining his eyes on my ass the other week.

Graham is not the husband and father I thought he was.

I don't have proof yet.

But I have a feeling.

A nagging feeling that drove me to circle Monarch Falls for three hours last night trying to find this man. A nagging feeling that kept me up all night, wondering, playing worst-case scenarios in my head. A nagging feeling that makes me want to disrupt the children's perfectly lovely afternoon snack just to scream in his face and ask him why the hell he's throwing away this beautiful life.

Whoever she is, she's not worth it.

I find myself huffing out loud, agreeing with my thoughts, and Daphne shoots me a quizzical look.

"Sorry. My allergies are bothering me today," I lie.

Graham's suited up in golf gear, head to toe. His hat matches his polo and his belt and his shorts and his shoes. They're all covered in the same logo. If he's lying, he's definitely going to great lengths to ensure she believes.

But I'm pretty sure she sees through it all.

I mean, who wouldn't?

We women are intelligent, instinctive. Men think with their penises. We think with our intuition. It's a superpower of sorts.

"Isn't it late for golf?" she asks, and I hear the disappointment in her voice.

"It's summer, honey," he says. "It doesn't get dark until almost nine. And we're just doing nine holes. I'll be home by dinner."

She offers him a faint smile, which I can tell takes effort, and tells him to enjoy himself. I don't know if she's being genuine or not.

"Be good for your mother tonight." Graham waves at the children from the garage entry door and disappears behind it a second later. The kids don't so much as bat an eye. It's as if they're used to him always being gone, always leaving. Coming and going. And that seems to be a pattern, I've noticed, over the last weeks. He pops in. He says hello. Hugs his children when he's not dressed to the nines and on his way out the door, and that's that. He frequently misses dinner. And I've yet to see him bring his wife flowers, which is odd, since she used to constantly snap these elaborate bouquets for her Instaface followers every week.

Maybe she bought them for herself all those times?

"Autumn." Daphne says my name loud and sharp.

I shake my head, my eyes flicking onto hers. "Yes?"

She laughs. "I said you could leave early. You're zoned out over there. You look exhausted. Kids wear you out today?"

I chortle, cheeks warming. "Yes, sorry. Thank you."

I give the children goodbye hugs, and Sebastian clings to my leg and Grace won't let go and Rose gives me a kiss on the cheek. I don't want to leave early. I want to stay. I want to stay longer and later. I want to stay until Graham comes home. I want him to bring her flowers and chocolates and tell her the reason he's been so unavailable lately is because he's planning their surprise anniversary trip to France, and then I want him to ask if I'm available to watch the kids for ten days. In my mind, we're all squealing, jumping, smiling, hugging. Happy.

Everything is as it should be.

But it's nothing more than a frivolous daydream. And I know that.

I slip my purse around my shoulder and ruffle Sebastian's hair.

"I don't want you to go, Autumn," Grace whines, following me to the front door.

Daphne stands back. "Grace, she has to go home. You'll see her in the morning."

Grace squeezes me again.

The feeling is mutual.

"Have a good night, sweet girl. Listen to your mom, okay?" I gently pry her hands from around my hips and give Daphne a nod. Her eyes are tired, makeup uncharacteristically rubbed around her eyelids, and her skin is paler than usual.

Daphne nods back, following me to the door and showing me out.

She says nothing.

I say nothing.

My chest squeezes and my stomach turns as I stand outside on the front stoop. Everything feels off-balance in a way I can't fully comprehend yet. What I thought I knew . . . what I think I know . . . . none of it adds up.

Grace peers out the sidelight by the front door, waving as I leave, her eyes despondent. At ten, she's old enough to know something's not right. And I see it in the way she looks at me . . . she wants to be with me.

She wants to come home with me.

Grace wants to get away from the impending maelstrom that is about to be her precious little life. A hand, Daphne's, wraps around Grace's wrist, pulling her from the window. I watch until she disappears.

I would take her away in a heartbeat if I could.

CHAPTER FORTY

DAPHNE

GRAHAM NUZZLES HIS FACE INTO THE BEND OF MY NECK AS THE TV flickers in the background, and his hand inches beneath the hem of my pajama top.

We haven't made love in ages, and honestly the thought of it makes me sick to my stomach now.

"Her name is Marnie, isn't it?" I ask a question to which I already know the answer.

His hands stop moving. "Why are you doing this? We've come so far. Things are getting better."

"Are they?" I ask. "Because it sounds to me like you still miss her. You still want to see her."

He retracts completely, lying on his back and dissolving into the mattress in a mass of frustration.

"Hacked my email, I see," he says, exhaling. "It's complicated, Daphne, it really is."

I smooth my hand down my thigh and inch away. "I'm sure it is, *Graham*."

"What's that supposed to mean?"

"Nothing." I sigh. "This whole entire thing is complicated, and to be honest, I'm trying to understand why you would act one way and say all these wonderful things and profess your devotion – but you're still out sneaking around with her, telling her you miss her. You know your words mean nothing now, right? You understand that?"

He doesn't cry. He doesn't break down. He doesn't show a speck of emotion.

"I'm still trying to end things," he says, his voice low. "I thought I ended things last time, but she wasn't handling it so well and I had to see her again, and things just kind of-"

"Spare me." I clear my throat and pull my shoulders back, readying myself to drop the bombshell that's been on the tip of my tongue since the moment he strolled through the door tonight. "Anyway, I saw her today. She was with another man."

Graham laughs. He doesn't believe me. Or maybe he just doesn't want to believe me.

"He drove a red Corvette," I say. "Salt and pepper hair. Dresses nice."

He's quiet now, and I sit here staring straight ahead, wondering why he isn't trying to talk his way out of this conversation.

I draw in a deep breath and turn to look at him in time to catch the faintest tremble of his bottom lip.

And then I know.

He loves her.

He loved her then. He loves her still.

"Let her go, Graham," I say, and for the first time in my life, I find myself wanting to physically hurt him. I wish I could smack him across the face and tell him to snap out of it. "Let her go, or I'll take away everything you've ever cared about."

He doesn't blink. He doesn't move. And in that moment, I realize, she's the only thing he cares about. The only reason he apologized before was because he was *scared*. He didn't mean anything he said. He never wanted to leave her. He doesn't want to spend his life with me. The kids are an afterthought.

He only wants Marnie Gotlieb.

CHAPTER FORTY-ONE

Autumn

"Can you do me a favor, babe?" Ben's voice pipes into my ear as I cradle my phone on my shoulder.

I'm distracted, and I can't stop thinking about earlier – about Graham and Daphne and the fighting and the awkward exchanges and the absence of affection. He clearly isn't vested in the relationship anymore, and Daphne clearly doesn't have the energy to fight for a man who isn't willing to fight for their marriage.

"How's Tulsa?" I ask, drawing up a steaming bath. I need to soak and think and wrap my head around all of this, and most importantly, think about how it's going to affect Grace going forward.

"Did you hear me?" he asks. "I need a favor. Real quick."

"Sorry," I say, peeling out of the day's clothes. "My mind was somewhere else. What do you need me to do?"

"Can you go check on Marnie?" he asks.

I stare at the tub, watching the bubbles grow higher and the steam evaporating into the air above.

"I'm taking a bath now," I say. "I can call her when I'm done."

"No," he cuts me off. "I need you to go to her house and check on her. Like, as soon as possible."

I laugh because he's being ridiculous. She's a twenty-four-year-old woman. She doesn't need a babysitter. In fact, I'm pretty sure she's holed up in some fancy hotel in New York City with her latest married mister, and a trip across town to knock on her door would be a complete and total waste of my time and energy.

"I'm being serious," he says. "My parents are in Seattle visiting my aunt Greta or else they'd do it. Mom said Marnie was supposed to take Grandma Peterson to a doctor's appointment this morning and she never showed. No one's talked to her in days. Something's going on."

"Maybe she went on that singles cruise?" I suggest, dipping my toe in the water. I perch on the edge of the garden tub, waiting for this call to end.

"Autumn, please." There's a boom in his broken voice unlike anything I've heard before. He doesn't appreciate my glibness. "Just knock on her door and see if she's home. That's all I need you to do. Please."

Twisting the handle of the faucet until the water stops, I exhale.

"Fine," I say. "I'll go."

"Will you go now?" He's breathy, impatient.

"Yes."

"Thank you. Call me as soon as you get there."

"Will do."

———

THE PARKING LOT OF MARNIE'S TOWNHOME COMPLEX IS FULL, BUT I manage to grab a spot between a Chrysler and a Lexus a few doors down from hers. Gathering my keys and bag, I check my phone for the time and climb out of my car.

Several spots away, a car alarm wails for a few moments, and when I turn my attention toward Marnie's Kelly green front door, I see it swing open partway.

There's nothing but blackness between the door and whatever's inside, and I freeze, watching and waiting.

A minute later, a man exits. It's getting dark now, but he pulls a cap over his head and yanks her door shut. The door swings wide a minute later and Marnie emerges, a black lace negligee barely covering her gaunt body. The left strap falls down her shoulder, and she yells something at him. The man rushes back to her, cupping his hand over her mouth and leading her back inside.

They're fighting, Marnie and her lover.

I stay back, waiting. And when he emerges from the door the second time, she doesn't chase after him. The man takes wide strides, keeping his head tucked and eyes lowered, and it isn't until I see him jog toward a black Tesla that I get a clearer view of his face.

Graham.

My chest burns, the contents of my stomach threatening to rise.

I want to chase after him. I want to pound my fists against his chest and scream in his face and ask him why. Why is he doing this to his family? To Daphne? Why Marnie?

The Tesla quietly starts, and I wait for him to exit the parking lot before I make my way to her door.

That little *whore*.

A moment later, I'm pounding on her door with a balled fist, beating until my hand goes numb. Marnie answers after what feels like forever, her face washed in shock. It wasn't me she was expecting.

"What the hell are you doing here?" Marnie sneers, her lips drawn into an incredulous smirk. Her blue eyes are ringed in smeared mascara and her cheeks are cherry red, like she's been crying.

I shove past her, showing myself in. It smells like wine and perfume, and music blasts from an upstairs bedroom.

I don't care if she wants me here or not. We need to have a little talk. Immediately.

Marnie slams the door then storms toward me, hands on her bony hips. "You can't just come in here like this. This is a private residence, and you're not welcome here."

"Your brother sent me."

Her jaw falls, and then her lips press flat.

"Apparently the whole family's worried about you." I glance around her townhome. I've only been here a handful of times in the last couple of years. Always with Ben. Always for a quick visit. "You were supposed to take your grandmother to the doctor or something? I don't know. Maybe you should answer your phone when your parents try to call you? Least you can do for them considering everything they do for you."

She rolls her eyes and then ambles toward me, nearly stumbling. The closer she gets, the more I can smell the alcohol oozing from her tiny little pores.

"I'm going through some shit right now," she says, as if I should immediately sympathize with her.

Poor baby.

"Clearly," I say.

Her brows meet. "What the hell is that supposed to mean?"

"I saw you with him." My words come from deep within my chest, and it makes me sick to say them out loud.

"Who?" She's playing dumb, and she's terrible at it.

"Graham," I say. "You're screwing Graham McMullen."

"Ha." She laughs, throwing her hands in the air. "Oh, *him*. You caught me."

Marnie slaps herself on the wrist, and I wonder if she's ever truly had to deal with the consequences of her actions before.

Doubtful.

I see red. And then black. And then before I know what's

MINKA KENT

happening, my hands are pressed against her chest and she's flying backward. Marnie lands on her ass, stunned and breathless.

"That's assault," she says, emotionless. She's in shock. I've never touched her before, and she's never touched me. She didn't see it coming, but to be fair, neither did I.

I'm not a violent person.

"He's a married man," I say, my words short and emphasized, though something tells me I'm wasting my breath. "He has three children. And a beautiful wife. And you will never be good enough for him."

"Sweetheart, he wants to leave his wife for me," she says proudly, as if she's earned some kind of whorish bragging rights. "We had a little fight tonight because he keeps dragging his feet about it, but he's going to do it. Soon. And then we can finally be together."

"You home-wrecking little *slut*." My voice explodes, startling us both, and I suck in a lungful of gardenia-and-cabernet-scented air. There's a flickering candle on the fireplace mantle, and the image of the two of them screwing on the sofa earlier flashes across my mind and makes me want to vomit all over her hard-wood floor.

"He's not happy, Autumn," she says. "You work for them. Surely you've noticed their marriage is an absolute joke. Daphne is a control freak, and Graham needs someone who lets him be . . . Graham. Someone who appreciates him for who he is and doesn't micromanage every minute of that man's life. All of this is Daphne's doing, really. She pushed him. She pushed him straight into the arms of another woman. Ugh. If you only knew the half of it."

I imagine she fills her head with all kinds of things that justify what she's doing because she's an entitled, spoiled little brat whose parents treat her like a prized purebred, rewarded for being cute.

She's never had to pay for anything in her life: material things or mistakes.

"You know nothing." My chest rises and falls, and when I look at her, I have to keep my fists balled because all I want to do is tear at her soft flesh and gouge her big blue eyes and crack her bony little body in half.

Marnie Gotlieb is a deplorable human being who doesn't deserve to live.

A waste of clean air and good water.

The world would be a better place without her, of that much I'm one hundred percent sure.

And I'll be fucking damned if she becomes Grace's stepmother.

"End it," I command. "End it with Graham, and maybe I won't tell your entire family about your extra-curricular activities."

She lifts an arched brow. "No clue what you're talking about."

"I know what you do in your spare time. All those married men. All those hotel rooms and fancy clothes. Your family might be oblivious, but I'm not. All the things you do when you think no one's watching? I've seen them. And it would break your father's heart to know his precious little princess is-"

"You don't deserve my brother," she says, spinning this entire thing around. Over the years, I've learned that's what people do when they're in the wrong and they know they don't have a leg to stand on. They turn the tables. They take the heat off themselves with a good, old-fashioned distraction. "My brother only *thinks* he's happy with you. He doesn't know it's all fake, like you."

I didn't know it was possible to hate this woman more than I already did, but here I am, hating her with every strained, tensed fiber of my being.

"I met your brother," she says. My heart stops cold.

My chest tightens, cutting off my air and strangulating the words I'm trying to form.

"He told me things about you," she continues with a smirk. Marnie rises, arms folding as she stumbles toward me. "Really,

really fucked up things. And as soon as Ben gets back, I'm going to tell him. I'm going to tell him everything. And he's going to leave you, because you're fucked up in the head, Autumn, and now I finally have proof. You-"

There's a crack.

And then she's silent.

And when I open my eyes, I'm hovering above her, my hands in her hair, and she's not moving.

Her head slides off the marble-top coffee table that centers her living room, and I let her go. She slouches, her body limp and pooling at my feet.

I lift my hand to my mouth, harboring a breath. Frozen, I watch her chest, looking for a rise and fall that never happens.

And then I leave.

CHAPTER FORTY-TWO

Autumn

"Was she home?" Ben doesn't answer his phone with a "hello."

"No," I say, hands trembling as I drive home.

I never meant to kill her.

I mean, I've thought about it a hundred times before, but making it happen was never more than a daydream fantasy for me.

I'm not a killer.

I'm not violent or murderous.

I don't have those urges.

"Well, shit," Ben sighs into the receiver. "Where the hell could she be?"

"I'm sure she'll turn up."

"Nah, it's been several days. I talked to some of her friends tonight. They all said she's been ignoring them too. We're going to have to call the police and report her missing."

God damn it, Marnie.

I get that she was "going through some shit" and in a funk or whatever, but why'd she have to cut off the rest of the world? That attention-seeking, drama-thriving little bitch.

"Did it look like she'd been home recently?" Ben asks, his voice lifted as if he's subconsciously willing me to tell him what he wants to hear.

"Everything was dark," I say. "All the lights were out."

I think about the flickering candle on the mantle. Shit.

If I'm lucky, it'll burn out before the police arrive.

"Well, thanks for checking on her, babe," he says. He still has hope. And it breaks my heart. "I'm taking the next flight home."

Ben hangs up. He doesn't say he loves me. I imagine him calling his parents next, updating them. I imagine the Gotliebs worrying sick, booking early flights back, losing sleep and shedding tears.

They're good people. And I feel for what they're about to go through. They really loved their Marnie, and I can't blame them. They never saw the ugly side of her. They never experienced her dark side. All they ever did was love her unconditionally and treat her like a spoiled house pet, her smiling face repayment enough for all of the gifts they rained down upon her.

And in the end, she still had a rough life, and she was a miserable, ungrateful soul. And it was all her own doing.

I pull into the garage fifteen minutes later, sitting in the car until the garage door closes and the light goes out and I'm engulfed in pitch blackness.

I wonder where Marnie is now. If she's bathed in light or drowning in dark. I wonder if she's being shown her life in photographs and flashbacks, and if she feels any remorse for the way she treated people.

I pull in a breath and exit the car, feeling my way to the nearest door knob.

Ginger greets me on the other side. The house is cozy and comfortable. The only light illuminating the space is from the hood range in the kitchen. It's good to be home. I scoop her up in my arms before heading to the medicine cabinet to grab another little yellow pill in a preemptive attempt to silence my mind tonight on the off chance I find myself awake at three AM, replaying Marnie's last moments.

A vision of her face, eyes open and staring dead ahead, her blonde hair wild and hanging in her face, floods my memory.

The pills are almost out.

If I want more, I'll have to go back to Dr. Josh.

I take one, chasing it with a sleeping pill and a glass of milk, and I wonder if any of this is normal. I wonder how many people have killed someone with their bare hands and went straight home to bed afterwards.

I determine it doesn't matter.

And then I determine that I don't actually know if Marnie is dead.

She was drunk, and she hit her head, that's all. She's probably passed out, and she'll probably wake up tomorrow with a killer headache and no recollection of what happened the night before.

I didn't kill her.

She tripped and hit her head.

If she is dead, the autopsy will show that. It'll show her blood alcohol content at several times the legal limit, and they'll take one look at the scene of the accident and determine she stumbled onto the coffee table; a young life tragically cut short by alcohol abuse and a string of unfortunate events.

It happens all the time.

CHAPTER FORTY-THREE

Autumn

GRAHAM AND DAPHNE ARE TWO PASSING SHIPS IN THE NIGHT THE following morning. His nose is buried in his phone, and she refuses to take her eyes off the made-from-scratch, whole wheat pancakes on the griddle. It's a late breakfast for the McMullens, and I wonder if they had a late night too. They haven't muttered more than a couple of formalities this morning, and the tension between them is dense and ripe.

I watch as Graham thumbs out a text message on his phone, his eyes moving between his screen and the back of his wife's head to ensure she isn't paying attention.

She isn't.

It's as if they've reached an impasse in their marriage, neither of them trying. Neither of them caring. Both of them in limbo until one of them makes the next move.

Ben came home from Tulsa earlier this morning, several days ahead of schedule. He was going to meet his parents at the police station as soon as they land so they could file a missing persons report on Marnie.

I rise from the table, leaving Grace's side and retrieving a bib for Sebastian from one of the kitchen drawers. I fasten it around his neck a moment later, staring at my hands: the hands of a killer. They look exactly as they did yesterday. No marks or scuffs or bruises. No unfamiliar notches or creases. Cream-toned and baby smooth.

The hands of a possible killer will be tending to these children today, and despite that fact, I would protect these babies with my life. The irony is not lost on me.

"Autumn, can you please set the table?" Daphne calls out, plating pancakes.

"Of course." I make myself busy, watching as Graham fires off another text. His jaw sets. His lips flatten. He exhales through his nostrils.

"All right, I'm off," he says a moment later. No one responds. Daphne doesn't tell him to have a nice day, and the children are too preoccupied with their impending breakfast to notice he's halfway out the door already.

Graham's Tesla veers out of the driveway in under a minute, and I tend to the children, telling Daphne I'll take care of clean up in a second.

"I'm volunteering today," she says, though she doesn't say where and I don't ask. "I've got to leave here in thirty minutes."

I'm not sure if she's talking to me or the kids or to herself. Her tone lacks enthusiasm and energy, and I wonder if today is one of those days when she's just going through the motions.

My stomach twists when I think of Graham and his hands all over Marnie and her mouth all over all the places on his body that Daphne should only know. I wonder how much she knows? Surely she's aware. A man doesn't just slip away from a marriage for no reason. He's always going to someone.

Daphne slips upstairs quietly, and the children share knock-

knock jokes and giggles, like it's any other day, and I can hardly stand here pretending like everything is fine.

How lucky they are to know the gift of living in the moment.

The doorbell chimes.

"Stay here," I tell the kids. "I'll be right back."

It's much too early for a delivery, but sometimes one of the neighbor kids stops by wanting to play. I'm willing to bet it's the little red-haired boy from down the street.

"I've been trying to call you all morning." Ben stands on the other side of the McMullens' door. His forehead is covered in worry lines, and he's out of breath. His car idles in the drive.

"Ben, I'm working," I say with a gentle chuckle. "What are you doing here?"

"The police are going to Marnie's now. If she doesn't answer, they're breaking down the door. I'm headed over there." His shoulders rise and fall.

"Okay, keep me posted." I glance over my shoulder, down the hall and toward the children. They're still eating at the kitchen table, giggling and being perfect little angels. Daphne's footsteps echo from upstairs. She'll be coming down any minute.

"Come with me." He isn't asking.

"Ben." I tilt my head.

"Autumn, I need you." He reaches for me, then stops. "I've never asked for anything from you."

That's a lie.

"Please," he begs, and begging looks horrible on him, but I look into his pale blue eyes, and I know what lies ahead. I picture him seeing his dead sister's body on the ground, lifeless, cold and dressed like a common prostitute. I picture him standing beside her casket, his arm around his mother. Ben checks his watch, then glances at me, his brows lifted as he waits for my answer. The circles under his baby blues tell me he had very little sleep last night, if any at all.

"Fine. Okay." I exhale. As much as I don't want to do this, I know I owe it to him. "Let me go talk to Daphne. I'll be out in a few."

I close the door, turn on my heel, and stop in my tracks when I see Daphne standing at the top of the stairs.

"Who was that?" she asks.

"My boyfriend," I say, fingers intertwined. "There's been a family emergency."

Her brows lift.

"I'm so sorry, Daphne." I place my hand on my chest. "I have to go. I'll try to be back later."

I make a promise I know I can't keep. If we go there and Marnie is dead, I don't know when I'll be back. I'll be expected to remain by Ben's side every waking minute of every hour of every day, at least until the funeral.

"Is everything okay?" she asks, a dumb question from an intelligent woman.

"We think his sister is missing," I say. "No one's been able to reach her for days. The police are going to her house now, and we're going with."

Daphne pulls at the pearls around her neck. "My goodness. That's awful. Yes, go be with him. And keep me posted."

I'm not sure whether she means to keep her posted about Marnie or to keep her posted as to when I'll be returning, but I nod, and promise to, and head toward the kitchen to tell the children I'll see them later.

Grace whines and Rosie asks where I'm going, and Sebastian doesn't seem to care either way.

I grab my purse and pass Daphne in the foyer. She's on the phone, cancelling something, and she waves as I leave.

A moment later, I'm climbing in the passenger seat of Ben's car. His knuckles are white as his hands grip the wheel, and we back out of the long driveway and head east down Linden street under a picturesque canopy of ancient oaks.

He's unusually quiet.

"Have the police said anything?" I ask. "Are your parents back?"

He shrugs. "They've pinged her phone. It's at her place. So either she left it or . . ."

His voice trails, and he doesn't finish his thought, and I don't blame him.

"Maybe she went on that singles cruise, after all?" I can't believe I'm making light of this situation. Maybe it's a defense mechanism? A distraction? My stomach twists harder with each turn we make, leading us closer to Marnie's street. "I doubt they have cell service in the Atlantic Ocean."

"Autumn," he silences me.

"We'll find her," I say, reaching for his hand. I try to pry it off the wheel, but he won't let go.

This isn't him. This isn't Ben at all. I don't know this man. He's sick with worry and fear and doubt and his body is tense, like he's expecting the worst. And he should. His entire world is about to change.

What is it about someone dying that makes people forget that they were deplorable assholes? It's like someone dies, and you only remember the good, even if there wasn't that much good to begin with.

I don't own many pleasant memories of Marnie, but in this moment, my mind is blank. I'm not fixating on how much I hated her or how much she deserved what she got. I'm not ruminating on what a home-wrecking little whore she was or how entitled she felt to Graham or how she blamed Daphne for everything.

My mind is void of a single thought, and it's as if reality is temporarily suspended. I'm not sure how many minutes pass or what songs have been playing on the radio or if the radio was even on. The second we pull into Marnie's parking lot, we see two lit squad cars, a fire truck, and an ambulance.

Marnie's door is wide open.

Two EMTs wheel a stretcher inside.

Everything happens so fast, and before I can stop Ben, he's already out of the car, sprinting toward the door, and he screams. And then I know for sure, one hundred percent, that Marnie's dead.

And I killed her.

CHAPTER FORTY-FOUR

DAPHNE

"OH, GOD. WHAT DO YOU THINK HAPPENED TO HER?" I MUTE THE TV as Graham crumples on the edge of the bed, his eyes rimmed in red. He's distraught over the death of his mistress, and I'm still trying to wrap my head around the fact that she was the sister of our nanny's boyfriend. "Did you know she was connected with Autumn?"

"I tried to end it with her several times, and every time she threatened to kill herself. I went there that night, trying to calm her down."

I don't believe him.

"When I left . . . she was fine. And then Autumn was there."

"So Autumn's the last person to see her alive?"

"I don't know. I don't fucking know." His eyes are bloodshot and he watches the TV, replaying the same segment over and over again.

"Are there cameras in her complex?"

"Why would that matter?"

246

"If they check them and see your vehicle leaving her town-house the night of her death and if anyone finds out you were screwing her, you're going to be a suspect. You know that, right?" I hold zero sympathy for him.

He hides his head in his hands. I don't know whether he's mourning Marnie or mourning the life he's about to give up the second he's named the suspect in her murder.

"What about that guy, the Corvette guy," I say. "You think maybe he did it?"

"I think she killed herself," he says, jaw set. "She always said she was going to do it. Guess she finally followed through."

"Anyway, you need to pull yourself together," I say. "As soon as the police find out you two were together and she was seeing other people, that gives you motive. And as soon as they review the security footage and see you leaving, the case practically solves itself."

"They haven't even said how she died. We don't know anything yet, but I swear to you, Daphne, I didn't do it."

I say nothing, folding a basket of clothes on the bed. I secure a pair of socks together and toss them in the top left drawer of the dresser we share.

"You don't believe me, do you?" There's a rush to his words, a sheer panic.

My mouth hangs, and the truth falls out so easily. "You've told so many lies, Graham. I don't know what to believe."

CHAPTER FORTY-FIVE

THE GOTLIEBS' PERPETUALLY WARM VICTORIAN IS FILLED TO THE brim with people that evening. Someone has placed an 8x10 photograph of Marnie on a coffee table in the living room. She's smiling, clear-skinned, white-smiled, and blonde-haired, and she looks peaceful and young and carefree.

I imagine she's happier now than she was here. Her earthly existence was sad, when I think about it. She lived a self-serving kind of life. In a fucked-up way, maybe I did her a favor.

Anywhere has got to be better than this place.

"Debra, did you want some water?" I offer Ben's mom. She's seated on the sofa, her sister's arm around her, and she glances up at me with bloodshot eyes and a red-tipped nose.

"Please," she manages to say.

I squeeze between the friends and neighbors, past the pastor from the Methodist church and the Gotlieb family doctor, and maneuver through a string of other family members.

Everyone came the second they heard about Marnie. Everyone

248

is crying, saying how they can't get over how tragic this is. How unfair it is that her life was cut so short. And the ones who aren't crying are waxing poetic about all the wonderful times they had with their dear, sweet Marnie.

I wonder if she was ever nice. Maybe she was a nice girl once upon a time? Maybe life turned her bitter and angry and jaded?

Guess I'll never know.

I pour a glass of filtered water for Debra and pass through the dining room on my way back where Ben sits with his father, who hasn't been able to look at anyone all day. He doesn't do well with emotions, Ben says. And Ben, the dutiful son and now only child of Darren and Debra, has yet to leave his side.

"Can I get either of you anything?" I stop to ask, my eyes falling on a pile of crumpled tissues. I'm not sure if they're Ben's or Darren's or both. Ben glances up at me, the rims of his eyes red and watery, and he shakes his head no, so I carry on and bring his mother her glass of water.

"Thank you, sweetheart." Debra takes it from me, and her appreciation breaks my heart. Our hands graze in twisted irony . . . the hand that gave Marnie life touches the hand that took Marnie's life.

I immediately think of Grace. And how I would feel if someone hated her. If someone hurt her. If someone murdered her. My lip trembles, and I close my eyes and turn my back toward Debra.

All the seats in the living room are taken, and I need fresh air anyway, so I head outside and take a seat on the porch swing. Alone. I can't allow myself to feel guilty – not yet. The second I let the guilt take a hold of me, it'll be oozing from every pore and everyone will know, and then all of this will have been for naught.

When I boil this down, I convince myself that I'm not a monster. I did what I had to do to protect my daughter and her family.

A white BMW pulls into the Gotliebs' driveway, and the

driver, a young girl with straight auburn hair, climbs out. She looks like she's been crying, her face puffy and her eyes swollen, but she's pretty, and she looks like the kind of girl Marnie would've run around with, though I never did figure out how many friends Marnie had. Many of them seemed to come and go, fading into the distant background the second they saw her true colors.

She was a tough person to like. It wasn't just me.

"Hi," I say to the girl as she climbs the front steps. Her hands are in her back pocket, and she wears a white cotton tank top with LAGUNA CABANA scrawled across it, the name of a private pool club Marnie always frequented. "Can I help you?"

Her jaw falls and her lips tremble. She tries to speak, then looks down. When she takes a breath, she tries again.

"I'm Megan," she says, "a friend of Marnie's."

She looks like she needs a hug. And she seems nice. And I'm not soulless. So I rise to my feet and wrap my arms around her. She hugs me back, squeezing tight and burying her head against my shoulder. Megan seems like a sweet girl, and I'll never know if Marnie ever knew how lucky she was to have this girl for a friend in a world where most people are shitty dickheads.

"I'm Ben's girlfriend," I say. "Autumn."

Megan pulls away, and for a second, I think it's because Marnie has spoken about me, tarnished my reputation before this girl had a chance to meet me. But she doesn't flinch. She doesn't act repulsed by me. And I realize there's a chance Marnie kept all of that family drama stuff to herself like a good little WASP.

"It's probably not a good time," Megan says, inhaling air like she can't get enough of it. "But I had some information, and I wanted to tell her parents."

"What . . . kind of information?" I ask carefully, ignoring the hard drum of my heart against my lungs. My mouth turns dry, and I can't swallow.

"Autumn was seeing this guy," she says, glancing to the left. She wraps her arms around her sides, her face twisting. She didn't like him. I can tell. "He was married. And he was just using her, if you ask me, but they'd been screwing around for years . . . ever since she interned for him back in college. He'd actually gotten her pregnant once, but she lost the baby. Or that's what she says. Anyway, I couldn't stand him. But she was obsessed. She said they were in love, but I don't see how you could love someone if all you do is fight all the time."

Megan wipes a rogue tear from her cheek.

"I'm rambling," she says with a sad laugh. "I'm sorry."

She runs her palms along her arms. She's trembling, her body overcome with emotion like it's trying to escape from the deepest part of her. These things she's telling me, she feels very strongly about them.

"I hated him," she says, teeth clenched. "He was selfish and arrogant, and he lied about everything all the time. Anyway, I saw Marnie last weekend." Megan shivers. "She was different. She seemed sad and withdrawn. We were supposed to do lunch at Palmetto's Deli a few days ago, but she cancelled. She didn't say why, and I didn't ask. But for the past couple of weeks, she would talk about how this guy was going to leave his wife soon, but he'd been telling her that for months. I think everything was coming to a head, honestly. You know, last year, she threatened to kill herself if he didn't come over immediately and stop her. And he did. He spent several days with her. I think he told his wife he was out of town or something. That was always their cover. They had the strangest relationship, Marnie and Graham. It was like a constant power struggle. I think that's why they fought so much. Anyway, her parents don't know. They don't know any of this." She looks down, jamming the toe of her Converse sneaker into the concrete beneath us.

"Graham, you said?" I study her face and wait for her response, hoping I misheard her. I'm not sure why I'm so surprised. I saw him there. I saw him with my own eyes.

"I gave his name to the police," she says, as if it's no big deal. "I just want them to look into it, just in case. And I wanted to come here and give the Gotliebs a heads up. I don't think they knew about Marnie's boyfriend."

Boyfriend.

Graham McMullen was Marnie's *boyfriend*. Not her married lover. Her *boyfriend*.

The idea of Marnie strutting around in her expensive clothes with her designer handbags and bleach blonde hair, bragging about her married *boyfriend* at lunch with her girlfriends makes me sick to my stomach.

If the police look into this information . . .

And if he gets pinned for her murder . . .

The kids will grow up without a father . . .

And Daphne will be a single mother of three, struggling to make ends meet . . .

And Grace will know a childhood no different from the one I knew . . .

Daphne will struggle, and Grace will suffer for it. All of this will have been for nothing.

The weight of what I've done hits me hard, and I'm sinking. I need to sit, but I'm frozen, unable to move.

"Are they inside?" Megan asks, glancing over my shoulder toward the front door.

"Yeah, but, Megan . . ." I pull in a deep breath. "Now's not a good time to break it to them."

"But maybe it'll give them hope?" Megan's brows lift, and I realize she's probably more idiot than sweetheart, and maybe that's why the two of them were friends. "If they know there's a lead, that there's a chance we could find out who killed Marnie, maybe it'll help?"

"Help what?" I cross my arms. "Marnie is dead. Nothing's going to change that. Marching in there and telling them that their daughter was," I lower my voice to a whisper, "screwing a married man isn't going to make this situation any easier for them to stomach."

Megan looks away, unsatisfied with my answer, but she has to admit I have a point. And besides, if Ben catches wind of Marnie's connection to the McMullens, I'll have no choice but to leave my job with the McMullens, and that can't happen. Not yet. I'm not ready. And Grace needs me.

"Megan, why don't you go inside and offer your condolences," I suggest, "but please don't tell them what you just told me. Let them get through this one step at a time. And if there's something to your little . . . theory . . . I'm sure the police will tell them."

Megan pulls in a breath, her shoulders sinking, and then she nods, as if she trusts me. I stand back and get the door for her. And then I return to the porch swing, burying my head in my hands as the reality of the situation sinks its teeth into me.

Fuck.

CHAPTER FORTY-SIX

MY PHONE RINGS THE NEXT MORNING AS SOON AS I STEP OUT OF the shower. When I told Ben I was going to go to work today, he didn't object. He grunted in bed and rolled over. The poor guy has hardly slept in days. Marnie's funeral is Saturday, and tonight is her visitation.

Everything's happening so fast. The autopsy has been performed and they're waiting on toxicology now. So far no official cause of death has been determined.

"Hello?" I answer after drying my hands. I'm wet from the shower, water soaking the bath mat beneath my feet, and I'm shivering.

"Autumn," Daphne says. "I'm calling to let you know we've decided to send the children to my mother-in-law's for the week. We figured with everything that's happened with your family lately, you could probably use some time off, and we usually send the kids up around this time of year anyway."

"Sure," I say, hiding the disappointment in my voice. I miss

254

those kids. I miss Grace. I just want to hold her, breathe in her soft scent. Hear her impish giggle. "Thank you."

"The kids will be staying until next weekend," she says, her words curt and her tone impatient. "I'll touch base with you then."

She knows about Marnie. In fact, I sent her a text that same day, when Marnie's body was discovered, and Daphne sent a bouquet of yellow roses the following morning. It was thoughtful of her, but I don't understand why she's being so short with me now.

Unless she *knows* about Graham and Marnie and Marnie's connection to me, and somehow I'm guilty by association?

"Sounds good," I say, my gaze flicking to my naked reflection in the mirror. I'm still tan and toned from swimming all summer, but when I meet my own stare, I'm taken aback. I look tired, withered. It's as if my body is reacting to the things my brain chooses to ignore. I'm literally wearing the very feelings I'm trying to suffocate.

I end the call and dry off, slipping into comfortable clothes before crawling back into bed with Ben. He rolls over when he feels the bed dip on my side, and he pulls me into his arms. He's been extra clingy lately. Touchy feely. Quiet, but needing more from me in every sense of the word.

I'm trying to be sympathetic, I am.

I'm trying to be what he needs.

But my mind is preoccupied with this impending maelstrom, and I'm trying to anticipate which direction this is going to go if that's even possible, and I don't have the energy to be his amenable door mat right now.

Ben's phone vibrates on his nightstand, and he pops up, rubbing his eyes. He seems disoriented for a second, and then he follows the sound, reaching a long arm across the bed and plucking it off the table. It drops onto the carpet, bouncing off the edge of the mattress. I never knew one person could make so much noise answering a damn cell phone.

"Hello?" His voice is an exhausted exhalation, and he rolls to his back. "Yes, this is he."

I sit up, trying to hear the other half of the conversation but with zero luck.

Ben climbs out of bed, pacing the room in his sweats and a wrinkled t-shirt, his thumb and forefinger rubbing his eyes as he says things like, "Mm, mm-hm, and really?"

I remain planted, watching as his fist clenches and he exhales and asks, "How long do you think it will take before we know?" and then, "Okay. Perfect. Thank you."

Oh, god.

"Thank you," Ben says just before ending the call. "The preliminary autopsy report will be ready later today."

He turns to me, and I've never seen a grown man cry before, but Ben looks like he's going to cry now. Maybe the phone call made this real for him. Maybe it wasn't enough to see his parents in shambles or to identify his sister's body at the morgue.

He's held it in the last couple of days, but at this point, he's too exhausted to be strong. I open my arms and let him come to me, and he bawls like an actual baby, his entire body convulsing and shaking as he wails. I don't think he knows how to cry in front of anyone. He doesn't hold back. He lets it go. It's an ugly cry, and I hold him tight.

Offering a wordless apology, I kiss his cheek and stroke his hair and let him get it all out.

When he's had his cry, he peels himself off me and stomps to the bathroom. He blows his nose and uses the toilet and washes his hands and brushes his teeth, and when he returns, he perches on the edge of the bed. His eyes are swollen and his face is red and he misses his little sister.

"I'm so sorry, Ben," I whisper into his ear, running my fingertips through his soft, chocolate brown hair.

He pulls away, his brows furrowing now. "Are you, Autumn? Are you sorry?"

"Wh-what?" I lean back when I see the crazy look in his eyes.

"Marnie's dead. And I don't think you give two shits." His accusation is pointed, and it stings.

"You're hurting, Ben. Please don't speak to me like this right n-"

"Everyone knows you hated Marnie." He climbs off the bed, arms crossed and pacing the room again like a crazy person. "You're probably happy she died."

"Can you even hear yourself right now?"

"I've been falling apart, Autumn. Falling apart." He grabs a fistful of his hair and shoots me a look. "And you're taking everything in stride, like it's just another day for you. Fuck, you were even going to go to work today."

I realize now how insensitive that looked.

"I'm sorry," I say. "I'm not good with death. Not a lot of people who were close to me have died. We all respond differently. They say it's good to get back into your normal routine after . . ."

My excuses fall on deaf ears. He's ranting and rambling.

"You don't understand the meaning of family," he says.

"What are you *talking* about?" I fold my arms. "Ben. Come on. Stop it."

I'm beginning to miss the days when we were just Beer and Wings Ben and Girl Next Door Autumn. I took those days for granted, and now here I am.

"I've been with you for two years," he shouts, holding up two fingers. "*Two years*. And you've yet to introduce me to your family."

"Maybe they're not worth meeting," I say without hesitation.

"You don't even talk about them," he continues. "You won't tell me their names, who they are, where they live. It's like they don't exist."

"I never knew that bothered you, Ben. You should've said something. I thought you were okay with the fact that I don't like to talk about my past." I draw my knees up to my chest, making myself appear small, and then I bite my lip, making myself appear scared. And I kind of *am* scared of him right now. He's never behaved this way before.

"Of course it bothers me," he snaps. "But I never brought it up because any hint of a mention of them and you clam up and change the subject."

My eyes avert. I never realized he noticed.

"It's bullshit," he says. "I love *you*, Autumn. I love you so much I was looking at engagement rings two months ago. I love the person you are now. I could give two shits about your past or who you were before. But don't you think not talking about it at all is a little extreme? It's not normal."

He points his finger at his head and turns it, a wordless gesture insinuating that I'm crazy.

"I don't talk about the past because it makes me uncomfortable."

"What, are you going to tell me you had a rough childhood? That you went through some shit? Forgive me for sounding insensitive, but you seem pretty damn well-adjusted now. You don't seem traumatized. You don't seem damaged. Or is it all an act?"

My jaw falls. Ben has never spoken to me this way. I clasp my left hand over my right to try and steady the shaking.

"Listen to yourself right now." There's a tremble in my voice, and in the ground. "You know *nothing*."

"Marnie always said there was something off about you." He stares at a painted portrait on the wall, one we picked up one weekend in Sag Harbor at an art show. He chose it because it reminded him of us. Everything was light and blooming and fresh and new, and that was us, he said. "I defended you every time. And now I'm not so sure. Seeing you lately, how you're acting like it's just another day while my sister's body is frozen in some morgue downtown . . . it disgusts me."

"I'm not a crier, Ben," I say. "When have you ever seen me cry?"

THE MEMORY WATCHER

"You don't have to cry to look sad."

"You don't have to look sad to *be* sad."

He's quiet. And then he lifts his fingers to his chin. "Are you, Autumn? Are you sad?"

"Of course I'm sad," I snip at him, feeling my nose twitch like it has a mind of its own. Once again, my body betrays me.

"Get out." He points to the door, and for a moment, I think he's joking because this is dramatic and over the top and this isn't Ben. He storms to the door, pulling it open so quickly the door knob smacks the wall and the knob leaves an indentation.

I don't gather anything.

I go.

I get the hell out.

I'll come back when he's calmed down.

CHAPTER FORTY-SEVEN

Autumn

I TIPTOE THROUGH THE BACK DOOR SATURDAY MORNING, NOT
expecting to see Ben seated on the sofa, his head in his hands. He
peers up at me, and my body clenches.

"I've been trying to get a hold of you since yesterday," he says.

"You told me to leave," I remind him. He doesn't ask where I
went, and I don't tell him I used his credit card to check into a
five-star hotel in uptown Monarch Falls.

He rises, sighing, and he ambles toward me. "I'm sorry,
Autumn. Yesterday . . . I've never felt that way in my life. And you
were there. And I took it out on you. And I shouldn't have. You're
the love of my life."

He wraps his arms around me. This Ben and yesterday's Ben
are complete strangers who have never met.

I hug him back. "It's okay. You're hurting."

"It's not okay." He buries his face in the crook of my neck and
breathes me in. He smells stale, like he hasn't slept or showered in

over a day. "I'll never speak to you that way again. I promise. I love you so much, Autumn. You're my world."

He's back to clingy again. But clingy is better than crazy, so I'll take it.

"The autopsy is done," he says, pausing and squeezing me tight. His pause nearly gives me a heart attack.

"And?"

"They think she was under the influence," he says.

I exhale. She did smell like wine that night.

"Drugs and alcohol," he adds. "Her blood alcohol content was twice the legal limit, and they found *heroin* in her system."

"Heroin?"

"They think she was on a bender, and that's why we didn't hear from her for days," Ben continues. "They think she fell and hit her head, and that knocked her unconscious, but they suspect it was the heroin that killed her. They won't be able to determine a cause of death for sure until the secondary toxicology report comes in, and that could take a month or two."

"Oh, Ben." I lift my fingers to my lips. I'm shaking for a myriad of reasons, but he doesn't notice. I'm slightly relieved. And horribly confused. "Marnie was a *user*?"

I had *no* idea. Zero. None.

His watery blues lift onto mine. "She was into heroin pretty good back in college. Mom and Dad had to send her away to some place in Malibu a couple times to get help. Guess it's why we were so overprotective of her all the time. We thought she was clean but . . ."

I wrap my arms around him, and he melts into me, taking a second to just exist in the confines of my hold, as if I'm all he needs in this world right now.

None of this makes sense. She seemed drunk that night but nothing else. And she was wearing only a lace nightie. I didn't see track marks on her arms, and there were certainly no questionable odors lingering in the air. And I can't imagine Graham fooling around with a drug-addicted woman. That's not his style.

Then again, what the hell do I know?

Apparently nothing.

Apparently I know absolutely nothing.

CHAPTER FORTY-EIGHT

DAPHNE

"WHEN ARE YOU GOING TO STOP MOPING AROUND?" I TRY TO MAKE the bed this morning but he's still in it. "Someone died. And in some roundabout way, you had something to do with it. Own it. Fix it. Move on."

"Fix it how?" He clearly isn't interested in owning it or moving on.

"I don't know. Go to the police. Tell them you saw Autumn there after you left. Tell them about the affair and make an honest man out of yourself for once. If you didn't do it, you have nothing to worry about."

The house has been empty this week, and I've had more time to myself than I've had in over a decade. It's been glorious. And I've been giving everything some thought, coming up with an exit plan.

I'm going to stick this out a little longer and wait until a few financial matters are handled, and then I'll strike. I'll serve him with divorce papers, clean him out as best as I can. Knowing my exodus is just around the corner gives me hope, and it makes it slightly easier to stomach all this casual discussion about his mistress' untimely end.

"You know we can't let her work for us anymore," he says. "She could be a murderer."

"She isn't a murderer, Graham." I roll my eyes and make my half of the bed, fluffing and arranging pillows. In this world there are sinners and there are saints, and Autumn Carpenter is absolutely the latter.

"Neither am I." His hands fall in his lap, knocking the remote off the bed. Now he'll be forced to get up. "I still think we should let her go. I mean, she was there the night Marnie died and so was I, and maybe that looks bad?"

"Yeah, it looks bad," I say. "But it is what it is, and if you didn't kill Marnie, then you shouldn't be so concerned with how things look. The police will sort it out, I'm sure."

Graham chomps on his thumbnail, an old, disgusting habit I thought I'd broke him of years ago.

"You're right. I should go to the police and tell them everything," he says. "That last article in the paper said that no one had seen her in days, that her friends and family were worried about her, but Autumn was there that night. I saw her."

CHAPTER FORTY-NINE

<small>Autumn</small>

I wake up before my alarm this morning. I haven't seen the McMullen children in over a week, and today they're back. I'm supposed to arrive at my usual time, but it feels like Christmas morning, and the sun's not out yet and already I'm dressed and ready to go.

I flip on the TV in the living room, keeping the volume low. Ben's still upstairs sleeping. He's taking bereavement leave from now until further notice. His boss told him to take as much time as he needs and that everything will be covered until he gets back.

Marnie's funeral was last week, and it was an awkwardly beautiful disaster to say the least. It was nothing but pink roses and baby's breath, and Debra hired a string quartet to play the most depressing classical music I've ever heard. Chopin, I think most of it was? It felt more like a morose wedding-for-one than a funeral, and it went on forever. People came out of the woodwork to talk about Marnie Gotlieb, to share fond memories, and fawn over the beautiful soul she once was.

As soon as the service was over and everyone moved to the community hall for refreshments, I snuck out back and bummed a cigarette from a cousin of theirs, Payton. She was tall and lanky and wore too much black eyeliner. She was maybe nineteen and the cigarettes were slim and wrapped in black paper and tasted like strawberries, but I was grateful for the company the second she said, "God, she was a fucking bitch, wasn't she?"

We laughed, then Payton cried a little. And then she lit another cigarette, offering me a drag.

I told her no thanks and continued to puff on the first one she gave me. I didn't inhale. Smoking is stupid. I just needed something to do. I needed to escape everything happening inside.

Payton and I talked about how lovely Marnie looked in her casket, dressed in white like she was some kind of angel. And then Payton told me stories from their childhood. Marnie used to tease her and tell her she was ugly and that she needed a boob job and her nose fixed, and then Marnie filled the family full of rumors about Payton, getting them all to believe she was depressed and taking street drugs, which led her family to find a bag of magic mushrooms she'd been hiding in her room for months (because someone gave them to her but she was too afraid to take them), which then led to Payton being sent away to some military school for a year.

Fucking Marnie.

Payton's stories made me feel better, and I silently thanked her for being the realest person there. I told her never to change as we headed inside, and she looked at me with the most quizzical look I'd ever seen. But I get it. When you're young like Payton, all you want to do is change.

It'll make sense to her someday, when she's older and I'm long gone and she can't, for the life of her, remember my name.

I head to the McMullens around a quarter to nine. It's raining, so I bring my umbrella and watch for puddles on the sidewalk.

There'll be no swimming today, which is a shame because I know how much the children love to play in the pool.

Daphne answers the door in a floral robe. It's paper thin and clings to her frame, which is looking gaunter than usual. She isn't wearing makeup and her hair is pulled back into a low bun. I hardly recognize her.

She waves me in, staring at the pouring rain behind me. The sound of the wind and rain rustling the leaves on the trees is one of my favorite things to listen to. As a young girl, I used to stare out the window whenever it would storm, watching the way the rain made everything clean again.

"Did the kids have a nice time in . . ." I know where her mother lives. Albany. But I only know that from Instaface.

"Albany," Daphne tells me what I already know as she re-ties her robe. "Yes. They had a wonderful time."

She doesn't seem to want to engage in conversation, and when she moves to the foot of the stairs, she rests her hand on the banister and turns to face me.

"The kids are eating breakfast in the nook," she says. Her stare lingers, her gaze narrowing in my direction. "You knew that girl? That one who died?"

I nod. "Marnie Gotlieb?"

"Yes."

"She was my boyfriend's sister."

Daphne's eyes flick to a painting on the wall. "So sad. Do they know . . . do they know the cause yet?"

I shake my head. "They have an idea, but it's going to be a while before the final toxicology report comes in. Thank you for sending the roses by the way."

"Of course." Daphne presses her lapels together then flattens her palm against her chest. She says nothing more as she climbs the stairs and disappears around the corner at the top.

When I find the children, they're seated with their father. I'm shocked to see Graham since he's usually at work by now, but he's sandwiched between Grace and Sebastian and he's dressed in sweats. His hair is messy and there are bags under his eyes. He looks as if he hasn't slept in ages.

"Morning," I say, taking a seat across from him.

He reaches for a mug, pours some black coffee, and takes a careful sip. "Morning, Autumn."

He doesn't look at me. I bet he knows. I bet Daphne mentioned to him that I'm connected to "that girl who died" that the whole town won't shut up about for two seconds.

"We missed you, Autumn!" Grace comes to my side, giving me a hug, and Rosie brings me a picture she drew last week that she'd saved just for me. Sebastian gives me a smile from across the table.

"I've missed you too," I tell them. My gaze passes over them all, landing on Graham who's staring vacantly ahead, unblinking. Without saying a word, he rises and shuffles to the sink, pouring out what remains of his coffee and heading out of the kitchen. His house slippers scuff on the hardwood, his feet dragging. Grace watches him, her expression laced with worry. I give her an extra hug and ruffle her hair until she smiles.

"I wanted to stay here with you, Autumn," Grace tells me, her voice a soft whisper. "Mommy wouldn't let me. She said we had to go to Grandma's."

"It's okay to spend time with your grandmother," I tell her.

Her lips bunch at the side and she rolls her eyes. "Not when she's mean."

"I doubt she's mean."

"She doesn't like kids," she says.

I laugh. "Sure she does."

I glance up to see Daphne standing in the doorway, fully clothed. Her complexion is warmer now, blush on her cheeks and mascara on her lashes. Her lips are tinted in a healthy shade of pink, and she's wearing expensive yoga attire.

Grace returns to her seat and grabs her spoon, returning to her bowl of oatmeal with zero commentary.

"Children and their stories." Daphne chuckles, gathering her keys and wallet and placing them inside a new purse by the desk hutch in the far corner of the kitchen. "You can't believe everything they tell you."

"Isn't that the truth?" I ask with a natural chortle. I don't tell her I believe Grace. I don't tell her that Grace is keen and observational, and she reminds me of myself as a child. Grace doesn't miss a thing.

"I'm heading to yoga," she says, as if the hundred-dollar Lululemon pants didn't give it away. "And then I'm heading to the farmer's market. I'll be back around noon."

"Sounds good." I give her a wave and watch her disappear behind the garage entrance door.

"Autumn, can we play Barbies?" Rose asks.

"Take your dish to the sink, please, sweet girl," I say. "And yes. Once everyone is finished with breakfast, we can play Barbies."

Fifteen minutes later, the kitchen has been cleaned and wiped down and the dishes have been loaded in the dishwasher, and the children are quietly watching Sesame Street in the family room. I grab a box of Barbies from the toy chest and spread them out in the middle of the room. The girls, and Sebastian, lunge for them, divvying them up like baseball cards.

I take a seat on the sofa, watching them play.

I love that Grace has a little sister, and I hope they're always going to be this close. I'd always wanted a sister growing up. An instant friend. A constant companion. Instead I had a jerk brother who made it his personal mission to make my life as miserable as possible.

"How could you do this to me?"

I glance down to see Grace holding a Ken in her left hand and a Barbie in her right. Barbie is shaking, and I imagine she's the one doing the "talking."

"It's always about you, isn't it?" Grace says, shaking Ken. She lifts his arm, making him point at Barbie. Barbie responds by slapping Ken across the face. "When did you stop loving me?"

My heart stops hard, and I'm glued, watching Grace act out an exchange that is better suited for two contentious adults. This kind of conversation would never originate in the mind of a ten-year-old.

"I sacrificed everything for you, and this is how you repay me?" Grace makes Barbie slap Ken a second time, and I'm stunned.

Does Daphne strike Graham? And does she do it in front of the children? Did this happen when they thought no one was looking? Did a fight prompt them to send the kids away for all of last week?

"You stopped loving me years ago," Ken says via Grace. She repositions Barbie. "That's not true. I never stopped. And for some insane reason, I still love you."

"Grace?" I interrupt her little exchange, and she whips around, her cheeks glowing warm when she realizes I'd been watching her. "Everything okay with your Barbies?"

I offer a humored chuckle, and she tucks her chin against her chest.

"They're fighting," she says.

"I see that." I lift my brows. "Did you see that on TV? Were you watching soap operas with your grandma last week?"

She bites her lower lip, choosing not to answer me. And then she turns around, her back toward me, and reaches for another Barbie.

"Hey, guys, you want to go swimming?" the new Barbie asks via Grace. "Okay, let's go to the pool today! I can drive us. My car's over here."

She's embarrassed.

And I shouldn't have pried.

But now I know.

Trouble in paradise is officially a tropical storm.

———

THE CEILING FAN WHIRS OVERHEAD THAT NIGHT. BEN'S WEIGHT IS over on top of me, sinking me into the mattress as he plows away. He grunts and groans and sweats, shoving himself in and out of me, and I dig my nails into his back the way he likes, but I'm not here. And I hardly feel a thing.

Earlier today, Daphne came home from running errands and Grace ran up to her to give her a hug. Daphne rolled her eyes, telling Grace her hands were full and she'd have to wait. Grace waited patiently, and when she finally got her hug, it lasted all of two seconds before Daphne flitted off to the next thing.

Later in the afternoon, Grace drew Daphne a picture of the two of them. She was so proud and had taken so much time and added so much detail. Daphne halfheartedly asked why her hair was green and then set it aside on top of a stack of mail.

Before I left the McMullens today, Grace pulled me aside and hugged me, the way she normally does, and then she whispered in my ear, "I wish you were my Mommy."

A wave of emotion rolled over me, and I could hardly keep myself together. If she only knew. If she only knew how connected we were, how I'm the one who gave her life. If she only knew how badly I wanted to be her mother when I had the chance.

I gave her away because I loved her. And because I had no other choice.

Ben pistons harder and faster, a sign that this will be over in 5 . . . 4 . . . 3 . . . 2 . . .

He finishes with a groan and lingers inside me until he softens. His lips press against my neck, our skin sticking together until he rolls to the side and then disappears in the bathroom. And I lie awake, all night, thinking about all the ways I could make Grace mine again.

We would need new identities. And we'd probably have to leave the country. Maybe I could sneak her to Mexico. Or Cuba. I'd have to cash out my 401k and what's left of my savings, but that should be enough. Maybe I can convince Daphne to let me take Grace somewhere . . . to the mall or to get her ears pierced. And we'll just go. We'll get in the car and drive and drive, and we'll change our hair and buy a used car along the way and throw them off our scent.

I imagine Grace in the seat beside me, giggling and playing with the radio, and I'd let her listen to anything she wanted. And I'd tell her the truth. I'd tell her everything. I'd tell her I am her mother, her real mother, and I'd tell her no one has ever nor will they ever love her half as much as I do. I'll tell her that Graham and Daphne haven't been doing a very good job, and that it was time for me to take care of her now.

She'll understand.

And she'll grin.

And then she'll ask for mint chocolate chip ice cream.

And I'll teach her Spanish in the car.

And when we get to the border, we'll adopt new names.

Maybe I'll be Maria and she can be Eva.

And we'll have our entire lives ahead of us.

We can make our way to Panama via Costa Rica and Nicaragua.

No one will ever find us.

And we'll be happy.

And loved.

Ben climbs into bed beside me, smelling like soap and cinnamon toothpaste, and he slips his arm over my hips and pulls me against him. Ever since last week, when he freaked out on me and told me to leave, he's been overcompensating.

But his words still echo, playing on repeat in my mind in

certain still, small hours. Everything he's ever wanted to say to me came blurting out in a fit of rage. He thinks I'm different. He thinks I'm cold and that I don't know what the meaning of family is.

I may not have had the perfect upbringing. I didn't have a mother who remembered every birthday and never missed a basketball game. I didn't have a father who taught me how to drive. I didn't have a close group of friends or a brother who chased away bullies.

It was always me.

And fuck Ben for judging me.

I tuck my pillow under my arm, thinking of Grace snuggled warm in her bed. I pretend I'm beside her, breathing in her sweet, perfumed hair and the fabric softener scent of her cotton pajamas. I imagine my arm around her. And I imagine her whispering, "Goodnight, Mommy" as she drifts to sleep.

CHAPTER FIFTY

AUTUMN

"AUTUMN, CAN YOU COME IN HERE FOR A SECOND, PLEASE?"
Daphne calls for me the next day, moments before my
shift ends.

"Of course." I make sure the kids are busy in the family room,
and I meet her in the foyer.

"I don't know how to tell you this."

My stomach sinks. I can't breathe. She's firing me. This has to
do with Marnie, I just know it. Fucking Marnie fucking me over
even when she's fucking dead.

Oh, god.

"Graham and I have decided to enroll the kids in a summer
educational program," she says, clasping her hands in front of her
waist, her mouth tugged into a phony frown. "We think the children need more structure and more interaction with other kids.
You're not doing anything wrong, you should know that. And this
was a last-minute decision. There's a program at Brinkman Academy, and they just had a family leave, so three spots opened for us.

We've been on the wait list, but I had no idea they'd be placing us so soon."

None of that makes any of this easier to swallow.

The foyer walls spin, Daphne's marble console and oil paintings and flower urns melting into a dizzying shade of cream.

"Autumn." Daphne places her hand on my shoulder, and it's cold, bony. "We'll still pay you for the remainder of the summer. This isn't about money."

No. It's not. It's not about money at all.

Daphne hands me my bag and offers an apologetic smile.

"I almost forgot." She disappears into the kitchen and returns with a check written for eight thousand dollars; lost wages and then some.

"Daphne." My lip trembles. I don't want to cry in front of her, but this is the absolute worst thing that could've happened to me today.

"You can see the children whenever you'd like," she says. "I know you have quite the bond with them. Grace informed me last night that she would rather you be her mother than me."

Daphne snickers, glancing away, and I wonder if *that* is what this is all about.

I'll never know.

"Is there any way you could reconsider?" I ask, feeling my chest rise and fall in quick succession. "The kids are so attached to me now, and we've really settled into a good rhythm."

"Thank you for everything." Daphne takes a step toward the door, ignoring my plea, and I take the hint. "You've been amazing, really. If you ever need a reference or letter of recommendation, I'd be happy to help."

"What if they attended part-time?" I ask. "And I watched them the other half of the time? I'm just worried about the kids, Grace in particular. She doesn't seem to do well with changes in her routine."

"Grace will be fine. The staff at Brinkman happens to be very familiar with her." Daphne pulls the front door wide, and her eyes trail toward the sidewalk before returning to me. She wants me to leave, and she's growing impatient with this conversation. "Thanks again, Autumn. Enjoy the rest of your summer."

I take the first step, my back toward the McMullen's home, and the soft click of the door and the clink of the lock follows a moment later.

I'm stunned and speechless, my hands trembling and the check shaking. I walk home in a daze, and when I turn the corner of Linden and Maple, the tears spill down my cheeks. I can't contain them any longer.

My daughter.

My Grace.

Just like that . . . I've lost her all over again.

The sidewalk turns into Willow street, and our home is up ahead. Ben is home. He's going to see me crying. And he's going to want to know what happened. And I won't even be able to give him an answer because I don't fucking know.

Moments pass and I find myself standing before the front door, swallowing the thick, mid-summer's air and drying my cheeks on the back of my hands. I can hear the TV inside, and through the curtains, I see Ben perched on the sofa, his elbows on his knees and his face squinting at the screen. He needs glasses, but he refuses.

Twisting the knob, I step inside and brace myself for a million questions and a giant Ben hug.

"Autumn." He seems surprised to see me, naturally. I'm home slightly earlier than he expected. Ginger runs to my side, and I drop my purse on the console table by the front door, and then Ben rises, his body twisting to the side as he grabs something off the sofa beside him.

A box.

Not just any box.

My secret McMullen box.

From beneath my bed in the guest room.

"You want to tell me what the *hell* this is?" he asks.

There are no words for this moment.

I have no explanation–at least none that would appease him.

"These pictures. These things. They all belong to that family, don't they?" he asks, flipping the lid of the box open. "There's jewelry in here. Addresses. Recipe cards. Pieces of mail. Small toys. Crayons. What the fuck, Autumn? Why do you have all of this stuff? Are you stealing from them?"

I close my eyes. At this point, stealing for the sake of stealing almost seems like the lesser of two evils. And maybe it's something he would understand, as opposed to the truth of the matter.

"Cut ties with them," he commands. "You're done working for them or it's over between us. And throw this shit away."

I don't tell him Daphne fired me. There's no point.

Ben is all I have now.

My lip quivers. "Okay."

CHAPTER FIFTY-ONE

Daphne

"I'm going to have to say something to Sebastian's teacher," I tell Graham over lunch. "That's the second swear word he's said in the last two weeks. I thought Brinkman had higher standards. Maybe they let just anyone into the summer program now, I don't know."

Graham nods, spooning his soup and staring vacantly into the bowl of steaming liquid.

"And they come home filthy every day," I add. "Dirty fingernails, stained clothes."

"Talk to the headmaster," Graham suggests, and I will, but for now I want to vent. I miss Autumn, and I miss the days when we could roll out of bed and not have to cart the kids anywhere and hope and pray that we get them there on time, but this is the way it had to be.

Graham went to the police. He told them about the affair. And he told them he was there the night Marnie died. And then he told them about Autumn. It's only going to be a matter of time before they look into her as a suspect, and if she were to find out Graham was the one who dropped her name at the detective's feet, it just seemed like a conflict of interest to have her continue to watch the children.

"I miss having a nanny," I say, forking through my salad and picking out the acceptable parts.

"It's good for them to be around other kids," Graham says. He seems to be going through the motions these days, dissonant and distracted. He's still mourning her. His heart is broken.

I still have zero sympathy for his loss. The entire situation is tragic, and I feel for that young girl's family, but I don't feel for Graham. In fact, if anything, I'm frustrated with him for moping around like a piece of *him* died that night.

"Anyway, I thought we could try to sneak away next week-end?" I try to place excitement in my tone, but the truth is I'm anything but.

All I can do right now is make him think we're going to recover, that we're finally putting all the pieces back together. He still has no idea I'll be leaving him soon, and I'm afraid the slightest little slip might set him off.

When you're about to go to war with someone, the last thing you want to do is tip them off so they can prepare for battle.

If he knows I'm filing, he's going to move money around, hide it away, and screw me over.

Divorce is strategic.

Hell, *love* is strategic.

Whipping my phone from my purse, I snap a picture of our bread basket and the adorable little butter pats cut and molded into sea stars, and then I post it to Instaface with the hashtag *#lunchdate #daydate* and *#lovemyhubby*.

Forty likes instantly.

My social media game has been sorely lacking these last few weeks, and I blame him and this massive squall he's roped us into.

But my mood is hit with the start realization that I'm probably wasting my energy.

If for some completely insane reason Graham gets blamed for Marnie's murder, her family will sue for wrongful death and take us for everything we have, and then all of this will have been for nothing.

CHAPTER FIFTY-TWO

AUTUMN

BEN HAS BEEN DETACHED THESE LAST TWO WEEKS EVER SINCE HE found the box under the bed. Sometimes when he looks at me, it's as if he's looking at me for the first time. I feel him studying me when he thinks I'm not paying attention, and at dinner, when we eat together, he's quiet and stiff.

"Marnie's headstone is up," he says out of the blue after dinner tonight.

"Oh, yeah?" I glance up at him. He's seated in his armchair, the one Marnie always used to steal when she'd come over, and he's staring blankly ahead at the flash of the TV screen.

"Thought we could go pay some respects tonight." His words are monotone.

"Of course." I rise from the table and finish cleaning up our dinner mess. He doesn't offer to help, but that's nothing new. "Give me ten?"

I keep my voice chipper and light. Now I'm the one compensating these days.

"I'll be in the car." He disappears into the garage after slipping into his sneakers, and I hear the door rise and the engine start.

Shoving the last of the dishes into the dishwasher, I grab my purse and slip into some flats and meet him out there.

He's quiet as we drive toward Crestwood Lawns Cemetery, his knuckles white around the steering wheel. He's like that lately: tense and overwrought. Always on edge. We stop at a flower shop on the way and grab a dozen pink roses, and then we continue on our way, finding a parking spot beneath a weeping willow when we arrive. We glance around for Marnie's spot, and it takes us a while to find our bearings. It looks different now, without the tent and the chairs and the blinding midday sun, but we find a fresh mound of dirt covered by patchy grass and a shiny, granite headstone bigger than all the ones around it.

I follow Ben, keeping a careful distance behind. I don't know if he wants me to hold his hand or give him space, so I keep back. He'll let me know if he needs me. The second he reaches her site, he lowers himself to his knees, placing one hand on top of the stone while the other traces her name.

MARNIE ELIZABETH GOTLIEB - *Beloved daughter, sister, and friend*

There's her chiseled-in-stone likeness that oddly makes her look more like Anna Nicole Smith than Marnie Elizabeth Gotlieb, and next to that are chiseled flowers and a cross.

My chest squeezes. For him. For Ben. Only for Ben.

Any day now we should be hearing back on the final toxicology report. I'm still scratching my head over the heroin in her system.

Approaching her stone, I lean the bouquet of roses against it and step back, jamming my hands in my pockets. Ben hides his face from me, as if I haven't seen him cry a dozen times in the past weeks, and I take that as a sign that he needs me to give him space again.

Peering around the cemetery, my eyes catch a mausoleum in

the distance. It looks like it's been there for a million years, with creeping vines growing over the door and a giant oak giving it shade and shelter.

A shadow moves behind the limestone façade, and when I look again, I see the profile of a man standing beside it. Stepping away from Marnie's site, I move closer because it feels like he's watching us, and I wonder if it's one of her many ex-lovers.

He disappears behind the building the closer I get, so I walk faster, my shoes snapping small twigs in the grass with each step.

"Hey," I call out, keeping my voice low.

When I reach the mausoleum, I expect him to be gone, but he's standing there, leaning against an exterior wall, and when our eyes lock, he says my name.

"Graham, what the hell are you doing here?" I ask, my yell more of a whisper.

His eyes water, and he glances down. There's a small bouquet of flowers, mostly daisies, in his hand, and he says nothing. And now I know. He loved her. For some completely insane reason that I'll never understand, Graham loved her.

"I know you were having an affair," I say.

His eyes lift onto mine.

I don't dare tell him I saw him there the night she died for the same reason police don't go around yapping about all the evidence they have when they're trying to solve a major investigation.

"How?" He seems genuinely shocked, and his eyes search mine. He's contemplating something.

"One of her friends," I say. "She mentioned it."

He's shaking, paler than usual, and it's as if he's been reduced to a fraction of the successful, confident man he once was. There's a bluish tint beneath his eyes. He isn't sleeping.

"Did you know Marnie was using?" I ask.

His blue eyes flick into mine and then narrow. "No. Using what?"

"Heroin." I cross my arms.

Graham shakes his head with vehement force. "Never. I . . . never. No. Marnie wasn't like that."

"Are you sure? Because the night she died, she had a lethal dose of heroin in her system." I don't know that for sure, but I'm testing him. Baiting him the way cops do during interrogations. If you make him think you're one step ahead of them already, often times you'll get a confession where there once was none.

"I'm one hundred percent positive," he says carefully, "that she was not on drugs. I've known her for years. I *loved* that woman. I knew her, inside and out. Hell, I was going to . . ."

His voice tapers off. I already know what he was going to say, and he knows better than to finish his thought in front of me.

"Don't tell Daphne any of this." His eyes plead, and he isn't asking. "Autumn, it's very important that you not tell anyone I was here."

I cross my arms. "Why, Graham?"

"Because-"

"*No,*" I cut him off. "*Why?* Why would you do any of this? Cheat on your beautiful wife? Abandon your beautiful children? I don't understand. You have no idea how good you have it, and you were going to throw it all away for a piece of ass."

His jaw hangs. I've rendered him speechless. He's never seen me like this. This isn't pliable, amenable Autumn who used to watch his children with a benign, helpful smile on her face. This is angry Autumn who was wrongfully terminated from her job because the children were getting too attached and/or the McMullens were worried about an outsider having a front row seat to the dissolution of their picture-perfect marriage. This is broken, jaded Autumn who feels disenfranchised because the one thing she loved more than anything in the world turned out to be a carefully crafted mirage.

"You don't know me." Graham scoffs, folding his arms and looking away. "You have no idea what my life is like."

"You'd be surprised. I know a hell of a lot more than you think I do."

He laughs. He doesn't believe me. "Let me guess. You follow my wife on social media. God, we look like the perfect little family, don't we? All dressed up. Smiling. Laughing. Happily married. Adorable little hashtags."

My chest burns.

"Pictures lie, Autumn," he says. "Especially when the person taking them is the biggest manipulator of them all."

"What are you talking about?" I glare at him. I refuse to believe his little manipulations. He's delusional and he's grieving and he's trying to believe his own lies, that Marnie was worth it all.

His fist clenches in the air. "I wish you knew Daphne the way I know her."

"Daphne is a wonderful person. She loves those children. And she loves you. And she works so hard to-"

"You know nothing. You see only what she allows you to see."

"Autumn!" Ben calls for me in the distance.

Shit.

"I have to go," I say.

He calls my name again, louder. He's getting closer. I can't let him see Graham, and I sure as hell can't let him see me talking to him.

I jog around the mausoleum and flag him down, walking in his direction to keep him from walking in mine.

"Hey, sorry," I say, slightly winded.

"Where'd you go?" He scratches at his temple, his other hand hooked on the loop of his jeans.

"I was just walking around . . . I thought I'd give you some time alone."

He squints for a second, then reaches for my hand. "I wanted you here, with me. I needed you."

"I'm sorry." Sliding my palm against his, our fingers interlace, and I follow him back to the car. "You're so quiet lately. I'm not sure what you want from me half the time."

He looks up as we walk, toward a pond surrounded with ducks and geese. "I just want you to be you."

Ben stops, turning to face me.

"Can you do that for me?" he asks.

I don't know.

"After the other week . . . I feel like we're strangers all over again." His voice is low and calm. We reach his car, and he opens the door for me, something he never does. "I feel like I need to get to know you all over again, Autumn. Maybe we could start over?"

"Start over?"

"Yeah," he says.

"Ben, you already know me." I playfully nudge his arm. "None of this makes sense."

"See, I don't feel like I do. Not anymore."

"What are you talking about?" I laugh, and I'm nervous, and I'm not sure why he's acting so strange all of a sudden. "You've had a rough day. Let's go home and relax. Maybe we can watch that show you like with that superhero guy, yeah?"

Ben nods, and I climb into the car, buckling up. He doesn't speak much on the way home except to ask if I want to get out of Monarch Falls for a few hours tomorrow.

I tell him I do, that getting away for a while sounds nice.

And he holds my hand, but he doesn't give it a squeeze and he doesn't tell me he loves me. In fact, he hasn't told me he loves me in almost two weeks, now that I think about it.

We're both ready . . . ready to get back to the way things were before. And maybe that means different things to each of us, but one thing's for sure, we can't keep treading these same murky waters. We have to move on. We have to move forward. And maybe I was wrong about Ben. Maybe he's the best I'm ever going to do. Maybe I could learn to love him fully, completely, the way he loves me.

CHAPTER FIFTY-THREE

AUTUMN

THERE'S A POLICE CAR PARKED IN FRONT OF OUR HOUSE WHEN WE get home Saturday afternoon. We spent all day in Harmony Springs shopping and dining and catching a matinee like it was any other day, and the last thing I expected was to come home to this.

Ben says nothing as he pulls into the driveway, and two officers climb out of a squad car. A third, in plain clothes, steps out of an unmarked Crown Victoria.

"What's all this?" I ask Ben.

"No clue." His brows furrow as he watches them through the rearview mirror, and then he kills the engine and steps out. When he heads toward them, he extends his hand. "Officers?"

"We're looking for an Autumn Carpenter," the first officer says. A voice comes over his radio, and he adjusts the volume as he looks at me.

I press my finger into my chest, feeling the weight of their collective stares. "I'm Autumn. What's going on?"

"We need to bring you in for questioning," he says, his hands hooked on his duty belt.

"Questioning? Can I ask what this is about?" I release an awkward chuckle.

"We're investigating the death of Marnie Gotlieb," he says, his eyes flicking to Ben.

"Are the toxicology results in?" Ben asks, stepping toward them.

"They just came in yesterday," he says.

"Why didn't anyone call me? Have my parents been called? Why am I just now being told?" Ben exhales, speaking a million miles a minute.

"The final cause of death hasn't been determined yet, but we're suspecting foul play so we're doing some preliminary investigating," he says.

"What does Autumn have to do with any of this?" Ben's question is genuine, and I love him for that.

"She was seen at Marnie's townhouse the night of the . . . incident." The officer shifts his weight, his eyes moving between the two of us.

"Of course she was," Ben says. "I asked her to check on my sister. We hadn't heard from her in days, and we sent Autumn over to knock on her door."

"Ben, it's fine." I turn toward him and place my hand on his chest. He's getting worked up, and I don't want this to become a big thing. "I'll go talk to them. They probably just need a simple statement for their investigation." I turn to the cop. "Isn't that right?"

"Yes, ma'am," he says.

"See?" My hand smooths over his chest and down his arm until it finds his fingers, and I give them a squeeze. "I'll be back as soon as I can, okay? We'll get everything figured out."

Ben closes his eyes slowly, tucks his chin, and then nods. "Sure. Yeah. You need me to come with?"

"No, it's okay. I'll ride with them." I lift on my toes and cup his face in my hands and kiss his tight lips, and then I say, "I love you."

"I love you too."

This can only go one of two ways.

CHAPTER FIFTY-FOUR

DAPHNE

THE KIDS ARE SWIMMING OUT BACK WHEN GRAHAM COMES HOME. The police called him in today for more questioning.

"How'd it go?" I ask.

"I told them everything," he says. "Again. Hopefully they took better notes this time."

"Do you think it was Autumn?" I watch him closely.

He shrugs. "To think. she was watching our kids all summer and she may have been a murderer."

"Do you honestly believe that? I just don't see it."

"She was the last one to see her alive. I'm just saying, you never know." He shrugs, dipping his hands in his pockets. The kids splash and giggle before us. "You know they're saying on the news she had drugs in her system. They're thinking it might be an over-dose. Did you know you were screwing a girl who did drugs?"

"I had no idea. She never seemed . . ."

"Anyway, I'm tired of talking about this. About *her*. You've put me through enough, don't you think? I hope next time you'll kindly think twice before removing your dick from your pants in the company of women to whom you're not married." I rise. "Watch the kids, please? I'm going to go inside and start dinner."

Graham sinks into a lounge chair, arms folded across his chest and staring toward the pool. Seeing him so miserable makes me feel incredibly vindicated. Knowing he can never see her or touch her or kiss her fills me to the brim with quiet satisfaction.

This is karma.

And this is the end and the beginning of it all.

CHAPTER FIFTY-FIVE

Autumn

THEY'VE STUCK ME IN AN EIGHT BY TEN ROOM WITH A TWO-WAY mirror, and despite the fact that they've offered me coffee and water and told me to let them know if I'm too hot or too cold or hungry or if I need a break ...

They're being very accommodating, so that has to be a good sign.

One of the detectives, Barnes is his name, pulls his chair out and plops down, sending a whoosh of cheap cologne in my direction. He's averagely attractive, with thick, sandy hair and eyes that smile even when he isn't. A plain gold wedding band rests on his left ring finger, and he seems like the kind of man who plays catch with his sons after work and kisses his wife goodnight every night and tells her he loved her lasagna even if it wasn't her best.

"So Autumn." He pulls out a yellow legal pad, flipping to a fresh page, and clicks the end of a cheap ballpoint pen.

"Yes?" I fold my hands on the table in front of me, eyes alert.

"What can you tell me about the night of Marnie Gotlieb's death?" he asks.

I drag in a lungful of stale air and release it, buying time. I don't want to seem too rehearsed or too quick-on-the-draw.

"Ben was out of town for work," I say. "He called and asked me to check on her. I drove across town, knocked on her door, and she didn't answer, so I left."

He's quiet. He doesn't take down notes. When he pinches the bridge of his nose, I worry I've fucked up somehow.

"Autumn, I'm going to cut to the chase here," he says, squaring his shoulders. He doesn't look like a nice guy anymore. He looks like a guy who's had a long day and is stuck working on a Saturday when he'd rather be watching his boys play ball, and he looks like he doesn't have time for any bullshit. Specifically, my bullshit. "Someone saw you at Marnie's that night."

"Right. I checked on her. Like I said."

"No," he cuts me off. "They saw you go into her home."

"Who?" I laugh, though I want to cry. "What did they claim they saw?"

"Our witness saw you enter Ms. Gotlieb's townhome. They said you were in there for about ten, maybe fifteen minutes. And they saw you run out after that."

I glance down, picking at my fingernails and racking my brain.

The only other person there that night who could've possibly seen me was Graham. Had it been one of her lovers or one of her friends, they wouldn't have recognized me. They wouldn't have been able to give my name to the police because they wouldn't have had it.

"It was Graham McMullen, wasn't it?" I ask.

I hate to throw him under the bus and I understand the repercussions of that, but right now, it's either him or me, and it sure as hell isn't going to be me.

"How do you know Graham McMullen?" The detective sinks back in his chair, playing dumb.

"I worked for his family this summer," I say. "I saw him that night, leaving Marnie's."

"Did you talk to him?"

"No."

"Did you tell anyone else that you saw him?"

"No."

"Did you take a picture? Do you have evidence?"

"Do I need evidence?" I scoff. "Clearly he told you that he saw me, so you know he was there too. I hope to God you're questioning him better than you're questioning me, because that's where your focus should be."

He doesn't respond. His pen scribbles against the paper.

"What do you know about Marnie Gotlieb and Graham McMullen?" he asks.

"Um," I glance up at the ceiling tiles. They're stained and mismatched. "They'd been sneaking around for a couple of years, from what I've heard. They fought a lot. He was thinking of leaving his wife for her. That's about all I know. Did Megan talk to you? She's the one you want to talk to. She was one of Marnie's friends. She knows more about their relationship than I do."

"Mm hm." Detective Barnes brushes his hand against his mouth as he takes notes. "Okay, real quick, let's circle back to that night. I'm curious, Autumn. Why did you tell Ben Marnie wasn't home? The way it looks now, you're the last person who saw her alive. You understand withholding evidence is a serious crime, don't you?"

I hunch over, resting my elbows on the table and staring him straight in the eyes.

"You don't understand the Gotliebs," I say. "I was only trying to protect them. I went inside to check on her after Graham left. She was drunk and belligerent, and I was trying to get her to calm down before she hurt herself. And she said that. She said she wanted to hurt herself. She wasn't making any sense. I didn't tell her family because I didn't want them to know that in their daughter's final hours, she was sleeping with a married man, drinking hard liquor, and threatening violence."

"I understand you wanted to spare the family, but you should have come to the police," he says. I don't like his tone. He's scolding me, and I'm not a child. "You understand how this looks, don't you?"

My brows meet. "No?"

"You and Marnie had a bit of a contentious relationship, isn't that right? The two of you didn't ever really see eye to eye?"

I see he's spoken to Ben's mom.

"There was some friction at times," I say. "Early on. But we grew closer. We sort of let things happen naturally, slowly. No, we weren't best friends. But did I wish she were dead? Absolutely not."

My voice trembles the harder he stares at me.

"Do you have any idea who would've wanted to hurt her?"

"Not at all," I fire back. "So are you ruling this a homicide now?"

He covers his mouth and exhales. "We are, Autumn."

"I don't understand. What changed?"

"Toxicology showed a lethal dose of heroin in her system shortly before her death. And pathology showed she'd been clean up until then."

My hand flies to my mouth, and I'm engulfed in genuine shock.

Someone *did* murder Marnie.

And it wasn't me.

And I'll be damned if I go down for it.

"Marnie didn't have a lot of enemies," he says. "At least not from what we've been able to find. She didn't really have a lot of friends either. The numbers in her phone mostly belonged to . . . men."

Tell me something I don't already know, Detective Barnes.

I nod. "I'm not surprised. She was ... troubled. She had ... issues."

There's a knock on the door, and Barnes excuses himself for a moment. When he comes back, I ask if he's talked to Ben yet and if Ben knows Marnie's death has been ruled a homicide.

"Someone's with him now," he says. "In fact, they just got the search warrant. Because you withheld evidence, we have to-"

"Search warrant?"

"We're searching your place, Autumn," he says, brows lifted. "That shouldn't be a problem since you had nothing to do with this, right?"

"Of course," I say, hand pressed over my heart. I did not poison Marnie with drugs, of that I'm one hundred percent certain. "Whoever saw me that night must have stuck around, waiting for me to leave, and then went inside to shoot Marnie with the heroin bomb. And from what I gather, it sounds like they're framing me for it. Or they're trying to. But you can search my house. Search everything I own. Search my phone calls and text messages. I've never purchased drugs in my life. And I wouldn't even know where to go to get them."

Detective Barnes clicks the edge of his pen on the table.

"Tell me, was Graham your witness?" I ask. "I saw him yesterday. At Marnie's grave. He told me not to tell anyone he was there. You should talk to him. If anyone has anything to hide, it's him."

"We've spoken to Mr. McMullen." His words are dry and disinterested. "He's already come clean about everything. The affair. Their ongoing relationship issues."

"So he admitted to you that he was there," I say, needing clarification. "And then he told you he saw me."

Barnes doesn't immediately answer.

"We have a photo of you leaving Marnie's townhome at eight oh seven the night of her death," he says, laying down the hand he'd been keeping close to his chest since the moment he walked in here. "Mr. McMullen supplied the photo."

My jaw falls.

That dirty son of a bitch.

I hate him.

I fucking *hate* him.

"That doesn't mean anything," I say. "Just because I was there, doesn't mean I did anything. Am I being . . . ? Do I need a . . . ?"

I can't finish my thought. My belly is twisted into tight knots, and I want to cry, but I have to keep it together. If they'd have marched me in here and said *"Marnie died of a blunt force trauma to the head and we have DNA evidence that it was you,"* then they would have me and there wouldn't be a damn thing I could do about it.

But *this?* This I did *not* do.

This I will *not* go down for.

Graham is throwing me under the bus. That whole sad-faced production he put on yesterday was nothing more than a ruse. He was trying to throw me off. He wants me to take the fall for what he did, and I refuse.

He doesn't get to make his little problem disappear.

He doesn't get to pin it on me.

And he sure as hell doesn't get to be Grace's father a minute longer.

I won't allow it.

"Are we finished here or are you arresting me?" I rise. My lips feel like hot gelatin, and the room spins.

"You're not under arrest, Autumn." His words wash over me, allowing me to breathe again. "You're free to go. For now. But stick around town in case we need to bring you in again, you understand?"

I snatch my purse from the table and sling it over my arm, and then I remember I need a ride home.

"Come on," he says, waving toward the door.

CHAPTER FIFTY-SIX

Autumn

I speak zero words to Barnes on the way home, and I thank him by slamming the passenger door when he pulls into my driveway. I don't appreciate the fact that he doesn't believe me. I see it in his beady eyes. He's just waiting to pin this on someone, and he thinks he's *so* close. He does seem like an insecure asshole who thrives on accolades and pats on the back from the higher-ups now that I think about it.

What a good boy, Barnesy! Good job solving the crime! Here's your Nylabone!

The squad car from earlier is still parked out front, and then I remember the search warrant. They're going through everything, just like they said they would. I'm not sure what they'll find, but I'm sure Ben is freaking out.

I run inside to be with him, to assure him everything's going to be fine.

He needs me.

And damn it, I need him too.

"Ben," I stop short inside the doorway when I see an officer in latex gloves holding a wooden box in one hand and its lid in the other.

"I thought you threw this out?" Ben's jaw clenches, pulses. His eyes burn into me.

I promised him I'd throw it out weeks ago when he found it and demanded that I cut ties with the McMullens immediately. I'd meant to get rid of it, but when it came down to it, I couldn't. Those memories in that box are all I have. I don't have yearbooks and photo albums and fond recollections of some idyllic childhood. My past is a series of years I'd rather forget.

I couldn't part with these things.

I tried. And I failed. And I hid them in the garage in a box labeled "Winter Clothes" because Ben keeps all of his clothes in one closet, never rotating anything out as the seasons change, and he'd never need to look in a box with that label.

"Why do you still have this?" he asks. "And did you know? Did you know my sister was having an affair with Graham McMullen?"

The hurt in his eyes sears my soul. I hesitate. And then I nod. "I didn't know until recently. And I didn't know how to tell you."

"How could you keep that from me? And how could you continue to work for that family knowing what you knew?" His lips snarl. He's disgusted with me. I knew he wouldn't understand. And I can't tell him. I can't tell him about Grace because ten years ago, when I signed those papers, I agreed to stay away, and there isn't a living, breathing soul who knows the truth . . . that I found her seven years ago, and I haven't stayed away since. Not once. And if I want to be there for all the rest of her sweet little life, I can't tell Ben a thing.

The officer rifles through my box of McMullen memorabilia. And that's fine. There's nothing in there that would pin Marnie's death on me. Nothing. All this does is create minor complications with Ben, but I can deal with them when all these nitwits finally leave our house.

Sure, it makes me look obsessed, but it doesn't make me look like a murderer.

"Get your things and get the fuck out," Ben says through gritted teeth.

"Wait, what?" I laugh. "Don't be like that."

I move to him, placing my hand on his forearm, but he brushes it away.

"Ben." I tilt my head, and I feel the officer watching us from his periphery.

"I mean it. We're done. You lied to me once, and then you lied to me again. I don't know you. I can't be with you."

"You're overreacting. It's just a box with stupid things in it. It doesn't mean anything."

"It's weird, Autumn. It's not normal. You know that, right? Normal people don't have boxes of other people's shit hidden in their houses." He has a point, and I'll admit it looks bad at surface level. "And to think you worked for them. You took care of their kids. You were in their home every day. This . . . this is fucked up."

"Ben, it's not as bad as it looks."

I know my words are false the second I speak them. I didn't expect him to react this way, and I'm not sure I'll be able to fix this.

"What if I had a box of some random family's photos and . . . and . . . and cards and recipes and jewelry?" he asks. "That would be insane, wouldn't it? You would think I'm some kind of creep."

I don't nod, but I silently agree. On the inside. If this were anyone but me, it would be insane. But I'm not crazy. And I don't know how to convince him right now. Desperate. Lonely. Heartsick. But not crazy.

"Get a bag, get your shit, and get out." He moves away from me, breathing hard.

I do as he asks, padding across the living room and heading for the bedroom we once shared. I throw as much as I can into a bag. Hopefully, in a few weeks' time, I'll be in Mexico. With Grace. And all of this will be a cloudy memory.

CHAPTER FIFTY-SEVEN

Autumn

"Name, please?" The woman at the front desk of the Bleu DuBois Hotel in downtown Monarch Falls peers over her wire-framed glasses. Her mouth is painted pink and her lipstick bleeds into the fine lines around her thin lips.

"Hannah," I say, pulling a name from a hat in my mind. "Hannah Gable."

I don't need to give her my real name. All she needs is a valid, signed credit card and my signature on the dotted line. I decide to be someone else tonight because I don't want Ben changing his mind and begging me to come back to him. I could imagine him crumpling to the ground after the police leave, feeling the weight of loneliness sink into him when he realizes he's literally all alone now, and I don't want him calling every hotel in the tri-city area looking for me.

I have a plan. And I'm putting that plan into action. I'm leaving this life behind. Shedding this skin for another, and this is my most important metamorphosis yet because this time, it isn't about me.

I can't leave my daughter with a murderer.

I can't sit idly by, watching as her life falls apart when Daphne can hardly afford to care for them. She'll be working two jobs just to get by as Graham rots in a jail cell, and my beautiful baby's Technicolor life will turn to ash and dust.

"Here you are." The woman assisting me hands me my credit card and prints a form for me to sign before handing off a plastic room key. "Third floor. Room 345."

"Thank you."

I wheel my bag to the elevator and follow the signs. The faint scent of chlorine fills the hall, and it reminds me of summer days with the children, swimming and laughing and splashing around without a care in the world.

My eyes water with bittersweet longing when I realize those were some of the best weeks of my life.

I swipe my card through the lock on my door and wait for the green light. My room is dark and smells of bleach and industrial-grade cleaning supplies, but I flip on the light and hoist my bag on one of the spare beds and collapse on the other.

Emancipation sinks into me, marinating through to my bones.

I'm no longer Ben's girl.

I'm no longer Autumn Carpenter.

It's been a long time since I've felt this free.

I'm anyone I choose to be, and my options are limitless.

————

At five in the morning, I sit up straight, lucid yet disoriented. The room is pitch black, and I can't see enough to see my hand before my eyes, but I feel around and crawl out of bed until I reach the nearest lamp.

My pajamas are soaked and the sheets are soaked, and I must have been having a nightmare, but I'm wide awake, and all I can think about is Daphne and the marijuana cigarette I found in her makeup bag.

Massaging my temples, I rock back and forth on the edge of the spare bed. If Daphne had access to marijuana, she could've known how to get her hands on harder drugs.

I don't know why I didn't think of this before.

Pacing the room, I piece it all together until it makes perfect sense, and then I call down to the station and ask the secretary when Detective Barnes will be in.

CHAPTER FIFTY-EIGHT

AUTUMN

"AND IF DAPHNE KNEW ABOUT THE AFFAIR AND KNEW ABOUT Marnie, she would have every reason to want her dead," I finish telling Barnes my theory. Today we're in his office instead of the interrogation room and the playing field feels slightly more level than before, but not by much. "Graham loved Marnie. I saw it in his eyes. Do you think a murderer would visit his victim's gravesite and cry?"

"But you don't know if Mrs. McMullen knew about the affair," he says, chewing the end of his pen.

"Trust me. I worked there every day for weeks. I saw the way they acted, the way she'd slink away at odd hours and he'd find every excuse not to be around her," I say. "And the kids! They'd repeat things all the time. Grace said her parents fought all the time and she thought they were going to get a divorce. Trust me, she knew."

"Welcome to marriage, sweetheart." He chuckles, like I'm kid with a Nancy Drew complex. "You ever been married?"

"I don't think you're taking me seriously, Detective Barnes, and that concerns me. I want to solve this case just as badly as you do."

"Of course you do."

I rise from my chair, rolling my eyes. "If I'm wasting your time, I'll gladly be on my way."

"No, no." He motions for me to sit then checks the clock on the wall when he thinks I'm not looking. "I'm interested in this little theory of yours."

"Really?" My head cocks. "Is that why you're taking such diligent notes?"

Our eyes meet at the blank sheet of paper in front of him. Maybe I underestimated him. Maybe he doesn't care about accolades. Maybe he's lazy and one of those assholes who is really good at making themselves look proficient when they're really just going through the motions.

"Anyway, I suggest you look into Daphne's alibi that evening," I say. "And then I suggest you dig a little deeper, figure out who supplied her drugs."

God, I could do his job in my sleep. I really could.

"Will do." His lips press together and stares at his still-empty sheet of paper. I hope he's lost in thought, but he could be reminiscing about last night's baseball highlights for all I know.

"All right, well." I stand, gathering my bag and eyeing the door. "You have my number if you have any more questions."

There's a tap on the door, and another officer waves for Barnes.

"Autumn, would you mind waiting here one minute?" he asks.

I frown. Yes, I do mind. I have things to do. Lots of planning and preparation ahead of me. Tomorrow's the first day of school, and Grace is attending a new 5-8 middle school three blocks from Linden street. I vividly recall a conversation from this summer in which Daphne agreed to allow Grace to walk to and from school from now on, since it's such a short distance.

That will be my shot. I'll pull up, flag her down, and ask if she wants a ride, and she'll trust me because she loves me. She wants me to be her mother now, she said so herself. I can't imagine a scenario in which Grace would go running and screaming in the opposite direction.

I know her. I know my daughter.

Barnes returns a few minutes later, and my eyes flick from the clock to his concerned expression.

"New development in the case?" I ask, half joking. My arms are folded.

"Yeah," he says, exhaling. "We're going to have someone look into Daphne's alleged involvement in all of this…"

"Thank god."

"But there's something else." He speaks slowly, carefully, and it's killing me.

Just spit it out!

"I need you to come with me," he says.

"Go with you where?" My feet plant firmly on the concrete floor of his office.

He motions for the door, and I follow, though every fiber of my being is screaming at me to run. Running would be very bad for me right now. Running would point their scrutiny directly at me instead of where it needs to be: on Daphne.

And so I follow, because I don't have a choice.

CHAPTER FIFTY-NINE

DAPHNE

THIS LATE SUMMER SUNDAY IS PARTICULARLY CHILLY, AND TODAY I've got the fireplace crackling and a warm cup of coffee in my hand. The children play in the family room, and the morning news displays across the TV.

They're talking about Marnie. Again.

The caption on the screen says, *"Breaking news. . ."* so I grab the remote and tap the volume button a few times.

"New details in the mysterious death of Monarch Falls resident, Marnie Gotlieb, have police scrambling to identify a new suspect. Gotlieb's death was ruled a homicide last month, declaring the cause of death to be a drug overdose which was not self-administered. Police have also analyzed security footage of Gotlieb's residence and confirmed that someone left the back door of her townhome shortly after eleven PM the night of her death."

My heart pounds in my ears.

He was supposed to be careful.

And he told me there were no cameras behind her house.

Hands trembling, I grab my phone and text Mitch. The message turns red and I get a failed delivery notification.

Resending, I wait, shaking.

It fails again.

Grabbing my phone, I carry it to the other room and call him, getting an automatic greeting on the other end telling me the number I have dialed is no longer in service.

"Son of a bitch."

CHAPTER SIXTY

Autumn

"Autumn, hi." A middle-aged woman with white, cotton-candy hair and kind chestnut-colored eyes extends her hand when Barnes leads me to a small office at the end of a hallway. I don't think this is her office. Nothing about it is personal. There's a laptop, some folders, a plain white mug full of navy blue pens, and a scratched oak desk but not much else. "I'm Dr. Whitmore. It's nice to meet you."

I turn to Barnes, a single brow lifted as if to ask, *"What in the ever-loving fuck is going on?"*

"Do you need me to stay?" he asks her, his voice low as if this is a question meant only for the two of them.

Why would *she* need *him*? Certainly not because of *me*.

"We'll be fine, thank you." She gives him a warm smile and sends him off with the flick of her wrist. A gold watch jangles against a silver and turquoise bracelet. I can tell she wants so badly to be eclectic or funky or free-spirited, but it's just not working. She's too academic. The doctor pulls her chair closer to me, her fingertips pressed against a manila folder that rests between us, and then she peers across the desk in my direction as if I'm the most fascinating thing she's ever seen.

"I'm sorry," I say, clutching my bag against my stomach. I've yet to sit. "I'm confused."

"It's okay, it's okay," she reassures me so casually I almost believe her, but nothing about what's going on right now makes me think this is all going to be "okay." Dr. Whitmore points to the seat across from her. "Please, have a seat. I'll explain everything."

Barnes closes the door behind him, and I watch through the sidelight window as he lingers outside the door.

"I want to show you something." She opens the folder carefully, her modest diamond ring glinting under the fluorescent lights above. Dr. Whitmore retrieves a piece of paper and slides it across the desk, flipping it around for me to see.

It's an 8x10 photo of a girl dated approximately ten years ago.

Her teenage face is chubby and lightly freckled and she's not smiling. Beneath the photo are the words PATIENT 00765, and at the top of the photo is the name SARAH THOMAS.

"Do you recognize her?" the doctor asks, and it feels like a trick question.

I say nothing.

"Sarah," she says a name that feels vaguely familiar, but it doesn't register that she's speaking to me until she says it again. "Sarah."

"Why are you calling me that?"

The doctor lifts a finger, pressing her lips together as if she's not sure how to explain what she's about to explain.

"*You* are Sarah," she says. "Your name is Sarah Thomas."

I shake my head. This feels like a dream. A nightmare. And I want out.

"Ten years ago, you were hospitalized in the psychiatric ward of Saint Andrews hospital in Stamford, Connecticut," she says. "This is a copy of your file, which I've read. The Monarch Falls police department called me in to speak with you after your brother saw you on TV and came forward."

I'm motionless, unable to speak or move, pinned down by the weight of what this woman is suggesting.

"What are you saying?" I flip the photo over and scoot my chair away from the desk. I can't look at that face anymore. That girl. She's unstable, miserable. I see it in her eyes.

"Ten years ago, you were hospitalized for severe depression, and while you were there, you were also diagnosed with dissociative identity disorder," she says. "And during your stay, you made a friend by the name of Autumn Carpenter. Autumn gave birth to a baby girl while she was an inpatient, and the two of you were very close. The best of friends. You told each other everything, even read each other's diaries because you didn't want to have any secrets. Autumn gave her baby up for adoption, and it was a very difficult thing for her to do. You helped her get through it. You never left her side. You even helped her choose the family. The two of you were discharged around the same time and you moved into an apartment together, but within a month, her family reported her missing. And *you* were no where to be found."

My face pinches. "I don't know what you're talking about. *I'm* Autumn."

Her eyes soften. "This is part of your disorder, sweetheart. Your personality is compartmentalized. It's a coping mechanism. It usually stems from a traumatic or abusive childhood, both of which are detailed here in your history."

She rifles through the papers in the folder, licking the pad of her finger. The stack is thick.

"You can read them if you'd like, if you absolutely feel the need to," she offers. "Though I'll warn you, it could trigger unpleasant memories, ones your personality has been blocking out, apparently, for years. I'm told you've been living as Autumn Carpenter for several years now?"

I shake my head. I don't want to read. I don't want to believe any of this.

"Anyway, your brother reached out to Benjamin Gotlieb, whom I understand is your long-term boyfriend?" she says. "He said he saw you on a news clip standing with Marnie's family and recognized you, and when he reached out to Ben late last night, they started piecing everything together. Ben made a phone call to Barnes and Barnes made a phone call to me, and now here we are. I'm so glad you were able to come into the station today. Your family has missed you. They're anxious to see you again, Sarah."

I press my finger into the desk. "I'm here because Barnes needs to look into Daphne McMullen as a suspect in Marnie's murder."

My words shock even myself. They taste different on my lips than they felt in my mind.

"Yes, I'm sure he's doing that, sweetheart. He's very good at what he does. Very thorough." She pushes her glasses up her nose, and she smells like cookies and fabric softener, and I officially resent her boringly comfortable life and easy-going attitude.

"This is *very* important." I raise my voice at a complete stranger, and I'm not proud. "Daphne McMullen had access to drugs, I saw it with my own eyes. Marnie Gotlieb was poisoned with heroin. Daphne's husband was sleeping with Marnie. Do you see what I'm saying here? Everything adds up!"

My daughter.

I *cannot* have my daughter living with a murderer and an adulterer.

I have to get out of here. Immediately.

I never should have come.

"Yes, I do. I see what you're saying, and that's a very interesting theory, Sarah." Dr. Whitmore reaches for my hand, placing her palm over top like that one little move could possibly calm me down. "But sweetheart, right now we need to focus on you. Your family has been searching for you for years. Your brother's on his way to the station, and your parents have been called."

"No!" I don't recognize my own scream.

Everything goes black.

CHAPTER SIXTY-ONE

AUTUMN

I COME TO IN A ROOM WITH GRAY CINDERBLOCK WALLS AND A THIN mattress. The clothes on my body are not the ones I dressed in this morning. There's a heavy metal door with bars on a small window, and I run to it, yanking on the handle, but it won't budge. Two voices on the other side of the door, a man and a woman, grow closer.

The iron lock on the door creaks, and I step back, watching as it swings open and Dr. Whitmore stands with her arms wrapped around a clipboard.

"Why am I in here?" My words are animalistic in my throat, and I reach for my hair. It's knotted and tangled. My stomach grumbles, and the sky outside my slit of a window is black.

"You're awake," she says with a jovial smile.

"Why did you lock me up? I don't understand." I try not to cry, but it's nearly impossible when you're being treated like a caged animal. A criminal.

"Sweetheart, you lost control in my office," she says gently.

"You were banging your head on the wall and screaming and you blacked out. We had to call an ambulance. You were committed because you were a danger to yourself and others. I hope you can understand, it's only protocol. You won't be here forever, I promise."

She steps into the room then stands aside, allowing a man to follow. Our eyes lock, and my heart stops. The taste of red pepper flakes on my tongue and the feeling of trying to breathe through a wet washcloth comes back to me in sensory memory form. The closet. The one with the lock on the door and a burned out light-bulb. The threat of a red hot cigarette lighter. A urine soaked mattress. Everything's flooding back to me at once, and I'm going to be sick.

I need to sit down.

"Sarah," a man with familiar brown eyes says. I recognize him now. He is my brother, and his name is Travis. "My god, look at you."

He moves toward me and I flinch, drawing into myself and stumbling backward toward the bed.

"Hold on, Travis," Dr. Whitmore says, extending her arm. There's a pen in her hand and her eyes are on me. "She hasn't seen you in a very long time. You'll need to keep that in mind."

"Sarah," he says, and my name feels familiar coming from his voice. His eyes look older than I remember, wrinkly at the sides, and he has less hair than before. It's thinning and darker now. He wears faded, ripped-up jeans and a dirty t-shirt with a mechanic shop logo across the front. His fingertips are black, oil-stained.

I can't recall the last time I saw my brother, but I know it's been years. My memories are fragmented, but when I look at him, my body trembles and I want to throw up.

He's not a good person, that much I remember.

"Sarah, we've missed you so much. Mom and Dad have been worried sick about you," he says with a breathy smile that I don't trust. He stares at me like he's staring at a ghost, like I'm transparent and he's trying to wrap his head around the fact that he finally found me again. "We thought you were . . ."

I close my eyes and feel his weight over mine. I feel his fingers around my neck, pressing until I blacked out. I remember the closet with the lock. I remember the names and the punishments and the humiliation in front of all his friends.

But it isn't Travis who's hurting me. It's our older brother, Adam.

I close my eyes and I'm transported.

Travis is watching. Laughing. Pointing. His hands don't torture me, but he's just as guilty because he never tries to stop it.

I'm crying, begging him for help as Adam pushes me to the brink of death for his own amusement.

He does nothing.

And when it's over, his eyes are dead, and Adam threatens us both.

And it never stops.

All I ever wanted was to escape, even if I could only escape in my mind.

Dr. Whitmore watches me tremble and then turns to Travis. "I think we should try this again, when she's feeling more . . . herself. This may be too much for her."

She directs her attention to me.

"Sarah, your parents will be here soon," she says. "And when you're feeling better, there'll be a detective here from the Stamford PD who would like to ask you a few questions about Autumn Carpenter. I won't let him talk to you until you're ready. I just wanted to let you know."

Pieces of memory float back to me like little flecks of dust. I think I can remember her now. She was pretty; blonde hair and blue eyes. And insecure. Privileged. Clingy. I was her only friend.

And I think I killed her.

Yes . . .

I remember now.

I held her under the water. We were walking the beach adjacent to her parent's Hamptons beach home. It was midnight and the sky was starless with a sliver of moon. It happened so fast. She was complaining about the things she was always complaining about—mostly first world problems—when I lunged at her from behind, my hands around her neck, and held her beneath me my weight. I was shocked at how little she struggled. It was almost as if she wanted it, welcomed it. When she finally stopped moving, I pushed her further out from the shore, and she floated away so peacefully, her body beckoned by gentle waves.

She wanted to die anyway.

She'd written it in her journal a hundred times.

I'm on my bed, the room spinning, and then I feel my body swaying. I'm rocking back and forth, my knees pulled against my chest. My eyes close tight.

"Get him away from me," I whisper. When I open my eyes, they're still standing there, staring. "Now!"

My scream echoes, bouncing off the cinder blocks and filling the small cell that contains me. Dr. Whitmore scrambles toward the door, pulling Travis with her. A male orderly stands in the hall, keeping his eyes on me as the doctor whispers something to my brother and pulls him out of the way.

"I want out of here!" I scream. My voice feels as if it's outside of me.

An orderly charges in the room with a syringe in hand and another comes to pin my thrashing arms and legs, and Travis watches the way he always did. He couldn't wipe the amusement from his face if he tried. A third orderly rushes past them, pinning my opposite arm down until I feel a sharp poke and then . . .

. . . nothingness.

CHAPTER SIXTY-TWO

Daphne

"Can I help you?" I climb out of my car and stride across my driveway toward the attention-grabbing cop car currently blocking my garage stall.

A tall man with thick, dirty blond hair takes heavy footsteps in my direction, his hands on his hips and a badge hanging around his neck.

Swallowing the ball in my throat, I say, "If you're looking for my husband, he's at the office. He'll be home after five, though I'd appreciate if you met with him when the kids aren't around."

"Are you Daphne McMullen?"

"Yes." I straighten my posture.

"You got a minute?"

My gaze moves toward the trunk of my SUV. "I have groceries in the back that need unloading, and I've got an appointment in an hour across town."

He bites his lower lip, squinting at me, and his forehead is lined in wrinkles. "You're going to have to cancel the appointment, ma'am."

"Care to tell me what's going on, detective?"

"I'm sure you're aware of the investigation into the homicide of Marnie Gotlieb," he says.

I nod. "It's all you hear about anymore on the news. That poor girl."

"And I'm sure you're aware of your husband's relationship with the deceased," he says. "At least that's what he said when he came in the other day."

Exhaling, I glance away. "I'm not sure what her death has to do with me. Graham and I have had our fair share of struggles, which we're still sorting out. Marriages take work, you know."

"Well aware, ma'am. Been through a couple of them myself." He chuckles, like we're friends, and then his expression fades. "Anyway, we just need you to come down for some questions."

Checking my watch, I sigh. "How long do you think it'll take? I've got to pick the kids up from school by three."

"It's going to be a while," he says. "Might want to call your husband and have him do the carpooling today."

"Is there any way we could do this in the morning? Tomorrow is completely free for me, and I'd be all yours." I smile, moving toward the trunk to start hauling in groceries.

"I'm sorry. We're going to need you to come in now."

Our nosiest neighbor, Mrs. Keller, walks by with her miniature apricot poodle, staring and mouth hardened into a disapproving frown, probably wondering why some strange man is hassling me in my own driveway.

How embarrassing.

Across the street, I catch a hint of a shadow behind a moving curtain.

They're all watching, waiting for me to be carted off in handcuffs in the back of his car because it would make for one hell of a story at Bunco this weekend.

"Is this a requirement?" I chuckle. "Is this how it usually works?"

"Look, ma'am, you need to come with me." He's growing impatient, forcing a hard breath through his nostrils and stepping toward me. His hands move to his backside, and he slowly retrieves a pair of shiny silver cuffs, moving carefully as if he fully expects me to run from him.

I laugh.

"This is a joke, right?" My arms are weighed with grocery bags, and I'd give anything, *anything*, right now to go back to my perfectly boring life with my two-timing husband and my non-minding children.

He shakes his head. "Drop the bags."

"Don't do this." There's a whine in my voice that I can't help. I feel them all watching; the entire neighborhood. I'm sure they're snapping photos and sending texts and making calls. And tomorrow my children will be teased at school because someone else's mommy saw their mommy taken away in a police car.

"Daphne, I didn't want to do this here," he says. I lower the bags to the pavement, lip trembling and knees buckling. "But since you're unwilling to cooperate."

He slips the handcuffs around my wrists. They're cold and weighty, and he tightens them until the metal digs into my bones.

"I'm sorry, but I don't understand what this is about." I'll deny.

Deny, deny, deny. My answers will be nothing but "I don't knows" and "I don't remembers," and as soon as I get a hold of Graham, I'll have him send in the best defense attorney money can buy.

I didn't kill Marnie.

"You're being charged with murder," he speaks like we're talking about the weather, about the St. Louis Cards, about donuts. "You hired Mitch Illingworth to execute the intentional overdose of Marnie Gotlieb. The guy he hired to do the job was booked this afternoon on unrelated charges and gave a full confession and any evidence he could provide."

My jaw hangs. Fucking Mitch. Fucking drug dealers.

He sold me out.

And of course he would.

I was just some rich bitch with deep pockets, and the jackass he hired was just some street thug trying to get off on better charges than the ones he was facing.

Still, I'll deny.

I don't deserve to rot for this.

I was only a woman, trying to keep herself together the only way she could, and I did what I had to do because it was the only way to end all of this: I destroyed the only source of Graham's happiness because she destroyed the only source of mine.

CHAPTER SIXTY-THREE

AUTUMN

"WHAT ARE YOU HERE FOR?" A GIRL WITH LONG LEGS AND A COVER Girl smile and green eyes that sparkle takes the spot next to me in the TV room one Friday morning in September. I haven't seen her before, so she must be new.

I don't tell her a thing. I smile and turn my attention back toward the morning news. Some man in a black suit is rambling on about the weather, and I hope I get a chance to go outside this morning before it rains.

I've been immersed in intensive talk therapy for the last several weeks. They tell me I have some kind of branch of dissociative personality disorder. It's rare and it needs to be studied more. It isn't textbook, they tell me. They want to send me to Portland, Maine to speak to some world-renowned psychologist as soon as I'm better.

I don't know when I'll be "better" or what that entails. So far I've woken every morning as Sarah, though I'm told I have an alter ego named Autumn who's based on someone I once knew.

They tell me I lived as her for at least the last seven years. They also tell me I confessed to her murder, but they're still trying to determine which of my memories are fact and which are simply a product of my disorder. Besides, without a body, there's no murder to formally investigate.

They also tell me I hid behind her identity as a defense mechanism, as a way to forget the trauma of my childhood. Dr. Whitmore says I need to face the trauma head on. It's the only way to overcome any of this.

I don't know how this is going to go or how long it'll take me to "face the trauma head on," but I do know that I hate being Sarah. Sarah is nervous and boring and anxious and her mind wanders all day every day, and she isn't happy. She doesn't know who she is or what she wants, all she knows is she doesn't want to be Sarah.

The girl next to me is rambling, talking a mile a minute. She's pretty and she seems nice, if not excessively chatty, but compared to everyone else in here, she seems relatively "normal." And I could use a friend. It's lonely in here.

"I'm Kerrigan," she says, extending her hand. "Like the figure skater from the nineties. Nancy Kerrigan?"

I offer a polite smile. I've never heard of "Nancy Kerrigan" before.

Kerrigan smiles more than I've ever seen anyone smile in my entire life. She seems happy and chipper, overly so, and I have no idea why she's here. I'm guessing she's manic. Off her meds. Needing to get stabilized.

But I like her. Or I think I could.

She's talking about nail polish now, asking if I'd be interested in doing each other's nails later. She's dying for a manicure and she's terrible at painting with her left hand. Also, she could use a friend, she tells me. No one wants to talk to her so far, and she thinks I seem nice.

"Want to be friends?" She laughs, but she's serious.

"Sure," I say.

Kerrigan tells me she's twenty-three, and she's an aspiring actress. She's been an extra in several Broadway productions, and she once had three lines in a production of Rogers and Hammerstein's Cinderella.

The news flicks to the next story.

A local woman has been indicted on murder charges after having hired someone to kill her husband's mistress via drug overdose. They have three children. The husband, a local businessman, is said to be devastated. The woman is facing life in prison with no chance of parole.

They show the woman dressed in orange, her hands cuffed behind her back as she stands before a judge. She's very beautiful, but she shows no emotion. Her expression is ice cold, and then they flash to a family portrait from better times. They have two girls and a boy and the photo shows them in front of an enormous Christmas tree, grinning ear to ear with a background full of beautifully wrapped presents.

I feel bad for them, my gut punched the same way it gets when I see one of those animal shelter commercials. They seem like any other family next door, relatable and functional, only they're the picture perfect version.

The anchor moves on to the next story, the demolition and relocation of a local youth shelter, and Kerrigan's still talking.

"As soon as I get out of here, I'm moving to California," she says. "LA. That's where all the good acting jobs are. Broadway is for the assholes who take themselves way too seriously. They think they're classically trained, but they're just a bunch of poor wannabes waiting for a big break that's never going to happen."

I laugh for the first time in weeks. I like the way she thinks. And I love her brutal honestly.

"The cool thing about LA, too, is that everybody reinvents themselves out there. You can give yourself a new name, a new persona, and nobody bats an eye. They even have personality coaches, can you believe that? Anyway, I'm ditching New York and hitching a ride to warmer winters and palm trees."

In a blink of an eye, I picture myself in LA with Kerrigan, laughing and drinking and leaving all of this bullshit behind.

"You can be anyone you want to be out there," she says, bouncing giddily in her seat and twirling her long blonde hair.

"Mind if I join you?" I ask.

"Oh, my god, are you kidding? I would love it! We can be roomies!"

"All right, it's settled. As soon as we're out of here, I'm coming with you."

Kerrigan wraps her arms around me, squeezing tight. "We're going to have so much fun."

"Yes, we are."

CHAPTER SIXTY-FOUR

One Year Later

Sarah

I SLIP AN OVERFILLED BACKPACK OVER KERRIGAN'S SHOULDERS, ROLL her to her side, and take the spot beside her in bed. This has become our Saturday night routine—she parties her way through the hottest LA nightclubs with her friends-du-jour and comes home plastered at three AM. And I see to it that she makes it to her room in one piece and doesn't choke on vomit in her sleep.

Our friendship is as simple as it is symbiotic: she pays the rent on our West Hollywood apartment—and I keep her alive.

I also do all the cleaning, cooking, and laundry, but this place isn't cheap.

It's fair and square enough.

Kerrigan moans, and I glance down to check on her, brushing the hair from her forehead before patting her back like a mother comforting her child. It's unlikely she'll remember this when she wakes up ten hours from now, but I'm trying to be the best version of myself ... whatever that may be.

I give it a few more minutes before trudging to the kitchen to grab her a bottle of her favorite blue Gatorade plus two Advil. Normally I have them ready to go, but she came home an hour earlier than usual tonight, and we barely made it down the hall before I had to all but haul her over my shoulder. If she stirs again, I'll remind her to take them. If not, she'll be looking at a massive Sunday hangover.

I grab my phone and ear buds before returning to her room. A minute later, I place her pills and drink on her nightstand before settling next to her once more. Sliding the white buds into my ears, I queue up a true crime podcast and stare out the window to my left—momentarily appreciating the view of a twinkling city filled with so much beauty, grit, tragedy, and hope.

It's been less than a year since we moved here, but already I've met some of the most fascinating people. Almost everyone here is from somewhere else. And almost everyone here came here to *be* someone else.

Except for me.

I came here to be myself—though I'm still learning exactly who that is.

The last eleven years have been mostly wiped from my memory. I *know* they happened. I know *what* happened. But I have no recollection of any of it. It's like driving from one point to another but not remembering the journey. The doctors and specialists tell me my mind was, quite simply, checked out.

I keep hoping something—*anything*—will come back to me one of these days, but a steady cocktail of psychotropics and talk therapy has only kept me level. No improvements, no regressions. My memories have scattered to the wind like autumn leaves ... which is ironic, given the fact that I spent a decade living as Autumn Carpenter.

I'm told I confessed to her murder shortly after being admitted to the psychiatric hospital—a fact that has haunted my every waking moment for the past year, but I have no recollection of that now. Doctors said I was in a frantic state, that coming back into myself was a traumatic process, and that I said a lot of things that couldn't be confirmed or denied. In the end, because there was no body and no evidence of a crime, there was nothing they could charge me with. Both relief and guilt have lived in the marrow of my bones ever since.

If I took someone's life, I'll never forgive myself.

Closing my eyes, I lean back against Kerrigan's headboard and focus on the female podcaster's voice as she talks about a string of disappearances that took place in the Stamford, Connecticut area a little less than a decade ago. All of the missing women were seventeen to nineteen, many of them at-risk or mentally ill—especially vulnerable. Each and every last one of them fit Autumn Carpenter's description and the timeline matches up.

This is the fifth podcast to cover these disappearances and so far they've all shared the same disturbing details—bloody panties in the woods, strands of hair stuck to tree branches, grainy security cam footage showing a man dressed in all-black overpowering unsuspecting young women in the middle of the night. He almost always took them in dark alleys, behind gas stations, or between abandoned businesses in the less desirable parts of town.

Bloggers and true crime aficionados refer to him as The Stamford Night Watcher, because he always took his victims at night and always seemed to be prepared—as if he'd been watching, lurking, and waiting for the right time to strike.

A chill runs down my spine the way it always does when I imagine him, though in my mind's eye he never has a face.

I've never told anyone this, but I've made it my life's mission to find Autumn—or to at least find out what happened to her. We were friends, roommates when she disappeared. Odds are I was the last one to see her. I stole her life, for crying out loud.

I should be the one to find her and bring her family peace or closure.

Six months ago, I wrote them a letter asking if they'd be open to a meeting since they hadn't returned my calls. I wanted to apologize, to offer my assistance in any way. I wanted them to know I *care*. A couple of weeks later, the letter came back to me; the words *return to sender* hastily scribbled on the envelope in black Sharpie.

I don't blame them.

Maybe I'd have done the same thing in their shoes ...

Drawing in a long breath, I check on Kerrigan once again, holding my palm close to her nose to ensure she's still breathing.

This sweet summer child had dreams bigger than the stars in her eyes when we first moved here. She wanted to be an actress, and she had all of these plans and ideas and strategies. The second our feet hit the dusty LA soil, she hit the ground running. She'd read every book on how to make it "big" here, signed up for every acting class she could find, joined online forums, and attended various actor meet-ups.

Within the first few months, she landed a (questionable) agent and a handful of auditions, but her excitement wore out with every rejection, and while Kerrigan is (unquestionably) beautiful, so is everyone else is the so-called City of Angels.

She doesn't stand out.

She fits right in.

It's both a blessing and a curse.

Forty-three minutes later, the podcast ends, and I'm no closer to finding Autumn than I was when it began.

A handful of months ago, I reached out to the family I nannied for ... the McMullens. Fully expecting to be avoided like the plague, I almost lost my breath when Graham answered in the middle of the second ring.

After I told him who I was, he was quiet for a beat, and I

almost thought he'd hung up on me, but he was still there—speechless but very much still there.

For fifteen minutes, he listened to me ramble on, spouting apology after apology. I told him my intentions were never to hurt him or his family, that I was sorry for any stress I'd caused during my time with them. To my surprise, he met me with compassion, telling me I was the least of his family's problems.

He also added that the children adored me, that I took great care of them, that they still ask about me, and that he understood that I had an illness and he would never hold that against me. In the end, he wished me well, but he kindly requested that I never contact his family again.

They were trying to move on, he told me.

His words stung, but I understood.

I didn't get a chance to talk to him about Autumn—his oldest daughter's birth mother—before the conversation ended. I had a handful of burning questions I'd hoped to ask … I wanted to know if she ever tried to reach out after the adoption, if they ever met her, or if there was anything he'd gleaned about her over the last year. If there's anything I've learned from these podcasts, it's that sometimes the tiniest speck of information can lead to the biggest breakthroughs.

Odds are he hasn't spoken to her.

But now I'll never know.

I tug the ear buds from my ears, check on Kerrigan yet again, and trek to the laundry closet in the hallway to quietly transfer a load containing my work uniform from the washer to the dryer.

When I'm not keeping Kerrigan alive or acting as her live-in personal assistant, I'm cleaning houses. I've managed to accrue a steady list of regulars to fill my twenty-hour-a-week schedule.

There's the middle-aged, recently divorced man who obsessively Facebook-stalks his ex-wife and her new French boyfriend. Then there's the single mom of five-year-old triplets, who occasionally pays me in free merchandise from her career as an influencer. And of course there's the moderately-successful B-list producer with the revolving door of aspiring actresses. And I can't forget the reclusive woman who wears dark sunglasses in her house and has yet to utter more than six or seven words to me the entire time I've cleaned for her. I've learned she prefers that I pretend she's not there, and I get it.

There's an odd sort of comfort and security in being invisible; in blending in with the scenery.

I start the dryer and return to Kerrigan's room, another Saturday night on the books. The same old questions dance through my head as I try in vain to chase a few hours of sleep before the sun comes up.

CHAPTER SIXTY-FIVE

DAPHNE

"YOU HAVE TWENTY MINUTES," THE UNIFORMED PRISON GUARD opens the door to the visitation area. I scan the sea of unfamiliar faces until my gaze lands on the pinched and tightened visage that could only belong to my mother-in-law.

"Daphne," she says when she sees me. There isn't a shred of emotion—pleasant or otherwise—in her tone. The fact that she's here speaks volumes, though I won't kid myself. She's not here for me, she's here because of me.

I take the seat across from her, ignoring the subtly disap-proving way she takes in my boxy, ill-fitting attire before settling on my pale face and grown out roots. I can only imagine the barrage of thoughts competing in her head as she compares and contrasts me to my previous self.

Not a day goes by that I wouldn't give everything I have—not that I have much—for one more day to hold my children again. One more ordinary bedtime routine. One more quick run to the grocery store. One more glossy manicure or evening glass of wine. One more exhaustingly jam-packed day of being the glue that holds our family together.

But my wings have been clipped, I'll spend the rest of my life in a literal cage, and I only have myself to blame.

"I brought some photos of the children." She lays out half a dozen matte, 4x6 photographs in front of me. The prison doesn't allow cell phones in the visiting area, so these are the only glimpses I get into the lives of my babies.

"Rosie's getting so big," I say, tears filling my eyes. "And Grace … she isn't smiling in these. Is she okay?"

My mother-in-law hesitates. "One could say that. She recently started therapy."

I lift a brow. "I had no idea."

"It was my suggestion. Graham has been a bit … overwhelmed," she adds. "Twice a week, Grace sees a children's psychologist at a very reputable clinic two towns over."

"What's going on?" Not being able to comfort my first child gnaws at my center with a fierceness so sharp it steals the air from my lungs.

Her mouth opens, but nothing comes out. Immediately, I grasp the idiocy of my question.

"It's been an adjustment," she finally answers. "For *everyone*."

Herself included; I presume. Last I knew, she'd moved in with Graham and the kids to help out, though her idea of helping out is to outsource all of the mothering and housekeeping to salaried individuals who do exactly what she tells them, exactly how she tells them to do it.

"And how's Graham?" I ask.

It would be easy for me to sit back and blame him for this. After all, he's the one who had the affair. He's the one who set fire to our happy home life first. But at the end of the day, he isn't the one who casually arranged someone else's death as if he was simply ordering a black market Birkin bag.

"Graham is … *Graham*," she says, squinting.

I imagine he's moving on in his own way and perhaps she doesn't want to tell me because what difference would it make?

"I wish he'd visit again," I say. Since my sentencing, he's only been here with the children once. It was a painful, bittersweet visit that ended in tears on both sides. "Please, tell him I'd love to see him and the kids. How's Sebastian?"

Her red lips tug up at the sides and her eyes light.

He's always been her favorite.

Her mini-Graham.

"Absolutely thriving," she says. "Smart as a whip and doesn't miss a beat. I've enrolled him in an exclusive Pre-K program where they let the children guide their own learning and he absolutely loves it."

I picture him in a little school uniform, his dark hair combed neatly with a side part and his giant dinosaur backpack bouncing as he heads off to school. It hits me, the way it does sometimes … a giant current of emotion too strong to swim against. Tears sting my vision, and I swipe them away as they fall.

Without a word, she rises from her seat, strides across the room, and returns with a couple of paper-thin tissues.

"I know this isn't easy for you," she says. "But you've got to stay strong, Daphne. Your children are going to watch you grow old in this place. You can't let them see you broken. It will haunt them. For the rest of your life—and theirs—they're going to remember you like this. Faded. Deteriorating. A sobbing mess." She lifts her palm. "And I get it. I don't know how you survive a day in here. But I'm telling you, you've got to toughen up." Leaning in, she adds, "Fake it if you must. Slap on a smile. Tell them about all of the fun you're having here."

I chuff.

I would never describe this place as fun in any capacity, but I understand her message loud and clear.

I don't disagree with any of it.

"Not everything is about you, Daphne," she says, her words soft and low. "The last visit was ... upsetting ... to say the least."

My lip trembles, but I stiffen it.

Straightening my shoulders, I nod. "It was the first time I'd seen them in months. They're my family. Forgive me for getting emotional."

I may be a murderer, but I'm also human.

I feel. I hurt. I regret.

I'll never forget the look in Ben Gotlieb's eyes when he read his family's statement at my sentencing trial. They loved Marnie. She may have had a hand in wrecking my life, but she was the light of theirs. I could hardly bring myself to look them in the eyes, but somehow I managed.

It was the right thing to do.

The three of them hugged and all but cheered when the judge sentenced me to life behind bars with no chance of parole.

I can't say that I blame them.

"I'm not trying to make you feel worse than you clearly already do," she says. "I'm just trying to offer you a bit of advice for the long road ahead ..."

Studying the photographs on the table before me, I fight another groundswell of waterworks.

"No matter what happens, Daphne, they're all going to be okay." Reaching over, she places her hand over mine in a rare moment of comfort. "I'll make sure of that."

CHAPTER SIXTY-SIX

SARAH

"YOU'RE NOT MY USUAL GIRL," AN AGELESS, RAVEN-HAIRED WOMAN with emerald-green glasses answers the door of my first cleaning job Monday morning. "What happened to Emma?"

"Emma quit last week." I hoist my cleaning caddy under my arm. "I was asked to take over."

The woman scans me from head to toe, her palms framing the doorway as if she's hesitant to let me in.

"You can reschedule if you'd like someone else," I say.

She exhales, peering back into the semi-cluttered abyss of her stucco and stone storybook home. "No. It's fine. I'm hosting a book club tonight so I need this place sparkling."

She steps out of the way and I lug my vacuum and supplies inside.

"You need me to show you around?" she asks, locking the door behind me. If she's locking me in or locking someone out, I can't be certain. "It's pretty self-explanatory. Kitchen, living, dining, office, three beds, two baths—and a partridge in a pear tree."

I smile and nod. "I'll figure it out, thanks."

"If you need me, I'll be in my office," she points toward the hall, the bracelets on her wrist jangling before she disappears from view.

I begin in the kitchen, as I prefer to tackle the biggest jobs first. Working my way from one end to the next, then from top to bottom, I'm deeply in the zone when she appears in the doorway of the dining room and startles the life out of me.

I gasp, my hand splayed across my chest.

The woman's full lips curl into a coy smile. "I didn't mean to startle you … was just coming out to refill my coffee."

She strides to the little strip of countertop that houses her Keurig machine, places her mug into position, and pops a coffee pod into the top. A second later, she presses the button on top and the machine whistles and whirs.

"Deadlines," she says with a huff, one hand on her hip.

"Are you a writer?" I ask. If there's anything I've gleaned since living here, it's that one out of every four or five people in this town are a writer of some kind—screenplays mostly—though occasionally I'll come across a movie critic or tabloid journalist.

"Isn't it obvious?" she asks with a soft chuckle. "The bags under my eyes, the swollen wrists, the hump in my back? That's what I get for living behind a computer monitor ten hours a day."

She must be delusional, because I see none of that.

In fact, this woman is beautiful—incandescent almost. Sparkly irises that can't decide if they're green, gold, or something in between. Smooth sun-kissed skin. Hair that glistens and practically drips down her shoulders in slow motion like a shampoo commercial.

But everyone in this town seems to be striving for unattainable perfection.

"Good god, I could use a massage." She rubs the back of her neck. "You don't happen to know a good masseuse, do you? My last one up and left. Apparently she reconnected with her high school boyfriend from back in Wisconsin and decided she was sick of LA's shit. I don't blame her. It's not for everyone. You from here originally?"

I spray two squirts of orange-scented antibacterial cleaner onto her countertop and wipe it down.

"No," I say.

Her coffee machine sputters, and she reaches for her mug. "Figures. No one is. Everyone's an import here. Where are you from originally?"

"East coast." I move to the sink next. I've already cleaned it, and I'm ready to move to the dining room, but she's perched in the corner, sipping her coffee and making small talk. It seems rude to walk away.

"You like it here?"

"I do." I eye the doorway to the next room and grab my cleaning caddy, hoping she gets the hint. But she remains planted.

"So what's your story?" she asks, cupping her mug in both palms as she lifts it to her lips.

"Beg your pardon?"

"What's your story?" she asks again. "Everyone has one. California's like one big magnet. But it only attracts a certain type."

"And what type might that be?" I'm curious.

"People wanting more," she says without hesitation. "But there are all different types of *more*. More sex. More money. More attention. More hope. More escapism. More distance. More everything. What's your *more*?"

I rest my caddy against my hip and glance up at the popcorn ceiling above. "I guess I've never thought about that before."

"Well, what brought you out here?" She takes a sip of coffee, her eyes electric.

"Didn't you say you're under a deadline or something?" I tease. If we weren't complete strangers, maybe I'd tell her about my abusive childhood. My relentless brothers. My detached and distant parents. My stints in psychiatric hospitals. My dissociative identity disorder.

She laughs. "I'm sorry. I'm inquisitive by nature. Too inquisitive. I've built my entire career on sticking my nose into other people's business."

"What kind of writing do you do?" I bring the focus of the conversation back to her and check the clock on the microwave. I need to leave for the next job in an hour and a half to make it there on time.

"I write true crime books," she says, fighting a semi-proud little smirk. "I don't suppose you read anything like that, do you? Most people don't. We're a special breed."

"I'm more of a podcast person."

She swats her hand. "I don't have the attention span to sit and listen to other people jabber on for an hour straight. My niece showed me how to play them faster, but then it just sounds like a bunch of chipmunks in my ear. Anyway. I'll be in my office if you need me."

With that, the onyx-haired woman disappears once more, her sheer, cashmere duster flowing behind her.

I get to work on her dining room before moving on to the living room, bedrooms, and bathrooms. I finish in her office, where she's crouched behind an enormous monitor, her fingernails clacking against the keyboard before she exhales and sinks back.

"I'm sorry," I say.

She turns to me, her face wrinkled in confusion. "Oh. No, honey. I wasn't frustrated with you. I just hit a wall with this damn manuscript. There's an interview I've been chasing for the better part of the year, and I need that to finish this section of the book."

I grab my feather duster and head toward a crowded bookshelf on the far wall. Amongst haphazard stacks of books crammed into every inch of shelving are a slew of matching covers, all of them bearing the name Dianna Hilliard.

"Are these yours?" I ask, pointing.

She turns back to me and nods. "They are."

"How many have you written?"

"Seven. Nine if you count the two I ghostwrote for another true crime author in my early days," she says. "Working on my tenth right now and it's kicking my ass."

"That's amazing," I say.

"If you want any of those, help yourself. I've got boxes of them in my garage. They're promotional copies."

I slide a thick blue tome off the shelf, flipping it over to check out the cover.

Lies for Sale: The Tina Todwell Story by Dianna Hilliard

"Ever heard of Tina Todwell?" she asks.

"Can't say that I have."

She shudders. "Consider yourself lucky. That project gave me nightmares for months. If you want something a little lighter, maybe grab the one with the green cover beside it."

I place the Tina Todwell book back on the shelf and check out the one next to it.

Missing Brides of the Gothic South

"That's a collection of historical crime stories, all of them set in 19th century rural Georgia," she says. "There's a bit of a paranormal element to those tales so take them with a grain of salt. They're still considered true crime—at least based on witness testimonies from that time."

"So a bunch of brides went missing?" I ask. "All in the same place?"

Her lips press flat. "Pretty much. Happened over a span of ten, fifteen years in a tri-state area. Then it just stopped."

I tuck a copy into my cleaning caddy. I'm not an avid reader, but I don't want to offend her.

"Thank you," I say before moving on to the next shelf, though with every brush of my feathers against book spines, I can't help but feel the weight of her stare on my back. I'm nearly finished when something occurs to me. "Dianna, right?"

"In the flesh." She winks.

"Have you ever heard of The Stamford Night Watcher?" I turn back to her.

She plucks her glasses off her nose, rests them upside down on her desk and crosses her legs. "I can't say that I have?"

I check my watch and drag in a jagged breath. "Then have I got a story for you."

SAMPLE OF THE WATCHER GIRL

Grace

I shouldn't be here.

The swell of nausea in my middle intensifies with every step toward the front door of my childhood home. When the taxi disappears from view, I tell myself there's no turning back. And then I remind myself this isn't about me.

I park my suitcase at the welcome mat, clear my throat, and wait for my father to answer the door.

A moment later, heavy footsteps are followed by the rasp of a deadbolt and the swing of the heavy door I used to run through a lifetime ago.

"Grace?" His tortoiseshell glasses are crooked on his nose, and his salt-and-pepper hair is tousled on one side. Safe to bet I woke him from a nap. Judging by his white cotton-poly pants and olive-green golf polo, it's also safe to bet he played a round this morning. "What are you doing here?"

My mother's peonies bow in the early June breeze, their frilly heads blooming with resilience despite my mother's twenty-years-and-counting prison sabbatical. The lush Kentucky blue-grass is edged to meticulous perfection along the double-wide sidewalk. The elms are taller than I remember, naturally, but their canopy of shade still extends across the driveway, painting my father's vintage Porsche a darker shade of platinum.

I should have called—but I talked myself out of it a dozen times, knowing he'd have questions I wouldn't be able to answer without changing my mind about coming here. Buying a nonrefundable airline ticket and shoving my things into a suitcase seemed like the path of least resistance in this scenario.

"Surprise . . ." I force a smile and splay my hands, a cheap attempt to make this exchange as lighthearted as possible.

His narrowed gaze eases, and the lines on his tanned forehead fade as the corners of his mouth curl one by one.

My father has an impressive knack for acting like nothing happened. It's an art form, really. The man is bulletproof. Scandal and misfortune have a tendency to ricochet off him and hit the innocent bystanders instead.

And he just . . . carries on.

He *always* carries on.

Sometimes I wonder how the man views himself when he looks in the mirror—truly views himself. What does he see when he strips back that perfect, persevering outer layer? Does he see a man who failed his wife and family by chasing after a younger woman? A man whose infidelity ultimately cost that young woman her life? A man whose ex-wife rots away in a prison cell an hour from here all because he couldn't keep his dick in his pants?

Something tells me he sees none of that.

His ego won't let him.

"Was hoping it'd be okay if I crashed here for a bit?" My palm dampens against the purse strap digging into my shoulder. I relax my gaze, tamping down the disgust that always forces its way to the surface anytime I hear his voice or find myself unavoidably in his presence.

"I just . . . you never . . . this is . . ." His expression morphs from wrinkled to relaxed and back. Despite everything we've been through, his softness for me has never wavered. I both love and hate him for this, but now is not the time to litigate old memories. "Of course you can stay here. Forgive me, Grace. It's been so long . . . You're the last person I was expecting . . . but yes, please stay. We'd love to have you."

We.

He and his girlfriend, *Bliss.*

I know all about her despite our never having met—what I didn't know, however, was that she'd moved in.

My father reaches across the threshold to take my luggage, and I follow him in.

The house no longer smells of my mother's ostentatious floral arrangements. Nor does it retain a hint of her French perfume that used to leave invisible trails from room to room, since she could never sit still for more than thirty seconds.

My lungs fill with a cocktail of scents that represent someone else's life.

Lemon dusting cleaner.

A hint of lavender.

An unexpected trace of sandalwood.

Leather dress shoes.

Stale air.

Vintage rugs.

Time.

I think of my mother now, confined to a cinder block cell with a roommate named Angel. There are no flowers to arrange. No windows to open when she craves fragrant petrichor after a hard rain. There are no children to chase after. No mile-long grocery lists or elaborate dinners to make. No company to entertain. No designer-filled closets to organize or dry cleaning to grab between school runs. No coffee shop stops. No neighborhood gossip to secretly enjoy. No summer afternoons lazing by the backyard pool, hardback bestseller in hand.

No handsome, philandering husband to kiss her good night . . .

I imagine her lying on the bottom bunk, reading one of the many used books my sister, Rose, sends to her, her silky blonde strands now gray streaked and straw-like. Her skin paper thin. Her eyebrows finger plucked to nothing. At least that's how she appeared the last time I saw her, ten years ago. The only reason I visited was to confront her about a true crime novel called *Domestic Illusions: The Daphne McMullen Story.*

While my mother's murder conviction legally prohibited her from profiting off her crime or the death of Marnie Gotlieb in any way, it didn't stop *Chicago Post* bestselling author Dianna Hilliard from taking a stab at it. She even had the audacity to dedicate it to my brother, my sister, and me.

We'd never met the woman a day in our lives.

The finished product painted my mother as a saint—a slave to her beautiful, privileged life. And it smeared my father as a sex-addicted narcissist. After tearing through paragraph after paragraph of family details only my mother could have provided, I was forced to pause our estrangement so I could share my disgust with her in person.

She sold us out.

My father may be a self-serving man with severe codependency issues—but he's no murderer. Graham McMullen's hardly a saint, but he'd never throw us under the bus.

Not like that.

"So . . . what brings you here?" His tone is pleasant, but his eyes squint as he studies me in the blue-green twilight of early evening.

The truth is complicated.

"Been gone long enough," I say on a long exhale. "Thought maybe it was time to come home."

Home.

I use the word for his sake. It makes him smile.

While I resided at 372 Magnolia Drive the first ten years of my life, calling it "home" would be a stretch at this point.

His dark eyes turn glassy, and his fingertips twitch at his sides. He wants to hug me, I'm sure, but he knows me too well. At least that part of me.

"Your room's exactly how you left it," he says instead of asking more questions. I imagine he'll space them out, fishing casually for tidbits until he has the whole picture. An investigational paint-by-numbers. "Good to have you back, Grace. I mean that. Stay as long as you need. We'll catch up whenever you're ready."

I thank him before grabbing my roller bag and climbing the winding staircase in the sweeping foyer. Every step rustles an unsettled sensation in my center, but I force it down with tight swallows.

I'm here on a mission, and as soon as it's over, I'm leaving again.

Stopping at the top of the stairs, I'm greeted by an outdated family portrait—the original McMullens dressed in coordinating navy-blue outfits, the children hand in hand, grinning against the autumnal backdrop of some local state park.

There we are.

Frozen in time.

Blissfully unaware of fate's cruel plans for us.

We were beautiful together—enviably happy from the outside.

Hashtag blessed.

My attention homes in on my parents, the way my mother gazes up into my father's handsome face, her golden hair shining in the early evening sunset, his hand cupping the side of her cheek. If I didn't know better, I'd think their love for one another was equal and balanced.

I trace my fingertips against the burnished-gold frame before pressing it just enough that it tilts, off-center. Noticeable only if you stare too long.

I have no desire to rewrite history, and I have little patience for those who feel the need to do so.

347

When I reach my old room, I flick on the light and plant myself in the doorway.

My father's right. It's exactly how I left it: Dark furniture. Blue walls. Pile of stuffed animals in the corner. Perfectly made bed complete with an ironed coverlet and a million pillows.

Aside from the fresh vacuum tracks in the carpet, no one's set foot in this room since the last time I was home my senior year of college.

I lock the door and collapse on the bed, digging my phone from my bag and pulling up the Instaface account for my ex from college and staring at his profile picture for the tenth time today—the hundredth time this week. Same coffee-brown hair trimmed neatly into a timeless crew cut. Same hooded eyes the earthy color of New England in autumn. Same dimples flanking his boyish smile like parentheses. He's exactly how I remember him, only with a decade of life tacked onto his face. Shallow creases spread across his forehead. A deep line separates his eyebrows. Maybe there's a little more hollowing beneath his jovial gaze. But other than that, he's the same as I remember.

I could describe Sutton Whitlock fifty thousand ways, but at the end of the day, I can sum him up in five words: he was a good man.

Eight years ago, I broke his heart—and not because I wanted to.

I had to save him from a lifetime of disappointment.

I had to save him from me.

But a handful of things have come up online recently—things that indicate he's not okay.

I need to rectify what I've done. I need to apologize for hurting him. Explain my reasons. Give him permission to move on, to be happy.

And then I'll disappear . . . again.

So this is how we meet.

I amble into the kitchen at a quarter past six the next morning

348

to find my father's girlfriend frying eggs, her back to me as she tends to the skillet. I wanted to grab a cup of coffee before my shower, but that requires riffling through cupboards to locate mugs and coffee pods. And now that *she's* here, I'm reminded of my guest status, and rummaging feels wrong.

Cracked brown shells rest in the sink. Unsanitary. My mother never would have done that. They'd have gone straight to the garbage.

I clear my throat and plant myself behind the island, fingertips curled around the marble edge.

Nothing.

Maybe she can't hear me over the sizzle of eggs?

My father shuffles from room to room above us. I guess he doesn't sleep in on the weekends anymore.

I clear my throat—louder this time—as Bliss turns from the stove to grab a plate from the cupboard to her right. She's lanky but in a feminine sort of way, the fabric of her Bandhani-print robe clinging equally from the protrusion of her bony shoulders to the nipping of her waist to the subtle rounding of her hips.

Her eyes widen, her lips curl, and she clutches her paper-thin lapels. "My goodness. Didn't see you there."

Bliss pops two white earbuds from her ears and approaches me without a hint of reluctance.

"I'm Bliss." She extends a manicured hand and offers a disarming smile. Her eyes are small but pretty, the darkest ocean blue and set deep behind a fringe of thick lashes. Her features are angled, German perhaps, a contrast against the silky-soft blonde hair piled on the top of her oblong head. Dare I say, she'd give my mother a run for her money in the looks department. But knowing my father, that's exactly why he's with her. He's always loved pretty, shiny things. "It's so wonderful to finally meet you."

"Your eggs are burning." I don't mean to be rude, but I know how my dad is when it comes to his food. Spoiled by years of my mother's perfectionistic ways in this very kitchen, the man has standards.

Without wasting a second, Bliss spins on her bare feet and pulls their breakfast from the fiery depths of burned-food hell before flicking off the gas burner.

"Oops." She laughs a humbled laugh, brushing a pale tendril from her forehead. "That's what I get for trying to multitask."

The human brain isn't capable of multitasking. It's a proven fact. She—a Princeton-educated-psychotherapist-turned-life-coach-slash-meditation-guru—should know this.

"Join us?" Bliss points to the unset table in the nook. "I know your father's anxious to catch up with you—and me . . . I've heard so much about you, I feel like I know you already . . . but I have so many questions. Just dying to pick your brain."

She's rambling, saying the kinds of things a person doesn't normally say to another upon first meeting. Is she nervous? I've been told some people find me intimidating, that my presence has a heaviness to it. It's quite the contrast from Bliss's lighter-than-air exuberance.

"Hope that's okay," she continues. Her movements are easy and relaxed. She's a sunny day of a human being. Clear and bright-eyed. Tepid, soothing voice. "I'm a curious person. Drives your father crazy sometimes, but I find everyone so . . . interesting."

Well, look at that.

We have something in common already.

Years ago, when this woman walked into my father's life, I scraped the internet in search of everything I could find. And with a name like Bliss Diamond, it wasn't that hard.

At first I assumed she was a retired adult film star, and given my father's past dalliances, I didn't think I was that far off.

But I assumed wrong.

Bliss Diamond—at least the internet version of Bliss Diamond—was a neohippie, self-made, meditation-guru influencer with a social media following that numbered close to a million. She's the antithesis of my father's usual bimbo Barbie, young-enough-to-be-his-daughter fare. Though with the help of fillers, Botox, and her natural lit-from-within vibe, she appears years younger than her legal age of forty-six. Five years ago, she successfully self-published a book on "aging from within."

Now that I've seen her in person, I'm thinking I should give it a read.

"Maybe another time?" I'm lacking the energy to be social this morning. I force a smile as I search for a coffee mug in the cupboard where my mother once kept them . . . only to be met with bottles of ibuprofen, jars of manuka honey and elderberry syrups, and various herbal tinctures. "Could you point me to the mugs?"

Bliss retrieves a ceramic teacup from a stainless steel carousel next to the sink, one that was hiding in plain sight this entire time. None of the mugs match, and their kitschy, exotic patterns suggest they've been collected from all over the world. My mother would gasp at the clash of color against her muted, neutral, classic kitchen.

Handing it to me, she lifts a natural brow. "At least join us for coffee?"

Her eyes are tender as they hold my gaze, and her lips relax into a hopeful smile.

I've never liked any of my father's girlfriends, and I don't intend to start now, but she's making this the tiniest bit challenging. It's next to impossible to be cruel to someone who has shown you nothing but kindness.

"Good morning, good morning." My father appears out of nowhere, his hair damp from his shower. "Bliss." He rests a hand on her hip and leans in to deposit a peck on her cheek before facing me. "Grace, how'd you sleep?"

I can't help but wonder what he's told her about me. Does he point out the fact that I'm adopted? Unlike Sebastian and Rose? Does he tell her why they adopted me? That my mother convinced him she was infertile because she wasn't ready to have kids? Or does he simply state that I'm his oldest child and then shrug off any questions about why we look nothing alike or why I'm so different from my well-adjusted younger brother and sister?

I roll the empty teacup in my hand as the two of them study me.

I loathe being on the spot, examined under an amateur microscope. The average person has no idea how to look beneath the surface, how to peel back layers upon layers of body language, how to read between the lines of the spoken word.

And even if I'm to believe everything the internet says about Bliss Diamond—and I don't—I doubt she's versed enough to take one look at me and think she has a snowball's chance in hell of figuring me out.

"Slept well. Thank you." I point to the mirrored gold espresso machine. "Don't want to be in your way. Was just going to grab a coffee and a shower and get to work."

It's the truth.

"Sure you don't want something to eat?" Bliss motions toward her half-burned eggs.

"You know, it's a gorgeous morning already. Why don't we take this outside? The three of us?" my father interjects before I have a chance to decline Bliss's invite again. "Surely you've got a few minutes to spare? Haven't seen you in years, Gracie . . ."

He's using my nickname to mollify my resistance. Only I don't feel soft—I'm entrapped by the guilt wafting off him and the way his expensive aftershave makes me think of different times. Not happier times. *Different.* I don't know that we were ever truly happy. Happy-ish? In an ignorant, unaware sort of way?

I pour my coffee and leave it black. "All right. I've got a few minutes."

He exhales, shoulders relaxing, and then he bustles about the kitchen with new life in his step as Bliss plates their food. My father pours two coffees, one for him and one for her, and we head out back like none of this is awkward.

The weather gauge by the pool house reads seventy-eight degrees, and the breeze is just light enough to tousle a few loose waves around Bliss's face.

She smiles and chews, smiles and chews.

Always smiling, this one.

Maybe it goes with the territory when your name is *Bliss*.

If I weren't crashing here, about to ask for favors, I'd ask her what her name used to be—before it was "Bliss Diamond."

The internet has no record of her until eighteen years ago.

But I keep my mouth shut.

I'm not here for her. Or for my father.

I'm here because of Sutton.

One sip of my coffee tells me it's expensive, but not the good kind of expensive—the kind where you're paying for the brand and the marketing. The bitterness lingers on my tongue after the first drink, making me long for the Turkish coffee place down the street from my apartment in Portland. The powder-soft grounds. The cinnamon and cardamom. The electric jolt of caffeine that wastes zero time hitting my bloodstream.

Soon, I remind myself, I'll be back there again.

This is temporary.

My father devours his eggs with his stick-straight posture, occasionally reaching over to pat the top of his girlfriend's hand.

I don't remember him being this affectionate with my mother. Then again, I'm sure there are a lot of things I don't remember. They say a child's memory can be grossly inaccurate and distorted. Some things I recall as though I'm viewing them through ripples of murky water. Other things I recall with terrifying clarity.

"So . . . Grace . . . what've you been up to these last couple of years? Rose said you were in Vegas? Phoenix? Colorado Springs? And then Billings for a bit?" My father pushes his eggs around on his plate, picking out bits of black. "Where's home these days?"

Rose has always been the information hub of this family, so it doesn't surprise me that he knows these things. It does, however, surprise me that he's been keeping tabs. I figured he'd have more important things to do.

"Portland. But not for much longer. I don't like to stay in one place for too long," I say.

"Where to next?" He brings his fork to his lips, pausing as if he has to will himself to take a bite.

Poor Bliss.

I shrug. "Was thinking Charleston, maybe? Or Charlotte. Kind of want to experience a different coast this time."

"Now that'll be quite a change of scenery," he says with the misplaced confidence of a man who was raised in New York and has spent his entire adult life in New Jersey.

I try not to judge him for never stepping out of his bubble because I know that deep down—beneath the McMullen family money, beyond the debonair features that have aged well, past the flashy car and the merry-go-round of stunning girlfriends and the country club social circle—he's afraid. Though of what, I'm not sure. All I know is that we all have our fears, and oftentimes those fears dictate exactly how we live our lives—whether we realize it or not.

My biggest fear was becoming my mother—a woman so desperate to hang on to her sham of a life, her carefully crafted illusion of happiness, that she was willing to kill for it. Or in her case—hire someone to do the killing for her. God forbid she got her manicure dirty. But in the end, fear got the best of her. It commandeered her decisions and drove her to do the unthinkable.

If I'd stayed with Sutton, he'd have given me a perfect life. That much I know. And he'd have loved me more than a person deserves to be loved. With each passing year, I'd have clung to him

—to our beautiful marriage and family—like lifeblood. And if anything so much as threatened to step in our path, I'd have snapped. Like my mother.

Maybe it's not in my blood, per se. But it's there. A learned unsteadiness simmering in my veins.

It's in all of us.

Some people simply control it better than others.

"Charleston is breathtaking. So charming. You'll adore it." Bliss's eyes light, and she splays a hand across her chest. "Oh, to be young and untethered again." She points her fork at no one in particular. "I remember those days. Cherish them. Once you settle down and have kids, you have to bloom where you plant them."

My father chuckles like he *gets it*, and I recall that in my quest to unearth the dirt on Bliss Diamond, I came across her website bio, which described her as a California-native-turned-entrepreneur living in New Jersey. No mention of kids.

"Do you have children?" I ask.

She looks at my father first, whose lips flatten, and then she shakes her head. "Wasn't in the cards for me."

He pats her hand again, as if this is a sore subject for her.

"Grace, your father says you do a lot of freelance work." Bliss frames her question as a statement. "Something online? Background checks or something?"

"My employer prefers I keep details to a minimum," I say. "But essentially I'm an internet sanitizer. People pay me to remove things they don't want online. Unflattering articles. Revenge porn. Harsh reviews. Outdated photos. Stuff like that."

I leave out the worst of the worst of the things I'm sometimes tasked with removing—things that require eye bleach, things that reaffirm my deep disappointment with society. Like the woman whose ex kept posing as her to post rape-fantasy requests on a dark web version of Craigslist, hoping a sick bastard would assault her. Or the husband who secretly attacked his wife's successful, homegrown bakery business with accusatory online reviews involving race and gender and religion so she'd be forced to close her doors and once again be financially dependent on him. There was also the mother-in-law who hired us to dig up dirt on her new son-in-law, who she was convinced was an ex-con living under a stolen identity, only in the process of digging up dirt on the man, I stumbled across the mother-in-law's secret involvement in a human trafficking ring. The son-in-law? Under-cover agent. The worst part was that the woman got off on some technicality. I'm not sure she spent a day behind bars. I'm also not sure where she scampered off to, but I'm willing to bet my life savings that wherever she is, she's up to no good.

If people like Bliss and my father knew how many truly sick and sociopathic individuals lurked among us, they'd sleep with guns in their nightstands, keep knives under their mattresses, and second-guess every word that comes out of another person's mouth.

Sometimes I find myself envious of that level of ignorance. Being able to turn a blind eye to all life's misfortunes. To go about my day like the sickest of souls don't walk among us.

But there's no going back now.

I've seen too much.

"That's fascinating." Bliss is finished with breakfast—appar-ently she has the appetite of a bird. It must be how she keeps her yoga-thin figure. She rests her chin on her hand and leans closer. "I've never met someone who does that before. How'd you get into that line of work anyway?"

My father smiles, and despite our finicky relationship, I still know him: he loves that things feel normal in this sliver-sized moment.

"It started as a part-time job in college. I worked for a major search engine, mostly removing things that violated copyrights, adding adult filters, recategorizing improperly indexed search items . . ." After graduation, I was approached by someone in senior management, who offered me double my salary and told me I could work anywhere in the world doing private assignments. I leave that part out. People always want to know how much this line of work pays, and it does nothing more than make for awkward conversation. Whenever it does come up, I typically say it pays enough to compensate for the dinners I've flushed down the toilet after digesting some of the more disturbing things I've seen. That tends to add a period to the conversation. "Made some connections, and it took off from there."

I peer across the picturesque backyard, over a thicket of manicured boxwoods, to the house behind us: a story-and-a-half bungalow that was once an agreeable robin's-egg blue. It's blanketed in a sunny yellow now, with white trim and a wooden butterfly wind chime dangling outside the back door. The new owners have added a cedar pergola out back, and a stainless steel grill rests uncovered, exposed to the elements. Lazy or carefree? It's anyone's guess.

Twenty years ago, it was home to a man and his girlfriend—a deranged and obsessed woman who stalked our family online and infiltrated her way into our lives. We would later discover she wasn't our neighbor by coincidence, though we couldn't have known that at first.

She had a plan, and when she began working as my family's nanny, she put that plan into action.

She claimed her name was Autumn Carpenter, which I later discovered was the actual name of my biological mother. Her real name was Sarah Thomas. And while she didn't give birth to me, she knew the woman who did—a woman who also happened to go missing a few years after the McMullens adopted me.

But while Sarah was sick, it wasn't a kill-your-husband's-lover kind of sick. She was more along the lines of an unmedicated-and-delusional kind of sick. She was sweet and gentle and especially fond of me. There were times, even as a ten-year-old girl, that I fantasized about Sarah being my mother. Sometimes I prayed for it. Made wishes on dandelions and shooting stars. I was convinced that if I believed anything hard enough, it would come true.

And it almost did.

At least according to a chapter in that *Domestic Illusions* book, where a police report claimed Sarah intended to kidnap me from school and drive me across the border to Mexico.

I'll admit there were years I wished it would've happened.

Sometimes I think I'd have been better off.

Even though Sarah wasn't my mother, she loved me in a way Daphne never could—another factoid outlined in great detail in that unauthorized tell-all. Daphne couldn't connect with me, it said. The bond felt forced. It was complicated. I was a handful, and while she gave me all she could, it wasn't enough.

I don't blame Sarah for what happened to us—or for the self-serving choices my parents made. She happened to waltz into our life during a familial cataclysm of the inevitable. Life as we knew it ceased to exist the moment that woman stepped into our world.

Pure coincidence, I'm certain.

She just happened to be in the picture.

If it hadn't been my parents destroying this family, it would've been me.

I was born with a darkness inside.

"Eyes like two empty black holes," as my mother described me in *Domestic Illusions*. I was a *"precocious child. Destructive. Hard to love."*

Hard to love.

I dig my thumbnail into the painted enamel of the perfect little teacup in my hand, leaving a noticeable scratch.

The urge to ruin all that is perfect is a sickness I've known my entire life, one I've yet to understand in my thirty years. And this sickness isn't simply relegated to things—people fall into this category as well.

The more perfect they are, the more I want to destroy them.

Sutton was perfect.

I left before I could ruin him.

358

Rising from the patio table, I palm the damaged ceramic. "I'm sorry—can we catch up later? I've got a few deadlines I'm up against . . ."

"Of course," Bliss answers for my father, waving her hand like she understands.

She couldn't possibly.

He gives a tight-lipped nod. "You let me know if there's anything you need. Just glad to have you home."

"Actually . . . there's one thing," I say.

I hate asking favors. *Hate.* Needing other people for any reason is a third-degree burn to my ego. But this request is minor enough, so the sting shouldn't last too long.

"Anything." My father perks up, happy to help. It's a desperate look for a man of his stature, but I appreciate it nonetheless.

"Can you give me a ride to the Enterprise in Valeria in a couple of hours?" I bite my lip. I should've grabbed a rental at the airport yesterday, but the never-ending lines wrapped and zigzagged, and I didn't feel like waiting two hours. On top of that, another minute of being shoulder to shoulder with smelly, grouchy, traveling humans would've had me coming out of my skin.

He checks his diamond-and-sapphire-rimmed timepiece—an antique that once belonged to my grandfather, whom I never met as he passed when my father was a teenager. Supposedly this is why my father pushed so hard to start a family when he was fresh out of college, before my mother was ready.

"Well, shoot," he says under his breath. That's my father—the most helpful man on earth but only at his convenience.

Bliss pats his arm. "Sweetheart, I'll do it. I'd be happy to."

Sweetheart.

They're like an old married couple, which is ironic given that my father doesn't know the first thing about long-term commitment. Bliss doesn't know it yet, but he'll be trading her in a year from now.

Maybe sooner.

None of his coquetries have ever lasted more than a small handful of years.

I give Bliss a showy couple of thank-yous—mostly to spite my father but also to illustrate my gratitude—before heading upstairs to start my day. She didn't hesitate to offer her assistance, unlike my father, who hemmed and hawed as he tried to come up with an excuse. I imagine he didn't want to have to move a tee time or cancel a lunch reservation. And I get it. I showed up unannounced after years of radio silence. I can't expect him to rearrange his schedule at the drop of a hat.

As soon as I wrap up a work email, I'll shower and catch a ride to the Enterprise downtown, grab myself a car, and start scoping out Sutton's life.

His *real* life.

His home, his work, his comings and goings. The things he does when he thinks no one's looking. Mundane or not, these are the things that tell you everything you need to know about someone.

I'm not interested in the version of his life curated across the front page of his Instaface account, nor am I interested in the version of his life summarized by a handful of internet searches.

If I were to take those at face value, then that would mean he's lost his mind. It would mean he actually moved to my hometown, married a woman with my uncanny likeness, and named his first-born child after me.

I hope I'm wrong.

I pray to anyone who'll listen that it's all a freak misunderstanding, a handful of eerie coincidences with laughably logical explanations.

I lock my bathroom door, strip to nothing, and climb under the hot spray of a pristine shower that likely hasn't been used since the last time I was home years ago.

My heart hammers beneath searing skin, the surrealness of this fading away as reality sets in.

Yesterday, I was three thousand miles away from the life I'd walked away from.

Now I'm back, elbow deep in Sutton's world, and he hasn't the slightest idea.

It would've been easier to call the man, to send him a letter or a message on social media as most people tend to do with ancient lovers.

But phone calls are easy to ignore, and messages are easy to miss, and the written word is easy to misconstrue.

I want him to know that I'm sorry, that he mattered to me—that he was the *only* one who ever mattered to me. And I want to see this with my own eyes—what I've done to him.

And then I'm going to make it right.

Whatever that entails.

AVAILABLE NOW!

BOOK CLUB QUESTIONS

Did the ending come as a shock? Why or why not?

1. What do you think Graham saw in Marnie? What was he getting from her that he wasn't getting from Daphne?
2. Do you think Autumn is inherently a good person with good intentions? Why or why not?
3. Aside from Marnie's jealousy and insecurity issues, do you think she genuinely picked up on something being 'off' about Autumn or was she just trying to scare her away from her brother for her own reasons?
4. How do you imagine the McMullen's day-to-day life now that Daphne is locked away? How do you think Graham is coping as a single father? How do you think the kids are doing?
5. Which running narrative did you enjoy the most: Autumn's or Daphne's?
6. What was your favorite line or scene from the book and why did it stand out?

7. Do you think Daphne acted in the best interest of her family ... or herself?
8. If you were to cast Autumn, Graham, and Daphne in a movie, who would play them?
9. What do you think happened to the real Autumn? Can Sarah's memory be trusted?

ACKNOWLEDGMENTS

Thank you so, so much to my beta readers, A, C, K, and M. This book was a monster of a project to tackle, and you all so generously offered your assistance, brutal honesty, encouragement, and valuable feedback. This book would not be what it is now if it weren't for you.

To Louisa, my cover designer. Thank you for bringing this book to life with such a breathtaking masterpiece. It's perfect. And you're the best.

Wendy, thank you for your kind words and eagle eyes. I'll never forget the email you sent me after the first pass. I needed to hear that.

To my husband, thank you, always. You may not be a reader, but you're always willing to let me bounce my ideas off you.

Last but not least, thank you Jennifer. Seriously. Your kind words and support over this past year has been a godsend, and I don't know if this book would have been possible without you. You're amazingly talented, your advice is solid gold, and our friendship is the unexpected gift I never saw coming. Thank you, thank you, thank you for everything.

ABOUT THE AUTHOR

Minka Kent has been crafting stories since before she could scribble her name. With a love of the literary dark and twisted, Minka cut her teeth on Goosebumps and Fear Street, graduated to Stephen King as a teenager, and now counts Gillian Flynn, Chevy Stevens, and Caroline Kepnes amongst her favorite authors and biggest influences. Minka has always been curious about good people who do bad things and loves to explore what happens when larger-than-life characters are placed in fascinating situations.

In her non-writing life, Minka is a thirty-something wife and mother who equally enjoys sunny and rainy days, loves freshly cut hydrangeas, hides behind oversized sunglasses, travels to warmer climates every chance she gets, and bakes sweet treats when the mood strikes (spoiler alert: it's often).

Click here to subscribe to her newsletter for sales, new releases, giveaways, and ARC opportunities!

If you'd like to contact Minka personally, please email her at minkakent@hotmail.com   or   head   over   to www.facebook.com/authorminkakent

Lastly, if you enjoyed this book, Minka would be eternally grateful if you took the time to leave a review at Amazon and/or Goodreads.

Printed in Great Britain
by Amazon